P9-CDS-574

Praise for

BLOODLANDS

"Effectively merges science fiction, horror, and the classic Western . . . [a] spectacular trilogy launch. Ingeniously subverting traditional themes, Cody skillfully builds near-claustrophobic suspense, finally revealing the true nature of monstrosity." —*Publishers Weekly* (starred review)

"A world of monsters that takes the reader on many plot twists and turns. Keep[s] you guessing until the very end. This is one to pick up." —*Night Owl Reviews*

"An excellent novel that touches on a dystop[ian] potential future, *Bloodlands* depicts the gritty nature of survival and secrecy, and sets fire to a fabulous new series."

—*Fresh Fiction*

Praise for

BLOOD RULES

"Developing a well-extrapolated dystopian future of urban hubs surrounded by chaos and a wildly creative collection of preternatural creatures, Cody offers a compelling glimpse into the varying aspirations and potential future of monsters and monstrous people." —*Publishers Weekly*

Ace Books by Christine Cody

BLOODLANDS
BLOOD RULES
IN BLOOD WE TRUST

IN BLOOD
WE TRUST

Christine Cody

ACE BOOKS, NEW YORK

THE BERKLEY PUBLISHING GROUP
Published by the Penguin Group
Penguin Group (USA) Inc.
375 Hudson Street, New York, New York 10014, USA
Penguin Group (Canada), 90 Eglinton Avenue East, Suite 700, Toronto, Ontario M4P 2Y3, Canada
(a division of Pearson Penguin Canada Inc.)
Penguin Books Ltd., 80 Strand, London WC2R 0RL, England
Penguin Group Ireland, 25 St. Stephen's Green, Dublin 2, Ireland (a division of Penguin Books Ltd.)
Penguin Group (Australia), 250 Camberwell Road, Camberwell, Victoria 3124, Australia
(a division of Pearson Australia Group Pty. Ltd.)
Penguin Books India Pvt. Ltd., 11 Community Centre, Panchsheel Park, New Delhi—110 017, India
Penguin Group (NZ), 67 Apollo Drive, Rosedale, Auckland 0632, New Zealand
(a division of Pearson New Zealand Ltd.)
Penguin Books (South Africa) (Pty.) Ltd., 24 Sturdee Avenue, Rosebank, Johannesburg 2196,
South Africa

Penguin Books Ltd., Registered Offices: 80 Strand, London WC2R 0RL, England

This is a work of fiction. Names, characters, places, and incidents either are the product of the author's imagination or are used fictitiously, and any resemblance to actual persons, living or dead, business establishments, events, or locales is entirely coincidental. The publisher does not have any control over and does not assume any responsibility for author or third-party websites or their content.

IN BLOOD WE TRUST

An Ace Book / published by arrangement with the author

PRINTING HISTORY
Ace mass-market edition / October 2011

Copyright © 2011 by Chris Marie Green.
Cover art by Larry Rostant.
Cover design by Judith Lagerman.
Interior text design by Tiffany Estreicher.

All rights reserved.
No part of this book may be reproduced, scanned, or distributed in any printed or electronic form without permission. Please do not participate in or encourage piracy of copyrighted materials in violation of the author's rights. Purchase only authorized editions.
For information, address: The Berkley Publishing Group,
a division of Penguin Group (USA) Inc.,
375 Hudson Street, New York, New York 10014.

ISBN: 978-0-441-02087-4

ACE
Ace Books are published by The Berkley Publishing Group,
a division of Penguin Group (USA) Inc.,
375 Hudson Street, New York, New York 10014.
ACE and the "A" design are trademarks of Penguin Group (USA) Inc.

PRINTED IN THE UNITED STATES OF AMERICA

10 9 8 7 6 5 4 3 2 1

If you purchased this book without a cover, you should be aware that this book is stolen property. It was reported as "unsold and destroyed" to the publisher, and neither the author nor the publisher has received any payment for this "stripped book."

To Morgan—to my funny and clever girl,
who never fails to make me happy. Love you!

ACKNOWLEDGMENTS

To the team at Ace: Ginjer, Kat, and the art, editorial, marketing, and sales departments! It's been a fun trip to the Bloodlands. To the Knight Agency and my critique partners, Judy and Sheri—you prop me up when I need it the most.

To people who are so entwined that they can't imagine life without each other. To people who strive for justice and right, even at the expense of their own safety and sanity. To everyone out there who has read my work and kept me writing!

In a work of fiction, there are licenses taken, and you will find many here. I hope you forgive any errors and flights of fancy. . . .

1

The Witches had captured a monster.

They stared down at it as they gathered in the only place they could go now—in a cave tunnel system underneath an urban hub that had been taken over by the beasts.

Seven of the Witches had survived the slaughter above. Seven, standing together over a creature that one of them had found while scavenging for food and spying on the monsters in GBVille, where moon-throttled darkness covered the curved buildings and nearly silent streets. Darkness brought on by some sort of energy-sucking bomb the monsters had used.

At least it was a positive sign that the Witches hadn't been deactivated yet. And at least they had undergone one last update before the monsters had attacked and the Witches had retreated from the massacre at the asylum site. They had only been trying to keep the monsters away from society—a task that had been programmed into their human bodies when they'd been identified as Special by the CIA.

Kids with some psychic talent, recruited, trained, and made over in pale camouflage colors into an elite unit.

They were still up and running.

The temporary leader of the Witches—the one who had been activated first—bent down to their unfortunate prisoner. It didn't take much study to see that they had captured a Cyclops, with its one eye blinking up at them, its unwieldy, long-legged body restrained by the other six Witches, who held the freak still with their mind powers, limb by limb.

The leader's second in command stood next to him. She resembled him, with her light curls, big clear eyes, scentless preteen body clad in white. The General Benefactors Corporation badge that they all shared was branded into her forehead—the sign of peace. The symbol of a new sentinel that had taken over for the old Shredder slayers after the latter had been retired.

The second in command used their enhanced mind-link to communicate in Witch shorthand while she inspected the monster.

Blood drinker?

No, the leader thought as the Cyclops blinked its eye, finally regaining consciousness from the nerve-pincher that had been used on it during capture. *Never bring down blood drinkers for study.*

The creature's eye flickered here and there as it took in the cave. Then that eye scanned the circle of Witches. The monster's thick lips were beginning to form words that weren't quite coming.

The second in command thought, *Confused, it. Cyclops not love blood?*

Right. Vampires, were-creatures . . . They love blood. Water robbers, them.

But teeth, his second thought, using her mind powers to force open the Cyclops's mouth. *Blood-drinker teeth?*

The thing's teeth were indeed sharpened to points, and it moaned and gnashed them while trying to get free of the second in command's psychic grip. When that didn't work, it started fighting against its invisible restraints, trying to jerk its meaty arms out of the mind holds that the others had on it as the group merely continued staring, their eyes wide, clear, and blank.

These Witches hadn't ever seen any Cyclops creatures in their asylum, and the uniqueness of it pulled at their linked curiosity. It had encouraged the Witch who had found it to break protocol and bring it to the rest of them so they could figure out what made it work. When they had initially been programmed with information about monsters, along with all the other infusions the government had given to them, the data hadn't *said* that Cyclopses loved blood. Yet common sense told this leader that these teeth had to be used for something, otherwise evolution would have phased out the feature during all the Cyclopses' years of hiding away from society, outside the GBVille hub.

Perhaps, after the world had changed, this mutant had begun to creep outside with the rest of the monsters, and it had found a need for teeth then.

Using his mind, the leader pulled the Cyclops's mouth open even wider, wishing for a better view of those teeth. But in his curiosity, he overstretched, and when he cracked the monster's jaw, the thing screamed.

None of the Witches around him flinched at the agonized sound. At least, they thought it might be agony, since pain wasn't familiar to them. Conditioning had rendered them serene and painless, the better for guarding.

They kept their psychic holds on the monster, pinning the thing down as it spazzed on the ground, its jaw unhinged.

The leader and his second moved in closer to see those teeth now.

Not fangs, the leader said.

Civil monster? the second asked. *Not a Red?*

Not a blood monster—not vampire, not were-creature. Not tik-tik, not gremlin. Not love blood, this.

But just to be certain of that, the leader knew it would be prudent to see just what the Cyclops's final meal had been. He . . . *they* . . . wanted to know if this type of monster collected precious water through the taking of blood from humans, or if it was one of the Civil mutants that didn't feed off people—a much less dangerous type.

Much less worrisome.

The leader finally used his hands, sliding a knife out of a holster at his side. He and the others could move only so much with their minds. Physical blades were always the most efficient when it came time to slaughter a beast.

He stuck the knife into the monster's gut, ripping it open.

Innards bulged out, the Cyclops's stomach laying itself wide to inspection and, as the thing made more noise, the leader blinked at the stench, then the spill of root matter.

Root eater, this? he thought to his group once they had all recovered from the smell together.

Not blood drinker, this, his second thought again.

One of the other Witches, a male with short light hair that curled around his face, thought, *Like us. Human?*

Not like us. The leader shot his comrade a pointed look. *None like us, them.*

They had been programmed to know that, like other humans, they were the superiors. They had been infused with Special liquids to make it so; it made them run faster, be stronger, and use their minds better, and it was only a matter of time before the monsters that were acting as if they had established a temporary new world order above ground would realize their moment was fleeting.

And *that* realization would come when the Witches made their way outside to find any surviving Witches who might still be in other hubs.

Other Witches . . .

The leader's mind clicked, then opened to a piece of data that the group had downloaded before the monster attack.

An image of a tall young man with dark eyes, dressed in a quaint old Shredder uniform with leathered armor, a bandolier, and elevated FlyShoes. He was holding a chest puncher as he peered into the camera lens of one of the few new Monitor 'bots that had recently been assigned patrol duty out in the New Badlands.

Johnson Stamp, the data read. *Shredder: retired.*

The leader felt a tingle of shared awareness travel around his circle of Witches. Besides other sentinels who might still be out there, perhaps there would be old Shredders, even if the government had done away with them after the monsters had been beaten into hiding and near extinction years ago. Even if this particular slayer, Johnson Stamp, was suspected of having gone against his government severance rules and taken up some rogue hunting out in the nowheres.

No matter what Shredders used to be and what Witches were now, they would all have a common purpose—to contain monsters. This would be their first directive   survival. Then, afterward, the Witches would revert to their usual priorities, which included replacing all the old Shredders, even if it called for eradication.

Do away with the old model in favor of the new for the sake of humanity.

The leader glanced down at the Cyclops—its broken mouth working as if to say something to the pale beings it saw around it, its innards bunched around its midsection. Its eye glared as if it, like the dying Monitor 'bot that had captured Johnson Stamp's image, were committing the Witches to memory.

The leader grabbed his knife from the Cyclops's gut, yanked it out, and stabbed at that eye, twisting the blade, blinding it.

Then, as one, the Witches walked away from the monster, efficiently shutting out its pitiful, fading moans.

2

Mariah

I woke up that night, my arms and legs tangled in the sheets of the bed that I'd been assigned to in our liberated asylum.

Even during the fog of post-sleep, I felt him right away, on my bare skin. Or maybe I should say *through* my skin—on top, under, in.

Gabriel.

As he lay behind me, still in the throes of vampire rest, he didn't make a sound. That was because none of the vampires I'd met so far needed to breathe to survive. Animation kept them "alive" or "undead" or whatever they chose to call it. But those of us in the monster community who lived under the title of *were-creature* were pretty much the opposite of a vampire, what with our strong ties to the humanity that ruled us whenever we weren't in creature form.

But just listen to me, claiming myself as a were. Hell, ever since I'd messed up and taken part in a brief exchange with the mysterious monster we'd rescued in this asylum a couple of weeks ago—a cipher named Subject 562 who turned out to be the mother and father of our blood monster line—I couldn't really call myself a normal were-creature anymore.

I, the stupid and impulsive Mariah Lyander, was now a curiosity for my community. I was even more of a pariah than ever, although the others—the Red blood-drinking monsters and the Civil non–blood drinkers—seemed to respect me for kicking 562's ass in the end with Gabriel's help.

We had psychically joined together and broken 562's sanity, using Gabriel's newfound ability to freeze minds. That full-moon night, when I'd first changed into a form that I could access only once a month, seemed so damned long ago.

I didn't like to think of what everyone had described to me: long teeth, a split tongue, flowing hair, four arms, and cravings that went beyond even a normal monster's.

Yeah, I'd really done it by allowing 562 to exchange with me. Hell, I wasn't even your garden-variety werewolf anymore when the moon *wasn't* full. I'd been testing myself over these last couple of weeks and, thanks to my origin, I could call up my new nonlunar form at any time, like when I got pissed off. Or when I got too excited.

This one featured big teeth in a huge mouth. Claws. Fast and mean.

No, in any case, I wasn't quite a werewolf anymore at all.

Now, as I lay here next to Gabriel in bed, I didn't move a muscle. I hardly breathed, wondering when he would sense that dusk had fully fallen. I pressed my face into my pillow while his mere presence sent my blood rushing, heating, as if it were waiting for him to put his fingers on my back, where the blood would gather at his touch. His imprint.

Our strange link.

My instincts told me that I should probably slide off the mattress before he did wake up. But when was the last time I'd listened to my conscience? It sure hadn't been present when I'd been off-guard enough for 562 to bite me in a rapid, willing exchange that I had barely even registered.

My heartbeat twisted as I heard Gabriel stir.

Awake.

I felt his fingertips skim over my spine, and I shivered as the blood rushed there, mocking the shape of his touch.

"I can hear your pulse," he said.

He'd told me once that my body's rhythms sounded like musical chaos to him, that it was like no other's. He couldn't resist the volatility in me; it was what drew Gabriel, but there were times I wondered if that could ever be enough in the long run for us. Or if it was *too* much, and it'd already led us to places we never should've gone together.

As I pressed my face into my pillow, he slipped his fingers over my back, to my waist, going even farther, inserting his hand between the mattress and my belly. My stomach muscles jerked. My blood did, too, as it tumbled from one part of my body forward, rolling over itself to get to him.

An ache pierced me low, stabbing and swollen. It was almost as if my blood were doing two things at once: trying to get out of me and go to him, as if it couldn't stand to be inside me anymore. Yet it seemed like it was also attempting to bring *him* into *me*.

When Gabriel traveled his hand a little lower, my blood jammed to a sharp point between my legs, and I groaned, burying my face in my pillow even more.

His thoughts mingled with mine through our link, which had always grown stronger when we did sex.

Give in to me, Mariah, just this once . . . give me everything . . .

No blood, I thought back. *Don't even ask for a taste.*

His vampire sway should've been enough to get me to surrender, but I was resolute these days. 562's blood had made me stronger than anyone or anything I'd ever known. Even so, I was already damp for him.

I resisted Gabriel, not wanting to lose control of my body, becoming that new nonlunar creature.

Even though the full moon and my more dangerous shape was twelve nights away, I knew that if my passions got the better of me tonight, I'd still regret it.

Got to stop now . . . I thought to Gabriel.

You won't change form, Mariah. I'll make sure you don't.

He was patient, waiting for my answer. But he wouldn't be that way for much longer if he kept rubbing me like this.

I told myself to pull away, but somehow, I wasn't doing it. I kept thinking that whenever we got together, we always managed to tear ourselves from each other before it got lethal, and we'd be able to do it this time, too. Gabriel would just go for his animal blood–filled flask at the side of the bed, drinking down the sustenance while he slid into me, giving me pleasure in that way while I held back my monster. It was a risky game that we'd won so far.

One night, though . . .

As I started to tremble, my mind kept grabbing at logic, even though it seemed as if emotion and need were eating it right up.

Gabriel had changed so much during these last months, just as much as I had, his bloodlust growing and growing as a maturing vampire. What we had wouldn't end up in a good place.

I'd first met him in the New Badlands, out in the nowheres, when he'd been able to masquerade as a human well enough. He'd contained his thirst, holding on to his humanity as best as he could back then. He'd even been a hero to our secretive were-community, going up against the Shredder who'd wanted to slay every last one of us.

But even as he'd been so noble and honorable, he'd met me, and I'd brought out the worst in him.

Maybe that wasn't altogether true, though. Since coming upon other vampires here in the urban hubs, Gabriel had been schooled proper. He'd learned that vampires eventually let go of their humanity, anyway, and his escalating need for blood and the lack of caring about it was only natural.

Yet something inside Gabriel was still fighting his instincts—I could feel the push and pull inside him even now through our link as he pulled me backward, closer to him, where I could feel the buzz of his bare skin. His remaining humanity was the only reason he still drank from that flask instead of sinking his fangs into me. Besides, he knew that if he tasted the blood of 562, he might get even nastier than any regular old vampire.

Obviously done with all the waiting, he coaxed his fingers between my thighs. I held my breath. Then, even though I should've stopped him, he delved between my folds.

Up, into me.

I sucked in that breath while my blood flooded and tingled, hurting in such a nice, scary way. He churned his fingers in and out, and my hips moved to meet every stroke.

I clung to my logic while I still could, but the heat was taking me over, a pounding that would lead to a burst, an explosion into my new form . . .

From the back of me, his stiffness probed between my thighs, and I knew that this was the time to leave that bed, but I didn't. I parted my legs, because I was his already.

My blood was his blood.

Thudding in every place that his skin touched mine, I started the change I so wanted to hold back.

First, there was a blue-tinged wanting . . .

Then something that had been building for the past couple of weeks—a bigger hunger that just got redder and redder by the second.

A craving unlike any I used to feel, and it split me down the middle in a streak of cruelty, a need to hurt . . . especially those who'd hurt me.

But somehow I shut out that hunger, angling my head into Gabriel's arm, where my cheek met his skin.

Smooth. Cool. No scent.

Vampire.

I bit into him, not rough enough to break his harder-than-human skin. Just enough to warn him that we were getting to a point of no return.

He growled, and if I turned round, I'd see that his eyes had gone from their usual silver to a blazing red, that his fangs had popped, changing him from a seemingly human drifter to a seething devil.

He pushed his fingers into me harder, and I groaned,

trying to hold back the meanness that was about to come out in me in a series of boiling, stretching, agonizing pulls.

His fangs scratched my shoulder.

"No," I said out loud now, my voice low, garbled.

God-all, he wanted a bite. I wanted it, too, but I wouldn't be limited to sinking my teeth into one of his veins. My bite would rip, tear, decimate.

And I had the feeling it wasn't regular blood I wanted, either. That split of cruelty prying me apart needed a certain sort of blood tonight—hot, violent, brutally earned—and I pushed back at the craving as Gabriel took his fingers out of me, using his hand to spread my legs even wider.

He probed at me from the back again, and I winced. At the sound, he teased a little more, slipping against me, sliding until I couldn't take it anymore.

"Gabriel." My voice on the edge, a warning. My vision gone to a pulsing violet.

Laughing low in his throat, he thrust into me, and I clutched at the sheets, yanking them off the corners of the bed, rocking my hips back against him, wanting him to go deeper so I would forget everything else.

But that was the human side of me, fighting this other . . . thing.

He rammed in again, and I moved with him—one drive, two, more, again . . .

My blood buffeted me from the inside out, forging toward him, beating against my skin like fists even as I drew *his* own blood to my skin.

He bent to my neck, fangs scraping my flesh.

"No!" I grappled for his blood flask, not really knowing where it was, only knowing it had to be close.

But then he drew himself back, in striking position.

I tried to move before he could bite, yet he was faster than I was in my mostly human form, and his fangs needled my neck before I dodged out of the way.

In a crash of white, our mind connection went blank, like a lightning strike that had wiped out all power. But I didn't need to read his thoughts to sense the anguish in him.

He had reared back from me, as if something had jerked him away, and when I got to my knees, one of my hands pressing against my slight neck wound, I saw that he was tearing apart the bedclothes on his way to where he'd stored his flask near the edge of the mattress.

My body rhythms were shredding me, my breath like icicles puncturing my lungs as heat wrestled with the coolness of my will to stay strong.

Stay human.

He spit out my blood, gulped from his flask, spitting that out, too, then drinking more. His back was to me, and I hunched down, shamed. A power within me was pressing outward, as if my monster didn't want to stay in. My gaze was still violet, beating and fuzzy.

No, I thought again, but this time it was to myself. *Just stop . . .*

He finished draining the flask, then slowly looked over his shoulder at me, his gaze a little less crimson, but not all the way back to its humanlike appearance. His short hair was tousled, his face a wounded scape boasting a nose that had been broken and hadn't healed correctly back when he'd been human. All in all, he was a bruised, haunted revelation of all the remorse he could muster.

But there was a terrible slant to his mouth that negated that.

"The way you taste . . ." he said.

He ran a bewildered gaze over me, and for a moment, I thought that maybe I had started to turn without having realized it. But with one scan of my body, I saw that I was still as human as I could be, considering the circumstances.

As I calmed my pulse—*don't think of the blood, think of breathing, just breathing*—I watched as Gabriel tossed the flask away.

"I can still feel your blood on my tongue," he said. "It . . . numbs me."

I still didn't get it. Not until I thought about the word *numb.*

"Like a poison?" I asked. My muscles ached a little, and

not only because I'd tempted my body to change. It was because I wanted him back inside me.

"Like a poison," Gabriel repeated.

I didn't think I'd heard him right, and I retreated to the wall, near my pillow. Before I'd turned into this new creature, he'd taken my were-blood. It had bolstered him, and I'd even thought . . .

Well, I'd thought that maybe I might be the only being in this world who could make him feel that way. But that was before I knew better.

Before I'd exchanged with 562 and become real poison.

My mind spun as he wiped the back of his hand over his mouth.

God-all, *poison*. Were-creatures worked that way with one another. We didn't yearn for each other's blood, because it pained us to taste and digest it. That was a good thing, too, because it kept the more powerful creatures, like the wolf I'd been, from attacking the weaker ones, such as the were-elk, were–mule deer, and were-scorpion who'd been a part of my Badlands community.

Had 562's blood changed the composition of mine to the point where Gabriel couldn't stomach it now?

I wasn't sure how I'd even been able to digest 562's blood in the first place, but maybe it had something to do with the way 562, my origin, had quickly and deceitfully taken my blood before I'd taken it from her/him.

Gabriel stayed on the other side of the bed, having turned away from me again. I wanted to reach out, run my palm over the lean muscles of his back.

"I don't get it," I said. "The night of 562's rampage, she/ he kept mentally appealing to you with the notion of feeding you with blood. Why would 562 have done that if it would've poisoned you?"

"Maybe its blood just tastes bad enough so that none of us would try to drink from it. 562 offered it out of love. That's what it kept thinking to me, anyway."

I'd always thought of 562 as more were-creature than vampire, with its snout and fur, its copse of long teeth, and its response to a full moon. Maybe that was why it had chosen me to be the drinker—because for the rest of the Reds, mother's milk wasn't healthy.

Besides, now that I thought about it, I *had* gotten sick on 562's blood, just as if it were a poison. But I'd swallowed it. I'd taken it right in, unlike Gabriel.

"Why did you take it from me?" I asked. "You knew that my blood could be dangerous in other ways."

His shoulders slumped, and the sight of such a strong man weighed down did the same to me.

"Whenever I'm with you," he said, "I tell myself I won't give in. But I did this time."

"Maybe we should . . ." What? I was out of ideas, and I couldn't stand the thought of never feeling Gabriel again.

"Tonight," he said, "it was a prick on your neck from my fangs. Next time . . ."

Next time he might get even more violent, and I could see . . . *feel* . . . that the part of him still clinging to humanity might survive only if he was miles away from me.

My blood gave one last desperate stretch in my core, then began to cool. My vision went from violet to blue as it turned back to normal.

When he stood, I looked away from him, hardly able to afford for my body to heat up again. I couldn't stand to see how beautiful Gabriel was, pale and streamlined, his belly flat, his legs long. And his skin . . .

I liked the coolness and hardness of it. I'd grown so used to it.

He gathered his dust-worn clothes—the beaten white shirt, the jeans, the boots that had always reminded me of a lost cowboy from the movies of yore. He put the articles on, one by one, seeming so far away already.

"I need to go to the cells," he said, as if we'd only been in the middle of some discussion and were just now taking it right back up again. "I've got to talk to Stamp."

"Now?"

"Me and the other vampires have to keep at it. We've got to chip away at him until he brings down his mind blocks to let us know if there're other security threats outside the hub, just biding their time to come in and attack. And Stamp *will* break. The old ones tell me that all humans do it at some point."

Johnson Stamp, the Shredder who'd tried to kill us more than once. He'd even chased our group out here to the hubs, although he'd gotten his due in the end.

When I didn't say anything else to Gabriel—what could I possibly utter?—he turned round, all dressed now.

I held a sheet in front of my body. I don't know why when he'd seen it all more than once.

When he came over to me, it seemed as if he were going to bend down, kiss me softly. But all he did was touch my neck, healing my faint wound just before he headed back to the door, walking right out of it.

I should've told myself that it wouldn't be the last time he would need to leave me hanging, either. Not if we wanted to keep ourselves—and probably every one round us—safe. I was so easily riled, and I had caused enough trouble in the Badlands to know better than to cross lines now.

Reassuring myself with that mantra, I set about getting ready for the night, aimless, restless, and even now under the thumb of a hunger that Gabriel had brought out in me but hadn't assuaged.

3

Mariah

I had to get out of the asylum, so I headed toward the gated doorway, onto the walkway along the top of a high brick wall that surrounded the massive stucco building that loomed over GBVille.

I'd decided that some fresh air would do me good, but there was another reason I wanted to take a stroll. I was actually going to a place that had offered me alone time more frequently these nights.

As I traveled over the walkway, I heard a measured pounding sound from the middle of the asylum—an outside area that acted as a sort of covered courtyard a few hundred feet away. It sounded as if someone was playing drums.

It almost even reminded me of the so-called music that the lowlords in the hub had been playing before we'd shut down GBVille, but this was more . . .

Primal?

Intricate?

Maybe I'd see what the others were up to later. But for now, I approached the main gate of the asylum's walls, where a couple of Civil guards were on duty. The ogre and a displaced Yeren man-monkey stood a little straighter when they saw me.

The ogre grunted something that sounded like my name, as good a greeting as I'd ever get from a gray-skinned, towering mammothite like him, while the Yeren merely looked at me with wide, dark eyes.

Thing was, that ogre had said my name as if he were investing some kind of heavy meaning into it—a definition that I was just coming to terms with. There was a gratefulness for how I'd beaten 562 in our head-to-head confrontation, when my origin had been snacking on monsters as she/he had rampaged through the asylum on the night of the most recent full moon.

But there was also a clear wariness, as if me and my new state of being were the second coming of 562, and all the Civils were just waiting for me to munch on every one of them.

Had the Civils caught on to the fact that 562 had been eating up only their kind that night, and not the Reds? Had they heard any rumors about how 562, the mother and father of all the Reds I knew, had possessed such love for her/his monster progeny that she/he had been willing to attack the Civils in order to put the Reds on the highest rung on the ladder of existence?

Had they worked out the notion that 562 even *preferred* to drink Civil blood?

I told the guards that I was only going out for a walk, and they apparently thought that I wanted to grab a wildlife meal somewhere just inside hub boundaries. And maybe that would've been a good idea, based on what my latest romp with Gabriel had brought out in me.

Changing to my nonlunar form and loading up on blood might just calm me down all the way. But I didn't wish to become that way tonight. I didn't even like to change randomly, since I didn't know what kind of tricks 562's blood might have in store for me, like new hungers in the pit of my belly that I'd need to address.

Then again, part of me wondered what I was capable of
now . . .

As I walked quickly away from the guards, toward the
fringes of GBVille, I still couldn't shake the odd feeling that
had been pumping through me while I'd been with Gabriel—
the cruelty, the thoughts that were simmering to my surface
and solidifying into stronger ideas only now.

Memories of my were-birth.

Blood . . .

Jaws, sharp teeth . . .

Pain so red and awful that I'd screamed and screamed . . .

The anger I still felt, even today, pushed me forward. It
always rode just below everything else in me, but I'd been
feeling it more and more lately. I just hoped my bloodlust
wouldn't ever explode into its fullest measure, as I'd seen it
do in 562 during the full moon.

I was even afraid that I might find an appetite for the
Civil monsters, just like the one my origin had revealed that
night.

It was only recently that my Badlands group had discovered that there were more monsters in existence than merely
blood drinkers, who were the children of 562. There were
a lot of others who'd obviously ventured into the open after
the world had changed; the government had caught some of
these Civils, too, keeping them in asylums for research along
with a lot of Reds. Word even had it that the government
had been preparing to sell monster blood to elite customers
who could afford to purchase longer life and immunity to
disease. But from the reports we'd just found in the asylum
labs, it looked as if our illustrious, shut-away leaders hadn't
gotten to the point where they had packaged that corporatized dream just yet, thank-all.

With every step, I walked a little looser, closer to where
I wanted to go. Behind me, under the murky moon, GBVille
was dark. Not a lit window to be seen anywhere—not even
in General Benefactors Corporation buildings that the hub
had been named for. There weren't even any flashing reflec-
tions from the now-deadened carnerotica public screens,

and surely no neon glares from the ads that had decorated transports before our group had used a power blaster to blow out everything.

Truthfully, it might as well have been the Stone Age, but I didn't think that the distractoids in the hub cared that much. The citizens were still running round in herds, high on adrenaline. Some had taken the "biological scare" pills ordered by the government for emergencies since we'd started a rumor about a rogue mosquito, just like the bug that had started the massive epidemic all those years ago during the Before era, when the world had changed altogether. GBVille had been barricaded because of those reports, and the populace was clueless as to the monster takeover because we'd been so secretive about it, with vampires imitating the voices of office-bound politicians and leaders, and other humanlike monsters masquerading as the powers that usually ran things. We'd also sent humanlike monsters as messengers to other fringe hubs already, just to get word out about the rogue mosquito. None of them had returned yet, but that was because they were searching out other monsters, gathering them, to begin rebellions in other places.

Even now, word hadn't gotten out about who was really in charge of GBVille—as well as an increasing number of other hubs as more monster communities followed our example here.

And it was about time we were at the top of society, too.

For a long while, what humans called "monsters" had been at the bottom of the totem pole, especially after the world had altered so much, what with melting polar ice caps changing the weather and the face of geography, and things like terrorists using stolen warheads to blow off a lot of the West Coast. Then the mosquito epidemic had hit, and it'd destroyed much of the world's population. But even then, our country wasn't the same as it'd been before—not with how places like India had leveled sanctions on us, messing up our economy until some mercenary private investors had started putting capital back into our interests. Me and my dad—rest his soul—had been sort of glad for the weakening of government, though, because it'd allowed us to move out to the New Badlands unnoticed by the bigwigs who'd cut back on some of their domestic surveillance programs. We'd even had a pretty good life in our were-community until Johnson Stamp had come along with his nosy employees.

We hadn't realized that he was an ex-Shredder at first, but our community hadn't exactly been up on getting to know outsiders, anyway. After the epidemic, people got real skittish round each other. They began to shut themselves inside their houses for the sake of their health as well as to avoid terrorist attacks, even if the government had started to actively execute offenders. Still, with the breakdown of society, bad guys had gotten ballsy, and their numbers grew and grew.

That was also when the stories had started going round—tales about how some of the people who'd survived the mosquito epidemic only did so because they carried a "monster gene," which allowed for immunity. It also allowed these types to obtain precious water through drinking blood.

They called monsters "water robbers," even if society wasn't exactly sure if we really existed or not. And you know what uncertainty leads to—paranoia. Monster hunts.

Monsters mostly responded by going into hiding, using hidden identities, secret sanctuaries, or staying locked up inside their homes, just like any other scared person. But some of us went to places like the New Badlands, where we dug the ID chips out of our arms, divorced ourselves from major technology, and lived in what we hoped would be peace.

Nobody much bothered us until Stamp and his ilk showed up.

Then Gabriel had come along out of nowhere, too, and me and my dog, Chaplin, had found out he was a vampire and . . .

Well, let's just say my Intel Dog, who'd been genetically bred and tooled with in my dad's lab, had overexerted himself in using Gabriel to bring Stamp down. He'd pitted the two against each other and it had ended up exposing our community, anyway.

I'd done my share to screw things up, though, mostly by

being so overprotective of my neighbors. Hell, I'll be clearer than that—I'd gone and killed a few of Stamp's men, but I'd been trying real hard lately to make up for that. I'd even taken 562's blood in the hopes that it would make me so powerful that I'd be able to protect my friends from every menace in the future. . . .

As I traveled down the main hill out of GBVille, past an abandoned sin alley where the prostitute altars and low-frequency vibration boxes had been abandoned, my heart started to beat in earnest.

I was getting closer to the place where we'd hidden 562, and I could feel my mother/father, even from this far away. Or maybe I was just anticipating seeing my origin.

I came to the little cave where we had secreted 562 a couple of weeks ago, and even though my pulse was shooting every which way now, I couldn't have felt any better.

Did that have something to do with the increased sense of power I had?

The meanness?

Blood still high, I tried to control what was going through my head, but my thoughts wouldn't mellow. In fact, they went in the direction I'd cut them off at before.

Blood.

Hurt.

A bite that had changed my life forever . . .

Under the thrall of those unforgiving memories, I entered the cave, making my way through the small rooms, back toward the space where we'd erected a panel of glass that served as 562's shelter for the time being, until we got round to piling rocks in front of it. I hadn't wanted to fully put 562 away yet, though. Our origin wasn't dead.

She/he was only sort of . . . sleeping. That's the only way I can say it. Mind broken, body stilled. By having 562 conscious and alive, we believed that our origin kept us blood monsters in a preternatural state. But that might have only been faith on our part, because we weren't even sure if 562's death would have erased all our powers and returned us to other, more humanlike forms.

We weren't even sure if 562 could die.

When I walked into the coffin room, I stopped in my tracks, totally unprepared for what I found.

Yes, there was 562 in back of the glass partition, all right—and her/his space was surrounded by what looked to be more offerings than me or any other Badlander had left, just as parting gifts, really. Behind that glass, she/he was in the regular, nonshift form: long silver hair hiding shattered red eyes and a face brushed with glinting down and a small black nose. Because there hadn't been another full moon since the last time 562 had gone lunar, we weren't certain whether our origin would be turning back into the four-armed beast shape that my own body imitated on a smaller scale. We weren't even sure a full moon *had* enough power to control 562's vegetative body.

But the community would sure be ready twelve nights from now, just in case.

We'd posted three older vampire guards in front of 562 as another "just in case" during the nights, using my fellow were-creatures Hana and Pucci by day while the vamps slept. But the vampires weren't what had brought me to a standstill.

It was their positioning.

All three were facing 562, as if they were statue copies of our origin; their legs were crossed in the same lotus position as sheathed silver swords rested on their laps, and their gazes were fixed on our relic with rapt, eerie attention.

They might have heard me enter, but they didn't do anything about it. They just kept their hands on their knees as they stared.

I heard a sound to my left, and I hunched, ready to be set upon. Then I realized that it was only Chaplin.

With the way he slunk toward me, my heart did a dip. He had that cautious, sad look in his big dark eyes, his head down. Even his brown fur, which had once seemed so shiny, looked duller.

I'd never seen him like this—not even when I'd been doing all that killing out in the Badlands. But he'd had faith in my improvement back then—and he'd also thought I could be controlled.

Out of habit, I got down on one knee, holding out my hand to him. He stopped short of it, and I battled a clenching in my chest.

An awkward moment passed before I asked, "Why're you here?"

With one glance at 562, Chaplin provided me with an answer.

He and my origin had never gotten along. 562 had attacked Chaplin once, and I knew that my dog often kept his distance from 562. Did he think he was protecting the community by watching over the origin?

Chaplin sniffed in my direction, as if he could smell Gabriel all over me. Whether Gabriel even *had* a scent didn't seem to matter, since an Intel Dog had powers of detection that went beyond even those of a were-creature in animal form. In this human shape, I didn't have the benefit of any preter powers, so I was at a loss.

My dog sat on his butt, still gauging me, still keeping a distance. But when he spoke in his typical yip-growl-yowl way, I understood him. I'd had him since he was a pup, and my dad had prepared me to take care of Chaplin just as well as he took care of us.

You've been bleeding, he said, barking out the sounds in low tones.

The vampires didn't seem to be listening, so I didn't do Chaplin the disservice of barring the truth.

I'd done enough lying in my life.

"I was with Gabriel," I said, touching my neck where the small wound had healed already.

Chaplin looked away.

"You disapprove?" I asked.

I had hoped you would learn to stay away from him, especially after your confrontation with 562.

"Funny. That wasn't your point of view in the Badlands, when you wanted him round, and when he promised to come with me here to the hubs for a were-cure we never discovered."

It wasn't because I wanted him with you, Mariah. Both times were a part of—

"Bigger plans. I know."

And those bigger plans had unintentionally ended up bringing out the wildness in me. For a while, me and Gabriel had gotten that under control, though, with the way he'd been able to give me the peace with his mind powers. Yet after Gabriel found out that I hadn't merely killed Stamp's men out in the Badlands, but I'd also brought about the death of the beloved woman he'd come out west to track down, he'd resented me too much for the peace to work anymore.

Our link had been contaminated by my actions, even if I'd killed Abby, a fellow werewolf, only because she'd challenged me to the death.

"Chaplin," I said, wishing I could put my hand on him, feel that comforting fur once again. "Don't worry about me and Gabriel. We're going to find a way, just like we did before. Just like we all have."

My dog shook his head. *Gabriel's a Red who still believes that he's got a human inside him somewhere. But all vampires are that way at first, Mariah. At least, that's what the old ones keep telling me.*

I couldn't say anything to that. But I could hope that Gabriel wouldn't be like the rest, couldn't I?

If anyone could save Gabriel from that fate, maybe I could, because I was special now—I had something no other monster had, thanks to 562. I just had to figure out how to use these new powers to our benefit.

Chaplin must've read my expression. *As much as I love Gabriel, you feed each other's bloodlust, and you know it.*

I shook my head, ready to argue, but he interrupted.

No—I saw that look on your face when you came in here. I've spent years seeing that look, Mariah, talking you through it, hoping it would go away for good one day. And I've seen it only get worse. Chaplin stood and started to circle me. *You've been thinking about the bad men who*

*made you into a monster again. I used to understand why
you couldn't forget about them, but now . . .*

"Now that 562 directly exchanged with me, even a little,
you're afraid I'm going to take advantage of what I might
be able to do to men like them."

Isn't that why you took 562's blood?

I shut my mouth, and that was as good as a *yes*. I
wouldn't lie.

Mariah, he said with a whine that crumbled me into what
felt like little pieces.

I tentatively reached out, put my hand on his neck. He
stiffened, but I didn't want to let go.

"Haven't you ever thought about it, Chap? Don't you
remember the sight of Mom and Serg after the bad guys got
through with them?"

I remember.

"A few of them escaped when my dad opened fire. If I
could do anything to those guys, I'd—"

*Don't say it. Don't think it. We've got a chance to live a
new life with this revolution. The tide is turning against the
humans. Don't do anything to turn it back.*

His words sank deep, enough to make me shiver.

But I didn't think it was just Chaplin's comments that
did it.

Out of instinct, I turned round, feeling extra watched.

The vampires had come to fix their stares on me—blank,
cryptic gazes that almost made me feel . . .

As if *I* were 562 and worthy of some dedicated attention, too?

One vampire, a guy with stubble on his pretty-boy face
and long, straight blond hair that came to his neck, smiled
at me just before they all went back to watching our origin.

I didn't like that smile.

"Why're they being weirder than vampires usually are?"
I whispered to Chaplin.

If a dog could shrug, that was what he did. *They're guarding. But if I didn't know any better, I would even say they
are . . . paying adoration.*

From the way Chaplin uttered it, I knew he'd noticed how that vampire had smiled at me, too.

What was going on?

There have been others who have come here, Chaplin added. *Only those who know that we kept 562 alive. In and out, never saying a word, only watching the origin.*

"Do they think 562's going to break out of this funk or something?"

As the blond vampire spoke, I startled, right along with Chaplin.

"It's doubtful that *562* will break out of anything, Mariah."

And he gave me another strange look that sent more chills down my spine, mostly because I could've sworn that he meant something that I just couldn't understand.

Not at that second, anyway.

4

Gabriel

As Gabriel moved through the asylum halls, flickering torches lined the way, much like the fellow monsters who stepped aside, allowing him to pass.

He didn't really look at them, not when it took all his energy to steady the chaos that was still winding through his body from his time with Mariah.

His blood was literally bubbling, his fangs scraping his bottom lip even now, so far away from her, his sight a dull red as he went toward the cells where he was to meet the other vampires for their nightly round of questioning prisoners.

Red. He could barely see around it. In his mind's eye, he could picture Mariah lying in bed, her hair knifed in a short line to her jaw, the color of it as red as his appetite. Her back smooth and pale as he went to touch it. Her eyes a brighter green than usual after she'd started to turn into the monster he always seemed to bring out in her.

He'd wanted Mariah's blood so badly, and he'd taken it like a thief. But he'd paid when his tongue had gone numb from the taste of her.

Was it some sort of cosmic punishment? Or was it nature's way of keeping all the vampires here from feasting on Mariah and her 562 blood?

He was so consumed by his remaining hunger for her—for her old blood as he remembered it during better times—that he came around a corner, nearly banging into the oldster.

Gabriel steadied the man, who'd found a long-sleeved white top and black pants somewhere in GBVille. His whiskers were longer than usual, making his stubble more into a beard these days. His posture was bent, echoing the slight hunch of his body when it was in were-scorpion state.

"Dang, Gabriel," the old guy said, immediately moving aside just as fast as the other monsters had done when they'd seen Gabriel glowering his way down the halls.

Gabriel sensed how the oldster's pulse had picked up, beating in that clean, unblocked cadence that distinguished the Badlanders from any polluted urban hubite.

"Oldster," Gabriel said by way of greeting.

But the other man just kept looking him up and down. "Looking a little rough tonight, aren't ya?"

He even said it with a certain amount of discomfort, but that was how it'd been lately between Gabriel and the Badlanders—the oldster, Hana, Pucci, and even Chaplin. And though the oldster didn't have to say another thing about it, Gabriel had the feeling that the man knew Gabriel's vampire had come out in full force because he'd been around Mariah.

Gabriel's olfactory buds—multiplied and strengthened by vampirism—caught scent of the oldster's humanlike skin. After turning his face away, Gabriel knew that the guy understood he was hungry.

Still hungry.

"Maybe you ought to take a run outside," the oldster said. "Work off some of that steam in you."

"I said I'd be here for tonight's questioning, and I keep my promises, Michael."

When the oldster lifted an eyebrow, Gabriel just about

whipped out some mind-reading mojo so he could find out what was going through the other man's head for certain.

It was second nature to do that now. After being with Mariah, especially this time, it seemed so easy to give in to what he used to consider so base.

And to be *better* at it than ever before.

But weren't all the older vampires—especially the eldest, McKellan—telling him that with the passing of years, humanity seemed less important to their kind?

Irrelevant, even?

The oldster gave Gabriel a wary glance. He would know how to block and even thwart a mind intrusion, anyway, because Gabriel had given him and the other Badlanders pointers when he'd first begun learning more about how his powers worked.

Jerking his chin toward another corner, where voices bounced off the walls, the oldster walked ahead, and Gabriel followed him, encountering more monsters. Only his blood relatives—fellow descendants of 562—failed to fall away from him as he passed: There were the tik-tik women who seemed normal enough while in their humanlike guises. You would never know that when they found their perfect meals—pregnant human women—the tik-tiks removed their heads and allowed this disembodied part of them to feed on the wombs, all while making that *tik-tik-tik* sound. 562 had first created them from the corpse of a dead woman, and they were the vilest of Red creatures.

The gremlins ran a close second, though, and as the sickly yellow-furred, slab-toothed rabbitlike creatures scuttled over the walls, chuckling in low, guttural giggles, they latched their bulbous, dark, long-lashed gazes on Gabriel and the oldster. They had been another one of 562's questionable experiments to raise the dead, this time with an animal.

Gabriel ignored a gremlin that hung down from the ceiling, dry-heaving at the monsters below as if it intended to barf on them. Classy. The stupid things had no fear.

He'd never considered himself biased before, but if he had to be a Red, he was glad he was a vampire, a creature that 562 had been proud of in its later years. 562 had been just as fierce about its were-creatures, too.

But the more Gabriel thought about 562, the more withdrawn he became, his fangs finally retracting, his gaze clearing. Musing about the origin of the Reds was just about as good as taking a precious cold shower, he supposed. But maybe that was because of how it hurt to remember the way in which he'd broken into 562's brain with Mariah, decimating their mother/father's motor skills.

Before that, he'd come so close to going over to 562's side, even when the origin had been killing all those Civils. He'd been so close to becoming a real menace before Mariah had pulled him out of it.

As he and the oldster approached the cells, Gabriel saw that an ancient group of vampires was staring inside some cages down the way, lethargic smiles on their faces, as if they were considering who should be their next meals in this fine buffet. Though they stood still, almost as if they were frozen in time, there was a stirring in the creatures. An excitement that fluttered Gabriel's blood, too.

Near them, a group of were-creatures lingered. Gabriel knew them well—the Badlanders, including Pucci, with his dusky skin and massive chest and shoulders, looking like the were-elk he was when the change came upon him. Then there was Hana, his dark-skinned consort, with robes and a head scarf that echoed her colors as a were–mule deer.

Gabriel tilted his head as he sensed the same sort of restlessness coming off them, too.

Was it because they'd all been cooped up in this hub?

Were they all just dying to let themselves loose on the captivated meals inside this asylum as well as out of it?

Just in back of the Badlanders, there was another patch of monsters—Civils—and Gabriel recognized Neelan, the half-man/half-serpent chimera, among them.

The oldster spoke to Gabriel well before they arrived at the groups. "While you and the other vamps were resting, the Civils reported that there's really nowhere else to look for 562's stored blood in the labs."

"It'll save them the bother of confiscating it in the future, then."

The Civil monsters all thought 562 was dead and that its termination just hadn't had any effect on the preter compositions of its Red progeny. So if there was still blood from 562 in the asylum, they didn't want any more Reds taking it and going as berserk as their origin had during the full moon.

A dead 562 was a good 562 because, by the Civils' way of thinking, the creature's powerful blood couldn't be taken anymore if none existed. It didn't even matter that Mariah, the community's hero and recipient of 562's blood, had been on the Civils' side that night.

No one knew how long that might last if her hunger grew to match 562's.

That was why it was a fine thing that no one but Gabriel, the Badlanders, and a few vampires knew where the vegetative 562 was actually being stored.

The oldster paused in his walking, still far enough away from the groups to guarantee a private word—unless you counted the vampires who'd be able to hear them.

"The Civils have been even more nervous than usual about what might happen if vampires or we weres got a hold of a 562 sample. Or—and I shudder to even think it—what would go down if a tik-tik or gremlin found one."

"It might make everyone as powerful as Mariah could ultimately be."

"Yeah."

Gabriel couldn't stop himself—he zapped out with his mind force and took a peek into the oldster's head, just to see if the man had gone so far as to imagine himself as a 562-type were-creature.

But there was only confusion in the oldster. A snowy storm of bewilderment in his mind.

What kind of price would we all *pay if anyone else dared take 562's blood . . . ?* he was thinking.

The oldster erected a mental block, shoving Gabriel out of his head while shooting him an irritated glance just for good measure.

Then they continued on.

Gabriel focused on the Civil monsters straight ahead as he drew near. Neelan, the chimera, was looking right back at him, stroking his beard. The half-man, half-serpent narrowed his eyes, too, clearly thinking that Gabriel looked "rough," just as the oldster had said.

"Evening, Neelan," Gabriel said pleasantly, but it came out a little jagged in spite of his best intentions.

"Gabriel."

With that, he and the oldster arrived at the cells, which mainly contained humans who had failed to be distracted by the government's pills out in the hub, the ones who were still aware enough to be a danger to the monsters who had taken over by stealth. And if the pills had worn off the distractoids who'd been susceptible to those pills, it'd been all too easy for the vampires to hypnotize them, leaving them out in the streets with the others.

Then again, there were also humans who had come here of their own free will, and these people were asking for blood exchanges to make them better survivors, just like the monsters.

Those were the cells that the vampires stayed closest to.

But Gabriel was aiming for yet another cell altogether, and when he stood in front of the silver bars that had come crashing down after the power blast in this corridor, the occupant slowly raised his head.

In Johnson Stamp's bottomless dark gaze, there was a hateful spark, and Gabriel liked it.

It reminded him of how Stamp's blood had tasted a couple of weeks ago, when 562's rampage had caused enough distraction and destruction for a crazed Gabriel to pounce all over it when the Shredder had been wounded.

Good. So good.

Gabriel smiled. When the Shredder had first tracked the Badlanders here to GBVille, he'd been all spit and shine in his slayer uniform. A young pup, just in his early twenties, slim as the barrel of an old pistol and just as full of explosion. Now he was minus a leg, but not any of his attitude, as he sneered at Gabriel from a corner of his cell, sitting with his arm propped on the leg he could still bend.

"My pal the vampire," he said. "I was wondering when you'd show again."

The oldster had taken up Gabriel's back. Pucci and Hana had even wandered over to add their support.

Feisty as ever, the old man said, "This ain't no courtesy call, Stump, and you know it."

At the demeaning nickname, Stamp's spine stiffened.

Gabriel stood in front of the oldster. This was still his war with the Shredder.

"Just thought you'd want an update, Stamp. I talked to your partner in crime before dawn, and she had something interesting to give up."

"Mags?"

It was the first time Gabriel had ever seen the kid invested in another person. His arm slid off his knee, his posture going into that of a protector's.

"What did you do to her to get information, scrub?" he asked.

Gabriel let the jibe bounce off him. "What do you *think* a vampire can do?"

He was just poking at the boy, but it worked.

Stamp gritted his jaw, his eyes darkening even more. "I'm going to fucking kill you."

Behind Gabriel, Pucci laughed. No one else did, though.

Then Stamp grabbed the post of his meager bed, dragging himself to a pathetic stand. He wobbled on his one leg.

"Where is she now?"

"With vampires." Older ones, and Gabriel had the feeling they had more in store for Mags than just questioning.

"If you went into her mind . . ."

Gabriel only smiled again. "Her mind. It's a cluttered place. She didn't want to give anything up, and she resisted doing just that for a while. But she let something loose."

Stamp launched himself toward them, reaching through the bars, and how a man with only one leg crossed the floor that fast, Gabriel didn't know. But that was a Shredder for you—quick, lethal, never to be underestimated.

"Check yourself," Gabriel said coolly, not flinching even an inch as Stamp's fingers nearly brushed him, "or you'll find that I've also become comfortable with freezing minds."

"I hear that's what you did with that 562 monster." Stamp pointed at him. "You messed that thing up good with Mariah's help. Hell, Gabriel, you're a *real* goddamned vampire now. Are you proud?"

That should've stung as much as the punishing curse that Stamp had thrown at Gabriel. But over the last couple of weeks, Gabriel had found himself weighing his true nature against the absence of humanity. The older vamps told him that soon, he wouldn't even miss it. Besides, now that monsters were taking over the hubs, there was no need to hide behind a human façade to protect yourself anymore—you could be what you were.

That had come to make perfect sense at times, too.

Gabriel had even occasionally wondered what had been so great about humanity in the first place, especially since he was able to borrow emotions from Mariah. And he was wondering that same thing right now as he inched away from what was left of his conscience.

Even so, a tug pulled low in his chest.

It got him . . . this time. "I'm not here to talk about me, Stamp."

The oldster had come around to Gabriel's other side, his voice loaded with sarcasm. "We got ourselves a little background on you ex-Shredders, thanks to your Mags. It seems that you two discovered recently that most of your other ex-Shredders—you know, the ones who were frakkin' paid off to live quiet lives after the government announced that monsters were extinct in society—advised you to stop hunting. Your friends even warned you that the government wouldn't take kindly to your resurrected enthusiasm for tracking and shredding."

Pucci spoke up from behind Gabriel, his voice booming. "Mags revealed that after the government got rid of you Shredders, they went from extermination phase right into preter experimentation. That's why they were putting the monsters who were unfortunate enough to get caught into these asylums."

The oldster leaned against the bars, just daring Stamp to reach through them again. "Now, putting all that together, why do you think the government switched gears in such a way, Stump?"

"I don't know." The kid glared past Gabriel, at nothing, it seemed. But Gabriel knew that he was barricading his mind from any reads.

He remembered the taste of Stamp again, and his animated pulse gave a small blast.

Hana finally said something, and Gabriel stepped aside to let her do it. Her robes swished around her, smelling clean from the refreshing tawnyvale herb they used in the rooms.

"Mr. Stamp, I think you know why the government turned aside from your type of Shredder. They replaced you with those Witches instead."

Stamp's jaw got harder, almost as if he hated the sound of *Witches* just as much as he did *scrubs*.

And the monsters had been banking on that. If they could get Stamp or Mags to give them more information about these new Shredder models, they could vanquish them. The Witches who had been guarding the monsters in the asylum might provide all kinds of trouble if any of them had escaped that first attack with the power blaster.

Gabriel stared at Stamp, willing him to look into his eyes.

But Stamp seemed to know that it would be over for him if he did so, and he backed away from the bars, turned around, then sat on the floor, facing away from them in flagrant contempt.

"Stamp," the oldster said.

But the young Shredder was immovable.

Without even summoning it, Gabriel's mind began to swirl—cold, vicious, the beginning of a brain freeze.

All he needed to do was to modulate his voice, command Stamp to turn around so he could catch Gabriel's eye . . .

But the oldster seemed to see what was happening, and he pulled Hana and Pucci away.

Was he thinking of that night, when Gabriel had gone too far in being a vampire and almost lost it like 562 had?

"Leave it to the more experienced vampires, Gabriel," the man said quietly, but with an authority that had really asserted itself since they'd come to GBVille. "*They* know how to contain themselves."

That last pull of humanity in Gabriel responded with a full-on yank, and he stepped back from the cell, gathering himself.

When he looked away from the bars, he saw the group of Civils, headed by Neelan the chimera, watching him.

Gabriel walked away from all of them, heading toward the older vampires at the end of the corridor, drawn by that pulsing restlessness that seemed to pull him in on an invisible line of red.

5

Stamp

Stamp had been waiting silently with his back to his captors, taking in every word, every nuance.

Cracks were beginning to show between the monsters and their different factions, even just a short time after the lot of them had taken over GBVille. There were fissures that Stamp had predicted would show, because monsters were evil, greedy things in general, and he expected they'd go animal on each other sooner rather than later.

Beasts didn't know any better.

As Stamp listened to the sound of Gabriel leaving, he imagined the vampire sauntering away, his arms curved at his sides like the gunslinger he thought he was.

Fangslinger was more like it.

Then he took a peek behind him, catching Gabriel's were-creature friends as they went in the opposite direction, trading discomfited glances, as if promising each other that they were going to keep tabs on their vampire pal.

After that, the corridor emptied in front of Stamp's cell, though he knew there'd be a Civil guard or two lingering nearby.

He made his way to the silver bars again, the thin hemp of his prisoner garb brushing the floor as he crawled over it. He moved so efficiently, as he'd been taught when he was just barely into his teens during Shredder training, that the woman in the adjacent cell didn't even realize he'd arrived until she glanced over at him, her eyes wide with surprise at seeing him suddenly appear.

Stamp merely grinned at her, one human to another. From listening to her talk with the monsters before, he knew her name was Jo, and that she'd done something to aid the scrubs in taking over GBVille. She was one of the humans who'd refused to take government stunner pills or to run the streets like an idiot, and the monsters didn't quite know what to do with her when she'd quite easily surrendered to their care.

The torchlight burnished the length of her tied-back auburn hair as she sat in front of the bars, looking down the corridor to see if any monsters were coming to chat with her.

"You seem out of sorts," he said.

Jo ignored him. Smart, if she wanted to get on the monsters' good side, because Stamp was a well-known rabble-rouser.

He kept trying to engage her, though. "I've heard what you've been telling the beasts. How you've been asking to join their ranks."

Sighing, Jo rolled her eyes, but she didn't move away from the bars.

"Do you have any preferences?" he asked, a taunting note in his voice. "You can't be turned into a Civil, since they can only be born. But what kind of Red would you want to be? A vamp? A were? Or maybe your tastes run to something more exotic, like one of those tik-tik women."

"Shut up, Stamp."

A response—now he was getting somewhere. "Of course, you'd have to be dead to be raised up as a tik-tik, wouldn't you? But anyone who turns on their own species to willingly become a scrub is dead to me, anyway."

Jo slanted him a look that told him she'd had enough of life as it was—being locked in her house, existing under the threat of everything bad outside. She'd been one of the good people he'd defended as a Shredder, making sure they never saw a monster, much less fell prey to one.

And, damn him, he still had a soft spot for protecting humans, mostly because he wished someone had been around to do it when his own parents had been blown up in a marketplace by monster sympathizers when he was a child.

The woman finally spoke. "Don't you see the way the world is going?"

"The way of the monsters?" he said through his teeth.

"Yes. They're survivors, Stamp. They've endured through massive hunts. They're stronger than any of us, the fittest, and they're the ones who'll be around years from now, when everyone or everything else has ensured their own destruction, just like we humans have."

"So you're casting your lot with them."

"It's a practical move."

"Who's to say monsters aren't just as dangerous to themselves?"

Now Jo smiled. "Everyone's dangerous."

She had a gentle face, heart-shaped, a little sorrowful yet strong all the same. A face like Stamp's mother.

Then again, Stamp could barely picture his parents most times. It'd been so long ago, and besides, the images he'd carried in his personal computer had been wiped out with that power blaster the monsters had used on GBVille.

He looked at the deadened screen on his arm, then rested it facedown on the stump of a leg that had been animated by gears and machine parts, until that 562 thing had torn it off during its full-moon freak-out.

Jo kept talking. "The difference between monsters and humans is this: They're just rising, and humans are the ones falling. If I want to survive, I'll go with the winners, not the losers."

"Good to know that I and the government sacrificed so much for people like you."

"No, don't misunderstand." Jo leaned forward. "I appreciate what kids like you did. It's just time to move on."

"*I'd* rather go down fighting as what I am, not as a vile monster."

He spit, and Jo's gaze filled with horror. Even though GBVille still had running water from corporate resources, it was the ultimate insult to waste it.

"Then down you'll go," Jo whispered. She already sounded like an old vampire—emotionless. Animated by something other than a soul.

Stamp's trigger finger itched. He'd been willing to extend one more chance to her, and she'd squandered it.

What he'd give for a chest puncher or a stake right now. But maybe monster-hunting weapons were even too good for a monster sympathizer—people who had turned on their own kind.

He burned Jo with a stare, but she didn't seem to care. And he would've kept right on staring except for the clatter he heard down the corridor.

Footsteps.

When his partner, Mags, came into view, he pulled himself to a one-legged stand, adrenalized. The Civil guard—a stone creature named Keesie who looked to Stamp like a cross between a mushroom and a statue—led her into her cell and locked her inside.

Stamp ran his gaze over her, but he told himself that it was only because he wanted to see that she was okay from this latest round of questioning she'd obviously undergone.

She leaned against her cell wall, her gray clothing just about hanging off her, her black hair pulled back to emphasize bladed cheekbones and an exotic, dark-skinned face. She clearly hadn't been eating much, and that pierced Stamp. Mags had always been cut by athletic curves, and to see her like this—thinner and less active—just about killed him.

When she turned her face to him, he saw surrender in her brown almond-shaped eyes. The scars she'd earned a couple of weeks ago from a tussle with Mariah before the Badlander had become whatever monster she was now had nearly healed, but there was something in Mags that hadn't likewise mended.

Was it because the monsters had left her and Stamp alive when they could've just killed them?

Was she grateful for that?

His disappointment was sharp, and it only brought his concern for Mags to a pinpoint. He told himself that he cared so much because they had to escape. She had to be up to it.

"What did they do to you?" he asked.

"Nothing much." Mags looked ahead of her again, expression a blank.

"You tried to keep them out of your mind. I know you that well, Mags. But divide and conquer—that's their strategy. They're keeping you away from me and thinking that'll put some distance between us."

He said it a little possessively, yet that couldn't be right. Mags wasn't his.

An unidentifiable weight fell inside him, but he didn't pay mind to it.

"I'm not sure what they meant to do," she said.

He lowered his voice. "Well, they won't do it again. We're gonna get out of here."

A beat thudded between them. Then she laughed, a serrated sound.

"You think we're just going to bust out?" she asked.

As she laughed again, Stamp wouldn't believe that Mags, his right-hand woman who'd been through bloody thick and thin with him when it came to hunting down these scrubs, had lost her will.

When she'd finished, she said, "Where would we go, John?"

"Anywhere. To another hub, just to see what's happening. Or to more ex-Shredders. Even if they were sitting on their asses when we came to some of them before, they'll change their minds now. No Shredder I know would stand for a monster takeover."

Mags sank down the wall, closing her eyes.

"Don't give up," Stamp said.

"I'm tired." Her voice was only a wisp. "Really . . . tired."

Out of the corner of his eye, he saw Jo resting in her cell, too. She'd obviously heard every word. And when her gaze met Stamp's, there was a clear *I told you so* there.

His lip curled as he heard vampires coming back into the corridor. They unlocked Jo from her cell this time, and she glowed at them, going willingly to wherever they were taking her.

Stamp crawled back to his bed, where he lay down, regrouping, believing with all of his heart that Mags was still with him.

6

Mariah

The second I stepped out of 562's cove with Chaplin, I heard those drumbeats from the asylum possessing the warm air like the footsteps of a fretting ghost.

"Are there lowlords somewhere?" I asked my dog, going back to my earlier suspicions about what could possibly be making the sounds.

Behind the asylum walls? he asked.

Chaplin was right. Lowlords—thugs who'd ruled gangs of bad guys in the hubs and had often done the bidding of politicians who refused to come out of their offices—would be just as run-out or drugged up as the rest of the distractoids right now. Besides, they wouldn't be in our territory—not unless they'd woken up and decided to take back GBVille.

We jogged up the hill to the hub, through the sin lane, to the asylum. By the time we arrived at the lower gates, where the ogre and the Yeren were still keeping guard, it seemed like more drums had joined the original one.

While passing those two Civils, I noticed that they kept looking toward the ruckus, as if the pounding were marching up their spines, making the gray skin of the ogre and the monkey fur of the Yeren stand on end.

Can you feel it? Chaplin asked as we left them behind. *In the ground?*

"Can't say I do." But my dog would be way more sensitive than me. Sensitive enough to recognize that we'd picked up some company in the shadows of the walls near us, as well.

Chaplin barked at them in greeting, and I searched for signs of life along the brick: a flutter of dark clothing here, a waving movement in the blackness there. Then Taraline seemed to come out and materialize in front of us before I even got a bead on her.

She wasn't so talented because of any preter skills—she was just one of the shadow people who'd blended right into wherever they needed to ever since they'd caught the dreaded dymorrdia disease, which had forced them out of society and into body-covering veils, gloves, and shrouded clothing. Some had remained in the hubs, hiding in plain sight, people who'd fallen between the cracks. But most had decided to retreat to near-distant necropolises, living amongst the other half-dead.

Taraline's veils fluttered in the slight wind. I'd seen her face only once, when she'd revealed it to 562 in an effort to tame her/him during the rampage. Her plan had worked, too, until 562 had turned her/his attention to sucking Taraline's blood in preparation for an exchange that I'd interrupted. In the end, I'd given Taraline my own blood to compensate for what she'd sacrificed to 562.

My blood had kept her alive, but none of us knew just what kind of effect it'd visited on Taraline since she'd pulled both of her veils right back over her afterward. All I pretty much knew was that 562 and I hadn't *exchanged* blood with her—we'd just let Taraline drink it—so she wouldn't have altered into a creature like either of us.

Had my blood allowed her human face to heal, though? Had it repaired the stripped skin that showed a few patches of skull? The pushed-in nose? We'd seen lingering signs of beauty in Taraline's face—hints of what she might've looked like before dymorrdia had rearranged her bone structure into grotesque arcs and splinterlike patterns; her eyes had still been a lovely blue, her mouth the kind that might make a normal girl with a normal life look into a mirror and practice old movie star poses.

Had she gone back to her former looks?

Taraline was the private sort, so if she'd healed, she was darn well keeping it to herself. Maybe she was also doing that because the other shadows might want me to give them some blood for mending, too.

Was she seeing what it fully did to her before she let anyone else know?

My dog sidled right up to Taraline, nudging her long black skirt. She was wearing her old clothing that still held traces of dymorrdia in its threads, according to Chaplin. He didn't seem to mind the off-putting smell, though, maybe because we'd just about mauled the cloth with tawnyvale lately.

When Chaplin peered up at her with those eyes full of the trust they'd lost with me, I took a hit right in the chest.

Taraline bent and petted my dog with a gloved hand. "It's an active time tonight, isn't it?"

Her voice was deeper than you would've expected from a lady, but that was because she'd gone through useless steroid therapy years ago.

"Do you know what's going on?" I asked.

"I'm not certain of what to call it. A celebration in the making, sponsored by the Reds?"

You would know, I thought. Gabriel had told me that Taraline had been hanging round the vampires pretty often lately, as if observing them closely. Then again, he'd said she'd been watching those tik-tik women, too. Maybe she and the shadows thought we Reds bore lots of observation.

Taraline added, "The Civils are staying away from the festivities, though."

Chaplin spoke up, and I translated for Taraline, who didn't speak Canine.

God-all help us if anyone outside the asylum hears us.

"Shadows are outside, monitoring," Taraline said. "If we can keep the noise to this level, no one will be any the wiser. The rumors of the mosquito have scared off those who used to be waiting to come into the hub, anyway, so no aware human should be near enough to detect it. Visually, if there's any satellite activity, the courtyard is covered. Hence, so are we."

I was just thankful that no one had picked up anything on satellites so far—otherwise, we'd probably have been overrun by the government.

"The distractoids sure wouldn't give a crap about noise," I said. "And the captured higher-ups that the vampires are controlling in the hub can't do anything about us."

As we began walking again, Taraline's veils belled out behind her. I could feel the presence of other shadows on the walls while they trailed us, no doubt undulating as they traveled, easing in with the night.

Now, I *could* sense the drumbeats in the ground. There was also an odd but somehow beautiful plucking and sawing sound, as if someone had found a few lengths of wire and was trying to make music on them.

My breath came shorter as the beats traveled up my legs, then through the rest of me. For some reason, it was as if I were back in bed, waiting for Gabriel to wake up with the dusk.

Or maybe it just didn't take much to get me back to that feeling.

We finally reached a part of the raised walkway that led to an open yet domed space between the burnished stucco walls. As the Gothic grandeur of the asylum loomed round, a gathering was indeed taking place below.

The primal beats were coming from three drums that some vampires were pounding. It looked as if they'd constructed them out of old leather that stretched over circled frames they'd probably found in the labs. They had also discovered what looked to be an archaic harp in the hub—I knew the sight of the instrument from my dad's knowledge books—and they were making discordant noises on that, too.

Whatever song they were playing, it reminded me of a

serpent weaving through the other Reds nearby, dancing, their hands above their heads, their bodies swaying to the *boom-boom-booms* and the lyrical straining. Most of them were half-undressed, torchlight glistening off their skin as hands explored chests, shoulders, arms. Young were-creatures nuzzled one another. Vampires skimmed their fangs over necks and stomachs.

My heartbeat joined with the drums in earnest now, my blood imitating the strange whispers of the harp. It was like all of us Reds were one down there, a pulsing entity . . . even a consciousness that was pulling everyone together.

Lured, I stepped closer to it, but Chaplin blocked me, instead directing me toward a sight that halted me cold.

A group of tik-tik women waited in a corner, the filmy dresses they preferred to wear looking like nightgowns in the faint light.

My blood curdled at the very sight of them. They seemed ready to explode, to break free and run out into the hub to search out any pregnant women to feast on. They needed to eat from fertile bellies only once a year, but, like the rest of us Reds, sometimes hunger wasn't just about survival.

Sometimes it was just about feeling better.

Round them, a few gremlins nipped at the tik-tiks' dress hems, just as if the little nasties were trying to pull the women into the larger group. Not too far away, more tiny creeps were dancing to the music, too, standing on their hind rabbitlike legs, thrusting out their pelvises in a parody of the bigger, badder Reds.

But then, as if by some signal, the music slowed, dying a bit, leaving only the thud of a lone drum as everyone discovered me standing above them.

Me.

My heartbeat played tag with the remaining drum while the vampires smiled, flashing their fangs at me, as if they'd been waiting for me to come. The were-creatures—all young ones, I realized as I surveyed them—rubbed their faces against each other. I could almost see the sweat on them as they contained their monsters.

The tik-tiks and gremlins shrank back a little, lowering their gazes to the ground.

All this because of me, the enhanced direct daughter of 562?

Chaplin whined once, then backed away toward Taraline, who whispered, "Mariah . . ."

She sounded just as confused about who I'd become as I was, but before I could sort that out, the drums started up again, even more frenzied than before. Someone—a werewolf—howled, clearly on the edge of a willed change, and a group of other weres descended on him, like they were keeping each other in check while playing the same kind of game I'd played with Gabriel earlier, tempting our natures, seeing how far we could go now that we had liberated GBVille.

As the beats took me over again, my vision began to flush with a tinge of blue . . . and it started going violet real quick.

It only got worse when I noticed movement in another corner of the party down below, as my gaze locked onto the one I'd been hoping to find down there all along.

Gabriel.

He'd stepped into the clearing, his long battered coat making him seem like a drifter amongst everyone else as they danced near him, leaving him space. He looked up at me with a craving that growled and gnashed through me. While he stood there under the torchlight, his posture and clothing beaten, yet a man still so strong in all other respects, I just wanted to go to him.

I descended a staircase, never looking away from him. He held his hand out to me. Just as I came near the bottom of the stairs, reaching out to him across that clearing, too, someone stepped in my way.

A Badlander who knew me well.

Pucci's barrel chest was heaving. I could see it clearly because his khaki shirt had been torn open, revealing his dusky skin.

"I don't think so, Mariah," he said, his breathing short, as if he'd been ripped away from his own dancing. "We don't need your kind of trouble tonight."

Unthinkingly, I bared my teeth. He did the same until his girlfriend, Hana, intruded, grasping his shirt and hauling him away.

"Antonio . . ."

Then he did something I'd been waiting for him to dare the entire time I'd known him.

He took a backhanded swipe at Hana, laying her out flat on the ground.

In back of me, Taraline cried out, and it seemed as if the music should stop again, but it kept playing on as my violet sight pulsed and my blood simmered.

Bad guy . . .

I leaped forward, but at the same time, someone else did the exact same thing, coming at Pucci in a blurring run and slamming into him. The only reason I didn't get to him first was that Chaplin had thrown himself against me, on his hind feet, pushing me back with his paws.

While I struggled with my canine, Gabriel grabbed Pucci by the neck, lifting him high as the bigger man choked.

"Lucky for you," Gabriel said over the music in his unruffled vampire voice, "I got here before Mariah did."

I panted as Chaplin batted me back up the steps. I wanted to punish Pucci for all the grief he'd given me in the Badlands, testing me with all his demeaning comments, always lobbying for my banishment.

Chaplin whispered to me in Canine. *Mariah-pup, Mariah-pup . . .*

He'd eased me to sleep so many nights with that song, cuddled in bed with me, and it soothed me now . . . but only far enough so that my change didn't burst out all over.

Hana had already gained her feet, grabbing Gabriel's arm while he still held Pucci aloft.

"Please don't, Gabriel. Please . . ."

I finally found my own tongue, but my voice was shredded. "How far is he going to push you, Hana?"

My friend—a Badlander who'd done her best to support me through thick and thin— leveled her liquid, dark gaze on me. A plea.

One I'd seen a hundred times before.

"God-all, Hana." I turned my face away from her. My sight rested on Taraline, who'd come to stand next to me like a lone jury, her veils hiding all expression.

"He didn't mean it," Hana said. "He never goes this far. He's just excited because of the dancing and . . ."

She trailed off. I didn't believe her, anyway.

Pucci choked while in Gabriel's hold, and he wrapped both hands round my vampire's wrist. He was starting his were-change, bones wavering under his skin.

Did he think he could take on Gabriel and win?

We'd caught the notice of the Reds nearest us, and some of the dancing came to a lull. Their stillness balanced my jittery pulse while the bloodlust that had never quite gone away from earlier in the night still boiled in me.

One of the bad guys, I thought, staring at Pucci. A brute, just like the men who'd broken into my family's home and forced that werewolf to bite me, the ones who'd killed my mom and brother.

And Pucci would keep on being a bad guy until somebody did something about it. . . .

But as Hana buried her face against Gabriel's arm, sobbing now, it was clear that my vampire wasn't so far lost that his logic defied reason.

He touched Hana's shoulder, tilted his head, and I knew he was thinking that she was capable of saving herself, if she ever chose to.

He released Pucci, letting him plunk to the ground.

Through the dust, the big man held his neck, coughing. At the same time, Chaplin dropped to all fours, coming up the stairs to Taraline again, as if I'd stopped needing a protector and she was his new duty.

But I couldn't care about that—not with the breath wedged in my lungs.

Gabriel spoke in a mangled tone. "If you've got enough balls to change into your monster right now, Pucci, I'm just gonna rip them right off you."

As if to challenge that, Pucci began to shake, allowing more of himself to turn, his skin absolutely flowing now with the changes going on beneath it.

Hana dropped to him, clutching his arm. "No!"

Her voice seemed to persuade him, and he closed his eyes.

"No, Antonio," she whispered fervently.

It seemed like forever, but he stopped his trembling, eventually huffing to his feet and stomping away, through a group of grinning vampires who'd obviously been entertained by the show.

After Pucci shoved past them, they went back to dancing with each other, grinding hips, their kisses moving up and down slick bodies as if nothing much had occurred.

As the drums kept on, Gabriel glanced in Pucci's direction. "Hana had better take over from here, because the next time I drop him in the dirt, it won't be in one piece."

Taraline spoke. "She needs help more than he does. I'm going to look after her."

She ascended the stairs, leaving us, her veils flapping behind her.

The drumbeats filled me up again, and when I turned back round, I focused on some were-couples just to the left of the staircase—monsters who apparently hadn't given much thought to our little Badlander drama.

They were using shirts to bind each other, forcing one another into willing, panting submission. It was an echo of how our bodies bound what was inside us—how we fought our restraints each and every pull of the moon.

Chaplin barked in back of me. *Come with me, Mariah?*

"No," I said. And I guess I said it in such a way that it was final, because Chaplin barked and yawped again.

You need some sense talked into you, and I guess I'm beyond doing that anymore.

He bounded up the stairs, following Taraline. What, was he going to bring back a bunch of Civils to haul me out of here, away from Gabriel?

I didn't think so.

I didn't watch him go because I was already locked onto Gabriel, whose irises had gone red, his fangs sprung.

Maybe I should've just listened to Chaplin, but seeing Gabriel step up to Pucci had made my sight go a deeper violet, my blood taking over like high, sharp, cold/hot screams through my veins. It killed me to be even this far away from him, and I didn't know what I would do if I ever had to be away for long.

The drumbeats had slowed, and from across the clearing, I realized that a mixture of ethereal voices had added themselves to the music.

Russian?

Perhaps, because we had a family of werewolves from that part of the world that we'd liberated in this asylum. I didn't speak their language, but I could've sworn it was poetry braiding itself into the chaos.

Under the spell of everything that had happened tonight, I finally went to Gabriel, resting my hand on the back of his cool neck. As I thought of what he might have done to Pucci—*blood, bad man, a reckoning*—I pulled him down to me, speaking against his lips, avoiding his fangs while testing the danger of them.

His thoughts coursed into mine, and I gasped with the thrust of our link.

I saw you standing up there, Mariah, and it hurt, wanting you so much . . .

The drums became my blood, drawing it toward my skin and to Gabriel with urgent need, making it so that I wasn't sure where the music ended and me and Gabriel began.

Our world was steeped in blood, defined by it while it tumbled in us, our rhythms racing until there was no more thought, just impulse.

We tempted each other, mouth to mouth, brushing, gauging. No kissing, just strained breaths, his cool, mine warm. His fingers were equally cool as he toyed with the lacings of my blouse.

I gasped, not expecting this. But it seemed natural with

the heat in the air, in *us*. With the exposed skin, the sensual swaying and the nuzzling and nipping, the rising aroma of lust round us as nails drew blood lines on flesh.

I wanted to be a part of it all. A part of him.

So very ready for more, even if it might harm me.

Gabriel understood that, and he undid my shirt. When he parted it, the air hit my skin. His palms covered me as he gripped my waist, his thumbs tracing my stomach. My shirt scratched against my breasts, making the tips go hard.

Behind me, an interested bystander ran a hand down my back, as if wanting to be a part of me and Gabriel, too, a real community of Reds.

Only Reds.

Nothing else mattered when Gabriel skimmed his hands upward, cupping my breasts. The creature behind me tugged down on my shirt and, for the first time I can remember, I didn't mind being revealed.

We were monsters who didn't have to hide now.

When Gabriel seized me by the waist and lifted me into the air, I couldn't breathe. Other hands grabbed at me, at the lacings on the sides of my pants, but their fingers didn't undo them. Maybe they wanted to be able to feel me as I exploded into what fascinated them—a form echoing 562's.

The daughter our origin had chosen to exchange with rather than anyone else.

Gabriel pressed his face against my bared belly, rubbing against it, absorbing my scent. Through our link, I could sense his temperature rising, adapting to my own.

By now, more Reds had gathered round us, whispering words I couldn't really hear. Most had shed their clothing, and trails of blood marked their skin—nail skids, appetizers for something that hung in the atmosphere like a brutal promise. It seemed that the drums were louder than ever, stomping on my chest, or maybe that was only my body giving way to what it should.

"Your blood," said someone in the crowd.

And, suddenly, others took up the chant.

Your blood, blood, blood . . .

I looked down at Gabriel as he looked up at me, fire in his eyes, his fangs sharp in his adoring smile.

He was going to bite me again, even if it would poison him. He wanted me that much.

No one had ever felt that way about me before.

In utter ecstasy, I leaned back my head, listening to the chanting—*your blood, blood, blood*—then spread my arms as if I could take flight. My shirt hung off me like wings.

Blood, blood—

I could feel Gabriel, ready to strike at a tender point in me, and not knowing exactly where it would be only added to my excitement.

Your blood!

I sucked in a breath . . .

But before I felt a bite, someone yanked me down, away from Gabriel, plunging me into a sea of bodies that forced me to the ground.

In the next fevered heartbeat, I felt silver links wrap round my limbs, restraining me, and I grunted in discomfort as it sent me to weakness.

A gunshot split the air. So did a familiar voice.

"Back off!" the oldster yelled over the cacophony.

The music had stopped, but the hissing and growling had just begun.

I strained at the bodies round me, but they were determined to keep me on the ground—older, wiser werecreatures who'd gone through a half change so that they were part animal, part human. Half-pumas, lions, tigers . . . They were all still capable of logic before it melted away with the reshaping of the bones and form.

The oldster fired his revolver again. I started to cool as I noticed that the older were-creatures carried stakes, too, and that a whole lot of Civils were down here backing them up.

So Chaplin *had* gone after help.

"Her blood is off-limits," the oldster yelled. "You hear me?"

From somewhere, a vampire hissed, "You weres want it."

The growling intensified from the monsters who were

guarding me. It sounded as if the younger were-creatures who'd been dancing were slinking back to their elders now, chastened.

I knew that the were-community was curious about what might happen if they tasted my blood, much less exchanged with me. And I knew that right before me, a power struggle was beginning between them and every other faction—the ones who couldn't claim me as their actual blood sister.

As I took that in, I went still.

Finally accepted, I thought, and I knew just how psychotic that was as tears started to blur my gaze. But after all this time being stranded on the outside of my Badlander group, I couldn't help myself.

I could see Gabriel through the bodies surrounding me, and I knew I needed him just as much as I needed everyone else. Even more so.

"Listen to you vamps," the oldster muttered, before saying even louder, "Nobody gets her blood. She stays one of a kind, got it?"

"One of your kind," said a vampire.

The oldster ignored him and spoke to his posse. "Take her away until these fiends calm down. You older weres corral the younger ones and give them a talking-to *pronto.* We need to stand together—all of us, Reds and Civils—or there'll be shit to pay if the humans ever start fighting us."

A pair of Civils, who weren't affected by silver, lifted me, carrying me toward the asylum, where I was pretty sure I'd get a talking-to, also.

The silver had cooled my half-changed body back to normal in record time, and I cooperated with the Civils as they brought me to my quarters and set me on the bed.

"She's kosher," said the oldster after inspecting me and tucking his revolver into a holster on his hip. I was sure the old-time weapon was full of silver bullets, which would poison a vampire, sucking energy and power just as surely as a shot in the heart would do away with a were-creature.

The guards unwrapped the chains from me, and I rubbed my skin.

"Thanks, Michael," I said.

Judging from the slant of the oldster's mouth, I could tell he wasn't sure whether I was being a smart-ass or not.

"I mean it," I said. "We just got caught up in . . . something . . . out there."

"Something? How about we just call it a near feeding frenzy? Do you have any idea what they would've done to you, Mariah? Chaplin's so pissed at you that he wouldn't even come with me out there."

I swallowed, then raised my chin.

"They wouldn't have done a thing I couldn't have handled," I said, surprising even myself with my cheek.

The oldster raised a gray eyebrow. "Cocky. Maybe you think you've become some kind of goddess who's untouchable or something."

The memory of what that vampire had proclaimed when I'd been visiting 562 slapped at me: It wasn't our origin who was going to "break out," he'd said to me with that strange vampire's smile. And when I remembered how those three guard vampires had *all* looked at me, I could almost believe I *was* untouchable.

The oldster put his hands on his hips. "Mariah, it'd be dandy if you'd avoid getting yourself into a situation like that again. We've got a passel of worked-up vamps now and a bunch of pissed-off Civils having to look over their shoulders. It'll be bad enough for them when the full moon hits and they'll have to team up with the other Reds to restrain you and us were-creatures. We need teamwork round here, girl, not bloodletting parties that threaten the Civils' comfort."

He didn't add anything about what might occur with the dormant 562 on the full moon. Not with the Civils still standing in my quarters right now.

I glanced at the pair of Civils who'd restrained me. Fauns. As expected, their human faces weren't amused.

"I'm sorry," I said, relenting for their sake.

One of them shrugged his bare, broad shoulder. In the torchlight, his chest glistened until it got to his hips, where the body of a goat took over.

"Not sorrier than I was when humans had *me* locked up in this place," he said. "But I sure don't want to go back to days like those with any community."

Okay, so he was a major diplomat. He wasn't even very convincing, but maybe there was a grain of truth to his comment. At least Reds weren't prodding and poking him in the labs, like humans would still be doing if we Badlanders hadn't liberated the place.

The oldster said, "What the hell happened to the concept of a honeymoon period after our great triumph over the humans, anyway?"

"We'll work all this out," I said, ever the optimist. Mainly.

"We have no choice." The oldster nodded at the Civils, and they left the room.

I remembered that my shirt was undone, and I held it together, suddenly not feeling so free or celebratory.

"I swear, Michael, it just . . . happened," I said. "We were having fun out there, like humans, and—"

"Not like humans, Mariah. Not the ones who weren't lowlords or their followers. Or religious zealots."

He was right.

What *had* happened?

And how had I lost so much control that it'd been simple to become such a part of it?

My questions were interrupted by a screech outside my door in the hallway, and just like that, the oldster had his revolver out again.

But when someone screamed "Murder!" as they ran by, he drew both of his pieces.

7

Gabriel

In a darkened stone hallway, lit only by the few working solar-powered lanterns that the Badlanders had preserved outside the hub during the power-blast attack, Gabriel stared through the haze of red covering his vision.

His hands.

Blood.

He wasn't sure how it'd gotten there. He only recalled the gathering, Mariah . . . then the oldster and a group of Civils and older were-creatures breaking them all apart before shooing them off. That was when he and some other vampires at the same early stage of development had grouped together while going back into the asylum. Then . . .

Gabriel tried to remember the rest of it. But he only knew that he and these other younger vamps had been restless after all the foreplay in the courtyard had amounted to nothing. They'd understood each other's torment, too, because, at their stage—"the gloaming," McKellan the elder called it—everything was a confused tug-of-war between what they'd known as humans and what they wanted as vampires.

Gabriel had genuinely believed that a nip of blood from his flask would help him get steady, so he'd been heading to his room to take care of himself.

But he'd clearly never made it. Everything in his mind was dark until this moment, when he'd heard a voice in the near distance scream, "Murder!"

Dizzy, he looked around the hallway. His red vision began to clear, and he realized he was on the floor, leaning against a wall, hearing sounds—slurping, moaning. Hissing.

Then he saw a swarm of vampires feasting on a body.

A . . . Civil monster?

A tide of horror reared up in his chest, sending his eyesight to a wash of dim, normal colors. Something like humanity had surged back to him, but it was too late.

As he kept looking on, he saw that the body *was* that of a Civil . . . a man who had the long neck of a giraffe and the spots of one, too. He was mangled, his throat torn out, his belly flayed open, his fur scattered and mixed with a pool of gritty red.

Then Gabriel's view was cut off as the young vampires who'd left the courtyard with him flooded over the Civil again, their heads bobbing, utterly animal as they drank.

Just like me, Gabriel thought as if his mind were detached from the rest of him. *They* are *me.*

One of the vampires, a woman with long brunette hair, reared back from the greedy crowd, blood dripping from her chin then to the ground as she hissed in pleasure.

Gabriel scented that blood as if it'd gone into him and taken hold, and he craved it deep in his belly. He shuddered. His appetite had gotten much worse during the gathering, when he'd been so close to Mariah . . .

As he watched the group, he felt as if the only remaining humanity in him were floating, isolated, a part of their hunger yet not a part of it. But then a jagged screech brought him out of his lull, and he clawed the floor as he saw the chimera Neelan, half-man, half-serpent, quickly writhing into view, breathing a stream of fire at the brunette vampire and pulling her by the hair away from the body while pressing a silver cross to her forehead.

She screamed while more Civils came out of the shadows, all with crucifixes that they used on the vampires, their skin sizzling as they cried out.

Gabriel didn't move as a Civil came at him, too. When the quasi-angel—its gray wings only for show, its disposition hardly heavenly—pressed a crucifix to Gabriel's cheek, he took it as his punishment, gritting his teeth, scenting the burn of his flesh.

"No," he heard someone say over by the victim's body. It sounded like the oldster.

The quasi-angel with the crucifix backed off Gabriel when he saw that he was getting no resistance from him. Gabriel's cheek flared with hot agony as he looked over at the carnage again.

The oldster was on his knees in front of the victim while the Civils pulled away the tamed vampires. He still had his revolvers in hand as he raised his arms, burying his face in the cradle of them, rocking forward.

"Just get them out of here," the oldster said, voice muffled. Then he lowered his arms and yelled, "Get them in silver restraints and keep them in the empty north cell block until I come."

Neelan spoke up. "You're in charge?"

"Who else?"

Neelan's bearded jaw stiffened, but his fellow Civils had already started wrapping silver chains around the vampires, roughly pushing them out of the hallway as the criminals stumbled along. None of the Civils had attacked them yet, though they kept glancing at the dead body with a mix of shock and rage on their faces.

As Gabriel's quasi-angel guard moved to bind him, the oldster barked out, "He's already calmed down—can't you see that he dragged himself away from this?"

"But—"

"I've got *him* for now. Go on with the others."

The Civil kept standing there. "You're a were. A Red. Why should I—?"

"Don't make this more of a fight than it already is." The

oldster took a breath, exhaled. "The community's gonna decide what happens next, and I aim to provide enough coolheadedness so that right is done. Understand? We need to find out who initiated this before punishment's wielded. You can't fault vampires for hopping on a spill of blood after it's out there."

"Yes, we can," the quasi-angel said.

"That's how vamps *are*." Then the oldster shut his mouth, gathered himself. He quietly said, "You need us just as much as we need you if we're going to band together against the people who'd hunt us."

The quasi-angel looked down at Gabriel with such venom that even a vampire might've withered under it, *if* that vampire weren't already decimated from self-hatred.

The Civil didn't attack Gabriel, but he remained close. "We'll take the matter to the community, like you said. We lock up the ones who were a part of this until we decide what to do. And when you isolate the vamp who brought down . . ." He gestured toward the bloody victim, grimacing. "When you do that, we take an eye for an eye."

The oldster nodded, his gaze slipping to Gabriel.

Hell, Gabriel thought, the word biting through him. There'd be hell and more to pay, and he wasn't so sure he and all the others didn't deserve it, no matter who'd brought down the victim first.

The oldster hadn't moved away from the body, his revolvers still drawn. As the quasi-angel slowly left, his breathing was ragged, as if he wanted to gut Gabriel but was forcing himself not to.

When he was gone, the oldster spoke. "Damn you . . ."

Gabriel flinched. From his friend's tone, it was clear that the man who'd been so kind in taking Gabriel into the Badlands community when he'd needed it the most was just about to lose all faith in him and maybe even the rest of the vampires.

He peered at the blood on his hands again, ached to taste it, ached and resisted with all his might.

Then he closed his hands into fists. "I wish I could tell you what went on. But I can't."

"Is this some sort of blackout, like the ones you used to have early on, when you came to us in the Badlands?"

"I . . . don't know."

It felt like centuries ago, another lifetime. When Gabriel was human, he'd had a habit of overindulging—alcohol, women, sometimes drugs. Like so many others, he'd been reeling from the world's changes, hardly strong enough to face them. Then he'd been chosen by his maker, saved by a near-anonymous exchange with her. She'd been on a mission to save as many people as she could from any more mosquito epidemics or other coming pestilence with her monster immunity, her vampire blood. She'd moved on to the next and the next, as far as Gabriel knew, without staying behind to mentor him.

He'd gone a little crazy back then, bingeing as if blood were booze, reveling in the numbness of it, blacking out most nights. Then he'd met Abby, and he'd embraced the humanity that all new vampires were said to be left with until it faded after a few years.

Soon enough, *she'd* disappeared, as well.

Then he'd found out her fate—he hadn't known until too late that she'd been a stealth werewolf who'd gone to the Badlands to hide. She'd died there, a figment of his memories now, since he'd finally come to terms with what she was and why Mariah had possessed no choice but to kill her in order to defend herself.

It'd been a matter of survival, just like bloodletting was for a vampire.

The oldster now leveled a look on him, and it would've been worthy of any vampire glower had the old man been one.

"What do you remember, Gabriel?"

"After we left the gathering, our hungers were stoked. I remember coming inside, with the other younger vampires, then . . . nothing. Just this."

He held up his hands, showing the oldster the red.

"You pieces of shit. I understand why there was a feeding frenzy when the blood was let, but that doesn't excuse the first vampire who brought this Civil down. This is murder, whether we're monsters or not."

Gabriel just stared at the body, the once grand giraffe Civil, with his long neck and patterned fur, with his gentle disposition, now reduced to slush.

Then he felt it.

Mariah's presence.

It dug down in his core, deep in his blood as she came to stand nearby. He scented her skin—the earthy perfume of it. He heard her rhythms, churning like violin strings in a stormlike symphony.

Back in the Badlands, she'd been the one defending the community and killing those bad guys . . .

The oldster seemed to catch Gabriel's musings.

"She was with me and the Civil guards the entire time," he said.

Gabriel hated himself even more for thinking that way.

She was next to him now, half in shadow from the light of the solar lanterns. He could also see movement on the walls. Shadow people.

Had any of them witnessed who'd attacked the victim first?

Had it been *him*?

As Mariah leaned against a wall, she wore an expression that spoke to Gabriel without words. Horror. Hunger.

He understood both equally.

"Just like 562," she said. "You went for Civil blood."

"No." Gabriel frowned. "We weren't hungering for a certain kind of blood, I remember that much. The Civil was just . . . here. Walking along. Available."

"Why?"

She wasn't asking why it was available. She wanted to know why they'd done it.

When Gabriel looked at her, she seemed to understand.

The bloodletting at the gathering had worked all of them up, and the only thing that had mattered was availability, not the type of blood.

Even now, the aroma from the small lake of red on the

floor was wafting to Gabriel. He could see that it was doing the same to the oldster and Mariah, too.

"Gabriel," the old man said with restraint. "When we arrived, you were sitting over there, apart from the feasting. Tell me that the blood on your hands is just accidental or that you tried to pry the other vampires off the victim. Give me a reason to let you off the hook."

He could've just lied, but the only decency left in him said, "I can't."

For all he knew, he could've been the one who'd brought down the Civil in the first place, and the rest of the uncontrolled younger vampires had scented the blood, taking advantage of the kill in their stimulated state. They hadn't been thinking, just *doing*.

The oldster sighed. "Hell's about to rain down, you know that, don't you?"

Stinging from the mention of hell, Gabriel started to respond, but the oldster raised a revolver and aimed it at him without even looking.

"Something tells me I should just get this over with now. We need the Civils if we're going to stay strong against bad guys. We don't need to become bad guys ourselves. . . ."

He hesitated, and that was all it took for Mariah to act.

It happened fast: She swung his arm over her shoulders and pulled him to his feet.

"Run," she said, pushing him.

Even in that split second, he felt the heat of her. Felt her choked reaction to the blood on his hands as well as the response to merely being near him. But before he could start berserking again, his logic took over.

So did the surety that he couldn't go anywhere without her.

It was as if the devil itself were nipping at his heels as he scooped her into his arms and turned on full vampire speed, zooming them down the halls, over the walls, out of the asylum.

Away . . . Going to someplace, anyplace, where he could

remember what had happened . . . where he could decide if he should even come back at all . . .

He didn't stop until they were on the other side of GBVille, near a General Benefactors building, its sleek lines sterile in the moonlight. Char burns marred the side of it, remnants of an abandoned bonfire from a lowlord's gathering. Pill-coma bodies lay around, dressed in the bland rags from a gang. No one—not even the few police that still roamed the streets, clueless as to the monster takeover—had bothered to remove them since they were so base.

That was when Gabriel realized that he hadn't heard the revolver go off behind them when they'd escaped. Was it because the oldster didn't want to shoot? Deep down, did he still believe Gabriel was the same guy he was out in the Badlands, when he'd been a hero, and that was why he'd hesitated?

Setting Mariah down on the ground, Gabriel changed direction and ran again, this time at the reinforced doors of the public GB building, where he wouldn't have to be invited in. He put a few dents in them before busting them open, then finding a bunch of higher-level humans propped against the white walls, passed out from the biological scare pills.

He spotted a water necklace on one of the humans; it was a luxury item, a symbol of prosperity to flaunt. Ripping it from the woman's neck, Gabriel broke it open, baptizing his hands with its contents, erasing the red as he then used the human's clothing to wipe them off.

He heard a sound behind him, a faint sliding.

Thinking it was Mariah, he turned but didn't find her.

Had it been a shadow person?

Or . . .

He remembered the night of the asylum power-blaster attack, when there'd been Witches who'd sounded just as quiet while they'd moved . . .

Fingers of discomfort crept over his shoulders as he finished cleaning his hands, but he didn't hear anything more.

He wouldn't have even scented a Witch, since part of their defenses included being odorless, so he kept his gaze peeled.

Nothing more.

Not until Mariah came into the room. He could scent *her*, and he went giddy with the aroma.

"Your clothes," he said, his voice sounding humanlike now that he was clean, now that he was away from that asylum. "I marked them with the victim's blood when I picked you up."

A faint rustling told him that she was removing an outfit from a passed-out human, then taking off her own shirt and pants. He couldn't bear to look back at her. It'd undo him for certain.

All the while, he felt the empathy flowing through her and, by extension, him. He'd borrowed so many emotions from her that he could identify them perfectly by now.

"Tell me you didn't do it," she said.

"I already said—I'm not sure."

"You didn't. I know it, Gabriel."

He completed one last scan of the room, and when he was content that they were alone, he turned to find her in one of the blasé, straight-skirted dresses that the hub women favored. But she was marked as a nonhub by the boots she still wore, and also by that red hair, recklessly shorn to her chin, giving her a waifish edge. She'd also taken a few water necklaces to wear, clearly anticipating her need for the liquid when she was in her human body.

It was a declaration that she still intended not to change form until she had to, at the next full moon.

Would they have to stay away from GBVille that long? And what was going to happen to his vampire brethren while they were locked up? Would the Civils carry out some revenge?

In a flash, his vampire logic took over, freezing out his humanity.

His fellow vampires could and would take care of themselves. No one was more capable.

Mariah had narrowed her green eyes at him. She'd sensed

the lightning-fast change. "Hopefully everyone will realize that it was just a small group of young vampires who lost control tonight. Either way, your older ones will know what to do with them, and how to talk down the Civils."

"Right. Everyone wants a monster society. Everyone will want to work this out so it doesn't happen again in the future."

He could feel a twinge of sorrow in her, and he thought it might be because she suspected a Civil killing *would* happen again, maybe even because of the were-creatures. With them, impulse ruled all, even logic, and she was the worst-case scenario.

But what were they inheriting, anyway? He glanced around the room, which was a monument to prosperity. Sculptures of peace and harmony. A glimmerfall frozen in midtumble behind a reception desk where a General Benefactors employee slumbered.

Mariah was so far away from him that she might as well have been another sculpture—but one that beat with the life and blood he couldn't live without.

"So are we running?" she asked. "Or are we going to stay here until they hunt us down?"

"Is there a choice?"

She sat on the ground, as if settling in for some planning before taking off again. "I think we need to go farther for the time being. Out of the hub. I, at least, can try coming back in a few days, when matters have cooled. By then, they might even know what happened with the victim. Surely some shadow people were round to witness it."

Gabriel didn't know if that would be a good or bad thing. "And if matters are still unsolved at that point?"

"Then matters won't *ever* cool." Mariah pulled her legs up, wrapping her arms around them, resting her chin on her knees. As her emotion infiltrated him, he knew that he'd never find anyone like her anywhere else. That he couldn't exist without her. It wasn't like Abby, where he'd thought he'd fallen into some sort of love brought on because of how he was clinging to humanity. Mariah had accepted what it was to be a monster. And she was the only one who could make him lose control and find it within the same heartbeat, only to cycle around again.

She was terrible for him, but he wasn't a person anymore. The same rules of love didn't apply. He needed what he needed now, and she was it—a poison. A drink he desired just as much as any blood.

Her expression altered as she read his face. Did his want for her show so much?

Her voice lowered to a thick whisper. "So where do we go?"

She was with him. His Mariah—the only one he had left.

"Now that we've heard that other hubs have been taken over, we have a choice in destination," he said. "We can go just about anywhere that the power is out."

"Without power," she said, "humans don't have much, do they?"

"No weapons, no surveillance. No hunting us down. We're probably in more of a situation here, as it stands."

She swallowed hard, and he could feel the rise of something in her. He'd felt it earlier tonight, when they'd been together in bed—a lightning strike of memory, anger . . . a need just as great as his own.

Without checking himself, he looked into her eyes, and even from this distance, he jumped into her mind.

He read where she wanted to go easily. "Dallas. You're thinking of Dallas."

She drew back from him.

Every fiber in him wanted to give her what *she* wanted, though she didn't seem as if she were champing at the bit to ask it of him.

"There's no good reason for me to go to Dallas," she said.

"That's a lie."

She blinked, flushed in mortification. The roar of her vital signs consumed him as he got to all fours, making his way toward her.

"We know from the monsters who've couriered messages back and forth between the hubs that Dallas fell already," he said. "It's probably even the closest hub that we know of that's secretly monster-secured. And it's your hometown."

The place where her very own bad men had turned her life upside down during the attack on her family.

"Forget it," she said.

"It makes sense you'd long to go there, Mariah. I came out to the Badlands to pick up my past. Why wouldn't you want to do the same one day, especially after you exchanged with 562?" He inched even closer. "You told me once that there must be a reason we were given these powers. That this is how nature works. That maybe it's up to us to balance things out if they weren't being balanced already."

"I think we should leave well enough alone, Gabriel." But her tone betrayed her true need. "We stay away a few days, then come back here when the time is right. If Chaplin were here, he'd say the same thing—no Dallas."

She had Chaplin to balance her, just as Gabriel had the clinging humanity. Night by night, both got a little further away from them.

"Chaplin's not the one who's here now, Mariah," he said.

Gabriel felt a plunging emotion in her that he couldn't quite grasp until it leveled into anguish.

Was it because she was just now realizing that Chaplin belonged to a different time in her life, before Gabriel had come along to encourage the beast in her that Chaplin had tried to make her face and tame?

She looked perplexed. "I suppose I've wanted to know if those bad guys who escaped my dad's weapons are still there. I want to know what happened to them, if they ever got what was coming to them. But that doesn't mean it's wise to go."

"And if you found out that they aren't there? Or that someone else took bullets to them?"

She lowered her gaze, trumped by his persuasion. "I might get a bit of peace from it."

Gabriel would give anything for that to happen. He, himself, had often wondered what he might be if he were to confront his own past—his absentee maker. Like Mariah, he'd been made and abandoned, except she hadn't been as willing as he was.

"I say that's where we head, then," he said, getting to a knee right in front of her, so close that her eyes went lighter in color as she shivered in his presence.

His appetite liked that—it liked that he could still be a hero to her in some way, too.

At her silence, Gabriel got to his feet, holding out a hand.

"We'll go there for a few nights," he said. "Just like you said. We don't even have to do any searching if you don't want to. We'll lie low in a place where other monsters are in charge." He waited a beat. "We have to go *somewhere*, Mariah."

She didn't agree, but in the light green of her eyes, he saw a glint of desire so strong that it tore through him.

A few seconds later, she took hold of Gabriel's hand, and they ran off.

8

The Oldster

The next night, the oldster sat in an anteroom of the asylum that had clearly been used as a lounge for the medical professionals who'd worked there. Round him were "live paintings," which had, when there'd been electricity, shimmered with images of lakes and ponds. Now they were just a bunch of burned-out pixels hovering over caffeine machines and plug-in stations where the humans had downloaded software into their personal computers.

He leaned forward in his chair, resting his elbows on a steel table. Across from him, a tik-tik woman named Falisha sat tall, her dark hair wound up into coils, giving her a faintly Grecian look, like statues you could see on a Nets museum. She was actually just as long-lived as those statues, too, because she had the same kind of existence as a vampire, animated until terminated. She wore a sheer white nightgown of a dress, a thick black ribbon round her throat and, up close, her eyes, deep-set and dark blue, were ringed by red. But it wasn't from exhaustion. All the tik-tiks carried that trait, and the color slanted up from the corners of her gaze like geisha makeup.

"I appreciate your giving me some time," the oldster said.

She merely inclined her head, but didn't utter anything.

"You seem to be the one all the tik-tiks look up to." No one knew these women all that well, as they kept to their lonesome most times. But the oldster was still observant in his waning years, and he knew that if he wanted to talk to the group, he should go through this Falisha first.

A gremlin scurried up her chair legs and settled into her lap, blinking its obscenely long lashes up at her. Its long two front teeth were comical.

She gave the oldster a considering look. "Michael . . . That's your name, isn't it?"

She had a frank way of talking that got the oldster's attention. And not necessarily in a good way since his gaze kept straying to her lips—lush, curvy at the top, like a bow.

"Yes, ma'am," he said, righting himself.

"You must be at the dead end of an investigation if you're chatting with *me* about the killing."

He kept to his poker face. There wasn't a need for her to know just what he was up to—especially that he hadn't possessed the guts to shoot a silver bullet into the main suspect, Gabriel, as the vampire had sped off with Mariah last night. Gabriel had made himself a fugitive, but damned if the oldster had given his friend—the savior of the Badlands—just one more chance and refrained from giving chase. *He* could've just as easily turned into his were-form, putting on his quickness, but he'd only watched Gabriel go, hoping against hope that his friend would get far enough away that it would give the Civils enough time to simmer down a notch. And to find out if one of the other vampires had attacked the victim first.

Not that the oldster wanted any Reds to be guilty. It was just that he'd promised the Civils that he would sort out this killing, and he didn't want to find out that his friend had been the cause of it. Besides, there was too much ill will quietly traveling through this asylum for this matter to go unanswered. So much of it that the oldster wondered if the monster community was about to destroy itself before they'd really even gotten started.

"I would think you'd be spending more time with the vampires than a tik-tik," Falisha added.

"As you might've heard, the vampires have closed ranks. They say they want to handle the situation on their own."

And when Gabriel returned—if he ever did—they would sort him out, too, *if* he was guilty. They'd also be giving their more unstable young vampires like Gabriel better training in controlling themselves and their bloodlust.

Meanwhile, the oldster couldn't get the image of Gabriel and his bloody hands out of his head. More and more lately, the old man was thinking of him as an other. Not one of his own kind anymore.

But was the vampire *ever* really one of the Badlanders?

Falisha rested a hand on the gremlin's head. "Are the vampires conducting their own investigation then?"

"Yup. And they'll be getting back to me with their findings soon enough. You can trust in that. They know what kind of stakes we're up against."

As Falisha petted the gremlin, its tongue lolled out of its mouth, its eyes rolling back into its head in delight. In a parallel world, the buxom tik-tik woman and the little nasty might've made for a portrait of a tainted scarlet woman with her lap dog.

"Listen," the oldster said. "I asked you to chat with me because I'm only trying to get at any angle I can to put together a full picture. I'm talking to everyone who was at that gathering."

"The tik-tiks will cooperate."

"Good. Did you happen to see that group of vampires leave the dancing last night? Do you know if there was one in particular that broke off from the rest?"

"No and no."

"Do you know if any of your women might've seen anything like that?"

"No. But you can ask them." She shot a question right

back at him. "Have you tried speaking to the shadow people about this?"

Damn, this woman was full of more curiosity than the oldster needed. "I do have someone taking care of that, ma'am."

He'd already rounded up Taraline. Last night, when he'd sought her out, she'd been watching over Hana in her quarters as Pucci had apologized over and over again to her. Taraline had been real quiet as she'd deserted that duty and gone off with the oldster. The sort of quiet that made a person walk a few feet behind a shadow.

Falisha stopped petting the gremlin, tapping it on the buttocks, making it jump off her lap with a grumble. It scurried out of the room, bitching in apparent complaint the entire time.

She scanned the oldster up and down, and he straightened in his chair. When had *he* been put in the hot seat?

"You wouldn't be interviewing us tik-tiks because you think we're somehow at fault, now, would you?"

"No, ma'am."

"Because I'll volunteer to have a vampire enter my mind, just to show that I and the other tik-tiks have no reason to lie, or even to kill a Civil."

"Ma'am, I know that you and your women enjoy one kind of meal, and one kind only. And it ain't got anything to do with a male Civil monster."

She smiled faintly, acknowledging that he'd scored a point. "Even so . . . you're here, picking my brain, as if you suspect we're somehow involved."

"Why would I think that?"

"Just a hunch." Her red-painted gaze was direct, no-nonsense. "If I can tell anything by the way the rest of the community treats us, it's that we're rather . . . unpopular."

He couldn't refute that. "My aim is to see that we all start to accept one another. That's why I'm busting my tail here."

"So we all can live happily ever after as one big monster family?"

If sarcasm could literally drip from a voice, he'd be steeped in it. "You don't think that's possible?"

"Not in the least, although I'd love to be proven wrong. I'm not a fan of humans—at least, not ones who don't provide for me—and living out in the open with other monsters would be my idea of Shangri-la. But, as in the myth, I'm pretty certain it's only a dream."

His expression had gone a little sour at her mention of humans that provided for the tik-tiks. Pregnant humans.

"Michael," she said. "I'm only offering honesty. Being dead at one time and resurrected by another tik-tik's blood exchange alters a woman like me. We become what we need to be."

"And if you don't give in to your appetites?"

"We degrade into what vampires would, I imagine. Shriveled, live corpses. So you see why we would subscribe to our bodies' necessities rather than starve."

That didn't make what they ate any righter.

He muttered, "And here I thought we'd have the opportunity for some normalcy in Monsterville."

"For you were-creatures, normalcy is going through your days like any regular human, unless there's a full moon or another circumstance that alters you. You're the most normal of all the Reds."

"I just can't believe I'm blood-related to you through 562," he said.

"Yes, if I were a were-creature, I would be disgusted, as well, Michael. I would hate to have a distant cousin who removes her head when she eats and is cursed to have a profane appetite that even other monsters find appalling."

He shut right up once again, and Falisha smiled bitterly, absently fingering the ribbon round her throat.

"I suppose," she said, "that puts an end to this whole warm, fuzzy family reunion theory."

He rustled in his seat. Time was ticking, and God-all knew if or when Gabriel would be coming back and whether the old man could gain some sort of control over the situation by then. "Since you don't seem to have any information, would you arrange some times for your other women to chat with me?"

"I'll do that. In fact, just as I mentioned before, it might be a fine idea to actually have a vampire or two go into our minds, just in case they're able to see something we're not consciously aware of—something that might help us put this matter to rest so we can all move on."

"That's gracious of you."

"I figure you've got the Civils breathing down your neck and you need to move on with your investigation. I hear they're loudly demanding justice for the victim, and that could very much put the upset on our efforts to establish a community."

Neelan, one of the Civils who'd seemed to step into the role of leader, had been preaching to his cronies that perhaps vampires should just be expelled from the hub. But that was a fine line to walk, since it was the vampires who had the mind powers and the abilities to keep GBVille running by imitating the office-bound human leaders on communication links as well as using their sway on distractoids and others who required it.

"I really do appreciate your willingness," the oldster said, starting to rise from his chair.

"As I said, of course. But I would ask something of you, too, if you don't mind."

The oldster rested his hands on his hips, just above his revolvers. "I should've known there'd be a quid pro quo coming."

"Your ability to think on your feet makes you quite the sheriff."

"Sheriff?"

The tik-tik had a gleam in her eyes, and damned if the oldster didn't think it might be some kind of appreciation for how he'd stepped in during this crisis for the Reds.

"You've been acting the part of the law for a bit now," she said. "It didn't go unnoticed when you kept venturing out in the night to liberate water slaves in the hub."

She was talking about the humans who'd indentured themselves to the richies who could afford corporatized water.

"Well," he said. "Now that just about every human is passed out from pills, running their feet off, hypnotized by a vamp, or in our cell rooms, it's easy to separate the slaves from their masters. I don't know how much good my efforts will do in the long run, though." Uncomfortable with her praise—she was a tik-tik, for damn's sake—the oldster got back to business. "What's that request you were going to make?"

"Some of my tik-tiks will need to feed. We've complied with the request to fall back while the revolution is occurring, but other monsters have been allowed to find food. We haven't."

"That's because the others go for stray wildlife round the area."

"Yes, but know this—we wouldn't be wanton in our feasting. Unlike a vampire, we've got strong control. That's because it's harder for us to find sustenance since our food must be . . . properly selected."

He read between her lines: Pregnant human women didn't come along every day, so tik-tiks wouldn't be like most Reds, hopping on whatever had blood. Even the gremlins were like demented mosquitoes, taking nips where they could off other animals on the outskirts.

The oldster's stomach turned a little at even discussing this, much less at having to give a tik-tik permission to comb the hub for their once-a-year meals. Not even a stem cell bank, if GBVille had possessed one, would've compensated, because tik-tiks needed their prey live from the womb.

But who the hell was he to judge when, every full moon, he had his own kind of cravings?

Maybe he just spent too much time as a human, not a were-creature. Still, when he answered Falisha, he did it reluctantly. "You'll have to run permission past the vamps and Civils first."

"Perhaps we need to put together a council."

"I tell you what—you work on that, Falisha. I've got my hands full presently."

As he left the room, he could feel her watching him, as if intrigued. Truth to tell, her straightforward manner reminded him a whole lot of Zel Hopkins, and that just didn't sit right, especially with the way the oldster had felt about her.

Loved and lost, he thought, trying not to dwell on how

she'd died at Stamp's hands. Besides, Zel, who'd been good through and through, wouldn't appreciate being compared to a tik-tik.

Not a bit.

He strode down the hallway as best as he could with this old man's body creaking and moaning. There was steam in him, though, an urge to clear Gabriel. He owed the vampire at least that much for what he'd done for the Badlanders.

And maybe he even wanted to prove to himself that he'd been right when he'd put his trust in Gabriel.

Not a minute had passed before he realized that he was being followed by something in the walls, and he stopped.

"Who's there?"

He heard breathing in back of him and turned to see Taraline, the torches providing a dim counterpoint to her black dress and veils.

He itched to lift those coverings, just to see how she was faring underneath—if she'd changed because of the introduction of Mariah's 562 blood—yet there were far more important subjects to broach.

"What's the word?" the oldster asked.

"The shadows have found . . . something, Michael. But nothing definitive."

As the oldster puzzled over that, Taraline stretched out a gloved hand. Chaplin came out from round a corner to nuzzle it. The dog whimpered at the oldster, as if saying a sad *hi* to him, too. He was just as concerned about Mariah's disappearance with Gabriel as any of them. Even more. To boot, their trail had gone cold outside of GBVille, because Gabriel had taken obvious care to cover any tracks.

"What do you mean you found something but nothing?" the oldster asked. "Don't tell me with all the shadows running round, no one witnessed what happened."

"We can't be everywhere at every time," Taraline said.

The oldster grunted. "Sorry to take it out on you. I'm just frustrated by the lack of answers."

"I understand."

Other shadows moved over the walls, but they could've

been from monsters walking in front of torches round the corner.

The oldster tried not to glance at the dark shapes. "What *did* they see?"

Taraline paused, as if she were firming up what she wanted to tell him.

Why wouldn't she just come out with it?

The oldster watched her expectantly until she talked.

"A shadow arrived at the scene just as all the young vampires with Gabriel were descending on the Civil. They actually witnessed Gabriel separating himself from the feasting crowd, as if he didn't want anything to do with it."

Her veils hid everything: expression, reaction . . .

"That doesn't mean he's innocent," the oldster said carefully.

"I know. It might even mean he was the one who attacked the Civil first. Afterward, he might have had a crisis of conscience, and it made him desert the feeding frenzy. We've seen him vacillate like that before."

She hesitated, and the oldster still got the feeling that she hadn't told him everything. He thought Taraline might've even noticed his doubts.

"And?" he asked.

"I don't want to raise your hopes or incriminate anyone, but . . ."

"Spill it, *please.*"

Chaplin winced and sat on his rear end. The oldster had never wished more that he or Taraline spoke Canine. Did the *dog* know something?

No, the oldster thought. Chaplin was smart enough so that he would've dragged him to a clue and barked at him to provide emphasis for any findings.

Damn, he was being paranoid about everyone.

Taraline folded her gloved hands in front of her. "A shadow did see . . . Well, I would call it a noteworthy detail."

"What?"

"A Civil, near the hallway where the victim was killed, around the time of death."

"A Civil?" The oldster's adrenaline pumped. "Who?"

"Neelan."

The half-man, half-snake chimera.

The oldster's mind went into overdrive, ideas taking form.

Neelan, who'd invited the Badlanders to the asylum after they'd carried out the power-blaster attack. Neelan, who'd welcomed them into this brave new world that the liberated monsters had begun to form. Yet, after Mariah and 562 had changed into their horrific forms at the full moon, Neelan had started to pull away from the Reds, as if he regretted ever bringing them here.

But . . . no. There was no way the oldster could even imagine that the Civil had done something like frame a bunch of vampires just to flush some Reds out of their community, especially by sacrificing a fellow Civil.

What had Falisha said?

Normal didn't apply anymore. They were monsters.

God-all.

But at least there was a new lead. Yet what if it didn't go anywhere? Worse, what if the oldster pursued this only to find out that Neelan hadn't done *anything*? Would he be stirring things up and starting a full-blown Civil-Red war?

Hating what had to be taken care of, the oldster said, "Where's the shadow who told you this, Taraline?"

"Follow me," she said, and he wondered if there was some relief in her voice.

Like a specter, she turned and walked away, guiding the oldster to the only salvation Gabriel might have.

9

Gabriel

The monsters of Dallas had given Gabriel and Mariah some grief a couple of nights ago after he'd sped across the miles while carrying her, keeping to the bushes and hills for cover, then arriving at the hub's wind-whistling borders.

A line of were-creatures had been subtly patrolling the outskirts, and it had only been after Gabriel had shown proof of fang and then used a bit of sway to persuade them that Mariah was on the up-and-up that the guards had allowed them past the barbed trenches—a souvenir from when Dallas had gone to the bad guys years ago.

Since Mariah hadn't turned into her monster, these Dallas guards had no idea that she was something other than a regular were-creature.

And just as well.

Inside the barriers, the streets held circa-millennium buildings that'd been fortified with steel, giving the hub a silver-capped sense of Western-movie quiet in the night. It was a boomtown gone to ghostliness, with remnants of public screens—like the ones that had featured ever-flipping advertisement channels—gone blank. The hub had been sponsored by a conglomerate of big oil companies that had been fighting for monetary survival with the green techno corporations when the world had changed, and their symbol—a white smiley face with sparkles for teeth—was etched into every building, on every corner.

It seemed that the streets should've been emptied, just like the bloody moments after a showdown, but the monsters here had decided that *they* weren't going to shelter themselves away in any asylum, even as their own vampires copied the model of GBVille, the first liberated hub, by swaying the humans in charge and imitating their voices to those outside Dallas who wanted to come in. That action had pretty much quarantined this hub, too, because, like GBVille, Dallas had also staged its own fake mosquito sighting. And there was no doubt in Gabriel's mind that the politicians in old D.C. were going a little nuts with news of all these so-called mosquitoes coming around after they'd supposedly been eradicated.

But that was why the older GBVille vampires had already thought to send a contingent to the capital to take the politicians over, after a new batch of power blasters was set to go off in about a week.

Yup, the humans were falling night by night, though they didn't know it. Thanks to how the vampires had infiltrated local leadership offices, first in GBVille and now in other hubs, they'd been able to collect and share sensitive information via monster couriers about human government and their plans for the future. One of the best tidbits they'd uncovered was the fact that humans actually hadn't been able to afford widespread top surveillance programs at this time, because of the recovery from Indian sanctions, though they'd constantly advertised the eyes in the skies and how these worked to keep humans safe.

Lies. Just lies.

This wasn't to say that surveillance programs weren't still operational—it just wasn't as prevalent as the monsters had always feared. Unfortunately, there'd been a program in the Badlands, yet they'd been careful out there.

But even gaining this intelligence hadn't told them every-thing about how the humans operated; they hadn't been able to access records about Witches. Not yet, at least. But that seemed a small matter as more hubs were covertly taken over.

Tonight, Gabriel looked out the window of a gone-to-pot energy booster café, with its neuroenhancer vending machines and white tables. He was watching humanlike monsters stroll past the sleeping distractoids outside. Clearly, more creatures had heard about the hub takeovers, and they were coming out of their hiding spots to join the movement inside the darkened hubs. Gabriel could sort the monsters out from actual people because he could hear the easy rhythms inside their bodies, unlike the processed-food-clogged people who littered the streets.

He'd awakened before Mariah, and when he heard her stretch to consciousness, desire rolled through him. He tried to counter it by talking.

"Texas monsters," he said while tracking a vampire who was gently kicking at a distractoid who lay on a sidewalk. "They don't give much of a shit about getting caught, do they?"

Mariah slowly sat up. Every breath she took reached right into him.

"Historically, Texans have always been up for a battle," she said.

She started to freshen up, but Gabriel just kept looking out that window, determined to stay away from her. He'd done pretty well refraining from her these past couple of nights, but maybe that was because he knew she was dancing on a razor's edge, having returned here to Dallas, her nightmare.

Sometimes he regretted suggesting this location for their temporary hideaway, but that was only during those times his humanity ran through him. Most moments, though, logic told him it was right to have her face the past so she could move forward, using what she was now for the purposes of good.

For the eradication of bad guys from this new world.

"How're you feeling?" he asked.

She exhaled. "I'm . . ."

"I get it if you don't want to go by your old house tonight.

We can just walk the hub again, asking around for information on your bad guys."

Not that wandering Dallas had done any good. Gabriel had
a sneaking suspicion that they'd have to visit her house to get
anything accomplished . . . if that was what she still wanted.

When he glanced back at her, she was hugging herself.

"Now that we're here," she said, "I'm dragging my feet.
It's more upsetting than I imagined."

She'd been fighting a change ever since they'd gotten to
this hub. Now that Gabriel had met his own vampire kind
and understood what they were about, he was finding it
harder and harder to understand her reluctance to be what
she could be, though he knew that she was only afraid of
how she might create a mess here in Dallas that these monsters would be unwilling to deal with.

When she locked her green gaze on him, his blood
chugged.

"Do you ever wonder what's happening back in GBVille?"
she asked.

Now that she mentioned it, Gabriel realized that he hadn't
thought about the Civil killing for a couple of nights.

He frowned. Just months ago, the Civil killing would've
torn him apart with remorse every waking moment.

Mariah continued. "There's something in me that misses
562. And Chaplin, but I suppose that goes without saying."

"Are you telling me that we ought to go back now?"

"No. We need a few more days out here, at least. But I do
need to think about where I should be when the moon gets full.
I'm not sure I feel secure turning into my moon form here."

It'd be one thing if the full moon lasted only a few hours
or a night, but it was usually a three-night phase—waxing,
highest power, then waning. Thank-all the moon didn't peak
all night long, either; Mariah had tried to explain to him
once that when the moon reached its full status, it remained
that way, even during daylight. But there was something
about the night reaching its darkest point that struck a were-
creature to madness.

Gabriel connected to her fear now, and not only because

he'd seen her and 562 in lunar bodies that had reminded him of the dark goddess Kali, with a couple less arms and a wickedly sharp, split tongue. Whenever the moon turned, Mariah would have to stay away from others.

And he'd thought it was bad enough when the moon *wasn't* full—when she turned into a weaker version of her most terrible state.

He lowered his voice. "I'll make sure you're safe, wherever we are."

He tried not to think about what had gone on the last time she'd turned. His bloodlust that night had made him even worse than she was.

She smiled at him, so close to happiness if he could only find the right words to continue with.

He gave it a try. "And I'll keep you safe, *if* you decide you want to go out there tonight."

Her body rhythms thrummed, terror in motion.

"If you want," he said, "I'll even go to your old place for you, just to see if there're any clues that I can pick up on—something that would allow me to hunt down any of your bad guys who still might be in the hub."

Her eyes lightened, just as they did whenever she was pushed. "I need to be the one to do that, Gabriel."

"But you're afraid of turning. You don't want to create a problem for these Dallas monsters if you get out of control."

He couldn't stop himself from going to her, lifting her to her feet, kissing her on the forehead, shivering from her scent.

"I'll try with all my might to protect you," he said.

"You can't promise things like that when we both know better."

"Would you rather spend the rest of your life like this? Afraid?"

"I'm not afraid."

As if to prove it, she headed for the door, going into the street.

Finally.

And she didn't hesitate in finding her old home tonight.

Maybe she'd just gotten to the point where the dread of waiting overshadowed everything else.

Whatever the case, they relied on her memories to guide them to the wasted suburb where her family had once lived. Now, instead of green lawns, there was scrub and tumbleweed among debris that had rusted under the gray-cloaked sun. Instead of fresh white paint on the walls, there were jaundiced flakes, like the skin of an oldster human who'd tried to crawl away to a hole but never made it. Iron bars survived on the windows, and locks rested against the stoop, neatly in line, so out of place with the rest of this dump.

As Gabriel and Mariah stood in front of her old home, the night wind groaned around them. Tears streaked her face. Gabriel could feel the fear hauling her down, but also the urge to cry because of what had been destroyed here.

Before he could ask her if she had enough courage to go inside, she stepped onto the path that led to the front door, which creaked on its hinges, half open, as if the last person to run out of here had left in such a hurry that they hadn't shut things tight.

At first, he couldn't go inside—not until she said, "Come in with me."

He followed her over the threshold, into what looked to be a living room. It was devoid of much except for a wire-harried camera perched up in the corner, its lens cracked. There was also a leather couch that drooled stuffing. A gutted flashlight lay next to it, along with the skins of some roots that someone had obviously discarded after eating the middle out of them.

"Someone's living here," Gabriel said.

Mariah sank to her knees, facing a wall. The outline of a pink stain scarred it, and Gabriel could still detect a trace of blood that someone had tried to wash off.

She was sobbing now, and Gabriel didn't have to ask why. Their link provided every image:

A red splash against white after her father had come in here to use a gun, to put her mother and brother out of their misery before the bites turned them into monsters . . .

Bleeding, bitten by the werewolf that the bad guys had been using to terrify them . . .

Then, the dead bodies of bad men sprawled, holes in their heads from where Dmitri Lyander had shot them . . .

Gabriel bent down to stroke Mariah's hair.

"It never goes away," she said.

She could've been talking about the bloodstain, but she wasn't.

Heat was pushing off her skin, and it scorched him also.

Any minute, she might pop, bursting into an angry reflection of 562 in the form it used to adapt when it was ticked off—a body unaffected by the full moon: huge teeth in a huge mouth, no mercy.

But, somehow, Mariah found the strength to just grit her teeth, her gaze a furious green as she looked up at that wall. She slumped, her body in a miraculously controlled half change while her teeth grew in number, the new ones coming to points.

Then, slashing away her tears, she stood, started to sniff. To growl.

Gabriel took in the scents from the weave of the rug, too, memorizing them. Very, very old aromas, barely identifiable. Two that he recognized in particular: Mariah and Chaplin. Many other scents that he couldn't identify, and maybe those were the ones that belonged to Mariah's bad guys.

Maybe those odors would help Gabriel to see if any of the bastards were still in Dallas. . . .

When he heard a sound near the door, he didn't hesitate in speeding over to it, grabbing whatever it was that had been peering in at them.

Gabriel brought the intruder up to his face, grimacing at the pale white man with scaly skin and pink eyes. In spite of his reptilian façade, his very humanlike tongue flickered in and out as he raised his clawed fingers to Gabriel.

But the guy didn't attack. Maybe because he was a Civil monster, Gabriel realized. And he was probably the creature who'd been using Mariah's old home as a shelter.

"Don't hate," it said in a mealy-mouthed voice. The aggression had obviously been all show.

But just because it was a Civil didn't mean it wouldn't cause trouble. Besides, there was something about the oddly sweet odor of the monster that was goading Gabriel, so he hauled it into the house and let go of it. Mariah was still hunched, her hands balled at her sides, but she wasn't even in half-change mode anymore, though it seemed as if it wouldn't take much to get her there again.

"Who's this?" she asked.

"Plattoh," the lizard-guy answered, slinking toward his torch and the discarded shells of food on the floor. "This is my home."

She kept at him. "And how long have you been living here?"

"Since Dallas went dark. A week. More. Less. Plattoh doesn't know."

The Civil's version of Old American speech struck Gabriel. Then again, monsters, shut-away humans, and elite business globalists were some of the few who'd clung to the dialect because they'd been in hiding, had cut themselves off from the changes in society at large, or spoke the common language with other corporatists; most humans who didn't hold the elite jobs that required languages like Chinese or Hindi or Old American generally used Text. But it could be that this lizard-man had ventured out of a hiding place recently and just started to learn Old American.

Gabriel spoke to Mariah. "His smell is the newest one in the room, so I think he's telling the truth about recently camping out here."

Then he stalked the guy, who'd raised his hands in front of him again. Months ago, Gabriel would've been taken aback by the Civil's fear, but now he reveled in it.

"Any idea who lived here before you?" he asked.

"Hmmm," Plattoh said, thinking.

Gabriel allowed his fangs to spring. "I'm doing you the courtesy of asking before I barge into your head."

"Ooo, no. Plattoh talks. Plattoh talks much and more more more." The lizard-man nodded, his long mouth stretching into a thin smile. "A lowlord gang lived in Plattoh's home before. They sleep now, in the middle of the hub, where business is done."

"They're under the influence of biological scare pills?"

"Yes, yes, that is right." Plattoh's voice thinned out. "You will kill me now?"

"Do I look like I'm going to kill you?"

"Yes, yes."

The darkest part of Gabriel was comfortable with that, even while something else inside died all the more.

The lizard-man took a long glance at Mariah, who had lost some interest in Plattoh and was staring at that bloodied wall again. She was clutching at her dress.

Gabriel lingered on her a moment too long—just enough for Plattoh to zoom out of the room on a girly sort of squeal.

Watching after him, Gabriel decided not to bother.

He sat on a part of the couch that wasn't ruined by a stream of stuffing. He was surprised he'd gotten inside this place if it belonged to the lizard-man now. Then again, Mariah obviously still moved around it as if it were hers, no matter who'd taken it over. She would always possess it.

Mariah's garbled tone was barely audible. "I keep seeing my family in here, and knowing that lowlords moved in after we left seems like a desecration. But even back when my father and me left for the Badlands, bad guys were moving in on everything. Why wouldn't they move in here, too?"

She walked to the wall, her hand hovering over the stain, not daring to touch it. After a moment she let her hand fall. Then she turned her back on the sight altogether.

"So what now?" She had blanked her mind, and maybe that was why she was so in control.

"We could track down this lowlord, wake him up, see if he or his gang knows anything about this house's history and where your remaining bad guys went off to after . . ."

He was about to say *the attack*.

Mariah was quiet for a while. She wandered away from the wall, rounded a corner, disappeared.

Gabriel got up to see where she'd gone.

He found her in a bedroom, where pink rags slouched

from a curtain rod over the iron-barred window. The bed's frame had crumbled, broken under the bare yellowed mattress and, behind him on the door, broken locks hung, useless, a reminder of how the bad guys had broken in to hurt the girl who'd slept here. In a corner, near a long mirror where he could see himself, a teddy bear rested, one-eyed, resigned, its fur matted.

Mariah went to it, held it. She looked normal. So human now.

"Chaplin's," she said.

Vampires didn't have real hearts to break, Gabriel thought, but this sight sorely tested his composure. So did the sadness emanating from her in slow waves that drenched him.

She added, "My dog tried so hard to save me that night, but they took him down, just before they loosed the werewolf on me."

He watched her, searching for signs that she was about to go into half change again. But something about holding Chaplin's stuffed animal was soothing her.

"I might never be able to close this chapter of my life," she said, as if that teddy bear had brought about an epiphany. "Now that I'm strong enough to finally face those . . . men . . . I may not ever get the chance. They could be dead. They could be in another part of the country."

"And they could be doing to other people what they did to you and your family."

She looked over at him. "It wasn't so long ago that you hated me for giving in to bloodlust."

"That was before . . ." What—before his vampire had fully kicked in? Before he'd been faced with more bad guys than he'd known what to do with, first with Stamp, then at the asylum? Before Mariah had come along to push along his natural progress?

She didn't put down the toy, just kept it against her chest.

"I've been learning more from the older vampires," he said.

She nodded, as if relieved that he was finally at the point where she wanted to talk about it.

"They call this stage I'm in *the gloaming*. That's an old

word for *dusk*, but to our kind, it means the time before darkness really settles in. It takes a while to get there, but once we do, it's a quick stage, and they say it's happening because our brains don't adapt as fast as the rest of our bodies after we're turned. The wisest of the vampires even told me something about how my psychological composition— my memories, my conditioning—is what's clinging to humanity. It's not actually humanity itself." He dwelled on that for a moment, but it didn't register much. "Once my mind fully adapts, the gloaming is over."

"I can't picture you being like them. Watching everyone all the time. So cool. Remote. Even though they're so hungry inside."

"Vampires consider the aptitude to separate emotion from thinking a gift."

She moved her thumb over the toy animal. "Maybe we were-creatures do the same, in a way. We can think more when we're in our human forms, but we lose it when we're not. It's only when we're in half change that we can do both at the same time." She hesitated. "But I remembered what I was doing when I went into lunar form this last time. That was different."

"We've all got our good traits. It's just a matter of accepting them for what they are."

Silence again.

Then she said, "Did you ever think that weres and vampires never hung out together before because we're just too different? That it's just as simple as that? And that it's the same for *all* monsters?"

Why did she say it as if she'd been discovering this with every passing night?

"Maybe for others it's always been that way," he said. "Maybe they never got as far as we did, though."

"And how far is that?"

Her gaze was wide, as if she needed to finally hear him say it. As if she suspected that he couldn't . . . or shouldn't.

But he wasn't going to let anything stop him from being with her.

He walked to her, got to his knee, cupped her face in his

hands. "I love you, Mariah. That's how far it's gone, and it's not going to matter when my gloaming's over and done with. You know that, right?"

A yanking sensation made him feel as if his blood had been pulled out of him, rushing toward her. And he would give her that and more.

He didn't think about how her emotions might be projecting onto him, how that blood might've been sacrificing itself because she was taking it, possessing it. What he felt had to be real, just this one time, and he wanted to hold on to it, even after he'd lost everything and gone full vampire.

Couldn't he keep just that one thing?

"I love you, too," she said, gripping one of his wrists, holding the stuffed animal with her other hand. "So much that I don't know what to do with it sometimes."

Already, the temperature was rising between them, the air seeming to waver as it reacted to the heat rising off her skin.

He should back away before it consumed him, too, calling his hunger, bringing on the self-destructive desire to drink the poison of her blood. Yet before they even got that far, something banged against the outside of the house.

The hinges on the front door screamed.

By the time a voice jarred both Gabriel and Mariah to their feet, someone had run inside, then halted at the bedroom entrance.

A man with brown hair that fringed his face, yellow eyes, and pointy teeth stood there. A man wearing all dark gray, his hands curved at his sides and his back curved into a hunch.

"I hear you're asking some rude questions," he said, breathing heavily.

Plattoh came to stand just in back of him, a grin on his lizard-man face.

10

Mariah

I'd been too deep into Gabriel—then too taken off-guard by the appearance of a were-creature in my old house—to change right away. It was just stunning to see a thing so blasphemous against the innocence that was somehow still lingering here in my bedroom, and I was floating in some sort of stasis.

But the were-man was under no such disadvantage: in fact, his face was moving, as if his cheekbones were shifting, his jaw priming up to lengthen and accommodate a set of big were-teeth.

Next to me, Gabriel's posture had gone feral, ready to bring on his own full change if the were-man went even a step farther.

All I could manage was to stare at Plattoh the lizard-man as two more were-creatures took up positions behind him, both in midchange, as well.

They must've carried the traitor here in a rush, I thought, *after he'd tracked his buddies down.*

Plattoh said, "Curious about the lowlord? Plattoh bring him to you."

"Thanks," Gabriel and I said at the same time.

Through our link, I felt him straining against his powers. But so far, the others hadn't attacked. Maybe he was thinking we could parley without bloodshed. A vampire's logic would've led him to that conclusion.

Or maybe nobody—not even the Dallas crowd—really wanted a confrontation since we were all-for-one, one-for-all monsters now.

When the were-man saw that we weren't forcing a showdown, he remained in midchange. But some brown fur had begun to sprout on his skin and he had a snout.

A werewolf.

"So why did Plattoh take it upon himself to fetch me for you two?" he asked.

The lizard-man answered. "Plattoh told you before, Tyree—newcomers asking about you. Plattoh only looking out for you."

"I suppose you were." The were-man dug into a pocket of his vest, took out a water bead that had obviously lost its way from the length of a necklace, then flicked it to Plattoh. To his men, he said, "Get him out of here."

His partners grabbed Plattoh and ushered him out while the lizard-man said, "This my home!"

"You'll have the run of it again," Tyree said to him without glancing away from us.

He was watching me in particular, and his intensity ruffled my skin.

What did he see? It was almost as if . . .

As if he were thinking that he recognized me?

Something revolved in his yellow gaze, and he smiled with those pointy teeth.

"Well, well," he said, suddenly the gracious host. "Just look at the variety of the company we get here in Dallas. I still can't get used to hearing monsters who speak the language and don't try to fool others by using Text. I got sick of Text real quick after the smart people took to their homes or went underground."

We didn't respond.

"Why *did* you come into Plattoh's home?" he asked.

"Looking for a place to rest our bones," Gabriel said, still terribly restless.

Behind Tyree, the were-man's cronies took up positions again.

"Why did you pick this home," he asked, "and no other?"

Gabriel shrugged. "Just lucky, I guess."

Tyree took a step into the room, his boots thudding on the rug next to the skeletal remains of a lock from my door. In my memories, I heard the sound of it breaking as the bad guys busted in.

"Maybe," Tyree said, "you're just stupid, not lucky. Sometimes it's a good idea never to walk through a door, no matter how open you think it might be. You see, Plattoh became one of my followers when he arrived in the hub, and he's been loyal enough for me to grant him a house in my territory. He's a bit of an immature tattletale, but he makes for some good eyes and ears."

Tyree gave me another strange glance.

Panic was welling in me, but I had to know whether I was on the right track about him before I allowed myself to freak out.

"You're a lowlord?" I asked. "How did a monster manage that?"

The were-man shrugged. "Before monsters took over here in Dallas, I was smart enough to hide in plain sight. I wasn't an idiot, though—I never changed in front of any human, but I had the grit that it took to run a gang. I learned Text. I acted just like them. And now that the monsters are boss, I made an easy transition to their side—the side I've always been on. I claimed this territory, mostly because it holds . . . memories."

I didn't want to know what he meant by that. Yeah, even after I'd come all this way to know everything.

Instead I said, "A lowlord was a perfect disguise."

"It was for years, ever since I got . . ." He gave yet another long look to me. ". . . freed."

My heart pumped, pumped, and pumped.

The were-man smiled even wider, the tips of his teeth seeming to gleam in the moonlight coming through the window. "Back when I was young, I got caught by some men. They kept me on a leash and used me as a weapon when they crashed houses. They kept the secret of what I was in exchange for what I did for them. Their deaths were what freed me."

The panic in me turned to a vibrating jitter.

I was so afraid of what he was going to say next that I was frozen again, my sight gone blue with more shock.

I felt Gabriel gearing up in response to me, but I threw a thought to him.

Don't.

I *had* to hear all of it from Tyree. Had to be a hundred percent sure in this new hub, in this territory that wasn't mine.

Tyree's gaze now held a familiar, rapacious gleam, and I knew.

God-all, I knew for certain, even though I'd hoped he was dead.

It felt as if I were changing backward now, shrinking into my human form out of utter and complete devastation, reduced to my weakest.

"Normally," he drawled, "I'd say you wandered into the wrong house, little girl, but it seems you found the right one after all."

In my mind's eye, I saw this stranger—this big, awful, surreal wolf named Tyree—coming into my bedroom, hovering over me, his saliva dripping over my nightgown as I struggled to get free from my captors . . .

"But my dad," I said weakly. "He stabbed you in the heart with silver . . ."

"And he missed my pumper just by an inch." Some of Tyree's smugness disappeared. "It was enough to disable me while you both left me for dead on the floor and ran out of here to who knows where. You never even looked at my face to see the pain I was in as I slid back into my human form. As for my owners? They soon died from those bullet wounds your dad put in them."

He took another step forward, and Gabriel's mind grabbed me.

Now?

No. This was mine.

I started coming back to myself, remembering just what I was, what I had, what I'd been planning to do if I ever met any of the bad guys who'd messed me up.

"But I remember *you*," he continued, just as cocky as I was, but for only a fraction of the reason. "You were a girl with red hair. I was in too much of a frenzy to recall the bite itself, but my, oh, my, as I lay there on the floor, you were burned into my memory. You and your father. I healed slow, and I had a lot of time to dwell on how you'd treated me. I even claimed this territory after the monsters took over because this house is where I was reborn, thanks to your dad. And, really, I'd be grateful for that if you all hadn't tried to kill me, too."

By now, Gabriel was shaking with his restraint.

But I was all ice.

"Aw," he said, tilting his head at me. "Looks like you haven't forgotten anything, either. What keeps *you* awake most often? Is it when I was with you? Or when your family's blood became a permanent decoration in the living room?"

That was enough for Gabriel, because he turned vampire all the way, hissing, opening his mouth to show how big his teeth could be, as well.

Tyree laughed while his two friends entered the room, hunching, their bodies flowing with a willful change.

"Bring it, sweetheart," he said to Gabriel. "After I have my way with you, I'll finish what I started with the prettier one, here."

This guy still thought he was only up against a vampire and his own begotten progeny, a werewolf like him. He had no idea about 562 and what he was actually baiting in me.

That was when I started to get real happy that Gabriel had brought me here.

Three-to-two odds. Poor wolfman. I was just sorry it wasn't a full moon and I couldn't give him all the justice I'd been storing up in me for years.

Gabriel sensed this in me, and he held still, seething next to me. His anger bled into mine, making me even stronger.

"You aim to claim me," I said, "just like you did this house and the territory round it?"

He and his men merely laughed.

When I exchanged a glance with Gabriel, his eyes red, his fangs readied, we smiled at each other.

Tyree's men came out from behind him, as if to manhandle me while leaving Gabriel to their lowlord.

And I let myself go.

My change seemed to take forever, but really only a split second went by. Even so, I had enough time to realize that when I'd changed during the full moon, it'd been like an explosion. Not now, though. Now, without the lunar pull, I was able to revel in the spreading sensation from my core, like pale balls of moonlight growing and banging against me from the inside out.

My heartbeat got so loud that I thought everyone in the room might be able to hear it. In the darkest parts of my head, I heard the worshipful chants from the other night.

Your blood, blood, blood . . .

My lust flipped over, focusing on these bad guys. Revenge—just the thought of it thrilled me.

Bad guys.

While I got closer and closer to my nonlunar form, the lowlord and his small gang were busy undergoing a full change themselves. I could see it in my blossoming violet gaze—how they panted and howled while they all slipped and slid into the stretched bodies of werewolves: huge, hairy, grotesque versions of a regular wolf that had adapted in this day and age to survive.

As for Gabriel—he was way ahead of everyone else, bent over, preparing to spring at the weres.

Everything kept going slowly to me, though, so slowly, while new teeth sprouted, going to daggers in a mouth that yawned to three times its normal size.

But, unlike my lunar form, I didn't feel another set of arms blasting out of me, nor a fall of long hair, nor the rotating of my eyes to vertical slits—not without the full moon . . .

As I let loose a scream, I saw myself through a shattered haze in the mirror on the wall—the mirror that used to show a young girl with long red hair that hid her face most times. A girl who'd slashed off that hair with a knife, knowing she'd never be the same again.

Now she was this: a reflection of 562 whenever our origin got mad. Huge teeth, huge mouth, and short-cut hair barely covering blazing green eyes.

Unlike my previous, more normal werewolf form, I could experience everything that was happening now in this state, and I turned to my enemies just in time to see Gabriel already springing at Tyree, who ducked, then batted my vampire into the other two werewolves.

That only allowed Gabriel to go to work: in a blur of speed, he made those werewolves resemble two bodies that'd been sent into some whirring blades.

Blood swished outward, covering the walls, soaking the carpet in pools.

The scent hit me hard as I launched myself at Tyree, who was crouching, then flying, his claws ready to rip.

Mine were, too, and I slapped his face before he got too close. It's just that my reach was longer than usual. Real long.

He twirled in the air, landing on his ass, splashing into a collection of his buddies' blood.

I waited.

I smiled, making sure he saw all my 562 teeth.

I thought he might have it in him to mindlessly dive into his friends' blood out of feral hunger, but he was fixated on me instead, and he got up again, his cheek raw with gouges that would start were-healing soon. Behind him, Gabriel had stopped motion, standing there with one werewolf in each hand, holding them by the hair as blood dripped from severed heads with faces that hardly existed anymore. They were more pulp than expression.

He moved to the door and tossed them into the hallway, casually coming back for the bodies and discarding those, too.

Pitiful Tyree was looking at me as if he didn't understand why I was like this instead of like him, since he was my maker.

"Slight malfunction in the gene pool," I said between my teeth.

He angled his head, an animal that didn't comprehend, and, again, I saw in him the creature who'd come into my room after the bad guys had broken in. I felt my gown being lifted as the men laughed, the hideous werewolf sniffing up my leg, then a scratch on my skin. . . .

Shame and anger impaled me, and I screamed, zooming toward Tyree, opening my mouth to give him my bite.

I munched down on him, sending bits of bone and blood everywhere, then spit him out of the bedroom, into the hallway with his friends where I could barely see what remained of him.

Poison . . . The taste of him hurt, nauseating, profane as I spit it out . . .

And, just like that, Gabriel was by my side, opening the skin on his wrist with a fang, pressing me to drink from him and wash out the bad.

I drank and drank, and soon I was flush with calm, my mouth and teeth receding until I was back to normal. But I was hot.

Still so hot.

As Gabriel's wrist healed, he looked down at me with an expression I'd longed for all my life. An expression made all the more intense by the red in the room.

My dress was soaked with the weres' blood, and it slicked my skin, hot, but already cooling. Still, I burned, my chest feeling as if it'd opened up for Gabriel, who'd protected me without my even asking him to.

Overcome, I pulled him down to me, and when his mouth

crushed mine, I sipped at him as if he were the only thing that could keep me alive.

In the harshness of our kiss, he pierced my lips with his fangs, flinching at the taste of me, then healed his mouth with a press of his fingers, his red gaze so ferocious that I dug my claws into his back. My mind—not so much my body—was still affected by my monster, still lusting.

Wanting.

"I can't kiss you like this," he said in that terrible voice.

"Then don't kiss me." Spiked by my desire—God-all, how I wanted him and didn't know if I could get enough of him—I rolled him to his back.

Blood haloed him as I ached, my clit sharp and swollen. I led his hand there, and when he touched me, my stomach flipped, as if I were going to turn again.

But I could keep it back. I *would*.

He stroked me, roughly, greedily, and I moved with every motion, riding him until he bowled me to my back, splashing me in a well of blood, his fangs at pierce points as he hissed over me.

He was dominating me, and I only smiled, taking hold of his neck and squeezing.

When he did the same to me, I slammed him down to the ground again, blood splattering. I laid my body against his so my breasts flattened against him, marking him with more blood.

I slid up his body, teasing him, feeling his hard cock between my legs and crying out a little with the agony of it.

I would've killed him for you, he thought to me as I grinded against him.

I know you would've.

He reached up, taking my dress by the collar. It stuck to me like a second, bloodied skin, and he yanked down, tearing it, exposing my chest. My skin was wet with red, too, and he sat up, rubbing his face against me.

I wasn't covered in *my* blood, and the smell had to be driving him crazy because he hadn't fed earlier.

"Gabriel," I whispered, holding him against me, urging him to take what he wanted.

And he did, licking at my breast, drinking the weres' blood, sucking, lapping, shivering. Then he went for more, laving at me, circling his tongue round my nipple and making me go so hard and hot that I felt the stab of it deep inside my belly.

While he sucked at me, roaming his hands over my slick skin, tearing off the dress until it hung at my waist, he undid his pants. Then he reached under my skirt, ripping my panties off.

I leaned my cheek on the top of his head. I saw the blood round us, and I closed my eyes.

His hair was thick and damp, and I buried my fingers in it as Gabriel thrust up into me, making me haul in a tight breath. He filled me, not only with his cock but with all the blood that was pounding at his skin in its frenzy to reach me.

Mine did the same to him, fighting to get where it couldn't.

He rammed into me, driving hard as I planted my boots on the floor for purchase. But even with that, he buffeted me backward until I arched, pressing one hand to the blood-soaked ground so I could meet him all the way, hammering back against him, churning, asking for more, although I wasn't sure how I was going to get it.

Or maybe I did. I wanted to devour him, but not in a monster way. I wanted him to be a part of me so completely that I didn't know how to manage it. Didn't know how I'd live without being able to do it.

The blood scent made me dizzy, but it was the screeching temperature of my body that almost made me so insane that I just about lost my tenuous hold on my calm.

It was as if I were holding a leash on a force so strong that all ties were snapping, strand by strand, and I felt every single break in my center, the popping sensation creeping up, up, up . . .

Just as the last hold was about to come undone, I moaned, cried out, asked him for more, and that was when *he* broke altogether, coming into me.

I came, too, hard and fast, an explosion of red, wet ecstasy.

As we recovered, we breathed together, and with every passing second, I realized how the blood cooled round us and against us. I held Gabriel to me, cold, hard skin and all.

I held him tighter than anything I'd ever held to before.

11

Mariah

Gabriel and me deserted that old Dallas house of mine right away. It seemed already vanished, anyway; it had to be if I was going to put my ghosts behind me. I'd gotten that reckoning I'd talked so long about, so I just kept telling myself that everything was squared.

So why, even now, did it feel so good to think about giving more bad guys what was coming to them in the future? And why didn't it bother me as much as it should've to know that me and Gabriel had done sex right after this last confrontation, cavorting in the blood as if it were the most normal thing?

While I grappled with all that, we found a location way outside Dallas to lie low. It was a mansion that didn't belong to anyone now, and I sat on the parlor floor while Gabriel lounged on a rickety swing on the front porch. I could see him through the smudged window.

I wasn't sure how many minds out there would interpret him as beautiful with his rough features and taciturn attitude, but just being this far from him cored me out, like there was a knife scraping round inside me. Good cuts. Good pain.

I decided to join him, willing to hurt even more.

As I came to the doorway, I saw that it was a peaceful sort of night, the moon sliced like a sideways smile that only grew with every approaching night to its fullest expression. The land was quiet, maybe even as far as Dallas, where the monsters in their hub were doing whatever they needed to do.

I just hoped that didn't include hunting us down for what we'd put on the wolfman Tyree and his men. I'd been expecting the rest of his gang, including Plattoh, to find us, even out here, but it hadn't happened yet.

But that might've been because we'd cleaned the scene and ourselves up well and good, trying to leave no traces of who we were, although any vampire or changed were-creature worth their weight in water would be able to follow my scent. Yet, maybe the monsters in Dallas were happy to be rid of Tyree's ilk. Or maybe Plattoh had found another sugar daddy to help him out and he'd already stopped missing this one.

Whatever the case, we'd relocated out of common sense, and here we were. When Gabriel saw me, his eyes glowed ever so slightly, silver caught by the moon. Neither of us seemed in a punchy mood, so I sat down on his lap, tracing a finger over the cool skin of his jawline. Gabriel had found me a new dress to wear, since we'd ruined the other one with the red and all the rips he'd made while getting to me and the blood. The length of the material dragged on the porch as his swing creaked back and forth, barely moving.

During the course of these past nights, we hadn't talked about what'd happened back at my old house—hadn't mentioned the blood play, the killings. It was as if we both should just accept it and go to the next night, then the next. And, away from my old friends, especially Chaplin, it seemed real simple.

"Do you think it's time?" I asked. We were six days off from the full moon, and I was getting itchy about having to turn into my lunar body, setting loose my most unstable form without a bunch of familiar monsters to contain me.

Then again, I wasn't certain it'd even be safe to turn lunar in GBVille. Probably I should just stay by myself in some isolated location where I could feast on wildlife, away from all others, with just Gabriel monitoring me until the full moon had passed.

He took hold of my hand and wound his fingers through mine. My warmth eased into his cool.

"*Should* we go back?" he asked.

I thought of Chaplin, our friends . . . 562.

He obviously felt the yearning in me, and I made sure he knew that I wanted to be round him most of all.

"You didn't murder that Civil, Gabriel," I said, "so I'm sure they've come to that conclusion by now."

Neither of us spoke for a moment.

Then he said, "And if they still haven't figured out who did do it?"

I paused. "If I go in alone at first, you could stay outside the borders of the hub, away from the guards, until I tell you it's okay."

"A man should face his own troubles," he said. But as he let go of my hand, I got the feeling he was just saying this—that it might even be a leftover sentiment from a few months ago, when he'd taken such pride in being so close to human, at least for a vampire.

"Sometimes," I said, "safe is better than sorry."

I rested my head against Gabriel's. Right now, it was as if the crisis at my old house had merely made something temporary explode in us—something that had calmed, although I could feel it building up again in the pit of my belly. It wouldn't be long until we were at another breaking point, but I wouldn't think about that during this lone moment of peace.

We left for GBVille a few hours later.

We sped along in faster time than usual, taking only a couple of nights to travel to the higher climes, then finding a location for Gabriel to hide far outside GBVille—a little cave that was dark enough so that he'd rest easy if I didn't return before dawn.

Knowing he wouldn't be easily found, I left him behind and was on the approach to our hub within a couple of hours. I'd stayed in my humanlike form, and as I came into view of the perimeter, I held up my hands as I drew near. My breath came harder, because of the altitude.

Even from hundreds of yards off, the group of vampires that had claimed this scouting spot located me, coming out from behind metal sculptures—a peace-sign garden of sorts—that had been built by General Benefactors.

By the time I got closer, the vampires had fallen to their knees at the sight of me.

That's right—just as if I were 562.

I slowed my steps. Their heads were bent, and they stayed that way until I got to within speaking distance.

One vampire, a woman I recognized because she seemed to always have an interested eye trained on Gabriel, peered up at me. She had ruby-colored lips and curly mahogany hair that fell to the waist of her fitted hemp dress. Her name was Rachel.

"Mariah," she said, not even asking why I'd just appeared out of nowhere.

Again, I got that same feeling I'd had when those vampires guarding 562 had looked at me . . . and when I'd been amongst the Reds when they'd been dancing and chanting, *Your blood . . .*

I cleared my throat, then rose a bit taller, taking advantage of my standing with them. It seemed the smart way to go. "Is it okay for me to come inside?"

Rachel exchanged a glance with another vampire, a woman who'd also been hanging round Gabriel when he'd first started getting close to the other vamps. Ilsa was this one's name, and she had black spiral curls that fascinated me ever so slightly.

I was sure that the females were silently communicating with each other.

Then Rachel focused on me again. "You're not the one

who's considered a fugitive, Mariah, so you'll be okay after a rough start, I imagine."

"Why?"

"We all know how Gabriel made off with you. You didn't run voluntarily."

From the jaded glint in her eyes, I could tell that she, and probably the other vampires, knew that I'd gone with Gabriel of my own free will.

Did all the other Reds believe the same?

Was it too much to hope that the oldster had spread this sort of story to the rest of the community about Gabriel spiriting me off without my agreement?

This wasn't necessarily a fine thing. There was a chance that the oldster, who'd likely reached his limits with Gabriel and the vampires because of this killing, had made Gabriel out to be the bad guy and I was the supposed victim. The oldster might've even gone too far in trying to protect me, his fellow Badlander.

"As you can see," I said, "Gabriel's not with me."

"Shrewd to have left him wherever he is right now," Rachel said.

Before I could respond to that, she turned to Ilsa, communicating again, while all the other vamps stayed lined up, still on their knees, watching me with those smiles. I tried not to notice, even though they made me feel as if I were the apple of their unsettling eyes.

Then Rachel and Ilsa stood, taking up both sides of me. Beneath a long, blasé coat that was probably filched from a sleeping distractoid, a sheath rested against Ilsa's thigh. Looked like she had a katana with her.

"Come along," Rachel said in a flat voice.

"Where're we going?"

"To the asylum, where your friend, the old man, has been conducting an investigation. He'll want to see you first off."

"The oldster's in charge?" Actually, it didn't surprise me that he was the one who'd ended up trying to sort this all out. He'd always wanted community more than anyone, even back in the New Badlands.

Ilsa glanced at me. "That's how the cards fell—right in front of your oldster. He's a go-getter, that guy."

As they led me up a dirt-caked hill, toward the rising, rounded spires of GBVille, I could feel the weight of the other vampires watching me as they remained behind.

Ilsa spoke with the lazy drawl of a coy girl, but since she looked the part with those spiral curls, it didn't clash with her demeanor. Still, it was a bit creepy to know that she was probably hundreds of years old and acting like a dollbaby.

"Your oldster's been busy, Mariah. He's been interviewing everyone—vampires, weres, tik-tiks, Civils, shadows. He even had some vampires venture into the mind of your doggie."

"Chaplin?"

"They didn't have you here to translate his Canine."

"Did my dog see anything about the killing?"

Rachel shook her head. "Nope."

I'd have to talk to Chaplin. He was good about blocking vamps out when he needed to. He'd done it to Gabriel back in the Badlands. He'd do it here if he saw anything that incriminated anyone he considered valuable enough to protect.

Ilsa added, "Your oldster didn't stop there, either. He actually interviewed demons."

I did a double take.

Rachel said, "The humans who were trying to get into GBVille have left because of the mosquito rumors, and demons have started to approach us. There're maybe three of them inside an alternate cell block right now."

No one considered demons to be monsters like us. They were possessed humans, a different breed altogether.

"Does the oldster think that a demon could've evaded guards outside the hub and come inside the asylum to kill that Civil undetected?"

"Doubtful," Rachel said. "We've guarded everything tightly out here on the fringes. They wouldn't have gotten past a vampire. Probably not a were-creature, either, if they were in beast form."

"Then who's the prime suspect?"

Ilsa rested her hand near the katana. She slid a satisfied grin to me.

"Neelan's on the short list," she said. "You know, the chimera Civil?"

I think my eyes nearly popped out of my head with the news. "Why would he do it?"

Rachel said, "To make the Reds look bad."

"A shadow saw him near the scene of the crime," Ilsa said, "and Neelan's been locked up ever since while evidence is being sought. And he knows better than to breathe fire to melt the bars. He's under rigid guard."

Now this *was* a fine thing, although I'd liked Neelan. But I'd prefer the killer be anyone but Gabriel.

"So Gabriel's off the hook?" I asked.

"No," both vamps said at once.

We were passing stucco-ridden general housing now, cluster upon cluster piled like sterile blocks.

Rachel said, "From what we know, there's not a strong case against Neelan. The oldster's keeping him away from everyone else for another reason."

"True enough," Ilsa added in that little flirt voice. "Before the oldster interviewed him and 'detained' him, that half-snake man was slithering around, stirring up shit, preaching about how vampires should be banished from GBVille. He was getting close to bad-mouthing the other Reds, too."

"Racist," Rachel said. "If it were up to Neelan, I think he'd advocate a Civil-only hub."

I almost defended the monster who'd come to us after the power-blaster attack, inviting us to live in GBVille with the rest of the liberated ones. But 562's rampage had clearly turned the Civil to a different opinion. I couldn't blame him, either, because we all were what we were, and *he* was a peaceful monster.

As the memory of me and Gabriel, covered in the blood of those werewolves, hit me, I stayed stone-silent.

It seemed that we all were what we were.

I could see the asylum in the near distance, lifted beyond

the brick wall. Chaplin would be in there. And, not so far on the other side of the hub, 562 would be behind her/his glass shield of a coffin.

I wanted to run to both of them.

Ilsa spoke. "The thing is that the Civils aren't aware that Neelan was detained, and they're wondering where he is."

"They don't know he's under suspicion," I said.

"That's right." Ilsa steered me toward the lower gate of the asylum, where two mummies were on guard. They hadn't seen us yet. "Civils are starting to get restless, wary of everything Reds do."

Rachel said, "Some are even following us wherever we go."

Were they insinuating that Civils were tracking Reds to 562's cave? I wondered if these two lower-level vamps had even been privy to the information about 562 still being alive, but before I could think about how to ask, Ilsa took hold of my arm, silencing me.

"Quiet now," she said.

At our approach, the Civil mummy guards straightened their spines. Rachel clasped my other arm, as if they were hauling me into the asylum after having found me.

One mummy followed me with its gaze as I passed by—I could see its bloodshot eyes through the slit in its bandages— and Rachel clucked her tongue.

"Don't fret, gorgeous, we've got her. You just keep guarding."

The women ushered me up the stairs, over the walkway, toward the innards of the asylum. All the while, I got varied reactions from the monsters: shock, then sneers, from the Civils; adoring smiles from the vampires; neutral gazes from the rest of the Reds, as if they didn't quite know what to make of my return.

Soon enough, the women brought me to a jail area I'd never visited before. The community had been centralizing our human "guests" in the cell block that had mostly housed Civil monsters back when the GBVille professionals had been in charge. But this space was obviously geared for Red monsters now, with backup silver-coated bars that had crashed down after the power had gone out to take the place of the laser shields. Most of the little rooms here were empty, except for a couple of what looked to be human residents.

Was this where they were keeping the demons who'd braved entry into the hub?

The oldster was talking with a group of monsters outside the cells, and at the sight of me, he blanched. Next to him, Hiram, a fellow were-creature—a puma in his moon form— went a bit pale, too. Keesie, a Civil who was some type of stone creature no one could really figure out, shaped her mouth into a little O. An old vampire—supposedly the oldest in this community—stood there, too, his hair the color of ink, his skin marble-white, a Vandyke beard his most distinguishing feature. McKellan was his name.

Rachel talked before any questions were lobbed. "Mariah gave herself up to us just outside the hub."

"Where's Gabriel?" the oldster asked me without preamble.

I shrugged.

"Mariah . . ." The oldster had his warning tone on.

Wordless, Keesie wrapped a stony hand round the bars of a cell and yanked the entry open. Good to know they'd reserved a place for me.

The oldster didn't make a move to shut it. Instead, he said, "Keesie, come on now. Mariah didn't have any part in the crime."

"I think," Hiram said in a drawl that always reminded me of a gambler's, "Keesie is indicating that she thinks Mariah became Gabriel's accomplice."

The stone creature nodded forcefully. She had scars— nicks and chinks—where 562 had wounded her during the rampage.

Hiram tipped back his wide-brimmed hat. "Michael, I guess you should take the opportunity to question Mariah, since she's here again."

The oldster sighed, and I saw what kind of wear and tear

me and Gabriel had given him. Didn't he know that we hadn't had any choice *but* to run?

And we'd do it again if we had to.

He motioned for me to get into the cell while Keesie held open the door for me to enter. My vampire escorts paused but then let me go. I had the feeling that the vamp women would be keeping lookout for me and probably Gabriel, too.

I was even sure the vampires on the perimeter were sending out a search party for him by now. Would Gabriel sense them and flee from that cave?

"Can we have some privacy?" the oldster asked the others as Keesie shut the door on me.

With some reluctance, the stone creature and Hiram left us. McKellan and his two vampire women lingered just long enough to show me that they weren't abandoning me, even if it seemed to be that way.

I stayed back from the bars and jerked my chin toward the residents of the other cells—three in all.

"Who're they?"

"Demons."

I'd been right. "This isn't quite privacy, oldster, having them in here still."

"And this isn't quite locking you up, either, when all you have to contend with are these bars."

He motioned toward my cell door, which would hardly hold me if I had a mind to change into another form, get up a head of steam, then barge out. The silver might give any other were-creature pause, but I'd get over it quicker than most, thanks to 562.

He added, "Putting you in here is just a formality, and you can be sure the Civils are going to be back with some bindings as well as a deep desire to speak candidly with you."

"But you already pointed out that I didn't have any part of the killing."

"That's what I keep telling them."

So I'd been right about the oldster, too. I inferred that he'd indeed protected my reputation by telling everyone that Gabriel had made off with me.

"He didn't do anything wrong, Michael."

He glanced about, lowered his voice. Demons weren't supposed to have heightened hearing in those human bodies, so we could talk. "They're on the warpath, those Civils, and they require appeasement."

"Sounds like you've been walking on your tiptoes the whole while. Especially when it comes to Neelan."

The oldster blew out a breath. "They think he's out in the hub searching for Gabriel."

"*Did* Neelan have any part in the killing?"

He shook his head. "Vampires went into his head and saw that he's innocent. He was close enough to hear the victim's screams, though, and to be one of the first to crucifix-burn the attacking vamps. I'm only keeping him locked away so he don't cause a riot, what with all the mouthing off he's been doing."

"Do you have *any* leads?"

"No. And the more time it takes to get to the bottom of this, the more fiery those Civils will be. They want justice right damn now."

I couldn't deny them that, either—not when I'd gone after my own justice in Dallas.

But I didn't regret it, and the oldster must've seen something in me that looked bold, unafraid, *un*like the scared little girl I used to be.

"Mariah," he said, "I get the feeling you came back here because you wanted to take the temperature of the hub before Gabriel returns. But you'd do well to just tell me where he is."

"Why—so you can lock him up, too, even if he's innocent?"

"That *would* be the most diplomatic move . . . for all of us."

And there it stood—the oldster on one side, me and Gabriel on the other.

My throat got tight as I refused to speak.

"Girl." The oldster loomed near the bars. His skin was ruddy under his longish whiskers. "I don't think you grasp the enormity of this situation."

"I do. Believe me, I do."

It bothered mc to even say that, because Chaplin, my friends, and 562 were important, too.

Just not as vital as Gabriel.

There was a new emptiness in me, right near my heart, at a corner of it. The oldster didn't seem to care as he turned away, toward the slap of paws hitting the floor of the corridor.

Chaplin appeared, halting next to the oldster. At first, my dog looked so happy to see me that I reached out through the bars to him.

But then the oldster said, "Maybe you can talk sense into her, boy."

It only took that for Chaplin to get the same look as the oldster in his eyes—ragged disappointment, helplessness at what to do with me. It hadn't even taken a second for that to happen, because I'd done so much to let him down lately.

My dog barked at the oldster, no translation required.

I lent one, anyway, whispering, "He wants you to leave us for a moment."

The oldster made a thwarted sound but still abided by my dog's wishes.

As soon as the oldster cleared out, Chaplin started in, yowling, woofing, and chuffing at me. In short, nagging.

Where in tarnation did you and Gabriel go off to?

Yup, he knew that I'd accompanied Gabriel willingly. And there was no way my dog would tolerate a big lie from me, even if I had it in me these days to give one.

"We went to Dallas," I said, finally feeling a bit of mortification. Regret.

Chaplin dropped to his belly, as if his legs had lost every ounce of strength. My heart went down with him.

He had to know that someday, I'd end up here. It was where I'd always been headed, and there was no stopping it.

Right?

"Chaplin . . ."

Dallas, he whined, and it stung like sharp wire whisking right through me. *Not Dallas.*

I didn't offer more, and that spoke volumes to Chaplin.

He didn't have to ask what I'd done, although I wanted to explain.

"You always said that our bad guys got away with so much," I said. "That someday, they'd get their just deserts—"

Chaplin jumped and barked at me with such vitriol that I moved back from the bars. He barked again and again, and with every admonishment I shrank away all the more.

But it was his final few barks that stole my breath clean out of me.

I've tried so hard all these years . . .

"Chaplin—"

I'm done with you, Mariah. Done.

When he turned his back on me and ran off, I knew in my sore heart that he truly meant it.

I sat on the cell floor, where all the adoring vampire smiles in the world wouldn't fill what Chaplin had left gaping inside me.

12

Gabriel

Gabriel was so far back in the cave where he was waiting for Mariah that he could feel the darkness in his very bones. His vampire vision cut through the dimness with a faint red glow and, to pass the time, he'd started to amuse himself with a bat that had winged through the cave earlier, when the colony had been disturbed by his presence.

He'd isolated just this one from the others with the force of his mind, holding it frozen, its eyes red in Gabriel's view as the animal struggled to get free.

He wasn't going to harm it. He was only curious. And it was as good a time as any to exercise his mind, as the older vampires—especially the one named McKellan—said he should.

What's in you? he thought to the mammal, reaching inside its head.

Its thoughts were impulses, not a language, and Gabriel felt the bat's instinctive fear rather than having to translate it: the urge to get from one place to another . . . The need to stay warm, to sleep, to merely go from this moment to the next . . .

Was this all that Gabriel would think about, too, one day, after he'd become full vampire? Would he be so tuned into rote survival that there wasn't much else to him?

He let the bat go, and it flapped away. He waited, knowing only a short time had passed since Mariah had gone.

Was she inside GBVille yet?

Was she okay?

Then Gabriel heard something in the otherwise silent cave: a sliding movement, the brush of clothing.

At first, he mistook the sounds for the ones he'd heard on the night of his escape from GBVille, when he'd caught something creeping around the General Benefactors building and wondered if the Witches were still about.

But these sounds weren't quite the same.

These hardly even existed. Instead, they were almost like what you might hear in a dream—the sort where you woke up and asked yourself whether what you'd just experienced was fake or real.

He tilted his head, listening, listening. Realizing now that it was only another vampire who'd come into this cave.

There'd been good odds that his kin would search him out. And, of course, they would've gotten here before Mariah returned, after they saw her enter GBVille.

"I had a feeling you'd have no problem finding me if you put your energy to it," he said into the near darkness.

The vampire showed himself.

It was the oldest one, McKellan, who didn't look a night past thirty. He'd lived as a human back when a great queen had died in England and left her throne to a Scottish king who wasn't even her son. McKellan had fought in world wars as a vampire, watched the years go by in cycles of destruction and rebuilding. Eventually, he'd come to this country, laboring his way across the States, just like other humans who'd wanted new chances, too. He'd pretended to be one of them—talking like them, working and laughing like them—until he'd been captured by a lucky Shredder years and years later and stored in this asylum for study.

Long ago, Gabriel had seen an image on the Nets of what

a kind, young god might look like—a man with shining dark hair and a smooth, understanding face sitting on a throne, his hand reaching out to a crowd of children. Except for the Vandyke beard, that very picture was McKellan in his beige hemp clothing, gazing upon Gabriel with serene pity right now.

The eldest vampire's Old American accent was flawless. "Your timing could not be better, Gabriel. We were going to institute a weekly Night of Rest for the first time tomorrow, and I would have found it trying to travel out here for you then."

Gabriel knew what McKellan meant. Ever since the vampires had started to visit 562 in secret, they'd been talking about this Night of Rest, a worshipful time to appreciate their good tidings.

But as McKellan sat near Gabriel, there was something else brewing in his gaze.

The old vampire opened his mind up to Gabriel, in fraternity, allowing him to see that their Night of Rest wouldn't involve only 562 . . .

He saw Mariah in McKellan's mind, too.

Gabriel contained a shudder. There were times he didn't like how the other vampires looked at her, smiled at her.

The older vampire held up a hand. "We have larger matters to weigh than that one. Much larger. Suffice it to say that Mariah is safe with your oldster right now."

McKellan noted Gabriel's relief with a flicker of interest.

"Still attached to her, are you?" he asked.

Gabriel nodded. During an instructional moment recently, McKellan had said that all vampires eventually learned not to have emotional attachments like the one Gabriel nursed for Mariah.

"It's our imprint," Gabriel said, trying again to explain it to the other vampire, though he knew his bond to her was even more than that. It had to be.

"Yes. The imprint. It should be enlightening to see how that develops. No vampires I know have ever taken the blood of a were-creature, then coupled it with bodily intimacy."

He sounded as bad as one of those human doctors who'd prodded and poked him might've been.

"But we digress," McKellan said. "It's *your* absence that was duly noted by everyone in the community, so we have made a few decisions while you have been away. In fact, your reappearance has already set much into motion."

With one glance, the elder conveyed current events to Gabriel: how the oldster had been investigating and hadn't yet come upon any answers as to who'd killed the Civil; how the other Civils were getting angrier by the night because of the lack of action from the Reds; how the vampires had pulled together and shut out the rest of the community in an effort to deal with this killing themselves. How they had waited to see when and if Gabriel would come back.

The killing. Gabriel hadn't thought about it for a while. As he did now, a pang racked him. A clang from his fading conscience.

"Have the vampires at least figured out who first attacked that Civil and started this whole mess?" he asked.

McKellan cut Gabriel off from his gaze for some reason.

"We did arrive at a solution," the elder said.

Why did that sound so cryptic?

McKellan was so still and quiet that it sent a scratch of discomfort through Gabriel.

Strange. He couldn't figure out why his conscience was back now, here in the dark, where it should be very easy to be a vampire.

Instead of explaining anything else, McKellan glanced over his shoulder. A second later, Gabriel heard another furtive sound, but there was also a familiar scent that he hadn't experienced in several nights. . . .

Soon, a shadow stood near them, holding a solar-powered lantern.

Taraline.

McKellan hardly seemed surprised by the arrival of this lady, whose clothing was steeped in the neutral tawnyvale herb so that the smell of dymorrdia wouldn't overcome them.

"Hello, Taraline," the old vampire said, recognizing her as an ally. Gabriel had vouched for her long ago, when he'd first introduced her to his kind.

She nodded to McKellan. "I noticed you slipping off from the hub, and I asked one of your men to speed me here undercover."

The elder addressed Gabriel. "She's been waiting for you to return, just as we have. Taraline believes she can be of some help to us, and she has been just that, running interference for us with the oldster and his questions."

"Why?" Gabriel asked.

It seemed as if she were averting her gaze from Gabriel's, too, though the veils made that hard to confirm.

"We don't need monster hunts in a new society," she said. "I *can* help in this situation, if you'll let me. You've gone into my mind to see how loyal I am to Gabriel. I owe him for bringing me here to GBVille from the necropolis."

McKellan shook his head. "I told Gabriel that we have already gone ahead with our own plans."

Gabriel asked, "And what would those be?"

McKellan didn't miss a beat. "Mind-screwing the Civils so they will forget the killing and 562 ever happened."

It took a second for the meaning to permeate.

Taraline leaned back against a wall that split the cave, as if her breath had been punched out. She obviously hadn't known about this.

"So it begins." She'd probably realized that she was a candidate for a mind-screw now that she was privy to the vampires' plans.

Gabriel's guts felt gnarled, tied up by the conscience that still hounded him. "Mind-screwing's a harsh measure."

A lock of dark hair dipped over McKellan's brow. "It will allow us vampires a clean slate, another chance with the Civils. Among us, we have already vowed that we will never go after a fellow monster again, *ever*, but we must do what we must this time."

His rationalization for using mind-screws sounded so

very vampire. But to Gabriel, going inside someone's mind and rearranging it was rapacious. Yet that was probably only the clinging humanity in him thinking so.

"That is true," McKellan said, reading Gabriel. "Mind-screwing is draconian. Yet effective. And that is not where we have to stop. Even before you left, Gabriel, we started to give in to the pleas from some humans who have been willing to join us. Most came to the asylum asking for mercy."

"They ask for more than mercy," Taraline said. "They ask for blood exchanges so they can have disease immunity and live longer lives, just like vampires, who seem to be the luxury-model monsters."

There was longing in her tone. Taraline had been toying with the idea of taking 562's blood in an exchange when the creature had offered it. The origin had sensed her mental battle between living with dymorrdia and the possibility of healing, and it had only been 562's downfall that had put an end to Taraline's decision to undergo the origin's exchange.

Gabriel turned to McKellan. He'd never been under any assumptions that he was the sharpest knife in the drawer, and he didn't want to assume anything now, but . . .

"Why would we want to exchange with humans?" he asked.

McKellan stared a moment too long, as if he were disappointed that Gabriel hadn't figured it out yet. Then he said, "If we give them what they have been asking for, we create more vampire allies."

"You want to produce troops," Gabriel said.

"No—I would call them sympathizers."

"And what about the jailed humans who *won't* be willing to exchange?"

"Gabriel, I have lived long enough to know how this will work. Eventually, most will come to see this as their only hope for survival for a variety of reasons, whether it is about longer lives, health, or even the chance to remain with loved ones. But not even a mind-screw would work to make someone a willing vampire—not if, deep in their soul, they are loath to give up what they treasure most about themselves."

He paused, then said, "Those are the ones who need extra motivation."

Gabriel must've looked torn, because McKellan went on.

"This is how society at large works: There is *always* one faction in power. They may be kind leaders or they may be greedy ones, but there is always a driving force that others follow because that is what they need—leadership. Capability. This pattern will follow even with monsters, whether it is in GBVille, Dallas, Gates City, the Northlink . . . Others need to look to us because each hub that falls does so due to vampires. We are the strongest and smartest. Surely you can see this trend already occurring."

Taraline was watching Gabriel through her veils. Like every other shadow, she was the eyes and ears of the community. Had she already seen who was the strongest and smartest? Had she been preparing for a showdown between the Civils and Reds ever since 562's rampage?

Was that why she was here, offering to help?

Gabriel dug his nails into his palms. Stupid. He was so stupid. It never failed that he was the last to see what was what—it'd happened back in the Badlands with Mariah and the were-community. It was happening here.

But then he loosened his fingers, emotion skittering away from him.

Soon, after his gloaming, he was going to be full vampire, smart and keenly perceptive. He wouldn't be the last to figure things out anymore.

McKellan leaned toward him, his eyes a blazing blue in Gabriel's vision.

"We *are* the most fit to lead," the eldest said. "And we knew that there would be a trigger incident that would show us the right time to take over. The killing and your flight made it clear that all us monsters will never be of a single mind and that one of our kind would need to assume control."

"Beyond what you've already told me, are there any other plans?"

"We should not need any."

Taraline broke in. "If you would just listen to me, I have

a way to have us all coexist in relative peace, without tearing up everyone's minds."

McKellan frowned as she wandered closer to Gabriel—so close that he could see the shape of her face under her veils.

Was it his imagination or were there rises of cheekbone and chin where there used to be none?

Once again, he wondered just what Mariah's 562 blood had done to her, if anything. Or if it had changed her in more than one way.

"In case you haven't noticed," she said, "shadows have been a neutral party in GBVille. We're not Reds and we're not Civils."

Human, he thought, *but just of a different sort.*

"And?" Gabriel asked.

"And wouldn't it make sense if the one shadow who was attacked and bitten by 562 momentarily lost her sanity and found herself hungry for blood?"

As her meaning came to Gabriel, decency kicked in him once again, taking the place of everything else.

"You're volunteering to take the fall as the one who attacked the Civil first," he said.

"Yes."

"I won't let you do that, Taraline."

She didn't look as if she were going to back down, though.

McKellan said, "Her plan is not as airtight as ours. After a mind-screw, the Civils would not even recall 562 or its rampage."

"But," she said, raising her voice, "it's not as final, either. Once you start mind-screwing other monsters, it's not going to stop. Don't you want a different sort of society in GBVille, now, while we have a chance to start over?" She spread her gloved hands. "Ever since dymorrdia's been such an intimate part of my life, I've been banished, and this is the first time I've been a part of a free society. I'm not going to stand by and see it crash because one faction takes advantage of another."

Gabriel couldn't believe this. "Taraline, if you confessed to killing the Civil, you'd be banished, anyway."

"No Civil would be vicious enough to demand punishment for me. I'm a victim, remember? 562 took my blood while I was trying to calm the origin down. I sacrificed myself for GBVille."

"Doesn't matter," he said.

"Even if I were to be banished, I would just go to another conquered hub, one where they wouldn't know me. There, I'd take great consolation in the fact that the monsters still stood united in GBVille, where the revolution started. The other falling hubs are looking to this place as an example of how to operate, Gabriel, and if they see that monsters can't live together here, *everything* will fail. Humans will rise up again in that void. Is that what you want?"

This was too much, her wanting to be the martyr. "You're forgetting one thing."

"What?"

"If you were to confess, the Civils could still blame the Reds. They would just point out that 562 *made* you a victim. The killing would still be our fault."

Taraline was looking at him hard—even through her veils he could feel the press of her gaze.

Was it because he didn't seem so dumb now after all?

Then something random occurred to him . . .

"Do you *know* who committed the crime, Taraline?" Was that why she'd been running interference for the vampires with the oldster? Was that why she was being so quick to volunteer? "Did you or one of the shadows see who did it, and you think the identity of the killer is going to cause a Civil-Red war? Then you came up with this scheme to avoid having anyone reveal the actual killer, ever?"

She paused a moment too long.

"No matter the identity of the killer," McKellan said, "we vampires will protect them. We have already decided it."

A bad feeling was enveloping Gabriel, just like a black fog where he couldn't see a step in front of him.

"Taraline . . ." He was about to tear off her sheer top veil so he could see her eyeholes, see her blue gaze completely so he could read her.

But memories darkened his gaze instead, images from that night: dancing with Mariah . . . hungry—so hungry . . . forced away from the blood, her blood . . . having to go back into the asylum for his blood-filled flask . . . stalking inside with the other young vampires, then—

Nothing.

Why had he blacked out?

What had happened from that point on?

"Gabriel." It was McKellan's water-flow voice, and the gush of it entered Gabriel, lending immediate peace.

Thank-all, peace.

The elder took Gabriel by the arm, his touch light as he directed a comment to Taraline.

"Although your plan was a brave one, it will not be required."

"But—" she said.

"Not," McKellan said, "unless *our* plans fail, which is not likely." Then he put his full attention on Gabriel as Taraline lapsed to silence.

"I will take you to the vampire house we have established in the hub," he said, "where others can mind you while I see to our progress with the Civils. I am keeping you out of sight because if the Civils see you before all is calm, we will already have lost the hub—and the fight against the humans."

"Have you already sent the vampires to the humans' cells to convert them?" Gabriel asked. "Have you started to mind-screw the Civils . . . ?"

"Upon news of your return, we commenced our plans."

Gabriel ran his hand down his face, as if he could wipe all this away.

The elder said, "Vampires have started to sway the Civil guards from cell block duty. They will get them into isolated areas of the asylum and put them away until every Civil has been wiped. We are doing this quietly, thoroughly."

"And what about any were-creatures who sympathize with the Civils?"

"Anyone whose mind reveals sympathies with the Civils

will have to be taken care of, only to ensure that no one ever remembers this killing."

Gabriel didn't move. At least with the mind-screws, Taraline wouldn't have to sacrifice herself, because the rest of the community would have forgotten the killing had even happened. But he felt as if he had started a new, ugly direction for GBVille. For their new world.

And he couldn't stop thinking about why Taraline would've volunteered to stage such a dangerous plan in the first place.

Just as he felt that thick black fog surrounding him again, McKellan tightened his hold on Gabriel.

After that, calm dominated him.

Calm and numbing logic.

13

Stamp

When the vampires came to Stamp's cell block that night, he had his back turned to the bars, his hands busy with the wire he'd extracted from the water sink unit near the screened-off loo section of his little room.

Idle hands make for the monsters' work, he thought, shaping that wire into a hook with his chapped, scraped fingers. He'd spent a lot of hours scratching at the stucco with his nails, extracting this wire from the wall, where the basin hid it. He just hoped that no monsters would be able to smell the blood on him as he formed a tool that might help him pick the lock on his door.

Good thing the power was out, because without these more primitive backup doors, Stamp wouldn't have otherwise had a chance.

Still, he wasn't only banking on lock picking to get out of here. No, sir. He'd also wound some other wires together until they looked like blades. He'd been sharpening those to points while no guards were near and had stowed them under his mattress.

When his trained Shredder hearing detected footfalls—plus the stealthy movement of vampires—he had to quickly stuff the lock wire under that mattress, next to the shivs he'd made. Then, using the bedpost, he hefted himself to his one leg and went to the sink unit to wash his hands under the trickle of liquid.

Whispers down the corridor. Vampire whispers—like silk over sand.

His Shredder instincts went on alert. Vampires didn't whisper unless they were up to something. And it was strange that he couldn't hear any Civils in the corridor; they were *always* guarding.

A chill scuttled down Stamp's neck, over his shoulders, as he caught the breeze-soft sound of vampires coming closer. The only thing that reassured him right now was that the Civils basically kept all the other monsters in check—it seemed that they respected life, human or otherwise, more than the Reds. But without Civils here . . .

Stamp glanced behind him at the corridor, seeing that Mags was already at her bars, a few inches from them, her dark eyes wide, wisps of her black hair escaping from the tie that held the strands back from her face.

She looked . . . excited.

Then again, she'd been different these past nights. Withdrawn. Refusing to talk to him and responding only when a crowd of vampires would come into the cell block to visit, standing in front of her cell, barring Stamp's view of her until they left.

It was as if they were conditioning her for advanced Stockholm syndrome, something Stamp had learned about in training. There'd been a case long ago in which a vampire tribe in old Europe had taken human hostages, attempting to win them over to their side. But before the humans had become willing enough to give up their souls, a band of Shredders had terminated the bloodsuckers.

As Jo, the monster sympathizer across the corridor, also came to the bars, Stamp kept a vigilant eye on her, too. She'd been visiting a lot with the vamps.

He turned back to the sink unit, but out of the corner of his gaze, he could see a group of vampires coming to Mags's and Jo's cells.

More whispers.

He'd cleaned his hands, drying them now. He still didn't pick up any audible signs of the tread-heavy Civils, nor the humanlike movements of were-creatures or tik-tiks.

Where had the other guards gone?

The clank of a cell door opening set him on alert, and he automatically lowered himself, holding to the basin to maintain his equilibrium. He'd been working on balance exercises, mentally picturing himself as a Shredder who could still be fast and efficient, even without one of his legs.

He scuttled to the bars, so quiet that not even the vampires in front of Jo's and Mags's cells acknowledged him. Clanks from other opening cell doors repeated down the corridor.

Jo was already being led away, vampires stroking her auburn hair, gazing on her with adoring, hungry smiles. And Mags . . .

She was in the corridor, too, but she wasn't looking at the vampires.

Her eyes were trained on Stamp.

As their gazes met, his chest pained him because she seemed so out of place—a fighter in the midst of those vamps. But maybe that was only because he knew she would battle them to the death if she had any odds of survival whatsoever.

For some reason, she sent a sad smile his way, and he gripped the bars. She wasn't looking so great, her skin sallow from all the time they'd been shut away.

"If they're questioning you again," he said, "hold strong, Mags."

A male vampire with skin darker than hers whispered in her ear, and it reminded Stamp of what a lover might do to a woman he was seducing.

Then the man touched her arm.

Stamp barked, "Get away from her, scrub."

The male vampire slowly turned on Stamp, his teeth white in the torch-hushed corridor.

Down the way, there was more whispering movement, then the heavier, less graceful footfalls of humans being led off.

The male vampire slid his hand to Mags's waist, and she peered up at him, as if she didn't mind being touched by a monster.

Were they here to pull all the humans out of their cells and question them tonight? Or was this some sort of blood feast that Stamp had to stop?

As the vamps led Mags away, Stamp threw himself against the bars, reaching through them to his partner.

"Mags," he said, hoping his voice would bring her out of the sway that the whispering vamp had put on her. Damn it, hadn't he trained her in how to avoid falling under their spell? She knew how to block.

She just didn't want to.

His partner sent one last glance over her shoulder as the male vampire took her by the hand, gently guiding her out of Stamp's sight.

Jo and her vampires trailed them, and he interpreted her accepting expression as a reminder of how he would no doubt be questioned again soon, too, if that was what the vamps were doing.

Stamp stayed planted. They wouldn't find him as compliant as these others, and that was probably why they'd saved him for last.

Two vampire women remained to the side of his cell while the other human jailbirds filed past. He wasn't even sure there were any more humans left in the cell block with him.

Fixing a rebellious *screw you* look on his face, he assessed the females. One woman had long black hair that fell down her back in spirals, a katana sheathed at her side under the drab distractoid coat she wore. The other pouted at him with scarlet lips against white skin and curly hair that was more red than brown. They were both centuries old; any Shredder would've known that from their talent at staying so still, as if every year made a vampire that much more detached from life's timeline.

As always, he avoided their gazes.

"What are you scrubs doing with everyone?" he asked.

Spiral Hair lowered her voice to a sway-filled whisper, but Stamp blocked it, just as if it were something being lobbed, like a quiet bomb.

"Darling, darling boy," she said, and all he knew was that if he were less mentally fortified, she would've sounded like soft chimes by a seashore before the country's beaches had been walled off, mined, and torn to shreds.

"I'm not a boy," he said.

The one with the red lips tried to get clever, and she bent low, attempting to snag his gaze.

No dice, because Stamp had already closed his eyes.

"You're no older than the first flush of your twenties," she whispered with the same tempting notes of her friend. "Still a beautiful human. You'll never be this beautiful again—but you must already know that."

Although Stamp's eyes were shut, he could feel how the female creatures had moved even nearer to the bars, their voices pounding their way into his skin.

The other vamp took up where her partner had left off. "Never again so beautiful."

"So beautiful."

They were repeating it often enough that the notion could've been easy to believe. But Stamp knew that he was more twisted wreckage than young man these days. He'd only been beautiful when he'd been at his best, wielding his chest puncher, slaying the monsters that haunted society, never asking for much in return besides the pride of nobility.

He heard the click of the lock on his cell door. The bitches were coming in.

Stamp thought of those shivs under his mattress.

"Bad move," he said.

A lilting laugh from one of the vampires. "Don't be that way, darling boy."

They should've listened.

"Go to hell," he said.

He sensed them flinching at the holy curse. He'd used it

to show them that he knew how a verbal assault would work against a vampire.

The girls recovered quickly, and one said, "Now, now. We're only here to ask you what we can do for you, then give you what you want."

"Or maybe," Stamp said, "you were left here to work on the most difficult human remaining. Did your old leaders think I'd actually be swayed by two crones?"

The other vamp decided it was time to stop playing around, and she lit into him with her full-sway voice.

"*I* know what he wants. It's that partner of his."

Hearing it said out loud chipped into Stamp, getting past his defenses for a splinter of a second. The image of Mags settled over the backs of his eyelids. He even felt memories of the sweat he broke out in during the onset of sleep, the only moments when he would allow himself to wonder . . . to want . . .

"We could see to it that she loves you back," a vampire said.

The other added, "Even *you* need love."

No.

No, he didn't.

Images of Mags were replaced by a ball of fire—the explosive devastation of seeing someone you loved fly into pieces in a marketplace while you watched, unable to do anything about it. Then, the abyss of loneliness afterward, when you wanted them back so badly but you knew you'd never, ever see them again.

Pushed too far, Stamp let loose with a barrage of curses, beating back the vampire women from his cell. As he heard them retreating, he opened his eyes, wheeling toward his mattress—

He made an awkward dive for it, then reached underneath, whipping out the pair of shivs. Spinning around, he flailed at the closest vampire, her red, red lips open in a silent cry as she even now recovered from the onslaught of his curses.

"Rachel!" screamed the other one, otherwise frozen in holy fear, too.

But Stamp already had her friend where he wanted her.

Flash-quick, he stuck the sharpened ends of the two shivs into her neck, and with everything he had, he pulled the makeshift blades apart, ripping her open.

Blood spurted out, followed by the wet thump of her body hitting the floor.

Balance restored, Stamp pounced on her, stabbing her again, slicing, dicing.

He'd stopped cursing, so that allowed the spiral-haired vamp to jolt out of stillness and grab her friend, yanking her out of the room so fast that Stamp's eyes barely caught it.

He lifted the shivs, blood dripping from them. "Now *this*," he said, "is beautiful."

The other vampire backed away from the cell, her gaze fiery, her fangs out.

"Animal," she said.

His heart was thudding so hard that he thought it might beat itself to dust. He'd just issued a suicidal invitation to get himself killed, but he didn't really care.

Born a human, die a human.

The healthy vamp hissed at him from the corridor, bending to her friend and holding her hands to Rachel's neck. He hadn't killed the scrub—he hadn't decapitated her, extracted her heart, or used silver blades or a stake or anything on her—but it would take a lot of healing for the vamp to come back around.

At least he'd reiterated to them that he wouldn't be an easy conquest.

As he sat there holding those shivs, just daring the vamp woman to come and get him, a streak of motion sped into the corridor, then solidified in front of his cell.

An old, old vampire Stamp knew by the name of McKellan took one look at Rachel bloodied on the floor, then at Stamp and his little weapons.

Without any visible reaction, McKellan said, "We have no time for this nonsense."

He joined Spirals in pressing his hands to Rachel's chest, mending her heart, then glanced at Stamp. "Leave him here for later."

"But look what he did—"

"*Later*, Ilsa." He nudged her out of the way. "Go with the others. We need all the numbers we can manage right now."

She sent Stamp a glare of such cold fury that he welcomed it, and then she zipped down the corridor, leaving the old vamp on the floor with the wounded one.

Gone. The Ilsa vamp had gone to wherever they'd taken Mags. Stamp just knew it.

McKellan was still tending to Rachel, both hands on her neck as her eyes flew open, fixed on the ceiling.

"There, my dear, it is just a scratch," he said.

As her throat wound closed all the way, he backed off from the woman and turned to Stamp. "That was not needed, my friend. All it would have taken was one word. *Yes.*"

But to Stamp, he'd made a better choice than to be ruled by the vamps, and he kept his shivs out, just waiting for the chance to make another good decision if either vampire decided to test him again.

They didn't.

As soon as the woman could move, McKellan didn't even allow her a glance at Stamp. In a blur, he closed Stamp's cell door, the lock clinking home just before he took the healed vamp by the hand and pulled her off in a flicker of speed down the cell block.

Alone, Stamp sat down, wondering what the hell was so important to the vamps that they hadn't even bothered to exact revenge on a Shredder.

Yet he didn't sit there for long, because who knew when they'd be back for him?

He tore off some hemp from the bottom of his trousers, wrapped the shivs in it, then stored the weapons in his waistband. Next, he got that pick he'd been working on and tried the lock.

It took him a while, and with every passing second, another bead of sweat joined the ones that had already gathered on his top lip.

Hurry, he thought. But he couldn't. Not if he wanted to keep his hands steady.

When he heard another sound down the corridor, he rolled his eyes. Looked like he'd never catch a break.

He furiously tried to force the lock just as someone came to stand just to the left of his cell, and when he looked up to see that it was Mags, he almost dropped the wire.

She was loitering, tilting her head at him, as if wondering what the hell he was about.

He looked at her empty cell, then at her.

Mags understood his question before he even asked it, and she righted her head, crossing her arms on her chest over her gray uniform.

"They didn't even notice I left," she said. "The vamps put us in the same old room as always, but then someone came to fetch them and they took off outside, as if there was some emergency. I heard only enough to know that they're mind-wiping Civils and were-creatures. They're out of control, John."

"Are you telling me they just let you go because of some monster emergency?"

"I doubt that. They know how easy it'd be to hunt us back down and they're depending on us to be there when they return."

Stamp paused, measuring her. Her story didn't make sense at all, and it sent his suspicion into overdrive.

What were the monsters up to?

Mags kept talking. "Really, you should see—everything's in shambles out there."

He turned back to the lock, finally getting it to cooperate. He sprung it with a click, and the door eased open.

Using that door for balance, he hopped into the hallway. Mags inserted herself under his arm, bringing it over her shoulder.

Their faces were so close that he could've kissed her, and he almost did—one big smackeroo that wouldn't mean a thing but a hurrah that they finally had a chance to run, albeit he didn't know how far they'd get.

He even had an idea of where they might go. Before they'd gotten jailed, Mags had wanted to travel to another hub, just to see if it was powerless, too, and to see if they could get help with Stamp's leg, which would now require a replacement rather than just simple medical attention.

It sounded like a fine notion at this point, because after they gathered themselves, and maybe even informed higher human leadership as to what was going on with the monsters in GBVille, he'd come back here.

Back to Gabriel so he could settle old scores, just as he'd always intended.

"Are the vamps so busy that we can make it past the perimeter of this hub without them catching us?" he asked.

Mags smiled, and for a snapping second, that smile seemed different to Stamp.

Then the smile turned normal. "Let's give it a go."

She started to walk, and he limped along with her, still thinking of that smile and why the hell it wasn't sitting very well with him.

14

Mariah

The oldster returned to my cell after Chaplin had left, and then he transferred the demons to yet a third block.

When he returned again, he didn't come alone.

If I'd had the emotional energy, I might've hit the ceiling when I saw Neelan in all his Civil chimera glory. For a half-snake who'd been behind bars a few days, he sure looked dignified with that stately beard and regal posture. But he was also intimidating as hell while he wove back and forth on his tail.

"Be nice," the oldster said to him. "I only let you out because we need to get a few things straight round here. Monsters listen to both you and Mariah, so if you can come to some sort of understanding, it'd be in the best interests of us all."

He had his hand on a holstered revolver. Tales went that a silver bullet would do damage to Civils, too, just as *any* bullet would, since those kind of monsters weren't as hardy as real preters.

Neelan looked down his nose at me. His eyes were those

sunken type, small, embedded in faint wrinkles that he'd earned over the years as something both mortal and mythical.

When he talked, it wasn't to me—it was to the oldster.

"I could get you into a great deal of trouble for putting me away as you did."

"But since I'm being kind, here," the oldster said, "I'm thinking you won't go that route."

He seemed to believe that the oldster would put him right back in the slammer, and he changed the topic.

"Where are the cell guards?"

"I told 'em I could handle watching a few demons as well as Mariah fine enough, so they left this quarter to me from the very beginning. No one will have seen you transferred here."

"You certainly trust everyone to obey—even the Reds." Neelan's nostrils flared, as if the very word *Red* made him ill.

"Right now," the oldster said, "I'm not one to much trust, be they Red or Civil or . . ." He glanced at the emptied demon cells down the way. ". . . anything else."

Neelan was still looking at me like I was dung on a boot heel.

I was still smarting from Chaplin's abandonment, so I felt like dung, too. "Don't worry—I'm not going to kill you, Neelan. That's not why the oldster brought you here."

"One never knows."

I let a sigh escape me, but the oldster was almost pleading with his gaze for me to just deal with the Civil.

Neelan shifted on his tail, and I hoped that the oldster remembered just how damned fast a serpent could strike.

Especially one with the ability to breathe fire.

"We'll want Gabriel in custody," the Civil said, coming right out with his terms. "Then, as a community, we'll want to go to council on plans detailing how we're going to manage crime and punishment among us."

The oldster looked him up and down. "Seems like you've done some thinking while you've been in the stew."

"Don't mistake me. In the future, I, for one, would be in favor of separate monster communities so we might avoid any more difficulties. I understand that this isn't the time to advocate for that, though."

He was acknowledging that it was the vampires who pulled most of the monster load when it came to containing the humans, but, as he'd noted, there'd be a better time to bring up post-rebellion issues in the coming months.

It was just that right now, he was demanding Gabriel. *That* was what held my immediate focus.

"What would you plan to do with Gabriel if he's turned over to you?" I asked.

"Don't worry about that," he said. "We'll treat your boyfriend with the respect he deserves."

"Somehow this doesn't console me."

The oldster paid no mind to that. "Just what would this sort of respect entail?"

"First, we would have to jail Gabriel for running away from the scene of the crime, because that in itself was worthy of punishment."

The oldster narrowed his gaze. "Running away doesn't mean that Gabriel is guilty."

"It doesn't exactly prove innocence." Neelan looked down at the oldster. "He hasn't been tried, but his actions have spoken loudly, Michael."

"Innocent until proven guilty," the oldster said. "That's how any good and just society should work."

The Civil seemed to pity the oldster for still believing that concept. "Wasn't that part of what went wrong in the past, sir? History tells us that the bad guys always got their share of the benefit of the doubt Before in this country. From that point on, things spiraled out of control and yielded a nightmare."

I clamped my mouth shut. Long ago, our justice system had been a thing of beauty . . . until criminal rights had gone too far. Eventually, during trials, victims had been put through the wringer more than the accused, both big-time and small, and that was mainly because the government had quietly supported most of the bad guys; corporate interests demanded it from the politicians for the henchmen who did most of their dirty work.

"Gabriel isn't a bad guy," I said, as if that were all the trial he needed.

Neelan only looked weary.

Ah, I thought. Here he was—the creature who'd been so courteous when this community had gotten started.

I backed off a little. "It's just that I know him, Neelan. He showed us what he was made of back in the New Badlands."

He didn't get superior on me this time. "You may not believe it when I tell you this, but I do wish there were a way around jailing him, Mariah. However, you have to understand my bigger view—we can't condone a place where Civils are hunted."

The oldster got sarcastic. "Maybe this community *should* separate, then. Right now."

"By doing that," Neelan said, "we halve our numbers against the humans."

"That's what I've been getting at all along," the oldster said, clearly at the end of his rope.

We were at such an impasse that there indeed didn't seem to be anyplace to go.

But Neelan tried again. "Mariah. Please. Gabriel won't be prosecuted without fairness. I can promise that."

I couldn't. Wouldn't.

So I refused to take part in it.

Neelan cursed under his breath and looked to the oldster.

"I say we convene a council now so we can bring about some better action. One representative from every faction, equal in number."

"Looks as if we have no choice," the oldster said, giving me the stink-eye, too. Then he planted his hands on his skinny hips. "I take this to mean, then, that I won't have to put you back into solitary, Neelan."

"I'm willing to be more diplomatic than I have been.

But"—he gestured to me—"I would have to insist that she goes nowhere, just as I couldn't."

The oldster sent me a glance that told me he was glad Neelan had turned a corner and I'd better not say anything to ruin the moment.

Yup, it looked like I'd be here until either I gave up Gabriel, which was never going to happen, or the real killer was found. . . .

A sound in the corridor made me look out of my cell, and I saw a dark-haired angel with gray wings. Or maybe I should say a "fake angel" because these kinds of Civils just had wings to make them fly—they weren't celestial, although for years, humans had mistaken them for that whenever a careless quasi-angel was sighted in the right kind of light.

The oldster didn't chide the quasi for being here after he'd issued orders to leave the area clear for this meeting. And when the Civil saw Neelan, he came right to his side.

"Where have you been?" the quasi asked.

Neelan exchanged a loaded glance with the oldster. I wondered if Michael had privately cut some kind of deal with the chimera, negotiating for his silence in return for more strenuous effort in looking into the killer.

The half-man, half-serpent kept eye contact with the oldster as he spoke to his comrade. "I've been out in the hub and beyond, watching for Gabriel. I should have left better word than just a message."

"We were concerned."

"I appreciate that, Tydeus. But I'm fine."

When other Civils trickled into the corridor, the oldster grunted, surrendering to circumstance.

"Don't orders mean anything to you all?" he asked.

A Civil creature with cushiony gray skin and tusks in his man-face said, "We heard Neelan's back, so we came."

They all looked at me, but I didn't receive the same sort of relieved welcome. As far as they were concerned, I was Gabriel's partner, former heroine status be damned.

But where were all the Reds? It seemed like the Civils were the only ones who'd broken the oldster's request.

Then I felt a breeze, and I noticed shadows on the torch-licked wall.

Shadow people? Reds?

Vampires?

Whoever they were, they were standing just in back of all those Civils, unnoticed, eerie in their quietude.

More of the Civils were arriving, calling out greetings to Neelan, and he kept having to explain his absence.

They were distracted enough for the Reds—yes, I saw now that they were definitely vampires—to gather.

And gather.

I never said a word, and when they sprang, chaos erupted.

Bam, bam, bam—

Before my next breath, the vamps had barreled into the Civils, shutting them and their own selves into individual cells. In the space across from me, where a male vamp had captured Neelan, I saw that he had gloves on his hands to protect himself from the silver of the bars.

A stream of fire flared out of Neelan's mouth until the vamp produced a metal cone.

He'd actually been prepared for a flame-breathing chimera . . .

The fire column sputtered out as the vamp smacked the cone over Neelan's mouth.

Other vamps clearly had cones, too, and the fire stopped from every shut cell it'd been coming from.

"Shit!" yelled the oldster, who'd knelt down, taking cover.

At the same time, the quasi-angel took wing, rising toward the ceiling as a vampire jumped at him and missed clawing him down by mere inches.

Across the way, I saw the other vampire already staring into Neelan's eyes, whispering.

Mind-screwing?

Had this happened because me and Gabriel were back, and this was how the vamps were protecting us? By wiping the Civils' memories of the killing and then this attack?

War. If any Civils managed to get out of this, there'd be a hefty price for us Reds. . . .

I kicked at the bars while Neelan struggled with his vampire. He was able to get out from his cone to scream one last thing at Tydeus.

"Go! Find that thing once and for all!"

Find that thing?

The quasi spread his gray wings to their full span, covering the width of the ceiling, just as Neelan blankly fell to the ground, and his vampire backed away, victorious.

I kept hearing Neelan's last words.

Find that thing . . .

562?

God-all, when Ilsa and Rachel had told me that the Civils had been following the Reds, *had* it meant that the others suspected that we'd been visiting 562 in that cave?

I yelled at the oldster while pointing at the quasi. "Stop him!"

But by the time the oldster heard me, the winged creature had zoomed down the corridor, gone.

In the cells round us, more Civils were dropping to the ground. I could hear the slump of their bodies just as easily as I could see that vampire bending over Neelan across from me, whispering again to him.

They had to be telling the Civils to sleep for the time being. It would give the vampires time to mind-screw all the Civils before they called it a night.

Then, one right after the other, the vamps came out of the cells, cool as assassins.

I yelled at the oldster again. "If you don't open my cage, I'm going to barge out."

I needed to get to 562 before that quasi did.

But a silver bullet might give me good pause if the oldster decided to skin his revolvers and use them.

He was hesitating to draw . . . and to open my door.

Was he afraid of what I was about to change into?

I didn't get it—he loved being a were-creature, and the destruction of 562, our Red origin, ran the risk of taking away his preterness. 562's death might strip the powers from all the Reds, so what was he waiting for?

At his inability to commit, I stepped back from the bars and called upon my monster.

A roaring birth inside, pushing at me to get out, making the world go blue, violet—

I screamed at the ripping burst of one stage to the other, then, completed, I ran at the bars, my huge teeth jutting out of a mouth that took over my face. With one push, I tore the door off its hinges and didn't stop going, not even as the silver from the bars stung my skin . . .

Past the vamps—

Down the corridor—

Outside where the night-shaded walkway was crowded with vampires looking into the eyes of Civils and whispering.

But there were were-creatures fighting vamps, too, as if . . .

I didn't have time to stop and figure out whether the vampires were mind-screwing were-creatures, because I was zooming to 562's cave, where I didn't even halt at the sight of Tydeus lying in front, pinned down by a vampire who'd obviously jumped at him and caught him in midair as he'd descended into the opening.

The vamp, a short-haired woman, was staring into the quasi's eyes, whispering.

I bolted past them through the cave until I arrived in the coffin room, where three guardian vampires were . . .

I cocked my head, panting as I got my bearings.

The same three vampires I'd seen guarding 562 before were still sitting in lotus position, their sheathed swords laid over their laps while they stared in adoring wonder at our origin.

My ragged breathing finally got the attention of the blond male with the stubble beard. Even in my horrible state, I had enough clarity to think how rough and beautiful he was all at the same time.

"You're here," he said lovingly.

Holding form was too much for me since there was nothing to spur me on—no blood, no need to fight anything off.

I sucked back into my regular body. My dress was stretched at the seams and I clutched it to me.

Weak. I was so weak from having to change suddenly and go back, so I got to my knees, my chest tight.

"They're coming," I managed to say. "The Civils . . . they know where we've been keeping 562."

"We figured that out from the kamikaze quasi who almost made it inside the cave," he said, rising to his feet so gracefully that he seemed like a demigod. "Luckily, Darby was on her way out as Tydeus was on his way in."

Darby, the vamp who was mind-screwing the quasi out front.

This vampire moved toward me, his white outfit consisting of boots, pants, a long-sleeved top, and a cut-off jacket.

"We've never been properly introduced," he said, and I couldn't believe that, in all this madness, he was acting like I'd just stopped in to say hi. "I'm Liam."

Then he motioned toward his two guard friends, strawberry blonds with spiked hair and freckles, both dressed in white vest uniforms like Liam's. The twins.

"This is Kemp and this is Kerr," he said.

None of the vampires had drawn their swords, which was crazy, because I was ready to get my monster back on at a moment's notice if any Civils strong-armed their way in.

"We've got to do something with 562," I said. "Move her/him. Hide again. And Gabriel . . ."

"Gabriel should be safe." Liam looked so unconcerned that it was bothering me. "That was the news Darby brought to us, along with updates on the mind-screws."

I blew out the breath I'd been holding.

Gabriel. Safe.

"The vampires are wiping the memories of the killing and 562 from the Civils?" I asked, guessing.

"Yeah. And anyone who has it in mind to make trouble for us."

"Including were-creatures."

The vampires didn't look ashamed about that as they nodded. But I hadn't expected them to get red-faced, anyway.

My attention wandered to 562, sitting there so wonderfully still with her/his hair raining over a face that would be expressionless underneath the silver fall.

I recovered. Looking at 562 helped. Maybe it did the same for these vampires.

"I almost wish . . ." I said, trailing off.

"What?" Liam asked.

"That 562 could be awake instead of waiting there like a sitting duck. It seems like there's such danger being in this state."

Out of pure instinct, I got up and went to my origin, rolling back the tattered sleeve of my dress. If vampires could hold their breath, that was what these would've been doing.

I walked round the offerings that had been left for 562—several water necklaces, one of which Hana had left for her/him. A comm device from Pucci, in memory of our fallen friend Sammy Ramos, who'd died back in the New Badlands. A stone with Zel Hopkins's name written on it from the oldster. Several woven weblike art projects and pictures from random vampires who didn't know how to express themselves to our origin otherwise.

I watched 562 behind her/his glass, wishing she/he were awake and thinking I might know how to accomplish that, insane as the notion was.

Liam came to my side. "Here," he said, gently guiding me to the side of the coffin.

Then he kicked, right into the glass, shattering it. In the next instant, he lowered his head in a gesture of obeisance as the last of the pieces tinkled to the ground, leaving 562 uncovered.

I didn't comment on how that glass was supposed to be unbreakable.

I only knew that there was something I had to do.

Holding out my hand to Liam, I made a silent request that he understood, and he used a nail to open some skin on my palm. Blood peeked out in a thin line.

I reached out to 562 as Liam dropped to his knees, looking away, as if seeing something too intimate to continue watching. Then I parted 562's hair and pressed my palm to her/his mouth, feeding my mother and father.

As I pressed against her/him, my origin's lips didn't move. None of her/him did.

But when I finally backed away, I prayed for a resurrection.

A second ticked past, and I felt Liam touching my wrist, healing it. Then another beat of my heart marked the time, seeming to last an hour.

Yet the rising never came.

That didn't seem to matter to the vampires as they gazed on me with even more fervid affection than before, their hands over their hearts.

Was it because I'd willingly shared myself with our origin? Or was it because, after failing to awaken her/him, I was the only 562-type monster who remained alive for them?

Liam stood. "We should go, at least until the hub is secure."

He meant that it'd be wise to return only after we were sure that the Civils had forgotten all about 562's existence.

I almost winced. Here I was, running away again.

Would it ever stop?

"Gabriel," I said. "What about him?"

Liam looked to one of the twins, and that vampire sped out of the cave, clearly under orders.

Then Liam returned his focus to me. "Kerr will update McKellan and try to get Gabriel to you. But it'll have to be outside hub limits."

The other vampire twin, Kemp, had gone to 562, cradling her/his body in his arms.

Meanwhile, my mind spun. *Where* would we go for now? And should we just bury 562 in another place?

I wasn't sure, but there was no more time to waste, and after I willed a change upon myself again, I led my vampire escorts west, away from the more populated eastlands.

West, where I'd escaped once before with my father, after the terrors of Dallas.

15

Gabriel

McKellan had brought Gabriel to the vampire house in the middle of the hub before he'd gone to check in with the asylum, where he was to coordinate the mind-screws and human-to-vampire conversions.

As Gabriel stood in front of a window in a bedroom, he thought that their headquarters wasn't half bad—a spacious home that had once belonged to the mayor who'd been tucked away here upstairs. The vampires swayed the public official often and also imitated his voice on megaphones with tubes connected to the roof—the better for the distractoids not to see their young leader while hearing his assurances. Back when there'd been people outside the hub waiting to get in, the vampires had even ushered the mayor to the outskirts, where the hypnotized man had shouted messages about the power outage and the mosquito threat to those outside who'd been waiting to get in.

He'd told them to flee far, far away, and they had.

Now, since most of the denizens of GBVille were either at the asylum, distractoided, or swayed by vampires into compliance, there wasn't much use for the mayor, and he was happily stowed here, a fey smile decorating his face as he looked out the window at his city.

Gabriel stood just in back of the man, who wore his hair slick and straight, his beige suit suffering from nary a wrinkle. There were waves of action coming off the hub tonight—sensory disturbances, really—and Gabriel couldn't put his finger on precisely where they were coming from.

He frowned. It could be that most of the disturbance was inside himself, though he couldn't say why. It might've had something to do with Taraline and how she'd volunteered to give herself up as the killer.

Or how she'd looked at him a moment too long when she'd told him her plan.

Gabriel closed his eyes, reaching into himself, trying to see once again just what had happened that night.

Mariah's scent while everyone had been dancing and chanting . . . the craving for her blood . . . walking into the asylum with the other vampires, then . . .

Still darkness.

Still nothing.

Downstairs, Gabriel heard a door bang open, and in the next second, he was joined by McKellan, who solidified in front of him with a whoosh.

The elder didn't waste any time in talking, though he was just as composed as ever. Even that dark lock of hair over his forehead looked planned and controlled.

"Progress," he said, then gave Gabriel a status update: vampires isolating then mind-screwing Civils into complacency while many nonloyal were-creatures were a little scrappier and resisting the wipes.

"But," McKellan added, "they all should be stabilized presently."

"And Mariah?" Gabriel asked.

McKellan's gaze betrayed an impatience with this continuing attachment. "She was locked up by your oldster, yet she was surrounded by vampires who watch her. She will be safe."

The oldster. . . . Gabriel wasn't sure where Michael's

allegiances lay anymore, or how far he would go to see a united community.

Were the vampires going to mind-screw him, too?

Not likely. If they made an attempt, the oldster knew how to shield. Gabriel had never predicted that the vamps would be laying the screws to them, though.

McKellan rested a hand on Gabriel's shoulder. "Soon, none of this will lean heavily on you."

"Because the gloaming will be over."

"Yes. As I have said before, what you have left of your so-called humanity is protected only by those parts of your mind that refuse to give up what it once treasured." He cocked his head, as if delivering a blow to Gabriel and wanting to cushion it. "Right now, the human-associated parts of your mind are even working to block out anything that might end your gloaming stage—any act that could send you over the edge."

Gabriel thought of his inability to recall the killing. But if his mind was dark because he didn't want to remember what had happened, it didn't make sense; not when he could recite every single detail while defending Mariah from her werewolf bad guy in Dallas.

Why hadn't his mind fought against *that*?

He wanted to know more from McKellan, but it seemed that the elder wasn't in the mood for teaching right now.

He looked into the other vampire's eyes—those dark blue oceans of experience, undisturbed by anything.

"After we wipe the Civils," he asked, "what are you going to do about the vampire who started all this? The killer?"

McKellan didn't break eye contact. "He will be taught. He will learn better control, just as the rest of us have."

He will be taught.

Gabriel couldn't stop a memory from the Badlands—when he'd learned that someone was killing a bunch of Stamp's men. He'd blacked out then, too, but it'd been due to a night of gluttony, overfeeding. Ultimately, he'd discovered that he wasn't the guilty one—Mariah had been behind the deaths—yet he'd sure believed himself capable of it.

Just like now.

"Who did it?" Gabriel asked, though he didn't want to ask at all. "Who's responsible?"

McKellan just kept looking at Gabriel, shielding his thoughts, unwilling to share.

Downstairs, the wind moaned, the prelude to another vampire appearing in the doorway and coming into solid form to reveal a red-gold-haired male with freckles.

Kerr. Gabriel remembered being introduced to him during those first days here in GBVille.

"562," the boyish-looking vampire said without further greeting. "The Civils found out where we were keeping the origin, and we've taken steps to evacuate, even with the mind-wipes going on."

McKellan nodded, already over his talk with Gabriel. "I assume your twin and Liam are already on their way out of the hub, just until we know GBVille is memory-free for those who need to be."

"Yes," Kerr said. "They have Mariah with them, too, but she wants Gabriel with her."

Mariah.

Gabriel needed to find her, be with her.

Protect her.

He moved past the statue-like mayor and then the elder, heading for the door. "I'm going to her then."

But McKellan was having none of it. "You will come with me to the asylum to mind-screw, Gabriel."

And, with that, the elder grabbed a fistful of Gabriel's shirt, speeding off and out of the house while Gabriel kept pace, still determined to find Mariah as soon as he could.

They were at the asylum within moments, on the high walkway circling the structure. Were-creatures, fully changed into forms like hulking pumas and bears and tigers who stood on two feet, slashed out with their teeth and claws at vampires who were darting about, trying to tame them. None of them were taking cover.

It was all out in the open.

Meanwhile, tik-tiks were conspicuously absent, but their

pets, the gremlins, were flitting out of the walkway's brick nooks and crannies, latching their teeth to were-creature necks; they tore and giggled and gurgled blood before vampires wrenched them away and glared into the were-creatures' eyes, whispering and mind-wiping.

As the were-creatures self-healed from the superficial wounds, red drops spotted the walkway, just like dots creating pictures Gabriel couldn't quite put together.

Blood.

At the heady scent of it, something in his mind thudded, sending a crash of those spots into a solid picture: *A torch-lit corridor—a flash of a giraffe-man Civil monster turning around as he sensed something creeping up behind him . . .*

Gabriel blinked, trying to get the creeping red out of his sight, trying to deny the lure of the blood calling to him as it filled his senses.

Then something tickled the hairs at the back of his neck.

He glanced behind him, preparing to spring while everyone nearby was engaged in clawing, jumping, captivating.

Against the moon, up in one of the watchtowers, he could've sworn he saw . . .

An angel?

But it didn't have wings or dark colors like the Civil quasi-angels. This was a young woman with long, light curls, and behind her, the arches and cranks of a chest puncher peeked over her shoulders while strapped to her back.

Witch?

Without another thought, Gabriel sped to the tower, clawing at it while climbing up the brick.

But once he arrived, she was gone.

Gabriel shook out his head. Hallucinating. Was this a part of his gloaming—the end of it, when he lost touch with the realities he'd always known?

Then again, McKellan had once speculated that Witches had been treated with the blood that the medicals had drawn from the vampires in asylum captivity—that this was what made them stronger, faster, and more psychic, though they were hardly at the levels of vampires. He'd even thought that

Witches might've been the test subjects for plans to sell monster blood to elite human customers.

Thank-all the humans hadn't known that they needed blood *exchanges*, not just infusions, to get the full benefits. . . .

Gabriel tried to scent out the Witch, even while knowing that the upgraded slayers used anti-odor treatments.

She really was gone.

The fighting was near-distant now, away from the watchtower, toward the asylum itself, and the vampires were winning.

Among the blood, Gabriel did lock onto an odor—two familiar ones.

As he scented more, he saw a couple of recognizable, fully changed were-creatures bounding and bouncing into view from a side door in the walkway, then stopping short when they saw the vampires attacking the other weres nearby.

The first was a hulking, bulky were-elk, with tannish brown hair above and darker hair below, long legs, a short tail, and terrible, sharp antlers. He stood on his hind feet, his eyes glowing in a face that was disconcertingly human. Behind him, a huge were–mule deer paused to check out the damage, too, her hair a dark gray-brown, a white patch on her rear near a tipped tail. Her large ears twitched as she stood on her back legs, as well.

Pucci and Hana. Had the blood brought them here?

The male's jaws seemed to be working with the desire for sustenance. Their digestive systems had adapted over the years because blood held water, and no matter what an elk and deer had eaten in the old days, their were-forms just weren't the same.

Blood was all, and it was here right now.

Pucci bent to all fours, licking the ground at a drop of red, but then he gagged.

Poison. He'd tasted a fellow were-creature's blood.

Both of them had no idea that Gabriel was perched on the watchtower, so when Hana leaped away from Pucci, disgusted at his behavior, the big elk-guy bared his teeth at her.

Hana's body shook as she stared up at her partner with wide, angry, light brown doe eyes that glowed in the night.

She bared her were-teeth right back.

The vampires put the finishing touches on the were-creatures over on the other side of the walkway, then glanced over toward Gabriel's area, as if sensing Hana and Pucci, and Gabriel lifted a hand.

I've got this, his signal said to them.

The vampires wandered off, in search of more victims to be tamed.

Below, Pucci opened his mouth, flashing teeth at Hana.

And that must've been it for her, especially after he'd hit her the other night.

She jumped, stiff-legged, all her feet hitting the ground at once, then turned around, kicking Pucci with her back legs and smacking him in the chest.

Gabriel stiffened. If Pucci struck back, it'd be the very last time.

And, lo and behold, the idiot was already rearing up on his hind legs, threatening Hana.

Blood. Tonight, it was going to be Pucci's.

But Gabriel paused as something else came out of the shadows.

Something that had obviously been trailing Hana and Pucci, watching. Always watching.

It was Taraline, and though she seemed so tiny next to the massive were-elk and his antlers, she wasn't powerless.

Quicker than Gabriel could believe, she took Pucci by the antlers, swung him around, and bashed him into a wall.

For the second it took Gabriel to process what had just happened, Hana let out an animal screech.

Pucci slumped on the ground, stunned, already receding into a less powerful half-form, his face even more human-esque, with crazy bright eyes and grotesque teeth. Swiping up, he snagged Taraline's veils.

He pulled them off and, in one baleful moonlit moment, Taraline's face was exposed.

She was still marred by fiberlike strands of skin over

cheekbones that had gained a little shape, and where there'd been the lack of a nose, there was a tiny push of cartilage now.

She pulled her veils back down before Gabriel could see more.

Healing. There'd been some mending from Mariah's 562 blood, and it had repaired Taraline's dymorrdia as much as it could. Yet it'd done something more, too. It had given the shadow woman more strength than any human could possibly hope for.

She wasn't a vampire. Wasn't a were.

Just . . . enhanced, Gabriel thought with distant wonder.

Hana had bared her sharp teeth at Taraline now, as if, for some sick reason, she were going to defend her man to the end, just as she always had.

Pucci was shaking it off, too, starting to change back into his worst form.

Not this time, Gabriel thought. *Not with Taraline.*

Gabriel jumped from the watchtower, landing between Hana and the shadow woman and just in front of Pucci. Then, with one slick movement, he darted out his arm, blading his hand so that it stabbed clean into Pucci's chest, straight to the heart.

He ripped out the organ, held up the beating mass of it, then, with his other hand, snapped Pucci's neck.

The half-changed were-creature's tongue unfolded from his mouth while his body slid back into its naked, human form.

It wasn't silver to the heart, but a spinal break would kill a were-creature fine enough.

So would a missing heart.

Gabriel peered at the still-throbbing organ in his hand as blood rippled down his arm, into his coat sleeve, soaking his shirt with red. Beyond control, he bit into it, so hungry, so . . .

Gone.

Hana screeched even louder—enough so that Gabriel

jerked, realized what he was doing, tasted the tough heart and the exquisite blood.

He swallowed, shuddered, because he wanted more.

But Hana was still screaming, all the way humanlike now, her dark skin bare in the moonlight, exposed and victimizing her in the extreme.

He dropped the heart and grabbed her arms, coating them with Pucci's blood.

Sorry, he thought, blasting into her mind.

But was he sorry?

As she screamed at him now, he pressed his blood-ringed mouth to her ear.

"Shhh," he said, swaying her.

Mind-wipe, he thought. *Shut her up.*

But with one slam of confusion, his humanity was back, his brain kicking in, and he couldn't screw her over.

Not Hana.

Not even now.

In the meantime, Taraline just stood there as she looked down at the dead Pucci, then back up at Gabriel.

She took a breath so deep that her veils sucked in, and that was when he knew that she *had* realized all along who'd killed that Civil more than a week ago.

A barking sound broke the air, and even before Chaplin bounded around a corner, Gabriel knew that the dog wouldn't be alone.

The oldster was behind Chaplin, his mouth parting in surprise when he saw Pucci on the ground, blood surrounding him like a shroud ready to cover his body after everyone was done looking.

Hana murmured, "Gabriel . . . ?"

And there was hatred just below the bafflement.

Chaplin, who'd probably been protecting the oldster during the vampire mind-screwing spree, posted himself in front of his newest charge. The oldster glanced at Gabriel, and he fumbled for his revolver, hardly forgetting who was a fugitive and who was a law-abiding monster.

Or maybe he was just worried that Gabriel had gone all the way over and was here to mind-screw them all.

Gabriel reached out to Chaplin, who'd been a familiar to him when he'd first come to the Badlands. Nowadays, not so much, especially right this second, as the dog went into a hunched pose, his hair on end, showing his teeth and growling.

Gabriel reached into the canine's mind.

Mariah, he thought. *We've got to go and find Mariah.*

But the dog shut him out.

Shut him down.

Unable to comprehend this, Gabriel looked around him, at the monsters who'd been his friends, his responsibility at one point in time when they'd needed him so badly.

Then he focused on Pucci's blood in his mouth, and with the taste of the man's blood and heart still lingering, that was when it all came roaring back.

That night.

The corridor, the giraffe-man turning around and opening his mouth to screech as Gabriel's fangs dug hard into the giraffe-man's neck, stabbing into flesh and releasing the red into his mouth, flooding it, sending a gush down his throat, through his body.

The other young vampires had swarmed over the victim then, just as Gabriel pushed away from the giraffe-man, his hands covered with blood as he wiped it away from his mouth, removing every trace with his clothing, too.

Then . . .

Darkness. His brain blocking it out, as if it could still protect him.

But the memory kept coming back now, once, again . . .

In the rotating void, McKellan's words ghosted through Gabriel.

Right now, the human-associated parts of your mind are even working to block out anything that might end your gloaming stage—any act that could send you over the edge.

The last of humanity had blacked everything out until now, as his friends all gaped at him in disbelief and crushed horror.

Except for Taraline.

She'd stood in front of him so the oldster wouldn't shoot.

Gabriel wanted to cry out, just as Hana had when she'd seen Pucci dead, but he couldn't. As something clicked in his mind—as if it were revolving to the last full chamber in an otherwise empty gun—Gabriel only backed away from them.

Hana.

The oldster.

Chaplin.

"Gabriel," the oldster said, as if he couldn't fathom how his former friend had done this. That this killing hadn't been perpetrated by Mariah, who was supposed to be the tetched, unpredictable one.

Gabriel couldn't stand that look in their eyes—the disgust in Chaplin's, the brokenness in the oldster's, the temporary blankness in Hana's.

The dead glaze in Pucci's.

"I'm the one," Gabriel said to the oldster. "I was wrong. I'm the one who should've turned himself in all along."

The oldster was still pointing that revolver at him, but there was one thing still left alive in Gabriel, and he felt it like the lure of a guiding star.

Mariah.

She was out there somewhere, ready to make him feel like he could still mean something good to someone. That he could still be . . .

Chaplin lunged at Gabriel, flying through the air over Taraline, his teeth bared and ready to rip out his neck.

Survival kicked in, and Gabriel put on his speed, slicing through the night, deserting GBVille for the second time in a week.

But this time, it was because he was a true outlaw, and he'd never be back.

At least, not as the man he'd been before.

16

The Oldster

As the oldster watched Gabriel speed off in a blur once again, he realized just how wrong he'd been. All the hope, all the things he'd kept telling himself about someone else killing that Civil . . .

Wrong.

He knew he should call upon his were-side and give chase, but he'd never catch Gabriel. Not until he regained his senses enough to track him.

Chaplin was barking at the oldster, but it sounded as if everything were wrapped in layers of hemp, cushioning him. Then the dog latched his teeth onto the oldster's pants, yanking him off balance.

Through that swath of muddled perception, the oldster realized that it wasn't because Chaplin was forcing him to go after the vampire.

It was because he was trying to get him off the walkway and down to a nook by the watchtower.

Vamps?

Were they coming after them for mind-screws?

As the oldster ran and took shelter down the way, Chaplin went back out to retrieve a stunned and naked Hana, who'd obviously stripped off her clothing so she could comfortably were-change. The oldster took off his vest and wrapped it round her before adding the protection of his arms.

Belatedly, he saw that Taraline had already darted off into the shadows, the only other witness to Pucci's death and Gabriel's vague confession to the Civil killing.

But what to do with all that now?

While Chaplin pressed against their legs, the oldster just held Hana, who was still quieted by the hypnotic *shh*-ing Gabriel had done to her. Soon, she'd be screaming again—the sound that had brought the oldster and Chaplin running in the first place when the dog had recognized it.

Chaplin stiffened, and the oldster knew that danger was real near. He held his breath while, on a wall close to where they'd just been standing, a shadow undulated past, going toward a corner that hid Pucci's body.

It was a dymorrdian shadow who'd blended with the night.

The oldster placed a hand over Hana's mouth, hoping she wouldn't choose this moment to come out of her vamp-given stupor.

But the shadow didn't return, and after waiting a few minutes, the oldster decided that they were in the clear—that it was okay to talk.

"Chaplin," he whispered, "do you think the shadows are tipping off the vamps to any of us who're hiding?"

The dog growled, as if to warn the oldster to shush. But, damn it, there was no way to be sure of Chaplin's intentions because they didn't speak the same language.

Would it be wise to turn into his were-scorpion form so he could fight off any more vamps?

No—silver bullets might be the best bet, seeing as they slowed down a vampire if the aim was true. Besides, were-changing might be seen as a sign of aggression that would pretty much guarantee a mind-screw for the oldster when, earlier, he'd barely gotten out of one.

It'd happened just after Mariah had taken off from the cell block where he'd been holding her. When she'd sped away in her new nonlunar form—what an ugly state, with those teeth and that mouth—the vamps had let her go without even a question. But right away, a woman vamp who didn't look much stronger than a stick had grabbed the oldster by the collar and held tight, her eyes red.

"Your turn," she'd said.

The oldster had realized that he was about to be mindscrewed, just as thoroughly as Neelan and the other Civils had been. The vampires were making a bid for their survival—and that of the community—in their own ruthless way.

The vamp woman had drilled into him with her gaze. It'd been as if she'd ripped open a dark curtain, peeking through it and showing him a sight more heart-jolting than anything he'd ever seen—a glance from a pair of red eyes blinking open in a dark canyon.

The oldster had scrambled to recall what Gabriel taught him back in better days about how to block or thwart a vampire mind attack.

Desperate to show the vampire that he didn't want to go against the Reds, he'd thrown up a mental screen, projecting onto it.

I'm on your side. . . .

And he'd believed it with all his might—at that moment.

The vampire's mental curtain had shut, and just like that, the oldster was back to rights, the vamp woman dropping him on his ass.

She'd left him sitting there, realizing that it was true. Deep down, he really *was* on their side, although he'd been playing the middle, acting as a peacemaker for the community.

Chaplin had found the oldster that way, still on his butt, surrounded by Civils who were in the other cells, stunned and content. They'd been told and persuaded that they'd been put away for their own benefit and would be let out soon.

The oldster hadn't corrected their assumptions. Surely it was better that no one would remember the Civil killing. The vamps had been right in doing this, although they were now clearly the faction in charge, which threw off the balance of GBVille.

But they could make this work, right?

Hell, he'd thought that much until he'd seen Gabriel in action.

Chaplin had been barking and carrying on, urging the oldster to his feet. Even before he'd followed the dog outside, he'd heard Hana screaming.

Then he'd seen Pucci. He didn't give a rot about the man—never had much, anyway—but he'd spied Gabriel, too, with Pucci's heart in his hand. With blood round his mouth.

Then Gabriel had taken off again, as fast as before, headed for Mariah, no doubt.

But where had *she* gone to so fast?

The oldster could still hear what Neelan had told that Civil winged quasi—*Find that thing once and for all!*—and how Mariah had split out of the cell in such a hurry.

Had Neelan been talking about 562?

He kept holding on to Hana, clutching the butt of a holstered revolver with the other hand. She and Pucci must've come out here because they'd been fleeing the vamps, or else they were merely seeing what was going on with the fighting—maybe the couple had even been thinking about how the vamps had been so carried away that Hana and Pucci had failed to take cover from any satellite footage that might reveal this carnage.

They'd just run into bigger trouble instead with Gabriel.

Everything had happened so damned quickly that the oldster didn't know what the hell to think now—what side he was even on at this point, in spite of what he'd shown the vampire who'd been about to mind-wipe him. There were so many sides. He wanted 562 to be okay, but he didn't like the division she/he caused. He understood the Civils'. concerns, but not at the expense of his kind's own good.

He knew it all came down to a choice all of them would have to make: try to alter and tame what came naturally to every monster, or divide and lessen their numbers so that the humans could pick them off all the easier if they ever found out the monsters had risen again.

There'd been no word yet from the monster contingent that had gone off to old D.C. to take down that most rotten hub of all, but the oldster supposed that the plan's success—or failure—would force the monsters in every conquered hub to decide if they wanted to compromise and live free or die out.

Now that things had been silent round them for a decent time, the oldster breathed the first sigh of relief that he'd dared.

He sat on the ground, bringing Hana with him, cupping her bared head and letting her lean on his shoulder. Her brown hair, without its usual scarf, was so short that her curls felt like clover under his hand. He was old enough to still remember how soft the very last of the clover had been.

They would wait here a minute more, just to decide what to do.

Just a minute more.

But much to the oldster's consternation, Chaplin stepped away from their hiding place, then started to heave.

Nothing came out of the dog's mouth, though. What was wrong with him? Too much adrenaline?

"Boy?" the oldster whispered.

When the canine stopped, he whimpered, lowering to his belly and resting his head on his paws. His brown hair nearly covered the sad moons of his eyes.

Mariah, the oldster thought. The dog wasn't sick from excitement as much as heart-ill at the separation between him and his mistress. The oldster didn't know what had gone down between them when he'd left them alone in the cell block, but he'd seen Chaplin skulking out of the corridor, so it couldn't have been good.

The oldster petted the dog. "Wish I knew how to fix what ails you."

Chaplin whimpered again, casting a gaze in the direction in which they'd left Pucci. Maybe this killing had been the last moral straw for the dog.

The oldster didn't dare discuss Gabriel and Pucci, though—not with Hana here. He didn't even want to think that they were still much too close to the man's naked, dead body.

God-all, half of him was actually glad Pucci had gotten his due. But half of him still wanted to go after Gabriel, whose bent heroism had curved far round from the oldster's conception of it.

His heartbeat wilted. Once, Gabriel had been a better man than any one of them.

Chaplin's head shot up, and the oldster put his hand near his revolver. If it was a vamp, he'd *act* mind-screwed and hope that it would work. His sight caught the image of what looked to be a frothy white cloud moving through the cover of wall shadows, just before he realized that he was seeing a line of flowing, nearly sheer nightgowns that revealed the hourglass shapes of women beneath them.

A group of gremlins sprinted in front of the intruders, snorfling as they pointed at the refugees in their nook.

One woman in front bent down and shooed the gremlins away, and the nasties tottered off, sputtering in glee when they saw Pucci's body nearby.

Shit.

"Call them off," the oldster said. Pucci had been a dick, but limits were limits, and he wouldn't see the dead desecrated.

When the lead woman moved out of the oldster's immediate line of sight, the moonlight showed her identity.

"Get going!" Falisha said to the gremlins. Then, to the rest of the women behind her, "Herd them away."

The others offered red-painted, moon-washed glances to the oldster, Hana, and Chaplin before they slowly moved on, keeping to the shadows again.

Falisha gave a pointed look to the revolver that the oldster hadn't quite reached for yet.

"Notice the quiet, Michael?" she asked. "That means you don't need to use a weapon on me. All's clear, and the vampires are starting to let the Civils out of their cages now. They've mind-wiped everyone they wanted to, except for any stragglers they'll pluck off as soon as possible."

He still didn't move his hand away from the firearm, even

though Chaplin wasn't growling at the tik-tik woman. That meant the dog didn't even perceive her to be a threat.

But what if the tik-tiks were in league with the vamps and the women were wandering round with the shadows in order to find the stragglers?

Then again, tik-tiks were definitely their own Reds. They'd never shown a major affinity for vamps over were-creatures. . . .

"Michael," she said again. "I'm not here to addle you. And the fact that you're hiding tells me that either you weren't mind-screwed by a vampire yet or they believe you're fine without a wipe."

So she had their number. "Didn't they get *you*?"

"Are you asking if the vampires mind-screwed the tik-tiks and gremlins? No. We're more like old Switzerland—the great In Between where immunity is offered and respected, so there was no need with us."

He still didn't move his hand from his revolver.

"And if you even think that *I* can mind-screw you," she said, "you're wrong. Tik-tiks don't have any wonderful powers like a vampire does. We have only one mental talent."

"What?"

She rubbed her fingers together. "Touch. When we come into physical contact with a woman, we know if she's carrying a child or not."

That was how they were able to choose a victim properly, he thought, getting off the subject as soon as possible.

"If you're not combing the walkway for mind-screws," he said, "then what're you doing out here?" Fear choked him. "Are you scouting the sky for government Dactyls?"

"Partly. The vampires were so steeped in bloodlust that they didn't take much care with staying out of the open. We can only hope that something's happening in old D.C. right now and there's no time for the government to be combing over satellite footage."

"Why're you out here, then?"

Falisha's coiled hair looked like black snakes in the night. "Surveying the damage. We Reds really made a mess of reorganizing the community, although I have to say that your friend's death was the only fatality." She glanced toward Pucci. "We've already taken the body away, so he's not merely left out here. The shadow people will bury him."

She glanced at Hana, who hadn't reacted. Even so, the oldster covered the ear that wasn't pressed to his shoulder, so she wouldn't hear all this.

"You don't sound too affected by a fellow Red's demise," he said.

She sighed. Had Falisha ever heard about Pucci's relationship with Hana? It hadn't been much of a secret that he was a jerk to others as well as to her.

"Death," she said. "We should have known it'd be all around us. Why are we surprised that it's happening so frequently?"

She was right, and it made the oldster feel like a naïf. He'd always been so hopeful about a sort of utopia, even if it was back in the New Badlands, where he'd brought together different were-creatures in the belief that they could coexist, just because their blood didn't suit each other's tastes and they wouldn't pursue each other. But that experiment had been shot to shit.

And he'd been silly enough to think there'd be a chance to prove nature wrong here, in an even bigger place with worse creatures.

Falisha placed her hands on her ample, nightgown-draped hips. "Why did a vampire actually destroy instead of just mind-screw Pucci?"

He finally took his hand away from his revolver. "I'm not sure what went on."

Although he could guess. Pucci had probably gotten up in Hana's face again and it'd goaded Gabriel, who was no one to trifle with lately.

"Well, I heard about Pucci's joyful personality," she said. "The shadows talk to us, you know. That's what happens between two low-class groups—gossip. We're entertained by the antics of the popular crowd."

She was talking as if the country still had high schools

instead of Nets think tanks and virtual classrooms. The oldster wondered how long ago she'd lived, how long ago she'd
been resurrected. She looked in her midthirties, although she
was a long-lived creature who would stay ageless.

When Hana sat up and away from the oldster's comforting hold, all of them stirred.

But it was her cold voice that caused a freeze.

"He killed Pucci . . ."

Damn it, she'd heard them talking.

The oldster, Falisha, and Chaplin hesitated, because it
was as if a fictional zombie had come back to life and they
weren't sure how to treat her.

"An eye for an eye," Hana added, her Somali accent coming back now in her quiet rage.

"Hana," said the oldster, his arm still round her.

When she jarringly shook him off, he lifted both hands.
Chaplin even cringed.

"My grandmother used to tell me that when one takes
from another, they are due payback. That is how it used to
be where she lived. That is how it should be now."

The oldster tried again. "You're in shock. . . ."

"Antonio was my love," she said. "My life."

Something in the oldster wanted to point out that Pucci
had hit her not even a week ago.

Falisha was the one who had the gumption to step up.
Falisha—a tik-tik who'd likened herself to old Switzerland.

"How did it work with you and Pucci?" she gently asked
as Hana narrowly stared at the tik-tik. "Were you addicted
to the apologies he made after every time he bullied you?
Did he, in turn, resent you for making him depend on your
affection?"

"Were you a brain doctor before you became a ghoul?"
Hana asked. Yup, Gabriel's sway had sure worn off.

Actually, the oldster had never heard her like this before.
But then, all of them had undergone some madness and
change: Mariah, Gabriel . . . even Chaplin as he moped
round, so different from his former self.

Falisha smiled. "I'm not a ghoul, Hana. We didn't even have any in this asylum. But, yes, you could say I had a background in dealing with the wounded. I was a social worker in the 1990s. I saw women like you every week."

"Women like me."

The tik-tik touched Hana's arm, but right before she pulled away, Falisha sucked in a breath.

Her expression was . . .

Hungry.

She seemed hungry.

She glanced at the oldster, reading his face. He put his arm round Hana firmer than ever, and Falisha's expression fell for some reason.

Without explanation, she stood, her voice shaking.

"You'll want to get out of here now, before the vampires see you trying to avoid them. They'll know something's amiss with you and they'll go into your minds to do what they need to."

Chaplin yipped, as if asking a question.

None of them understood, but Falisha had stepped back, anyway, encouraging them to come out of the nook.

"I mean it," she said. "Get out now."

There seemed to be something else bothering her.

The oldster came onto the walkway. Chaplin went to Hana, fronting her, the ultimate guard.

Falisha began to walk, glancing round. She hadn't been in this kind of hurry before now.

A gremlin was lingering near the pool of blood where Pucci had once lain, and it was sniffing at the red. The tik-tik woman didn't even chide him, instead bending down to whisper in its ear.

The nasty sped off, a blur of puke-yellow fur and long ears as a throttled sound escaped from Hana's throat. The oldster rushed her along.

"The shadows will be here soon to clean everything," Falisha said.

She was walking so quickly that all of them exerted themselves to keep pace.

"Falisha," the oldster said, but she cut him off.

"Move along, Michael!"

She pointed to the door of a second watchtower just as a crowd of gremlins ran past them and started to gnaw round the lock of the wooden door.

The iron device plunked to the ground and Falisha reached through. When she had opened the door, the gremlins sped ahead into the darkness.

"They'll look for shadows and warn us if they see any," she said, "or they'll chase them away."

Judging by her footsteps, she'd begun to descend a staircase.

Hana spoke. "Are you taking us to Gabriel?"

It was ridiculous, but the oldster just kept leading her down the stairs.

Falisha said, "I'm only showing you one of the many passages that no one has really found in this asylum, but maybe that's because tik-tiks and gremlins aren't busy with all the politicking. Where you go from there is up to you."

She circled down, down the stairs as the oldster hugged the wall as well as Hana, following the tik-tik.

When they got to the bottom, Falisha led them into a tunnel. It was dark, but she seemed to know the way, guiding them with urgings until they came to a rise.

Then she opened another door, moonlight filtering in.

She ushered Chaplin out first, and the dog peered round outside. The oldster saw that Falisha had taken them to a spot shaded by a stone tree forest, sponsored by General Benefactors. The pale art pieces were like frozen bones spearing toward the sky, clustered together, an attempt by GB to add some nature to the area.

Chaplin made a small yawping sound that served as an okay. Before the oldster guided Hana out, Falisha doffed her nightgown and handed it to the other woman, who'd already taken off the oldster's vest and handed it back to him.

He didn't look in the tik-tik's direction. She'd remained in the darkness, but propriety demanded that he still not acknowledge her bareness of skin.

She was a tik-tik, he reminded himself.

Hana didn't put on the nightgown, because she was already bent, her skin waving over her altering bones as she started her change to were-form.

She was just itching to catch up to Gabriel, the oldster thought. But they didn't have a chance. Since they didn't know where he'd gone, tracking would be their best option, if the vampire had left the earth disturbed.

Chaplin sidled up next to her, just as he'd always done with Mariah, watching the were-change, expressionless.

When the oldster made a move to join them outside, Falisha grabbed his hand.

"If you decide to come back," Falisha said, "don't do it for a while. And look me up before you make your presence known here."

When she'd grabbed him, she'd put herself into the moonlight. She wore the strangest expression: puzzlement? Yearning? Sorrow?

What? What was each of them about?

Much to his astonishment, she touched his face with her fingertips, brushing them over his skin. Her naked body was voluptuous—rounded breasts, arms, stomach.

The oldster shivered, and at first he thought it was because she was a repulsive creature.

But that wasn't it at all.

He stepped away from her, fast. So fast that Falisha seemed to know that she'd damn well been put in her place.

She didn't talk about what'd just happened between them, instead saying, "You care for Hana, don't you? You really care."

What was it to her? "Of course I do. She's a good friend. Almost even like a daughter."

Falisha sighed, and it seemed pained.

Then she put a hand on her belly. "When I touched her, I felt a child forming."

The words didn't come together for a few seconds. In that amount of time, a bunch of gremlins peeked from behind the door frame, their eyes glowing in the night.

The tik-tik woman began to shut the door, closing it on the eerie sight.

"Please get Hana out of here now," she said before she entirely disappeared.

She closed the oldster all the way out, leaving him grasping at the realization of what she—a hungry tik-tik—had given up for Hana's sake.

And, evidently, his.

17

Stamp

During their escape, Stamp and Mags had made it to the fringes of GBVille.

Evidently, so had a few others.

When the pair heard a door in a dirt-ragged hill moan open, they sought cover behind a boulder. Stamp reached for his only weapons—the shivs.

He pulled them out of their wrappings, and they were still slightly crusted from the gore of the female vampire he'd shoved the blades into. Mags took a step back, but he didn't ask why because, right then, Mariah's Intel Dog, then a naked woman, busted out of that door and into the shade of that stone forest.

He recognized the female right away—Hana—and her dark skin was flowing as she bent over, obviously racked by the intensity of a willful change to were-form.

Meanwhile, he could see the oldster talking to someone just inside the door. Stamp strained to hear, but all he caught were low murmurs. When the door slammed, the oldster came over to Hana, who groaned and panted during her alteration.

But she didn't change all the way. She was crying too hard. Actual tears from a monster.

Stamp chuffed, then shot a glance back to Mags, waiting so still behind him that he might've mistaken her for one of those stone trees nearby if he didn't know any better.

He flipped both shivs into his palms, gesturing toward the monsters with them.

Mags narrowed her dark almond-shaped eyes and shook her head. *Just stay quiet,* was what she would've said if they could communicate out loud.

Okay, so she wanted to hold their position and wait until they were in the clear before making their full escape from GBVille. Not a bad idea. It might even be prudent to see what was going down with these monsters and why they seemed to be running off, too. There had to be good reasons for that Intel Dog to be stomping around Hana with clear agitation and for her to be in half-change mode, her eyes glowing, her teeth long as she fell to the ground on all fours.

The old guy reached for a nightgown that lay by Hana's side and offered it to her, like that was going to cover up all her monster issues or something.

Then Stamp heard him say, "Hana . . ."

"Damn him!" There was a serrated wildness in her tone.

Behind Stamp, Mags moved sharply, and Stamp lifted a hand, quieting her, concentrating on how Hana's teeth were so white and long in the moonlight.

Who would've ever thought a deer would need teeth like that unless the creature had turned into a blood drinker somewhere along the line?

"I know you want to stop me," the woman said to the old man, refusing to accept the dress he was still holding out to her, "but I am going to find him."

This was getting more interesting by the moment.

"It's not safe, Hana."

The Intel Dog barked in obvious agreement.

"I do not care how strong he is," she said. "I can be stronger. I can be hungrier, because of what he took away from me. He *killed* Pucci and then ran away."

Stamp gripped the bases of the shivs even tighter. He recalled that Hana had a mate—a big guy who'd followed her around the cell corridors. Pucci.

But it seemed as if someone had wasted the guy and she was out to get the killer. That was probably even why these monsters were out here, ready to chase, unless they'd merely been scared away from the hub by those mind-wiping vampires.

Who'd killed Pucci, though? A random vamp?

All Stamp really knew was that he heard in her voice the same kind of vengefulness he'd cultivated after Gabriel had bested him back in the nowheres.

The same hatred.

The oldster had taken her by the arm now, as if holding her back from doing something impulsive.

"I'm telling you that you can't go on any hunts," he said. "You're in no condition to."

"Yes, I am."

"No. Falisha told me something . . ." He sat next to her, his voice softening. "You're pregnant, Hana."

The air seemed to bond into itself, twining around and around until it squeezed all the oxygen out of the atmosphere.

Pregnant, Stamp thought. A damned were-creature. It'd be born, not bitten, a curse on the world. It'd be some kind of hybrid between a deer and an elk, too. A mutant all around.

Just what this world needed—another type of abomination.

It wasn't until the oldster spoke again that things seemed to go back into motion.

"Did you hear me?" he asked the woman.

As the dog whined, Hana just stared at the oldster, and he leaned closer to her, making his point further.

"*That's* why it's not safe for you to go chasing after Gabriel. You might endanger your child—Pucci's son or daughter."

In spite of the other words, all Stamp heard was one. *Gabriel*.

Stamp glanced at Mags again. Her brows were knitted.

He didn't know why she seemed so conflicted—she'd been there when Gabriel and his pals had dealt their blows to them, when Gabriel had survived as Stamp had barely hung on to life. She should know what effect his name had on Stamp.

Or was she just reacting to the news of the murder, trying to figure out all the angles?

Hana hadn't gotten up from her spot on the ground yet. A slant of rogue moonlight shone over her dark skin, her short-cropped, curl-packed hair. Her eyes seemed to glow even brighter as she continued to process the news.

"A baby?" she finally asked.

"Yeah, that's what she told me. And tik-tiks know these things. That's one reason Falisha wanted us to scram out of GBVille. And that's why you're not going on any mission to get Gabriel back for what he did."

Chaplin the dog nosed her, snuggling up to her as if in a mixture of congratulations and condolence.

Hana slowly rose to her feet, stiff. She folded her arms over her bare, slightly curved belly, as if cradling it. She was round all over, so Stamp wouldn't have been able to determine any kind of pregnancy just by looking at her. She must've been in the very early stages.

"Would *you* go after him then?" she asked the oldster. "For me?"

The old guy paused, then said, "That's a complicated question, Hana."

"No, it is not."

"What would I even do with Gabriel if I caught up with him? He's a vampire, and even during my best nights in were-form he would—"

"Are you telling me that he has leave to kill anyone he feels like killing then? You and I both know that this is not to be countenanced. This is not how we have always lived, and it cannot be so in the future. We live by rules . . . order."

The oldster got quiet again, his tone a whisper. "Whose rules?"

Even though Hana didn't have a ready answer, Stamp did. The law of man had worked for a long time in this country—until the monsters had risen up. Now the world was shit. It was, as Hana had said, not to be countenanced.

It was all too much for Stamp, who was mired in the memory of the night Gabriel had bested him.

A vampire. A malicious force that couldn't be tolerated on this earth if the rest of them were to survive. It was just that these were-creatures were only now discovering what Stamp had known all along, now that they had to live with other monsters.

All of them were beasts, and they would end up destroying each other well before they could do it to the humans.

As usual, Mags gauged Stamp well, because she pressed a hand on his shoulder, keeping him in hiding behind the boulder. When he tried to resist, he found that her hold was stronger than he'd remembered it ever being.

"No," she whispered.

"This is too good an opportunity to pass up."

"You're going to take up with them, just to find Gabriel?"

"I was thinking of it."

She rolled her eyes. "I know how your mind works—how it always works, especially when it comes to that vampire. He was the only one who's ever beaten you, and if it takes you until the day you die, you're going to remedy that."

She pushed him back against the boulder, leaning so close to his face that he didn't know how to react. Even so, his body was doing enough responding for him: pulse firing off rounds of ricocheting bangs through him.

"I can even tell you every step of this plan you're formulating," she said in his ear, tickling it. "You don't have operational Shredder tracking devices on you, and you don't have any weapons besides these pieces of crap." She pushed aside one of his hands, which still held a shiv. "You're going to use a pissed-off preter to act as your tracking device, as well as a weapon against Gabriel. And don't tell me I'm wrong."

Yup, once again she had his number.

She took him aback when she let him loose, her dark gaze going liquid.

"Can't we just stay *here*, John?"

A fleck of emotion tinged her voice. He'd heard it before, but after all they'd been through—seeing her almost killed by Mariah, seeing her locked up in the asylum and becoming more hopeless by the night—it mattered more now.

She apparently knew that she was getting to him. "Please, just give this up while you can."

But the shivs were heavy in his hands. He'd decided the day he'd been put in the orphan camp that he would never, ever give up and, when he nudged her away from him, she opened her mouth, as if to protest.

He talked first. "I never thought there'd be a day when you gave up, Mags."

Her expression changed, as if she were about to tell him something he didn't want to hear. He got the feeling it might even be about how they were such great partners, and she didn't ever want to lose him.

But he couldn't hear it, because it'd bring on choices he didn't want to make. Shouldn't have to make, as a Shredder.

As he looked into her eyes, he thought he saw something else, too, until the sight disappeared just as quickly.

In his state of mind, he thought he'd seen a reflection of blood. Red, just like a memory that he was projecting onto her.

But that was impossible.

Gripping his shivs, he dodged Mags entirely, then used the boulder to come to a wobbly, one-legged stand, keeping the rock between him and the preters as cover. It seemed, though, that Hana, who was still in half-were form, had finally overcome her distracting emotions and gotten a whiff of him, and she was on all fours again.

She fixed her glowing gaze on him, screeching, revealing those pointed teeth.

Stamp almost laughed. Were-deer. Oooo—scary. Even the Intel Dog, with his bared teeth, didn't put the fright in Stamp, although he'd seen firsthand how peppy the canine could be when it came to defending his folk.

Before the oldster could initiate a were-change, Stamp spoke up.

"We're not here to fight."

The oldster's back was hunched, but he was still in humanlike form. "Then what're them blades you've got in your hands?"

Stamp didn't drop the shivs. "They're my security, and I'd like a little of that while I parley with you."

The oldster had a set of holstered revolvers, and his hands stayed near them. Behind Stamp, Mags took up his back. She was so contained, though, that he couldn't even hear her breathing.

"You want to parley, do you?" the oldster said as the Intel Dog bristled near him. "To my recollection, that activity doesn't suit you all that well, Stamp. You're more an action type of fellow. And I don't know what the spit you're doing out of your cell, but I suspect it bodes no good for the terms you'd like to discuss with us."

"Hana might understand my terms more than any of you," Stamp said, deliberately looking at her.

He meant her to know that he'd overheard everything about the baby, Pucci, and Gabriel. That he was an ally now.

Just until he found Gabriel.

She sat on her knees, her features melting back into humanlike form so quickly that she hugged herself, no doubt from the pain of going back and forth so often in such a short time.

Yet she'd heard him, all right, loud and clear, and from the look on her face, she was listening for more.

Stamp provided it. "If you're going after Gabriel, I'd like to offer my company."

Chaplin barked loudly, hopping to the front of Hana while the oldster raised a firm hand to Stamp.

"Stop right there," he said. "We have no need to listen to any more of your bullshit."

Stamp just kept appealing to Hana. "I'm not much to look at right now, but I've taken out a lot of vampires. And I have enough experience with Gabriel to know how he fights."

"You don't think I can destroy him myself?" the woman asked.

"I think that the child you're carrying might make you consider twice when it comes right down to it. In the thick of a fight, you might pull your punches in the fear of endangering him or her." He wouldn't mull over that abomination she was carrying. Finding Gabriel was bigger than any werebaby she was about to add to the world. "I, however, would have no such qualms about meting punishment out to Gabriel after you help me track him and corner him."

He felt Mags behind him, hovering. In spite of everything, she was still here.

The dog obviously didn't like that Stamp had enough gumption to be making this kind of offer, and the canine was going apeshit, barking at Hana. But Stamp could tell she didn't understand Canine.

The oldster's upper lip curled. "I oughta just put a bullet in you, Stamp."

"So why aren't you already doing it?" he asked, feeling his oats. Hana was his—he could tell because she was still looking at him, as if she'd already decided but just wasn't up to making the commitment yet.

Did she have it in her to join up with a guy who used to be the big enemy, just to get back at Gabriel?

The oldster spread his fingers, as if flexing them in readiness to grab a revolver from its holster.

But then he stopped. So did the dog's barking.

Stamp had the feeling that something else was going on, and it was probably even right behind him.

He peered back at Mags, finding that she was training a revolver on the group . . . and the weapon no doubt had silver bullets in it.

Sneaky lady. She'd grabbed a firearm somewhere in the asylum before she'd come back to him in the cell block.

Full of surprises, that Mags.

Now that there was a bit of order, Stamp made one last appeal to Hana. If she said no, he'd move on. After killing this bunch, of course.

"I'm with you, Hana. How about it?"

She never got the opportunity to answer, because the

oldster called on his were-form. His skin bulged with the shift of bones and muscle just before an exoskeleton took over his flesh, a tail and pincers springing out of his body while his face went hard, his glowing eyes still looking so very human in spite of their preter shine. His clothes and boots ripped, his gun belt dropping to the ground.

The dog yowled as the were-scorpion man pulled Hana to him in one of his long, curved arms, snagged his gun belt, then scooped up the dog in the other arm. Then he put on a burst of preter speed, disappearing down a hill, leaving just a trail of dust.

"Fuck!" Stamp yelled.

But Mags was already putting away her revolver, hiding it under the folds of her gray suit where he hadn't noticed it lurking before.

She sounded nonchalant. "I suppose that leaves us here, then."

"Not by a long shot."

He got out from behind the boulder, holding on to the side of it for balance.

Normally, Mags would've sighed in exasperation, but he didn't hear any such thing. He took that as a good thing as he got to a crouch and scuttled to where the were-creatures had been standing. There, he used the moonlight to inspect the shape of their steps, to smell any traces of distinctive odor that he might use if they ever slowed in their progress. Until then, he would use the disturbances they left in the dirt, wispy trails marking their haste.

Would they end up going after Gabriel? Hell, would Hana even break off from the others and go on her own?

He thought well and hard as he took up a fistful of dirt and allowed it to sift through his fingers. He'd need to move after them, and move quick.

Where could he get a vehicle that was in working order, far enough out of the range of GBVille so that it'd still have power, and near enough so that he didn't lose too much time?

He remembered the shack on the edges of the nowheres, where some ex-Shredders tended to gather. They would have zoom bikes. And, after hearing about the monster takeover of GBVille, they might just join him in his hunt for the bad guys, too.

He followed the progress of the monsters, using the oldster's were-scorpion trail as a guide.

"Let's go, Mags," he said.

And she followed, although it was more distantly than usual.

18

_____

Nobody had seen them this entire time, but that was usually the case when it came to Witches.

Two of them were using the white stone tree forest to camouflage themselves while, not a hundred yards away, the were-deer, were-scorpion, and dog faced off with the other pair: a dark-skinned woman with long black hair who backed up a male whom the Witches focused on the most.

Johnson Stamp.

The Witches were too far away from them to see the clear identities of the were-creatures or to hear what was being said, but they were doing their best to use their trained and enhanced hearing nonetheless. And they watched Johnson Stamp carefully as the retired Shredder had an unexpectedly civil conversation with the monsters.

What business did he even have with them?

Traitor, him? a female Witch mind-asked her male counterpart as they peeked out from behind the stone trees.

Perhaps yes, the male thought. _Perhaps no._

What they knew for certain was that their data files—which

still hadn't been updated since GBVille had lost power—had shown images of Johnson Stamp with that dying Monitor 'bot out in the New Badlands. Had he destroyed government property back then—a surveillance device that had only recently been put to use since the sanctions had worn off?

There was no good explanation for why an ex-Shredder would attack a 'bot, so the Witches wanted to find out the reason. And they had already taken measures to do so, because a few nights ago, a visiting Witch from Dallas had been able to make her way through the outskirts of GBVille, carefully avoiding all vampire guards in particular because if anyone would find the Witches, it was those monsters.

The new Witch told the GBVille slayers how Dallas had been taken over, too, confirming everyone's suspicions that the power-blaster attack here wasn't just an isolated incident. None of the GBVille Witches who had set out for other nearby hubs to see if they had also gone dark had returned yet, but without powered vehicles or zoom bikes, it would be a while before they got there and maybe even fetched reinforcements.

In the meantime, it seemed as if it were up to the Witches gathered here to save humanity.

A male sneaked in back of the first two, just as silent as they were except for his mind.

Ex-Shredder, him, he thought to them in greeting while he focused on Stamp, too, catching up to what his comrades were seeing.

None of them had data on these were-creatures or the dog because they weren't close enough for facial recognition. But they did know of the dark woman who seemed to be backing up Johnson Stamp. Deitra Montemagni, a corporate freelance hubite who'd gone off the social register over a year ago until showing back up here with Stamp.

No fighting yet? the new Witch asked, also wondering why Stamp and his friend were simply talking with the monsters.

No fight here, confirmed the male.

Just big fight earlier, thought the female Witch, who'd been casing the asylum not long ago, standing on a watch-tower to monitor the eruption that had broken out among the monsters. She had come close to being engaged by a vampire—name: Gabriel Bruce, age thirty-three, last officially seen in the Southblock area of the country. He'd been watching over a were-deer, much like the one who was down below now, plus a were-elk. But the Witch had been forced to desert her watch when Gabriel had noticed her spying.

Based on what other Witches had seen and shared this past week, he was the same vampire who had broken into GBVille headquarters in the hub nearly a week ago with his redheaded female friend—identified by remaining facial recognition scans in the Witches' brains as Mariah Lyander, age twenty-three, last seen in Dallas at age fourteen.

The sentinel who had been spying on them had retreated before getting caught, so the Witches didn't have a full idea of what Gabriel and Mariah had been doing out of the asylum. But they were piecing data together little by little, collectively spying on the monsters, noting weaknesses and troubles between them and mentally marking places where just a push would topple them.

Data collection before action—that was what training had taught the Witches.

Actually, just this evening, one of them had reported something that bore more investigation: Early tonight, down by a cave near Little Romania, a Witch had witnessed a quasi-angel Civil being pinned and mind-screwed by a vampire, just as all the other Civils and were-creatures were being wiped at the asylum. But it seemed as if this Civil had been going after a particular goal. Perhaps even a significant monster who might put an end to the mind-wiping?

Then the Witch had seen a blur run into the cave and matched one of the voices inside to that of Mariah Lyander's.

From listening, undetected, after the vampire had taken the quasi-angel back to the asylum, a Witch had heard the occupants talking about "562," as if this were a very important monster to the Reds.

As in "Subject 562," a creature that had been housed in the asylum before the monster break-in.

It was a Red creature that the data files deemed ultra-dangerous. Hence, the staff had set it aside for mere observation, in need of constant watching, especially whenever it turned into its hideous form during the full moon.

After hearing mention of Subject 562 in that cave, the Witches had watched the monsters speed away from the premises just about an hour ago. And when the Witches had investigated the abandoned cave afterward, they had discovered what looked to be gifts near shattered glass.

But there was nothing else.

No Subject 562.

Had the speeding vampires been chasing down this monster after it had run away in all those blurs of speed? Or had they *taken* it from the cave and were they relocating it somewhere else?

That would mean they were protecting it, and there had to be a good reason.

Down below, a new development caught the Witches' full attention: The were-creatures had fully shifted, and the were-scorpion picked up the dog and the were-deer, then sped off.

Johnson Stamp remained with Deitra Montemagni, who'd drawn a gun and was just now slipping it back into the waistband of her suit pants.

The male Witch accessed both of his associates' minds at the same time. He thought of a bit of data he'd received from his last download before GBVille had gone dark, showing them files of ex-Shredders who'd last been reported out west. There was even a shack where many of them gathered—out of work, lazy, turtlegrape-drinking castoffs.

When he was done, one female Witch thought, *Reinforcements?*

Perhaps. Then he showed them images of the zoom bikes most of them rode.

The other Witches understood. The ex-Shredders could supply them with fast transportation that had been too far out of the range of the power blast to have been disabled. The Shredders might not join the Witches in their hunt for the monsters—and perhaps even Subject 562 if the monsters had the creature with them—but they would be patriotic enough to at least provide vehicles for their country.

If not, then the Witches would just *take* what they needed.

Two will go, the male said, pointing to the female. *You, I.*

Then they rose as one, still watching below while Stamp came out from behind his boulder and began tracking the departed were-creatures.

Odd, though, the male thought as he focused on Deitra Montemagni. She stood so very still while watching over her partner.

So very still.

He shared that with the others, then filed the data away in his brain while all the white-clad Witches retreated from the stone forest, slipping back into nothing, just as if they didn't exist at all.

19

Mariah

We'd been speeding 562 out of GBVille for hours, heading west and racing the sunrise, when me and my vampire guards started to look for a good spot to rest for the approaching day.

We found it in some lowlands, at the base of mountains, where the dirt was abraded by brush and the cracked asphalt of old roads. Monuments seemed to rise out of the small hills: a faded sphinx with an open mouth and a long funneled tongue lapping over its paws, a three-headed dragon bleached to white and tangled in a network of slides.

A sign greeted us in front of it all: SLIPPERY SLOPES.

A water park where kids used to play the summers away, splashing and laughing. You could almost hear the echoes of all that now against the arid emptiness. A place of plenty reduced to just about nothing.

It was already warmer in these climes, away from the mountains where GBVille rested, out here where the sun started to bake the land during the days. It was also easier to breathe at this altitude. But all that affected me much more than it did the vampires.

Liam, the friendly, rough-and-ready blond one, had been carrying 562 with nary a complaint this entire time. As we ventured inside the water park, seeking a place to lie down for a spell, he held 562 as if she/he were a large infant, cradling our origin to his chest.

I was using a solar flashlight that I'd grabbed before leaving the GBVille cave, shining it over the inside of a building that had been dug into a hill. It'd clearly held some sort of tank for fish gazing, but the glass was busted out now, leaving the gaping emptiness of it with nothing but fake kelp still strung from the ceiling.

Liam gently put 562 in a corner, where she/he flopped in loose-limbed disarray until the vampire once again arranged her/his limbs into that lotus pose. Then he backed away and found a comfy area in which to sit near the broken tank. Both twins, Kemp and Kerr—the latter of whom had caught up with us well outside GBVille—took up positions on both sides of 562.

Liam said, "There're a couple of hours until dawn comes, Mariah. Why don't you rest before we vampires get knocked out?"

I would be keeping watch over 562 when that happened, just as Hana and Pucci had been doing during the sunlight hours before all the insanity had struck the monster community.

I removed some water necklaces that I'd taken from 562's altar from round my neck, breaking the beads of one open so I could relieve my thirst. The vampires had seen how changing form back and forth had taxed me, so they'd asked me to stay in my humanlike state while Kemp had carried me over the miles tonight. It'd reminded me of how Gabriel had done the same for me not too long ago, when the two of us had fled to Dallas.

I stopped drinking, held a hand to my lips. Gabriel. When would I be seeing him again?

And Chaplin? Would I ever get back to GBVille to make amends with him?

Liam's voice wove through the room, which was lit only by that lone solar flashlight. "You're sad. Is it because we had to leave the hub?"

The twins had been surveying me, too. In spite of their pale skin, it seemed as if they had windburn on their cheeks—patches of slight pink from all the speeding they'd done. It made them look like they were no more than teenagers, with their short, spiked strawberry-blond hair adding just an extra touch of innocence.

"I *am* sad," I said.

Liam looked at the shattered tank for a moment, as if he were trying to recall what sadness felt like.

"I can't hardly believe," I said, "that I had a whole different life only a few months ago, before we had to desert the Badlands."

No use in talking round it—all the monsters knew my history in the New Badlands, with how I'd killed Stamp's men for the safety of my community.

"You talk like blood is ugly," Liam said.

Through his voice, I saw me as *he* saw me—and probably all the rest of the Reds, too. He spoke as if the blood I had let was a matter of course, that I shouldn't think twice about having to do it.

I felt no better than Stamp. I was the bad guys I'd always hated. I was the rotten werewolf who'd sired me. I couldn't even think of a way that I was any different from the lot of them. Didn't they all have *their* reasons to kill, too?

But these vampires still looked at me with loving expressions, as if anything I did were okay with them. It was a far cry from how my neighbors, and now Chaplin, had pretty much shunned me, even though I'd always done my best for them.

I drank more from the beads of the water necklace. Then I asked, "How long do you think we're going to have to stay away from GBVille?"

"Are you talking about yourself or us?" Liam asked.

"Any of us."

"I don't know about you, but the more I think about it, the more I realize that it'd be wise to stay away for good. Keeping the origin close to the Civils is a bad idea, even if they've been mind-screwed."

So he'd come to the same conclusion. "You decided to rebury 562 and stay on as guardians?"

"Yeah. We vowed to be the watchers when the community first realized what we had on our hands. This is just part of the job."

One glance at Liam, so blond and gorgeous, then at the young twins, made my heart feel bruised. It seemed that they had no regrets about making this vow. They were confident that they still had plenty of time to live full lives, even though they'd volunteered to shut themselves away for a part of them.

"You're sad again," Liam said. "But I think it's for us this time. Don't be that way. Others will come to spell us someday. Besides, it's the least we can do for the mother and father. We wouldn't have any existence at all if it weren't for 562."

The twins grinned at him, just like younger brothers who hung on an older one's every word.

They were so cavalier, but maybe I saw it that way only because *I* had no real conception of how long vampires could exist. Unless 562 had done something to my mortality, I would still have the life span of a regular person. That was fine with me, though, because, to tell the truth, the idea of going on and on made me uncomfortable, just like thinking about the idea of forever and how it stretched into places that I couldn't even imagine. Places too big to exist.

But mortality would eventually matter to me and Gabriel. We'd see in a few years' time if we needed to address a longer life for me. Then again, we'd have to survive that long without getting into more trouble and ending up killed.

Liam leaned his head back against the wall. His throat was pale, corded, sensual. I wondered how many human women he'd lured to him in his time.

"What kind of vampires," I said, "would volunteer to shut themselves away like you three have?"

"I've never pondered that." Liam jerked his chin at his fellow guards. "Just what kind of vamps are we?"

Kemp laughed while Kerr shrugged.

Liam answered for them. "We defy classification."

"I suppose you do," I said. "Did you talk those boys into that vow you took for 562?"

"The twins do anything I do. No minds of their own."

"Hardly," Kerr said. "You're not *that* cool."

"Is that so?" Liam bent a leg and rested an arm on his knee. "And who were the two little vampires who didn't even know how to throw a mind block when I found them?" He talked to me again. "Back when there were still high school football games, these two were the stars of their team." He pointed to Kemp. "There's your all-state quarterback"—then Kerr—"and the all-state running back. Both these shitheads were from a privileged family on the East Coast before it was fully corporatized. They had their whole lives ahead of them watching that old MTV channel and choosing which college scholarships they were going to take."

The twins were listening intently.

"Then," Liam continued, "two pretty girls came along, strangers in town. Can you guess what happened next?"

Kemp grunted, as if he didn't want to hear it.

Kerr chuckled, apparently not minding the story himself. "So we took those girls under the bleachers after a game. What red-blooded American guys wouldn't do the same?"

"Were they vampire girls?" I said. Easy guess.

"Yeah, but we didn't know about vampires," Kemp said. "Not at the time."

Kerr interrupted. "You mean, we didn't *believe* in them. But there they were, with their tight shirts and pretty lip gloss, too good to resist."

They got quiet once more, as if they'd reached their word quota, and Liam started up again.

"After the blood exchange was complete, the girls told the twins that their parents wouldn't understand what they were now. So they staged a car crash and made everyone believe they died in it."

Kerr added, "Then we left town with them. Even before the funeral."

"It wouldn't have been a good idea to spy on our departure ceremony, anyway," Kemp said. His voice rode a note of confusion, like he was trying to access that feeling he'd still been able to create during his gloaming. Sorrow. The agony of getting to see his parents one last time before he and his brother left them.

Liam picked up a piece of glass from the tank, idly inspecting it. "Your makers were two greedy, careless little vampire slags. Young. Untaught. Finding their way because they had no one to guide them. Thankfully they mellowed with time."

"Were they in their gloaming when they exchanged with the twins?" I asked.

"They were in their first year," Liam said, "abandoned by their own creators and avoiding other vampires while they were at it. They were rogue. But this was long before the government started cracking down on monsters, and vampires were freer back then. Eventually, humans were even mightily entertained by us, romanticizing our legends. Those were the days. We could go just about anywhere and it wasn't a big deal. Eventually, the world collapsed and society became concerned about how we'd attack them for their water content. That's when vamps went back to being scary, like we started out."

All three vampires had their heads cocked, and I hugged myself, the solar flashlight casting shadows on the walls that made me feel far outnumbered.

I looked to Liam. "How were *you* born?"

"Same old, same old," he said.

Kerr broke in. "Liam was what they would've called an easy rider."

Liam chucked the piece of glass toward him, but Kerr ducked it.

Kemp seemed not to have even noticed the kerfuffle. "He walked into the wrong bar one night and got friendly with the wrong girl, so when he talks about me and Kerr like we're chumps for getting lured under the bleachers, he's full of it."

"What happened to Liam's maker?" I asked.

Kerr said, "She already had a partner, and he was an old, old vamp. Centuries. He didn't like Liam so much and he told him in no uncertain terms to get lost."

When I glanced at Liam, he just blew it off. "She didn't mention she had an old man until he showed up."

"And they left you alone during *your* gloaming?" I asked. "Yup."

I shook my head, thinking that there were some similarities here with Gabriel's maker. She could've very well been in her own gloaming. "Are there any master vampires who stick with their progeny?"

"Vampires don't normally like to band together," Liam said. "We're basically solitary creatures. Predators. But some of us don't mind the company, especially when it's necessary, like right now in GBVille. Some even take training their progeny seriously. But like I said, that wasn't the case for these freckle-faces. When I saw the twins for the first time, they were feeding out in the open in an alley by a movie theater, and I had to take them aside and teach them a thing or two about secrecy. They didn't know a thing about survival."

"He told us," Kerr said, "that he'd be gone after we became too annoying."

Liam made a slight gesture with his hand, dismissive. "But they kept following me. Couldn't get rid of them."

Kemp kicked a stone at Liam. "He means that we all went into hiding eventually, underground in GBVille while everything went to crap above us. You know the rest because you lived through it, too, with the threat of Shredders and eradication. When we heard news about the fall of GBVille a month ago, we were liberated."

And here I'd thought that they might've been captured by Shredders and brought to the asylum. But no—they were just a few of the monsters who'd been attracted by the rumors of the GBVille fall.

"So here we are, then," Liam said, looking at me expectantly, as if it were my turn now to provide more stories besides what everyone else already knew.

I plucked another bead off my water necklace.

Liam obviously understood that I wasn't in a talky mood when it came to myself. "You've gone a long way around what you really meant to ask us in the first place, Mariah. You're not really wondering how long we vampires will have to stay away from GBVille as much as how long *you'll* have to stay away."

Why'd they have to be so perceptive?

He added, "Too bad I don't have any answers for you. You're the one who's going to have to decide when it's okay for you to go back."

Kerr was obviously an optimistic vampire. "Don't worry, though—Gabriel's going to find you. When I told McKellan about your being jailed, Gabriel flipped. Mac made him go to the asylum first to do some mind-screwing, though."

Liam's tone was darker. "Don't be cruel, Kerr. He'll find her only as long as he's motivated to."

It was as if a spike had burst up from the ground and lanced my middle. "What does that mean?"

They all sent a long look to me, telling me that I already knew.

The gloaming.

"What he has for you now," Liam said, "is the closest to love he's ever going to get again. After he matures, he might still have certain attachments, but they won't be based on emotion."

They didn't know about our link. Our imprint.

And there were other points in my favor. "*You* love 562," I said.

"Love?" Liam ran a hand over his hair, pulling the long blond strands back from his face. "Someone who doesn't know any better might call it that. But I would say it's more devotion."

Was that what they had for me, too, whenever they gazed at me?

I hugged myself tighter. It'd gotten cold in this room, even with the warmer air outside.

"Sometimes," I said, "I get the feeling that *I'm* 562 for you guys, just because I have a little of the same blood in me."

"562 chose you," Liam said. "562 *is* a tiny part of you."

He couldn't have said it any more clearly. Then again, that night when the Reds had gathered, dancing, calling for my blood, it had been pretty transparent, too.

"So," I said, "am I going to end up behind glass somewhere someday, just like 562?"

"Doubtful," Liam said. "We fear that if 562 dies, her/his death will bring all us Reds back to a nonpreter state. But *you* aren't our origin. We'll let you rest in peace." He grinned.

That was a relief. I didn't have any children, and I didn't even want to dwell on what might happen if I exchanged with or bit someone. I'd never wanted to bring babies into this world—human or preter—so I suppose falling in love with a vampire, who couldn't produce them unless it was through a blood exchange, made sense.

Kemp took up where Liam had left off. "You're not our origin, Mariah. You're more like . . ."

Kerr finished for him. "The strongest child of us all."

There was that devotion in his tone.

But they seemed to sense some bewilderment in me about how exactly I fit in with the scheme of things, and they stood, going about their business as if our conversation had never happened. All of them removed their sword sheaths from their belts, then positioned themselves in front of 562, setting their covered weapons across their laps.

"You don't have much time to sleep, Mariah," Liam said.

My gaze wandered to 562, dim and frozen in the light from my solar flashlight. I could see a faint red reflection in her/his eyes, just behind the hair, so I snapped off the device.

But that didn't do much good, because now I could see all the vamp eyes glowing in the dark.

So I closed my own eyes, knowing Liam was right. I needed rest because, all too soon, I was going to be up again when the vampires went down for the day.

Slumber didn't come. I went back and forth on the ground, trying to find a comfortable position. But it wasn't my body that wouldn't relax.

It was my brain. My heart.

I kept thinking of Gabriel, if he would really find me.

And if it would happen before the gloaming ended.

That was too much to bear, though, so I tried to concentrate on my friends, especially Chaplin, whose rejection just kept getting heavier and heavier inside me, like a black mass that darkened every bit of light that still might've been burning.

I don't know how much I tossed and turned, but suddenly the vampires stirred, the sound of swords being drawn from sheaths making me go to all fours, listening. The vampires' eyes glowed in the dark.

Then I heard them put their weapons away.

I grabbed my solar flashlight and turned it on, only to see Liam smiling down at me, the twins in back of him looking just as pleased.

Did we have some friendly intruders?

Something zoomed into our room, materializing.

A man.

As I sucked in a breath and stumbled to my feet, Gabriel rushed over to me, almost knocking me over with his enthusiasm when he took me into his embrace.

He'd found me in time.

At least for now.

20

Gabriel

He'd tracked Mariah over the miles, but it wasn't her scent or the faint call of her vital signs that had led Gabriel to her.

Her vampire guards had left subtle hints for him: a piece of Liam's clothing here, a sliding vampire footprint there. And Gabriel had done his best to erase every one from existence on the way, though he knew that might not be possible.

When he'd gotten close enough to them, the trail signs had disappeared; the guard vampires had even thought to leave red-herring scents—a dead sand-rabbit or beakhead bird that might confuse the senses of others. But, at that point, Gabriel's link to Mariah had emerged like a piercing ache in the center of him, pulling, leaving him no choice but to follow.

Finally, he was holding her in his arms, unwilling to let go, stroking her hair, burying his face in it. Every twisted heartbeat of hers became his, completely and thoroughly.

To be apart from her again . . . He couldn't imagine it. Right here, right now, with her, he knew that he'd never find a more powerful solace.

Especially after tonight.

He put off telling her what he'd discovered about the Civil killing, about what had gone down with Pucci, just until he could get one more rush of her, his olfactory buds filled, making him drunk on her scent.

She backed away from him an inch, looking up at him, as if her memory of him didn't quite match up to what she saw now. But then she smiled, like he'd finally come together for her.

"They told me you were safe," she said, "but I didn't believe it until this second."

"Same here." He brushed her hair away from her face. In the near darkness, her eyes glowed like stars, deep lights that burned from within her.

Around them, he could see how the guard vampires had gathered near 562, their backs to Mariah and Gabriel so they wouldn't intrude on the reunion. But it seemed as if 562 were looking right at Gabriel with that vacant, hair-filtered stare.

Looking through him.

Emotion deserted him at that moment, just as if he were pulling away from his origin—his mother and his father.

Or coming *closer* to his parentage by going toward the blankness that he'd been trying to outrun ever since GBVille, when the truth had descended on him.

The killing.

The unnecessary murder he'd committed just because he could.

Thank-all when Mariah wrapped her arms around his waist again and a twinge of his humanity made him press his cheek to the top of her head, his gaze averted from 562.

Mariah seemed to feel the push/pull in him. The strain of the gloaming before it became the darkness that would define him for the rest of his existence. He was only inches ahead of it right now, and he could feel it creeping up in him.

"There's something wrong," she said. "What is it?"

He couldn't put this off any longer.

Holding her hand, he took her away from that room and guided her to another—one that had obviously held a few fake tide pools in the past. Starfish reliefs littered the walls, the shapes rough and raised out from the granite. Where water had once flowed down, the rock was discolored, almost like a torn, dirty bridal veil.

He sat her down on a flat rock, getting to his knees and placing the solar flashlight next to her so its glow would offer some illumination.

When she rested her fingertips against his face, he felt the thud of her pulse, hungering for the blood it carried.

He put some distance between them, and her hand remained raised, as if all she had left of him were a ghost.

She lowered it slowly.

He said, "The vampires have control of GBVille. At least, that's how it was when I left it."

"And you came out here to take me back?"

"No."

She wrinkled her brow, and he could see . . . feel . . . that she was getting worried about what he had to say.

As he searched for the words, she said, "Would you just tell me?"

"The Civil killing. I remembered, Mariah."

"You know who did it?"

When he stayed quiet, she started to shake her head.

Was it the look on his face that told her the rest?

"No," she said. *"No . . ."*

At her crumbling expression, something faded inside Gabriel. At first, he thought it was an impending heartbreak, but he didn't feel it as he'd felt it before whenever he'd made Mariah sad—the aching, just as if someone were extracting parts of him while he only watched, suffering under the invasion.

No, this wasn't the same at all, because now it was as if he were watching her from a floating distance, a dark hole that was swallowing him while he held on to only a thin thread that was going to snap at any moment.

"I'm sorry, so sorry." And it might even be the last time he meant it, because, already, the Civil killing—and even his termination of Pucci—seemed like abstract events. Stories that someone else had told him. "I didn't know until tonight, when there was some blood spilled while the vampires mind-wiped the Civils and the were-creatures."

And after he'd killed Pucci.

"How could you not know?" she asked.

He explained more about the gloaming: the way his brain had protected the last, innocent parts of itself by blanking out the terrible truths until it couldn't be helped anymore.

"But I don't forget everything I kill," he said, reaching for her knee before he thought better of it. "I remembered that werewolf in your Dallas home. It was justified, though— even a human would kill for the woman he loves. My mind wouldn't have been troubled by that."

Just as his mind wasn't troubled by taking out Pucci, who'd meant to hurt Hana and Taraline.

Mariah had started looking down at the ground, as if she didn't want to face him . . . or this. He didn't have to add that the giraffe-man Civil killing had been wanton—the work of a true vampire, which was what the last of him had been fleeing.

"I had to get out of GBVille for another reason, too," he said.

Even from over here, she seemed cold for the first time he could ever remember.

She'd shut herself off from him, and that was when he felt it—the *snap*.

The breaking of that last thread that'd been holding him together . . . and to her.

It was as if he'd been knocked over for a moment, only to be pushed back up in a different world—one where the sound of Mariah only translated into . . . food.

Just food. Blood.

Where were the effects of their imprint—the connection, the understanding?

With a new clarity, he had an answer: His link to her had vanished because his gloaming was officially over.

He didn't have the emotion to panic. Instead, there was just ice. Cool. Logic. He wasn't even hungry for Mariah as her heartbeat filled his ears. He'd had enough blood lately.

"It's Pucci," he said, his voice so calm that it didn't sound like his anymore.

He wondered at that. Analyzed it.

Accepted it.

Meanwhile, Mariah only stared at the ground. Was she asking herself where their link had suddenly gone, too?

"He started to go after Hana again," Gabriel said, "so I put an end to it."

There wasn't a lick of remorse in him now. He could even taste Pucci's blood, feel his teeth sink into the were-creature's heart after he'd pulled it out of the jerk's chest.

Gabriel's fangs prodded his gums, but he held back while he told her about Taraline, as well—how she'd been following Hana and Pucci outside, how she'd tried to protect Hana from Pucci's temper and had prodded him into attacking her instead.

Then, even while Mariah stayed silent, he told her about what he'd seen under Taraline's veil. "She's healing. Or maybe she's *healed*, as much as she can be. Your 562 blood made her stronger, Mariah, but it didn't turn her."

He considered the consequences of leaving Taraline behind. "I should've brought her with me," Gabriel said, cocking his head. "The oldster . . . he saw everything that happened. Maybe he'll jail her now."

Tears filled Mariah's eyes as she scanned his face for some emotion, *any* emotion.

"I think she knew, or suspected, that I might've killed that Civil," he said, unable to give much more than that to her, "and she was willing to take the blame for me, so maybe the vampires will mind-wipe the oldster and . . ."

"Is anyone coming after *you*?" she asked.

He considered that. "I swayed Hana, but not deeply enough. She'll remember how I killed Pucci. And if she decides that she wants me to pay, there's no way the oldster or Chaplin will let her come after me alone."

Mariah's gaze brightened slightly at the mention of her dog, but then clouds filled her eyes as the rest descended on her. And that was even before Gabriel delivered the crushing blow.

"Chaplin chose to stay behind with the others. He sided with the oldster when he could've come with me."

She choked on her words before they came out. "Didn't you tell him that you were going to find me? Maybe he didn't understand that."

"He understood."

Mariah let loose with a sob, and Gabriel thought that maybe he should touch her now. So he pressed her hands between his as her tears came, ruining the brave set of her mouth as she tried to fight them.

He should tell her that *he* was here now, not Chaplin. It was time to put away childhood things and move on, to him.

To the future. She was always going to be in it, because even though she seemed so far away from him now, he couldn't picture himself leaving her behind.

It didn't make sense to do so.

Was that what McKellan had meant by having an attachment after the gloaming?

"When you were chosen by 562, you had to know that it was going to bring you someplace others might not be willing to go," he said. "That's why Chaplin stayed behind."

"But you're going to be with me," she said, repeating the promise he'd made before to her.

"Yes," he said. "Yes, I am."

He had her hands in his, and it was as if she were expecting more—a kiss to her palms? A fervid vow of love?

As if disappointed that he was analyzing it, Mariah let go of him. But dawn was creeping up his veins, anyway. There wasn't much time for what she obviously wanted from him—affection, intimacy.

He'd realized early on that the guard vampires would be able to hear them, even from the other room; this act of privacy was only a formality. So when Liam entered, Gabriel wasn't surprised.

In Mariah's presence, the blond vampire got to a knee. "We need to be ready to move on at nightfall."

He was asking where they should go, now that Gabriel was with them.

Something happened to Mariah then—a resolute stiffening of her senses that completely barred Gabriel from her.

Was it because she was still fighting off the hurt from all the news he'd dumped on her? Whatever the case, it made her into something he'd seen only that one night, when the Reds had been dancing around her, chanting.

"We have to hide 562 in her/his new home," she said. "A place where no one much goes anymore."

Gabriel said, "But there shouldn't be any Civils at the asylum who even remember 562 by now."

Liam shook his head. "We can't bring the origin back there, Gabriel, just in case. And if we separate Mariah from 562, we'd at least have one of them, if anything should ever happen to the other."

He meant that if 562 ever did die by the hand of an enemy, they'd at least have Mariah's blood as a backup. Her blood might not do anything to turn them into the vampires they were now, but it would do *something* preternatural to them, if they survived the poisoned taste of her.

A thought struck Gabriel: Had 562's blood made Mariah more vampire than were-creature?

As that circled his head, she removed her hands from his grip.

Liam said, "I have a specific destination in mind, if I can suggest one. A long time ago, I used to travel the States."

"The easy rider," Mariah said, giving him a halfhearted smile that Gabriel assessed, then understood.

"That's right." Liam gestured southwest. "If there's a maze left in this world, it'll be at the Grand Canyon."

Most just called it "the Big Gape" nowadays, having no respect for history. But what mattered was that going there would put them near the south area of the Badlands, and Gabriel frowned, almost grasping what the expanse used to mean to him: the redemption he'd been seeking once upon a time.

The search for the soul he'd lost when he'd become a monster.

But again, those were just words right now, floating past.

Mariah no doubt felt his detachment, and it doubled her own as she stood, talking to Liam.

"Sounds good to me. I'll guard 562 while you all rest, then."

Liam bent his head to her, then rose to his feet, retreating from the room.

When Mariah turned back to Gabriel, her white dress seemed to glow in that solar-flashlight beam.

A white dress and Badlander boots.

He saw her as the others must have on that night they'd chanted for her blood: an earth goddess, a pleasure principle.

But now that he thought about it, she'd always been that to him, even as he'd fought the temptation of her.

"Go rest, Gabriel," she said softly. "We've got a lot of road ahead of us."

She hesitated, searching his face, but all she probably saw was a vampire trying to match her intensity of emotion.

Yet with the dawn overtaking his body, the darkness was stronger than ever, and she faded under his eyesight, her sterile white dress the last thing he saw.

21

Mariah

Night came, and we journeyed away from the water park, Gabriel carrying me while Liam traveled with 562 once again.

Even while I was in Gabriel's arms, I felt his coolness, and I knew for certain that his gloaming had ended. I'd seen the switch in him when he'd told me about the Civil killing—when our link had gone just as dark as GBVille after the power had been blasted out.

But I wasn't about to give up on us. What we'd had was too strong. How could that just disappear?

By the time we arrived at the Big Gape, the cloud-covered moon was just about ready to go full.

Tomorrow night, I kept thinking.

The time of truth.

I tried to distract myself by looking into the canyon, though. Nowadays, it was all but covered in billboard ads, washed of their own color and shredded from their frames. Long ago, in the Before era, I knew that you used to be able to see every cut of the rock, the red-and-sand hues, but then corporations had moved in, just as with almost everything else.

Saddest of all, nobody came here anymore. Why should they when you had to go out of your house and brave the bad guys? Heck, you could "visit" the Big Gape on your personal computer, anyway.

The twins and I wound by all those ad signs, exploring the canyon and its crusty trails, its ragged and rusted train tracks lined by broken power poles that had once looked like crosses but were now just collapsed pieces of wood and wire. Gabriel and Liam stayed with 562 under a rocky overhang, but it didn't take long for me and the twins to find what we were looking for and return.

When we came back to our party, Liam was cupping 562's stringy-haired head like that of a sleeping child's, while Gabriel paced. In the distance, we could see the mammoth steel walls that divided us from the ocean. Thanks to our proximity to the water, the weather was cooler here than it was in some places farther in, like the New Badlands. Ever since terrorists had blown off this part of the West Coast, the shoreline had been relocated and, miles beyond the walls, there were supposedly great juts of land and rock. Corporate water organizations like Saline-Free had erected those barriers with the government's permission because they didn't want anyone near their property with homemade desalinating devices.

"We've got something," I said to Gabriel and Liam as the twins stood in back of me. "It's an old hotel, but it looks like survivalists built tunnels underneath. Those can be blocked off, and there's an entire network that would give you room to move about with some freedom. There'll be enough wildlife outside for your blood purposes, too."

Liam and Gabriel were curious about the location, so we all went to the proposed shelter, which was a three-story building miles down the railroad tracks, complete with chipped columns. Dirt caked most of its white façade, giving it a bearded stoicism. Round it, you could tell there used to be lots of trees, because there were holes pocking the ground. I think I'd read once, in my father's paper books, that there'd been pines in the Big Gape, and they'd smelled real good.

Now the air was mostly dead, the aroma of dirt dominating, with just a hint of salt.

When we went inside, there was no need for the vampires to be invited. First, it'd been a public place, but more important, it didn't belong to anyone now.

It was as if we'd stepped back decades and decades, to a time when the hotel had been in use. A material I'd never felt before—Liam called it *velvet*—decorated the furniture, and the tables were made of that fancy mahogany wood, which was all glossy, even now. Dust caked everything, though—even the old pictures of stiff men with cowboy hats at their sides—but it was as if we could've settled here with a little cleanup, if we'd had a mind to.

A tiny flail-salamander hopped from underneath a table to a chair, where it stood on its hind legs and thrashed its front ones about. I didn't mind the creature. Actually, it only reminded me that we were genuinely back in the nowheres.

Close to the best home I'd ever had, for a time.

Kerr had opened a hidden door in a velvet-covered wall, and he waved us over. "This way."

We all followed him down the steps, to where those tunnels fingered off to different holed-out rooms, supported by iron beams and stocked with super old firearms, like the ones me and my dad had collected, plus canned foodstuffs. Both would be pretty incidental to vampires.

When we passed a closed room that me and the twins had already checked out, Gabriel decided to backtrack and open it. The floor was piled with bones and bullets.

I shut the door again. "Whoever decided to hide away here probably didn't last all that long."

"A suicide pact," Gabriel said, his voice emotionless.

I wanted to touch him, just to see if he would react—if I could *lend* some response to him, just as I always had been able to do with our tempestuous link—but I didn't want to see myself fail in that. It would be more than I could take.

I mean, I'd barely recovered from the news of what Gabriel had done to Pucci, as well as his being the Civil killer, even though I accepted those qualities in my Gabriel.

We moved on from the suicide room, going as far back in the tunnels as we could, to a space that seemed to have once acted as a meeting spot. There was even what looked to be an altar of sorts at the rear of it.

I was concerned that the vampires and 562—and maybe even I, with my 562 blood—wouldn't be able to enter, but it was no problem.

Liam said, "This is where they lost their faith, whatever it was."

Sure enough, you could feel despair in the very air.

"I'm not sure if they held to an organized religion"—like the kind that had fallen out of favor once people had turned their fervor to cultural and popular idols—"but, no matter what, the faith didn't work for them as the days got harder to live through."

"Same old story," Gabriel said, sitting on a big rock that acted as a chair. "What they used to believe in turned out to be empty. I wonder if death became their only hope."

I wished I could tell him that not everything ended up that way, empty.

I stood aside as Liam brought in 562, putting her/him on that altar. She/he looked right at home, sitting in lotus position, presiding over the room.

Liam crossed his arms over his chest. "Unlike whatever was worshipped here, 562 will always live. We'll see to that."

The twins took off their sword sheaths and sat on the ground, comfortable as they gazed upon the origin.

Liam doffed the strap that was holding a canteen at his hip, just over his sword sheath. I'd found out recently that it didn't merely hold blood. It was filled with *Civil* blood, just in case 562 came out of this vegetative state.

I never asked how the vampires had gotten it or when.

"So," I said, "this is it? You're going to stay here?"

"It's a good location." Liam took a seat on a rock opposite Gabriel. They were different in every way—one fair and dressed in white, the other brooding, with off-kilter features, put through the wringer of life. It was just that I couldn't take my eyes off Gabriel.

Liam added, "We'll do some work on fortifying this place in the coming nights, before you and Gabriel leave."

Kemp said, "Before others come."

"Like the vampires who'll spell you?" I asked.

"No," Liam said. "Others. Soon, more of our kind will know that the origin is here. They'll come to her/him, just like they started doing back in GBVille, and they'll keep it a secret. That's what you get with vampires who can communicate mind to mind—news that travels silently."

"They'll want to be a part of 562," Kerr said. "They'll want to just touch or look at her/him."

Gabriel said, "They think it'll empower them, just like any relic."

The vampires were all looking at me now, and I got the feeling I inspired the same notion. That night of the blood and dancing back in GBVille, when I'd felt other Reds touching me, lent some weight to their theory.

Did Gabriel feel that way about me, too? Or did I have the opposite effect on him, degrading instead of empowering?

The vampires must've been right about 562 luring others, because I still didn't want to go.

I wandered nearer to the origin. "What about during the days? Who's going to watch over her/him?"

"We'll construct some traps to keep anyone but vampires out," Liam said. "Maybe one day, there'll even be a vampire who finds a Red sympathizer who's willing to come here and take the day shifts."

"What if I stayed here to—"

"No, Mariah." Gabriel had come by my side without my even knowing it. He had no body heat, but I could feel every inch of him in me.

He still had the power to make me crazed, to raise my temperature and steal my control. Funny, because I left him cold now, literally.

Had this become a one-sided love affair after his gloaming had passed?

"We've got to go," he said.

"But the full moon," I said. "Since there hasn't been one since 562 went under, we don't know what's going to happen tomorrow night. What if she/he alters and goes on another rampage?"

"There aren't any Civils here to tempt 562," Gabriel said. "And the vamps have Civil blood handy. They'll be fine. 562 won't want its descendant's blood—not with the parental attitude it had about its Reds."

"What if 562 goes wild and tries to run off, then? We can't afford for that to happen. Remember how you and I controlled the origin last time?"

The vampires exchanged glances, leaving Gabriel out of their communication. But he was busy watching me with a baffled expression, as if he were trying to figure out how to connect to my thoughts again, connect to me.

Then Liam smiled patiently. "Maybe you could stay for the first night of the full moon."

It was a good enough compromise, and we all arranged the bunker to our satisfaction that night, stringing together bladed traps at entrances and exits for anyone who happened to stumble upon this shelter, fat chance though it was.

Gabriel kept back from me the entire time, but that didn't stop my desires from rising whenever I merely glanced at him across a room or thought about what we'd had together just a short time ago.

I was losing him, wasn't I?

The next day, the hours slouched by until they got to the deepest darkness, which would combine with the full moon's apex and make me go into my own turbo form.

I was happy when Gabriel sat with me in an empty room down the hall, not abandoning me. He hadn't bothered to bind me, since I'd been a force of good the last full moon . . . at least compared to 562.

When I told him that he might want to have one of the

vampires' silver swords on him, just in case, he wouldn't hear of it.

"I'd never put an end to you," he said.

See—it was times like this when I thought that there had to be something left in him, that I was wrong about him reaching full maturation. But then he'd go back to being still and remote.

The minutes ticked past, each of them offering a new crack to my heart. But then I started to feel the moon swelling in the sky outside, then sensation chipping away at all of me, taking me apart so it could build itself back up again as a different being.

As Gabriel came to a stand across the room, I had to wonder if, down the hall, 562 had awakened with the moon yet, her/his gaze snapping to consciousness, body swelling into something far more dangerous. . . .

My hunger grew along with the expanding force in my body, and as each second jarred by, the image of that canteen, filled with Civil blood, consumed me.

I realized that I didn't want just *any* blood this time.

A sob stuck in my throat. This couldn't be happening. I didn't want my origin's appetites, and last time, I'd been so sure that I'd avoided them.

Still, I couldn't deny it now as I thought of all the Civils back at the asylum: Sasquatches, chimeras, animal-type mutants . . . all so appealing.

All so easy to catch.

And there was another burn of need emerging in me— one I'd believed to be assuaged. The thirst for bad blood, the kind I *had* to chase down.

Bad guys. Anger. I wanted to tear, be mean, kill kill kill—

As the night's darkness grew, surrounding the full moon, my body seemed to explode, my eyes rotating into vertical diamond shapes, my sight going quickly to crimson, my hair sprouting long and red from my skin, my mouth yawing open to accommodate teeth so much bigger than my non-moon form. Then . . .

Then came my extra set of arms.

They blasted out of my sides while my tongue shot out, long and grotesque, split down the middle.

Thing was, every bit of this was marked in my mind. It was a cruel joke when, for so long, I'd been able to go blank during the worst parts of my werewolf change. I didn't want to know this kind of hunger when I'd always managed to blank it out before, didn't want to know what it felt like in its most extreme—

I sprang to my feet, roaring at Gabriel, my tongue waving out.

But he didn't run.

He didn't hide from me.

Just when I thought he was going to stay emotionless, shutting me out because he was trying to adjust to what I'd be for the rest of my life, I felt it.

A jerking sensation between us.

Our link?

As he took a step toward me, I shook my head, trying to access his mind so I could tell him to stay away. He should just go, even if all I wanted to do was bring him closer.

Then I saw the shine in his eyes. Tears?

Had seeing me like this again gotten through his growing layers of vampire?

"It's back," he said.

He reached up, and *I* was the one who flinched away from him.

Blood, I thought desperately, getting through to his mind. *So hungry. Civil blood. Any blood. Help me.*

I will, he thought, our link singing into me, because for some reason, it *was* here again, as strong as ever, during the full moon.

I held to the dirt walls, my claws digging in as Gabriel left me, opening the door, then speeding back within a second.

He handed the Civil-blood-filled canteen to me, and I drank long gulps. And as I did, I saw what 562 must've felt every time she/he assuaged those hunger pangs: Red domination. Ridding the world of anything but her/his own

progeny. The continued survival of her/his children through-
out the ages . . .

I let the emptied canteen drop to the floor, all my arms
grasping air, not knowing what else to do until Gabriel
clasped one of my hands in his. They were so ugly, those
clawed hands, so many of them, but somehow, he was enjoying the feel of them.

"Come here," he said, pulling me outside.

He brought me down the hall to 562's chamber—to where
the vampire guardians were circled round our origin.

She/he sat on that altar, silver hair still covering a serene
face.

The moon hadn't taken over 562 after all, as we'd hoped
and feared. *I* was the only one left moving.

The true daughter of 562.

When the guardian vampires finally glanced at me, I
could see they wanted to touch me, to be a part of whatever
made me so powerful, but they didn't dare.

They were devoted to me, yet they feared me now, too,
in this form. As what I sincerely was.

Gabriel seemed to be the only one who didn't.

He took me away from 562's shelter as the moon stayed
powerful, leading me over the miles as we sped far, far away
to a destination he wouldn't even tell me about. I didn't know
if I was ever going to see Liam or the twins again, but I
sensed that the idea of me and 562 was very different from
the reality for them, and they were relieved when I got going.

Imagine, vampires wary of something.

Me.

Near dawn, we slowed down in a desolate, sand-stretched
place that I recognized. A rise of hill near a diner where
we'd stopped during our journey to GBVille back when I'd
set out to find a were-cure. Now, we were going in the opposite direction.

Toward the Badlands.

"I can't think of a better place to rest for the night than

up ahead," he said. "We know there'll be food and especially water here for you when the day starts, and in your human form, you'll want both, badly."

I sank low to the dirt, all my hands brushing against it. It felt like a souvenir from a better time.

I'm glad we're going back, I thought, although I already missed 562.

He heard me think it, and I wondered if, from this point on, our link would work just when I was in this state. The end of his gloaming had changed him, flipping his inner world over, and it was as if the power I had in this form were the only thing that could bring him to me.

I didn't want to believe that this was the only time we'd ever be able to connect again, just three nights out of the month. That this was the only period when he'd be influenced by me and what our imprint had left us.

We sped the rest of the way to our first homestead, an abandoned spread under the ground that the oldster had founded and my dad had developed. My camouflaged trapdoor waited amongst the brush, and Gabriel accessed it.

After we jumped inside, we crashed onto the blankets where Chaplin had once slept. All my hands swept over the old material, which was threaded through with the familiar smell of him.

Gabriel shut the trapdoor above us and, through my red gaze, I surveyed the living area. It still had its old couch. The side room with a vault where my dad had stored his collectible geek dolls. The food prep unit . . . my quarters . . . the door leading to a tunnel that connected to a common hub, which was in turn linked to the quarters where my neighbors had lived. Another door that opened to a cave where we'd had a pump system to draw out the aquifer water, and where I'd raised hydroponic foods as well as shaped bullets for my outdated arsenal.

But my weapons were gone now, transferred to a second homestead that we'd used after Stamp had attacked us here.

"We'll stay just for the night," Gabriel said. "Then we'll think about where we should go."

I tried to smile at him, but it was all sharp, grotesque teeth, and I closed my mouth.

He didn't turn away. "You think I'm disgusted with you."

I nodded, my long hair swaying.

"No," he said. "I'm not afraid, either. You were sated with that Civil blood, and I'll bet it lasts for this entire moon cycle. You wouldn't go after my type of blood, anyway."

No, I wouldn't.

He grinned at me, and suddenly the old Gabriel was back—the stranger who'd stumbled into the sights of my visz monitors, his face cut and bruised. The mysterious man who'd charmed me and Chaplin, then revealed himself to be a vampire.

"Something happened with us tonight, didn't it?" he asked. "I can feel us when I didn't before. Why?"

I don't know.

It looked as if he were thinking about coming to me, but I shrank back from him. How could he even look at me? And when he got too close and our appetites took over, would he touch me again?

I stayed in my corner, hoping he'd stay in his. I changed the subject to something far less intimate.

What if, I thought to him, *Hana seeks you out here? She might predict that you'd want to go to the only home you've known in the last years.*

She just might.

My claws lengthened, my split tongue darting out instinctively. If Hana came at night for Gabriel, she had no chance, not with me during a full moon.

Power rushed me, and I thought, *Who in their right mind would ever challenge me?* I was more than a were-creature, and even a vampire.

The love in Gabriel's eyes didn't lie to me—it was back now, just as it'd been there before, during the gloaming.

Maybe we should never leave this place, he thought. *Why would we have to when we can take on anyone who comes here?*

I knew the truth in that. We *didn't* have to be afraid now.

Let anyone come.

At dawn, after he folded up his coat to use as a pillow and fell to rest on the couch, leaving me the blankets by the trap-door where I could smell Chaplin's old scent, my form shifted back to normal, my link with Gabriel disappearing.

But I knew without a doubt that it would be back when the second night of the full moon awakened us again.

22

Stamp

Hours Ago

Ever since Stamp and Mags had left GBVille, he'd had the feeling that something was following them.

Tonight, though, just near the border of the New Badlands—or the Bloodlands, as he'd called it after he'd tangled with the monsters there—the presence seemed closer than usual.

Near a stand of loto cacti at the base of a hill, he halted, putting down the padded rod that Mags had found for him a few nights ago from a hunk-of-junk old car that had petered out on the desert sand. He'd been using the rod as a crutch, and it'd been chafing his underarm, so he rubbed at the area now, then got out one of his shivs.

Casually, he stabbed a loto cactus. It moaned, bleeding a thin tan syrup that would have to do for water until they found the real thing.

He'd already cleaned the vampire blood off the shiv, unable to stand the sight of it, and this enabled him to lick the moisture from the blade as Mags went to the other side of the loto cactus, evidently preparing to get a drink from it, too.

"Our guest is getting bold," he said in a low tone, wiping a sleeve over his forehead. He'd forgotten how dry and dragon-breathed it could get out here.

"Sure is."

Out of his peripheral vision, he saw a scurrying shadow-like movement; it cast a reflection on the ground near a stand of some more boulders. Whatever it was knew how to hide real well, but not well enough.

"What do you want to do?" Mags asked.

"See what it's up to."

Stamp took more moisture from the loto cactus, whose prickles tried to stab him in order to protect itself. But he was too fast for it.

"I don't think it's a preter," he said.

"What makes you say that?" Mags was still behind the cactus, with its silhouetted arms. She was nothing more than a shadow in the coming of the full moon.

"The hairs on my skin tell me everything," he said.

"Is that so? Your hairs still work that well?"

There was something like amusement in her voice, yet as usual, Stamp couldn't be sure. Mags had always baffled him, but these past few nights, she'd doubled up on the womanly weirdness, giving him more room than usual while they tracked the were-creatures. It was as if she were watching him just as much as he was watching the trail marks on the ground.

But tonight, he was going to deviate from the were-trail. He was going to Goodie Jern's shack for some transportation and maybe a little aid, and they needed to get there before the sun came up. No sane person would be in Bloodlands daylight without a heat suit, which they didn't have.

As Stamp took another helping of loto cactus juice, the fluid dripped from the shiv, and he caught every bit of it in his mouth. He felt Mags watching him, and his skin warmed up. He turned from her, in the direction where he'd last seen the shadow.

He narrowed his eyes. "I hope it's not a were-creature. Not with the first night of the full moon on us. The less agitated our guest is, the better."

"I've got those silver bullets in my firearm."

"Then you can go ahead and shoot whatever's following us now."

He just wanted to get going and find Gabriel.

The talk of shooting must've turned a screw in their guest's head, because what looked to be a real shadow eased out from behind the boulders down the way.

In the blooming moonlight, Stamp spied a dark form in a dress. Veils.

He'd seen the shadow people around the asylum. Dymorrdians, some called them, because of the disease.

What was one doing way out here?

Grabbing his crutch, Stamp propped himself up. Mags didn't move a muscle, though, as if she were perfectly confident she could best anyone, even while lazing around a loto cactus.

"You'd better just tell us who you are," he yelled at the dymorrdian.

She moved toward them, seeming to float over the sand in that long dress. Her voice was huskier than he ever would've guessed it'd be.

"My name is Taraline, from GBVille."

"Are you here to bring me back to that cell?"

"No."

"So why're you dogging us?" he asked.

"Dogging?" She laughed, as if he'd pulled a joke. "I believe you misunderstand my motives. I'm merely traveling with you."

At his patent surprise, she added, "I know that you're trying to find Gabriel, and I'm doing the same. However, I don't have much in the area of tracking skills, so I'm just doing what I do best—following."

She was honest. He'd give her that.

"What's Gabriel to you?" he asked.

She seemed to raise her chin under those veils, but she didn't tell him a thing.

Not that he needed enlightenment. "Okay, I get it. If you were listening in on my conversation with Hana back at

GBVille, which I guess you probably were, you know that she's going after Gabriel for the murder of her boyfriend. And you . . ." He shot her a sidelong glance. "Are you pissed at him, too, for some reason?"

"He's a friend."

"Aha. You're going to save him, then."

"I owe him," she said. "He's always watched out for me, and I'm doing the same for him. What Hana wants to do to Gabriel isn't right. He was only defending me when he killed Pucci. He was defending her, too, but that's another matter."

"Miss Taraline, you do know that vampires are mean and capable, and Gabriel won't need your protection, right?"

"I realize that, yes."

"And do you know that a vampire probably wouldn't care if he's on the bad side of a were-deer, of all things?"

"Yes."

Mags had come out from behind the loto cactus now, but she was still watching him, not the dymorrdian. Stamp's flesh ruffled under her intense focus.

"All of that matters," Taraline said. "But I'm going to Gabriel because, even if Hana is a weak opponent, she'll never let up on him, not until he's truly dead. She's a woman wronged, and that's the scariest being I can conjure in my imagination, no less reality."

"And you can protect him."

"I can watch for her while he rests during the day. That's got to be of some value."

Mags laughed softly, and when Stamp looked over at her, he couldn't help noticing that the loto cactus needles were veering away from her, as if repulsed.

He got back to the business at hand. "I'm not interested in preter drama," he said to Taraline. "So you can take it right back to GBVille with you."

Yet the dymorrdian just stood there, as if she weren't about to be chased off by a one-legged ex-Shredder and his partner.

Her bravery made him weigh the advantages of her accompanying them. Would a shadow be beneficial to him and Mags as they traveled? She might prove a good scout or a nice backup who could sneak up on any trouble and surprise them, if Stamp and Mags were to get into a spot.

He tried her out. "I'm not sure if you're aware of the history between me and Gabriel. You might not be so eager to follow me if you were."

"Everyone knows about it."

"I wonder, then, what you might do when we find Gabriel. Attack me first so I don't get to him before Hana can?"

She paused, then much to his astonishment, leaned back her head and laughed again, clasping her gloved hands together.

"Oh, Mr. Stamp," she said. "The misunderstandings between us only continue. All I meant to do was follow you until we got close enough so that I could find my own way to Gabriel. I realized you both might catch on to my presence, being what you are, but I was willing to take that chance." She unclasped her hands. "I'm not inclined to *join* you. As I said, I'm following. It's what dymorrdians do best."

"I don't take to being followed."

"For the last few nights, it didn't do you any harm."

Mags finally said something. "Leave her be, John. She doesn't offer any kind of threat to us."

There was sympathy in her tone, but also a note of confusion. He'd never heard Mags like that, unless you counted her time in the asylum.

When he turned back to tell Taraline to scoot once and for all, she wasn't there anymore.

Mags started walking away from the loto cactus. "She'll be following us, whether you like it or not."

"You should've just used that revolver. One good shot and the issue would've been resolved."

"The last thing we need is to draw any shades to us," she said, referring to the carrion eaters who more often than not attacked any nearby living beings once their appetites got going.

"Ah, shades," Stamp said. "A Bloodlands specialty."

"I hear some disgust in that. Does it mean you're rethinking a trip away from GBVille?"

This again. "If you want to go back, go."

"Not without you."

Her candor made him speechless, and instead of answering her, he just took more loto juice. Then, putting the shiv away, he used that crutch to move on, staring straight ahead of him, not thinking about how tired he was or how far they might have to go to get to the shack and a zoom bike or two.

She was right behind.

It wasn't a mile later, though, that Mags brightened up, pointing to a hill.

"There, just over the crest, as I remember it," she said.

He didn't have to ask her what she was talking about.

Mags offered him a helping hand at the base of the hill, but with one lethal glance from Stamp, she withdrew the gesture.

"Excuse me then," she said. "I'd hate to break a man's ego just so he can climb a little easier."

She stomped up the slope, sand whisking around her boots. In her gray pantsuit, she made for quite a silhouette against the bulging moon—a first-night full orb that would be bringing out the worst in the were-creatures back in GBVille by now. Like last time, they'd be restrained; unlike last time, there'd be no damned 562 creature to take off Stamp's other leg or eat the Civils.

Stamp worked that crutch, climbing up the hill. He avoided looking at Mags, mostly because he was appreciating her way too much, his pulse quickening, his breath coming a bit short.

She reached the crest, waiting for him to catch up, and, when he got to the top, she spared a soft look at him—one of those that made him go weak.

With a big fuck-off to that, he made his way down the hill, keeping his gaze on the tiny shack just beyond. Four zoom bikes were parked outside.

"Hell yeah," he said.

He thought he heard Mags lose a step behind him.

"You coming or what?" he asked.

"Just leaving some space between me and your barbed tongue," she said.

He didn't engage her, instead making a hobbling beeline for the rotting porch where the door stood open, a flicker of candlelight welcoming and warm.

The moment he stepped into the doorway, all attention was on him. Behind the slab of a bar, a teen with her hair in prairie braids widened her eyes at Stamp, and he got the feeling that it wasn't just because he'd come in here with one less leg than he'd had when he'd seen her last time, when he'd tried to recruit her lover, Goodie Jern, to go monster hunting. The girl didn't even have her ever-present knife on the bar.

Struck by that irregularity, he looked to a corner, where a random passed-out drunk slept it off among broken chairs, his hat over his nethers. Then Stamp glanced at the two ex-Shredders sitting under a gutted chandelier at a rickety table with a lone, burning candle in the center.

He recognized Goodie Jern first off. She was a worn-down ex-Shredder who looked like an oldster with her stubbled head and used-up skin, albeit she wasn't too much older than Stamp himself. It was turtlegrape drink that had sucked her dry, probably just as much as the raw toughness that'd made her a good slayer in the first place.

Stamp expected her to say something cutting, like "The boy who cried wolf returns."

But all she did was nod her head at him, her eyes fixed to his as if there were more to it than a greeting.

The same could be said for the man sitting across from her—a thirty-something guy with a wild look, probably because one of his eyes was buggy while the other was sewn shut. The rest of him seemed to be all wiry black hair and dirty hemp clothing. On the back of his denim vest jacket, Stamp knew he'd find the patched image of a skull and crossbones, then his name. Dicing.

Stamp's instincts flared—everything was just too off-kilter for normal—and he went for his shivs.

A nudge from his side stopped him.

He held up one hand, grabbing his crutch with the other, putting his balance on one foot and bringing up the device to swing it.

But the thing that had poked him caught the crutch just before it made contact with its head.

Time seemed to suspend as Stamp took in the sight: a petite preteen girl with long pale curls dressed all in blinding white. She had big clear eyes, a peace symbol burned into her forehead, and a chest puncher strapped to her back.

He waited for Mags to deliver some kind of follow-up from behind him at the door, but it never came.

With a quick look over his shoulder, he saw that she wasn't even there.

Goodie Jern spoke from the table. "The Witches got here just before you."

If blood could simmer in a human, it'd be doing just that in him. Witches had taken over his career. His life.

Dicing said, "They aim to question us, Stamp, so you might as well take a sit."

"They're obviously on some mission," Goodie Jern added, and Stamp recognized her diplomatic voice, or the closest thing she had to one.

From the right corner of the room, where Stamp hadn't even had the chance to look yet, a young male spoke out, and his voice seemed gravelly from ill-use.

"Johnson Stamp, twenty-one, last seen near GBVille."

Next to him, the Witch girl grabbed Stamp's arm, disturbing his equilibrium and then quickly righting it. She pushed up the sleeve of his asylum suit, touching the power-blasted, blank screen of the personal computer buried on the inside of his forearm.

When it didn't boot up, she let his arm flop down.

"Dead," she said.

In the corner of the room, the male, who was just as blond, young, pale, and angel-white as his cohort, added, "Fried circuits."

Then the girl spun Stamp toward the table. He hopped to a chair before he fell, then sat in it, his hands up as he targeted an ireful look to the intruders. Somewhere along the way, she'd relieved him of his shivs.

He saw his weapons in her hands as both Witches went

to a corner of the room and looked at each other, communicating psychically. Stamp had heard that the upgraded Shredders would be able to do that.

His thoughts went into gear. Maybe this Witch visit had something to do with the Monitor 'bot out at the Bloodlanders' second homestead—the 'bot that the very dead Sammy Ramos had destroyed before Stamp had looked into its dying camera lens.

Had the Witches been waiting for Stamp so they could question him about the murder of government property?

No, that was too convenient a theory. They couldn't have known that this was where Stamp was headed . . . unless they'd been following him from GBVille and anticipated where he was going.

No way.

"What kind of mission are they on?" he asked the other ex-Shredders in a whisper while the Witches still communicated with each other.

"Who knows?" Dicing said. "They keep saying 'Subject 562' over and over again. I think they're after it, whatever it is."

Stamp didn't see the need to tell them about the uber-Red creature yet. It was gone, anyway. Disappeared.

So why were the Witches way out here searching for it when the last place the monstrosity had been seen was GBVille?

Goodie Jern seemed to have forgotten that she'd just about kicked Stamp's ass out of this shack the last time they'd met, when she'd told him that she was enjoying her retirement and he'd actually better do the same before the government took umbrage at his initiative in hunting monsters.

"What the hell's happening out there, Stamp?"

"You been having too much turtlegrape to stick your head out of the door and notice?" he asked. But the monsters had been good about stealth, taking everything over slowly, quietly. Nobody out here probably knew about the fall of GBVille.

He grabbed the edge of the table and leaned in, telling them about current events.

Afterward, he realized the Witches had been listening, gathering data from their discussion.

Then they must've heard something outside, because they stepped out the door to take a look-see.

Mags?

Goodie Jern said, "I've never seen a Witch before."

"That's because they guarded monsters behind the walls of asylums," Stamp said.

Dicing's one eye was wider than ever. "They say that their brains get downloaded with data. These new slayers are way more advanced than we Shredders ever were."

"I guess," Stamp said, "that their brains are even still filled with data after the power blast at GBVille because they aren't wired up like a regular computer."

"They're stronger than we were, too," Goodie Jern said.

"Can't you think about why that is?" Stamp asked. "I wouldn't be surprised if they were 'downloaded' with vampire blood in those asylums."

Every Shredder had learned that vampire blood infusions would invest humans with strength, a little bit of speed, and healing. And maybe any already-present psychic powers they had might be bolstered. Stamp was glad the government hadn't gone that far with *them*, the first models. Back then, there'd been some dignity in Shredding.

Goodie Jern cast a glance over to her braided companion behind the bar, then returned her attention back to the men. "This is a bad spot to be in, boys."

Dicing kept his eye on the door. "All we have to do is see exactly what they want, and then they'll be out of our hair."

"Don't be a turd," she said. "Do I have to remind you that Witches are government employees? And that the government gave such a shit about us retirees that, after they cut us loose, they warned us to stay out of the monster business for good at the risk of censure? They didn't kill us off at that time, but who knows what they have in mind now? These Witches might've been sent to tie up loose ends with us after they finish questioning us about this Subject 562."

Stamp kept his gaze on that door. What would those

Witches do to an ex-Shredder who might've been caught in the sights of a dying Monitor 'bot? Had the government interpreted Stamp to be some kind of rebel who went around harming their equipment, some kind of retired malcontent getting his revenge on them?

This situation was adding up to an uncomfortable sum.

Dicing said, "Then we've got to try to get away from them."

"No," Stamp said. "We've got to get *rid* of them, but not by assassination. They're too fast and strong for us to ever pull that off."

Taking the chance on assassinating them—and failing— would mean hell to pay if the government was still operational, and Stamp knew what kind of punishing tricks the government had up its sleeve. They hadn't made examples of terrorists in a while, mostly because nobody had done much public terrorizing lately, save for the secretive activities of the monsters. But killing a Witch would be considered an act of sedition. The Witches were obviously counting on that, too, or else they wouldn't be asking for info from ex-Shredders who might not be of a mind to cooperate.

"You heard me warn you about what's happening with the government and the monsters," Stamp added. "But if the monsters take over all the hubs, the Witches won't have any bosses." He emphasized this next part. "If these things ever go rogue, it's certain trouble. They're part monster with that vamp blood in them. How would it be with *them* in charge?"

"You're exaggerating," Dicing said.

"Am I?"

The man got real quiet.

"Stamp," Goodie Jern said, "if I find out that these Witches were tipped off to us because you tried to go monster hunting after you were told not to, I'm going to lynch you."

Stamp's patience was fraying. "I think you're both not thinking straight. We've got a solution to our problem right in front of us."

Now they were listening.

"These Witches are after Subject 562, right?" Stamp said.

"So if we had something in our possession that would help with the Witches' hunt for this monster, they'd no doubt keep us alive, in spite of any fears we have to the contrary."

"You mean, if we had something like information about this Subject 562 and its location?" Goodie Jern asked.

"Yeah. And I think I can eventually supply that."

She leaned in closer. "Do you know where Subject 562 is, then?"

"No."

Just as the two other Shredders looked ready to give up on him, Stamp said, "But that doesn't mean I lack the means to find out."

He explained about the vengeful monsters he was tracking, told them how they were connected to Mariah and the beast she'd become, and how she might be on the run with Gabriel.

"Maybe those monsters I'm chasing," he said, "would know Subject 562's location . . ."

"And," Goodie Jern continued, getting his drift, "your quarry would make for some fine leads in locating the Witches' target."

Exactly. "So the Witches would find it handy to have at least me—the one who's familiar with these monsters—around for the time being. And if I told them they should deputize *all* of us for that task, they'd weapon us up before taking us with them."

Dicing looked astounded. "You're suggesting that we turn on them at some point?"

Yup. Stamp had no problem in getting the Witches to give him a weapon or two and then using them to get to Gabriel as rapidly as possible on those zoom bikes that they were about to claim. That way, he'd also have Witches to back him up—an option that was realistic and necessary to a one-legged Shredder who had the guts to take on a vampire and his friends, especially Mariah. But as long as Stamp got Gabriel in the end, he'd be content.

"If you have a better idea," Stamp said to Dicing, "then have at it."

Goodie Jern was already on his side, though. "If they were to deputize us, we'd be beholden to our vows to support the government. The Witches wouldn't expect us to turn on them. Hell, that's why they're not all over us right now—because they think that we, as veterans, still have an affinity for them."

"Technically, we *wouldn't* turn on them," Stamp said. "Besides, we never took vows to uphold the government, per se. We promised to defend this country and its humanity."

And there was a difference, Stamp thought. Goodie Jern and Dicing seemed to realize it, too.

She was nodding. "Then what you're saying is that the monsters would take out the Witches for us."

"But," Dicing said, "we'd be honor-bound to fight our best alongside the Witches."

"Well, who knows how we useless retired old Shredder models would do against full-moon-turned monsters?" Stamp said facetiously. "We might be so out of shape and practice that we'd have to retreat and leave the Witches to do the heavy lifting. Know what I mean?"

"The Witches and monsters would wipe each other out," Goodie Jern repeated. "Two dead birds with one blow."

Stamp gave her an *Am I a genius or what?* glance.

They all thought over the plan and, in the end, Dicing had one last comment to offer.

"If this doesn't work, we're guaranteed death."

"But, as Goodie Jern pointed out," Stamp said, "we might be in line for the big sleep if we just sit here, anyway. We've got to think ahead, Dicing. Or maybe you've forgotten how to do that."

Dicing looked affronted while Goodie Jern peeked at her braided partner behind the bar again. The girl nodded, and the older woman straightened in her chair.

"I'd rather die trying than sit here waiting for a shot in the head, myself."

"Good," Stamp said. "I'm going to tell them that we need to get straight to tracking, too. No stops at other hubs to see how they're doing, no nothing. We need that full moon."

Before Dicing could fully commit, the little female Witch

walked back into the shack and came to the table. She was breathing a little faster than normal.

Had they been chasing Mags out there?

The male Witch had come back into the room, in the same state as his partner.

Time to put things into motion.

"I have a way to find out where Subject 562 is," Stamp said to the Witches. "I can track a vampire named Gabriel, and he'll be able to tell us."

It might be a lie, but it got their attention.

And the best part was that, with the aid of those zoom bikes outside, the Witches and the working tracking devices that they were sure to have in this ex-Shredder shack were about to take Stamp straight to Hana and the oldster, or even to Gabriel.

The girl Witch pointed at each of them in turn. "Shredder, Stamp, Johnson. Shredder, Jern, Goodie. Shredder, Dicing, Ronald." She went around the circle again. "Activate, activate, activate."

As the Witch walked away, Stamp said, "Well, how about that. Deputized."

The male Witch went for a locker behind the bar, pulling it open without even springing the combination. Inside, a bevy of weapons awaited: taserwhips, deathlock guns, guns with bullets that would open up enough to shred the hell out of any vampire in range, chest punchers, UV flash grenades, silver debris grenades, and field glasses. No FlyShoes, though, which was a pity.

Stamp just about salivated, anyway.

The male Witch threw a deathlock gun at Goodie Jern, and she swiped it out of midair. She pointed a finger to her companion behind the bar.

"She stays here."

Prairie Braids seemed ready to piss her britches as the Witch assessed her.

"Stay," the Witch finally said to her.

Goodie Jern's girl didn't disagree.

The male Witch finished doling out the weapons, and

Stamp held tight to his chest puncher, relishing the crossbow-like contours of it against him. He imagined shooting it at Gabriel, the puncher prying apart his ribs to get at his heart and set it on fire . . .

Outside, the sound of a zoom bike revved up, then took off, and the two Witches ran to the door, quicker than any human, but not nearly as fast as a monster.

Had Mags just taken off with one of the vehicles?

The Witches communicated, gaze to gaze, then efficiently went back to the weapons locker, stepping up the process of outfitting Stamp, Goodie Jern, and Dicing with all the weapons they could carry.

Then they sprayed them with scent killer and pushed the recruits outside, toward the remaining zoom bikes.

Stamp grinned. Mags would catch up with him at some point.

The girl Witch fixed her and Stamp's chest punchers to the bike, made Stamp sit right behind her on the seat, and took the controls. He stowed his crutch, plus his other weapons, then held to the sides of the bike instead of her.

The boy Witch took Goodie Jern with him, while Dicing was given his own bike.

Then they all blasted off, combing over the desert ground, the full moon shining down on them.

23

The Oldster

"Come on, Hana—did you really think they'd come here?" asked the oldster under the darkened New Badlands sky.

They stood in front of what looked to be a sand-blasted beaded necklace of desolate hills, the entrance to the last homestead they'd lived in before they'd been flushed out toward the hubs and ended up at GBVille.

Even after speeding away from Stamp there a few nights ago, Hana was still stripped of her clothing. The oldster was the same—wardrobeless, bootless, carrying nothing but his holstered guns. The night they'd run away from Stamp, the oldster had only stopped progress hours away from GBVille, where he'd finally put Hana and Chaplin on the ground and sunk to the dirt, so winded that he could barely move.

Of course, that was when Hana had sped away from *him*, forcing the oldster to chase her with Chaplin in tow. But he'd been slow, even while he'd tracked her, wasting time as nature ticked down to the appearance of the full moon last night.

Before it had come, they'd found Hana burrowed up in an abandoned church, near the border of the New Badlands.

She'd made it clear that nothing would stop her from tracking Gabriel, so what could the oldster do about it? At least she hadn't insisted on going back to GBVille to get Stamp so he could be her hunting buddy. She had that many wits still about her.

But she was bent on payback all the same, that was for sure, and the oldster wasn't about to see her get into more than she'd bargained for with Gabriel and lose this baby, much less her life. Surely he could prevent tragedy by sticking by her.

And he had done just that last night, after the moon had shown its full face and they had hunted, eating and drinking until the sun had risen and they'd had to go back to their resting spot in the church and out of the heat.

They'd journeyed on at dusk until they'd gotten here, and now Hana was leaning up against the wall of the hill, where an entrance blended in with the rock. Chaplin was right behind her, nosing round the spot where that deadened Monitor 'bot from the government had expired. Sammy Ramos had done the deed, changing into his were–Gila monster form and striking out at the machine. Later that night, Stamp had arrived and killed Sammy, may he rest in peace.

The oldster didn't think it a good sign that the 'bot wasn't here now.

Chaplin started barking as if he'd come to the same conclusion and was advocating for them to leave.

"If you are telling us to vacate," Hana said, "my answer is no. Ever since we entered the nowheres, you and I have not gotten a good trail on Gabriel, Chaplin. But I think he came here, to a familiar place. I would bet my life on it."

"He's got to be with Mariah," the oldster said. Judging from the way Chaplin had reacted recently, the dog had picked up her scent on the oven wind in these Badlands, only to lose it within minutes.

The canine whined while the oldster glanced up at the sky, where the moon was only strengthening.

"Either way you slice it, we do need to rest in a safe place until we change in about an hour, judging by the moon."

Hana pushed on a patch in the rock, and it rumbled open,

revealing a dark passage that branched off into different areas: an aquifer room, private quarters where their little community used to take rest, the central cavern where stalactites and stalagmites reigned. Among them, visz monitor screens would stare out, shut down and blanked from the lack of motion inside the hideaway, hardly useful in helping anyone keep watch now.

Ignoring those other rooms, the oldster headed for the water area first off. He'd only filled up on fluid from blood last night, from the scampering creatures that had tried to get away from him and his were-side. The sustenance hadn't lasted long enough with all the stress and activity.

Chaplin and Hana weren't far behind him, and they took advantage of those aquifer pumps, opening their mouths under the water that still came out, then washing themselves.

But soon after they were done, Chaplin began sniffing the air. The oldster took a better look round, too, drawing his firearms before going to his old quarters.

"Hellfire!" he shouted when he saw the state of them.

The clothing he'd left when they'd had to flee from Stamp was all over the place, some even torn to bits. Everything was knocked over, from his nightstand to his bed.

Hana and Chaplin arrived in time to see the oldster pick up his favorite pair of denims, ripped beyond recognition.

Then she rushed off to her old room.

When they got there, they saw that her essentials were also in shambles, and the oldster jogged right to the common room, where he found the visz screens busted in. It also didn't escape his notice that what they'd left behind of their weapons arsenal was stripped.

"It was Stamp," the oldster muttered. "He must've come in here and trashed the place."

Then again, the Shredder had been on their trail real soon afterward. How would he have had the time to do all this damage? And would he have cleared away that Monitor 'bot from outside, too?

Chaplin barked, but the oldster didn't get the gist of the dog's communication.

"Do you have another idea about who did this?" he asked. "Who would've even known there was a community in here at one time besides Stamp?"

Chaplin kept jerking his muzzle toward the entrance, and he even pantomimed a shape in the air, then fell to the ground as if he'd been gutted.

"The Monitor 'bot?" the oldster asked.

The dog woofed and bounded back up to his feet.

Chaplin had to be right. The destruction of the Monitor 'bot had probably attracted attention on a higher level, and maybe it'd signaled government workers to come here . . . or maybe even more 'bots had arrived and gutted the homestead.

Did that mean they were still nearby?

"Do you smell anyone who's been in here recently?" he asked the dog.

Chaplin sniffed and sniffed, then shook his head. But even with that assurance, he ran back toward Hana's quarters, as if to persuade her to get on out of the room.

When the oldster arrived there again, Chaplin was at the foot of her hemp-covered mattress, on his belly, probably reluctant to approach her for the time being.

She'd righted the bed, pulling the covers back up, all neatlike. Lying down, she was resting near the long, wide spot where Pucci had set his own body night after night.

Chaplin's head was on his paws, and he raised his brows at the oldster. There seemed to be a thousand things he wanted to say.

Hana put her hand on the pillow next to her, as if she could still see Pucci's face there. Tears wet her cheeks.

"I keep seeing it, over and over," she said. "Taraline throwing Pucci against that wall. Then Gabriel shoving his hand into his chest—"

"Stop that." The oldster didn't want to relive it. "You're going to torture yourself if you keep on, Hana."

She wasn't listening to him. "Taraline. Gabriel was saving Taraline because he thought Antonio was going to hurt her."

"Pucci *would* have."

Both Chaplin and Hana raised their heads, hardly believing the oldster had the balls to say such a thing of the departed.

He regretted it. Now wasn't the time to speak of Pucci's true colors.

But Hana talked before he could apologize.

"Something happened to Taraline after she drank Mariah's 562 blood. It had an effect, just as it might have on any one of us, if we had tasted it, too." Hana clutched the bedcover. "I wish now that I had tried."

"Why—so you could be some super freak, too?"

Hana lay back down, running her hand over Pucci's place as if it would summon him right back.

"Eh," the oldster said, making a dismissive motion at her. He regretted that, as well. "You know that all we would've gotten from a taste of her was blood poisoning. Mariah's still a were."

"No, she is not. We cannot lie to ourselves about that."

Chaplin closed his eyes, and it was the most painful sight the oldster had seen in an age. Pure heartbreak.

"She has *got* to be with him," Hana said. Back to Gabriel again.

"I wouldn't doubt it."

"Do you think they went to the first homestead and not this one, and that is why Chaplin picked up her scent in the Badlands?"

Hell, she was a terrier. "Could be, Hana."

"We should go there. It is not so far away, especially if we speed. And if we time it correctly, we will have the full moon at our disposal."

"But so will Mariah."

"So we will speed and get there before the darkness goes deepest on the moon and before Mariah can change."

That was it then. They'd be off and running again all too soon, even though the oldster's bones couldn't take much more speeding. It was bad enough the moon would force a change on him tonight. He was pooped.

Still, what he'd seen in this homestead presented a mighty compelling case to leave, should the vandals—Monitor 'bots or not—have posted a lookout and the bunch of them returned.

He told Hana about the damage in the other rooms and what he and Chaplin suspected had caused it. "We don't want to be here if 'bots are keeping watch on this place, anyway, but I'm just not sure about going to the first homestead, Hana."

"I am sure."

She got up from the bed and went to a hidden spring door she'd built in the ground. She stomped on it, and it flapped open, revealing a few weapons she'd had the presence of mind to keep there.

"The government's agents did not look around very well," she said, staring at the cache. "They must be the most ineffectual body on earth."

"Can't even find a trapdoor, can they?" he asked. "I'd say they couldn't even find their asses, either, if they hadn't had us monsters on the run for so long."

Hana picked up a silver machete, and the oldster frowned. She looked like a Shredder, especially when she got a belt out of the cache, wrapped it round her arm, then snapped the machete into its holster so she'd be able to hold on to it during a were-change.

The oldster tried to slough off the image, but it wouldn't let him be. This wasn't right—monster versus monster. But it wasn't right that a vampire murdered other monsters, either, just as Gabriel had done with the Civil.

With Pucci.

Hana said, "The Monitor 'bot will not have known about our first homestead, so it would not have led anyone or anything there. That is another reason for us to visit tonight."

"You don't think Mariah will do everything she can to protect Gabriel, even before she changes?"

Hana started to walk out of the room.

"Answer me."

"I will not stop trying to find him, Michael. I would scour this entire planet if need be, and she will understand that."

The oldster merely grunted, then left the room, too, unable

to hear more nonsense. He wished he could live out the rest of his were-life in peace, but that didn't seem to be in the cards.

Hana darted way ahead of him, running out of the homestead, already going into her were-change. The oldster gave one last look to the homestead where Sammy Ramos had died, saluted the memory of his friend, then looped his holster belt over his bare arm and chased her, his body thudding and stretching into its other form, too.

They sped over the sand and dirt, seeking the shadows— an emerging were-deer and were-scorpion followed by a dog who did his best to catch up.

A mile before they arrived at the first homestead, the oldster and Hana slowed, sucking back into their own shapes, naked as the day they were born.

"We still have time to reassess this notion of yours," he said, rubbing at his skin. His body hated him right now. "If we overstay, we'll be sorry. The moon's at its very fullest tonight, you know."

Hana let go of the machete belt, and it clapped to the dirt. Then she bent to extract the blade from its holster.

"Onward, oldster," she said.

They waited for Chaplin, but it took the dog a while to reach them. When he did, he didn't stop, instead running past them.

Fifty feet farther on, he skidded to the ground, rolled in the dirt, digging at it with his nose, whining. Almost crying in a way that made the oldster cover his ears.

Without the benefit of speech, he knew that Chaplin had caught the fresh scent of his mistress again.

Both the oldster and Hana moved past him, using the brush as cover, his silver-bullet-filled revolvers in his hands, the machete in hers.

24

Gabriel

Gabriel knew he and Mariah had company well before their guests even arrived.

It had nothing to do with his vampire senses, because ever since he'd awoken on this second dusk of the full moon, he'd been watching the visz monitors that Mariah had reactivated last night, after she'd turned back to her humanlike form.

And a few seconds ago, the screens had begun to show a disturbance in the near distance, by some brush.

Predators, sneaking up on them, under the moonlight. One of them was running on all fours ahead of the other two, just like a dog, and he was rolling in the dirt like a dog would, too.

Nothing about Gabriel's response betrayed caution when he guessed that this shape must be Chaplin. And Chaplin would be with Hana. And based on the third naked body that emerged from the brush to advance on the homestead at a purposeful walk, it'd be a good bet that the oldster had come here to back her up, as well.

Gabriel heard Mariah come up from the aquifer area, closing the door behind her, setting down a pack of water that she'd already pumped.

"They've come," he said levelly.

She hesitated, as if his distant tone were discouraging her from approaching him. Or perhaps she was staying away because he still whipped her up—made *her* pulse go haywire when his remained static. Made *her* want to lose control.

It could be that the full moon would change her mood, though. He'd never felt closer to her than last night when the orb was at its most lethal.

He recalled the old sensations—the scream of his blood when he got near her, the churning of her body rhythms. The link between them had returned, imploding within Gabriel the moment she'd burst into her full-moon form and had died just as quickly when the sun had risen.

Why?

How?

He didn't know, but he didn't need to, either, when just having the link back was good enough. He craved it as he longed for blood—as he had agonized for *her* before his gloaming had ended.

But that was all it was—another hunger.

She finally came over to the visz screens, which were posted on the wall near the food prep area. He scented, more than saw, that she'd donned some clothing she'd been forced to leave behind here when they'd vacated the premises; she was wearing an old pair of lace-up pants with her boots, a baggy white shirt. She'd washed off in the cleaning unit, too, her chin-sharp red hair still damp.

He waited for the flash of blood that would rush him at her proximity, but it never came.

But he would wait.

"Is that Chaplin?" she asked quietly as she watched the monitors. On them, her dog was getting to his feet, following Hana and the oldster, his head down.

"He's not here for your sake."

Gabriel's bluntness made her pull away from the screens,

then move toward the ladder that led to the ceiling-fixed exit door.

"Where're you going?" he asked.

"Out there."

"The moon's going to be at its strongest soon."

"And that's why I'm not going to wait. I'm going to talk some sense into Hana right now."

"She can still change into her were-form, even without the pull of the moon. You're walking into a bad situation."

"She's no match for me if I should change, too, even if it isn't to my worst state." Mariah leaned against the ladder. "Besides, I'm not the one she wants, Gabriel."

He went to the ladder, too. He could surprise and overcome her with his instant vampire speed and strength if he wanted to, trussing her up so she wouldn't go anywhere. Yet that'd only be a temporary solution. Even in her nonmoon form, she'd bust out of any restraints without much effort.

She wasn't about to listen to him, though, and she continued on her way out.

Not restraining her, he only focused on the visz screens again, girding himself for a fight if Hana advanced even one aggressive inch toward Mariah.

He watched her open that door, pulling herself out, and slamming down the hatch with athletic grace. She hadn't even armed herself, seeing as they had no weapons here because the arsenal had been moved to the second homestead during the relocation.

Gabriel studied the visz monitors as she came into view of them, the lenses tracking her movement.

Right away, Chaplin bounded over to her, but he remained a few yards away.

"Boy . . ." she said, her sorrow-edged happiness loud and clear over the visz speakers.

There wasn't even a sound from the dog as Hana and the oldster left a respectable distance between them and her. They were both buck naked except for the silver machete clutched in her hand and the revolvers he carried.

This was a showdown, the minutes thunking toward a forced change for the were-creatures and 562's direct daughter—and it was the second moon night, the worst of all three.

Strange that Gabriel didn't feel a part of any of it.

Mariah was still looking at Chaplin, who was just about planting his paws into the dirt in an effort to keep himself from going to her. Gabriel could easily read the dog's body language, maybe because, as a vampire, he had an affinity for canines, who could be his familiars. That explained his attraction to Chaplin . . . and his initial one to Mariah, the former werewolf.

Hana said, "Is Gabriel down there?"

Mariah finally pulled her gaze away from her dog. "Why does it matter when I'm not going to let you anywhere near the entrance?"

Hana's machete trembled in her hand. The oldster stayed rooted next to her, as if he weren't going to get between the two women.

But that was the oldster for you, Gabriel thought. The conciliator. The one who always seemed to be caught in the middle until he finally took a stand.

What side would he end up on tonight?

Mariah got to a knee, holding out a hand to Chaplin. When he didn't move, she kept it up there.

Hana wasn't about to be ignored, though, and she made a move toward the homestead's entrance. Rising to her feet, Mariah blocked her.

"You may have a blade in hand," she said, "but you'd be a fool to try to come round me, Hana. You know what'd be in store."

"How can you protect him?"

Mariah looked sympathetically at the pleading were-woman. "Coming from someone who spent years protecting a brute when she could've been protecting herself, that's quite a question."

"*You* are protecting a brute."

The oldster finally came forward. "Mariah, do you have any idea what Gabriel did back in GBVille? What he could do to any of us?"

The conviction in Mariah's voice made Gabriel cock his head.

"He told me the details about Pucci's death. And if you think he'd do the same to any of us, you're mistaken. *I* wanted to give Pucci a taste of his own medicine for a while, didn't you, Michael? Gabriel was only the first of us to have done it."

The oldster looked more uncomfortable than ever.

Hana reared back her free hand for a slap to Mariah's face, but Mariah gripped the other woman's wrist, holding it. The two stared at each other, Hana's arm shaking.

The oldster was looking straight into the visz lens now. He knew where it'd been hidden in the scrub and was talking to Gabriel directly.

"How about the Civil killing?" the old man asked.

"He told me," Mariah whispered, and it almost sounded as if the words had scratched their way out of her throat.

In the background, Gabriel could see the winged and ragged silhouettes of shades—carrion feeders—against the moon. They'd locked on to activity down below and were hoping for blood.

They'd get it, too, just as soon as night crested and affected the moon. It wouldn't be long.

"You should go," Mariah said, letting go of Hana, "before we're all worse for the wear. You walk your way, we'll walk ours."

The oldster held up his gun-filled hands, as if in some kind of surrender as he came toward her. "That's not going to end anything, and you know it as well as we do. To make matters worse, there may be enemies about. We were at the second homestead, and it looks like we had some guests there after the 'bot was killed."

He told her about the ripped clothing, the gutted arsenal wall inside the cavern.

"'Bots could be anywhere, Mariah," he said.

She was unshakable. "There's always going to be something after us, but this vendetta of Hana's . . . It *has* to end here, because you all will end up dying if you continue coming after Gabriel."

"Why?" the oldster asked. "Because *you've* decreed it?"

That shut everyone up. Not even Mariah seemed to know what to say.

The oldster kept on going. "Every time I look at you, girl, there's something else going wrong. First, you were the teenager who came to us, befuddled and crazed after getting forcibly bitten. Then you were the woman who didn't know what to do with the powers you'd been given, and you used them in the wrong way, although it was for all the best intentions. Now you're this—a monster on a head trip, thinking that you and your Gabriel are beyond any rules."

Gabriel couldn't help thinking of how the vampires had treated Mariah, how she'd looked in that white dress with the light of the solar flashlight on her when they'd been resting at the water park.

562's chosen one.

The oldster added, "If you'd only accept what's put on you by acting like a savior instead of adding to this self-implosion that the monsters have brought upon themselves, we'd all be better off. You ever think of that?"

No one said anything, maybe because the oldster had hit a nerve.

But Hana wasn't here for that sort of discussion.

"Bring him out," she said to Mariah. "Because if you do not do it tonight, I will *someday* pull Gabriel's heart out of his chest and stake it until it is mush." She held up the silver machete. "Then I will take a bite of it."

As Mariah reared away from Hana, Gabriel had a flash: the taste of Pucci's heart, blood dripping from it, wet and delicious.

Pucci had come close to tasting as good as Mariah used to before 562 had gotten to her—pure, untouched by the processed junk from the hubs. Hana might be just as edifying . . .

Hana's voice rose as she stepped toward Mariah, who still seemed to be reeling.

"Did Gabriel not tell you?" the were-woman asked. "Did he not describe how he extracted Antonio's heart and ate it?"

Gabriel realized that he hadn't taken sustenance tonight, and he could do with some blood now. But not animal blood.

Were-blood, just like Mariah's old life water.

He crouched, then launched himself upward, his gaze red, his fangs out as he crashed through the door, arcing through the warm air.

It was as if Hana expected him, and she immediately threw the machete. It spiraled at him while he contorted his body away from the blade, then landed a few feet from her.

Hana hunched over, willingly changing as fast as she could, eyes glowing yellow, teeth bared, hair bristling from her skin, face still retaining some human qualities—the intelligence in her fiery gaze, the high cheekbones. She stayed on her hind limbs, even as they melted into a mule deer's, and she screeched at him, pawing in front of her with those powerful animal legs.

She was getting ready to switch her weight to the front so she could kick the innards out of Gabriel.

The oldster screamed something in back of him, and whatever he said forced Mariah into motion.

She zoomed into Gabriel with a bang. He felt himself grooving into the dirt, pinned.

"She's pregnant!" Mariah yelled down at him, her voice warping in the midst of her change—her mouth expanding, her daggered teeth lengthening, her eyes greener than eerie lights.

He hissed at her but she held him tight while the oldster—already in his own were-scorpion form—and Chaplin corralled Hana.

But she was going wild, kicking out at the pair with her back legs in rapid time, making that terrible screeching sound . . .

All the while, Gabriel locked gazes with Mariah, but without the full moon, they had no link right now, and he was ready to tear her throat out because she wasn't anything more to him than a barrier.

As Hana kept caterwauling, Gabriel detected a purring noise just over a hill, and he locked his senses onto it.

A zoom bike?

Mariah had gone stiff above him, her long teeth white.

Let me up, Gabriel tried to think to her.

But it didn't take. She kept pinning him, even as the zoom bike appeared over the hill.

He strained against her, twisting with vampire ease so he could see an upside-down view of the vehicle coming at them, with a rider wearing black veils that flapped in the wind.

A shadow.

Taraline . . .

As she sped close, she jumped off the bike, skidding over the ground. The vehicle kept going, seething over the dirt, riderless, until it crashed into a small rise just ahead, crunching to the ground in a sparking mash of parts and gears.

All violence was forgotten as Taraline crawled to Mariah.

"Get inside!" she said, barely able to talk for lack of oxygen. "Witches—tracking you . . ."

The oldster had already scooped up Hana, speeding away, probably toward one of the other camouflaged doors that led to underground rooms that the Badlanders had lived in. Gabriel grabbed Taraline, going for Mariah's door.

He had just enough time to see Mariah and Chaplin looking at each other, long-toothed monster to dog, before the canine tore off with the were-creatures.

Gabriel had Taraline draped over his shoulder, and he was ready to close the door as Mariah stayed on hands and knees, looking after Chaplin, pain in her gaping, daggered mouth.

"Mariah!" Gabriel hissed.

She spared one more glance at Chaplin, then sprang toward Gabriel, who jumped the rest of the way down to the ground, landing and swinging Taraline to her feet.

"Witches?" Gabriel calmly asked as Mariah pulled the door closed behind her with clawed hands, following

Gabriel's progress and standing just in back of him, panting. From the way she was doing it, he guessed that she was slipping back to humanlike form.

Under her veils, Taraline focused on Mariah but didn't seem afraid of her in this nonlunar state. She'd witnessed much worse on the night 562 had attacked.

"I saw Stamp and his friend Mags leaving GBVille, so I followed," Taraline said, gasping for breath as Gabriel checked her over for injury. She brushed him off. "He headed for a shack where there were zoom bikes. The Witches were waiting for him there. I got on the roof and listened through the chimney the best I could, and I avoided the Witches when they started to chase something outside— I think it was Stamp's partner Mags. When they went back inside, I stole a zoom bike, then I waited for them to leave. When they did, with Stamp, I followed at a distance."

"Why, Taraline . . . You're a regular spy."

She stood still, as if wondering why he was being so removed and flippant. Then she went on. "They want to find 562, and Stamp told them that he'd track you and that finding you would lead them to the origin. But I'd heard him talking to his Shredder friends . . ." She took in more air. "Stamp's using the full moon, Gabriel. He brought the Witches here when the were-creatures would be at their strongest. He's setting up the Witches."

"He brought them here because he wants to get to *me*. He doesn't care about anything else."

"Even though he told the Witches he was going to use you as a lead to 562, I think he was going after Hana first, thinking *she'd* bring them to you. They spied her and the oldster a few hours ago." Taraline was plucking at her veil, the most agitated he'd ever seen her. "They just climbed off their bikes far from the second homestead so nobody with good hearing would catch them, and then they watched Hana and the oldster make their way over here with long-range field glasses. They were so occupied that they never noticed me watching *them*. Then Stamp led them off because I'm sure he's on a timetable with this fullest moon."

Gabriel was thinking of the bigger strategic picture here. "562 would be a real coup for the Witches. They'd probably already have information about the origin's importance and powers. Or they'd at least have an idea, from all the observations the medical staff did at the asylum. I'll bet they're working off the theory that 562 might extinguish Red preter abilities."

"Aren't you worried?" Taraline asked, looking at Mariah again.

She was back to humanlike, her clothing torn, but she was slouched against a dirt-packed wall. Quiet.

Too quiet.

Was she feeling the night's deepest time inside her?

"I've come up against Witches before," Gabriel said. They hadn't proven a problem. "Did they see you leave that shack with the bike?"

"I don't think so."

"And they're all banded together?"

"Mostly, but I lost account of Stamp's friend, Mags, at the shack—"

He couldn't care less about Mags, no matter what Taraline might know about her. "Those Witches must be loaded to the hilt with their weapons. Even with a full moon, they think they've got a shot, but they haven't seen Mariah. I wonder if Stamp has told them what she'll become."

Taraline went still again, as if she couldn't believe that he'd said it with such blankness.

"Gabriel?" she asked.

He cocked his head.

"It happened, didn't it?" She sat on the ground, her skirts a dark pond around her. "Your gloaming ended."

He didn't know why she seemed so sad about that. Apparently, nobody understood that maturation was natural, and it wasn't as bad as he'd feared.

"Yeah, it ended," he said. "The last time I felt anything on my own was when I realized that I'd killed the Civil."

At his casual mention of it, Taraline's voice became wobblier than usual. "I didn't know you were the killer. I only suspected, but I tried to keep suspicion off you. I tried to distract Neelan and the oldster from your trail because I kept telling myself that you *couldn't* have been the one."

"But I was."

"I still don't believe it."

He almost felt sorry for her. Kidding yourself was a waste of time. He knew that now.

Behind him, he heard a sound from Mariah, yet he knew it wasn't because of her beast's approach. He couldn't feel the link yet. Couldn't feel anything from or for her.

Taraline crumpled her skirt in a fist. "I had faith in you because I believed that vampires can do good. You and Mariah saved my life from 562 not all that long ago."

"Is that why you came out here after us, because you're repaying a life debt?"

"I . . ."

Her veiled focus strayed to Mariah, and Gabriel understood.

When Mariah had saved Taraline from 562, she'd given the dymorrdian her blood—her 562, Red, vampire-tik-tik-gremlin-were-birthing blood. It had taken root in Taraline, making her stronger, faster, more alive than she'd been in years.

And where Gabriel went, Mariah went, so Taraline had come, just as Renfield had longed to be with Dracula in the old story McKellan had told Gabriel back when he'd first come to GBVille.

He heard Mariah breathing heavily in back of him.

"I'm going to leave you with her now," he said. "You need a weapon, and I aim to get you one."

And he departed, going to Mariah's old quarters, where he wandered around. If things went south with the Witches anytime soon, Taraline would have to defend herself because the monsters might be otherwise occupied, maybe even with fighting each other.

After dismantling Mariah's bed so the mattress crashed to the floor, he fashioned spears by scraping metal against metal in fast motion. It took a while, too, but then again, he was waiting for that full moon to come, so he had some time.

Then he waited.

Waited.

When he heard a sound of distress from the living area, he brought out the spears, set them by Taraline's side, and watched the viszes with her.

A streak of white smudged across the lens, then revealed the landscape again.

Witches? Were they here?

"That's the second time I saw it," Taraline said. "Are they setting up some kind of ambush?"

"Probably. Stamp knows where the entrances are. He's had some experience with attacking us here." Gabriel glanced at the locked common tunnel door. He had more to think about than just Stamp. "I'm betting that Hana and the oldster are in one of their former quarters right now, and they've restrained themselves. They know that if they come over here and attack me, Mariah will tear them apart. The only reason I'm not going over there to take care of Hana first is because Mariah would never forgive me for it."

And right now, he needed Mariah in that full-moon form to ensure his safety against Hana, the oldster, and Chaplin.

Mariah panted even more heavily than before, as if she were holding back the change. Gabriel went to her, resting a hand on her shoulder.

He removed it quickly, as if burned.

With just a touch, his link to Mariah began to throb, and he knew that the moon and night were about to collide. When he touched her again, his blood rushed to her, and she drew in a long breath just as he did.

Alive. He was coming alive just as much as she was.

The emotion—the all-consuming love for her—bolted back into him. Here . . . It was here again, just as if it'd never gone.

As he tightened his grip on her shoulder—it felt so good to have his pulse beat in time with hers, to feel a part of her—he realized that he would do anything for Mariah. He'd even hold off any Witches who might have it in mind to breach the homestead, hold them off until Mariah was at her most powerful.

Could he lure the enemy away and lead them on a chase until Mariah turned all the way into her full-moon form?

"I'm going to keep them busy until you're ready," he whispered to her, stroking his knuckles over her cheek.

At first, she merely seemed gratified that he was back, and she rubbed against his hand. His mind was so muddled by his overwhelming feelings for her that, before she could protest, he zoomed toward the door, banged it open, shut it, and greeted the moonlight.

Up in the sky, clouds threaded over the round yellowed orb, as if getting ready to roll away and reveal its worst side.

Gabriel then waited until someone saw him.

He scented them first—the aroma of skin that had rubbed against clothing before being rendered odorless by something like Shredder scent killer.

Then he heard the rustle of a chest puncher being cradled and aimed from a hidden foe, and Gabriel hunched over, ready to buy Mariah the time she needed.

25

Mariah

On the visz screens, the full moon hovered, close to its peak, but not close enough.

"Gabriel?" I asked, so swamped in my oncoming change that I'd barely noticed him flying upward and out the ceiling door a moment ago. I'd felt our link go live, and it still tugged at me, as if I needed to go to him.

Taraline was in front of those viszes, and she gasped as one of the lenses locked onto Gabriel, who was just standing there as casual as you please, testing the air with his senses.

"What is he doing?" Taraline asked, angry and afraid. "He's going to get himself killed."

"Cocky," I whispered, clutching my midsection. "That's a vampire for you."

I looked at him on those screens and compared him with the guy I'd first met—the wounded stranger who'd peered into these very same visz lenses and begged me and Chaplin to take him in. Then there was this vampire, who was just about daring anyone and everyone to come and get us now.

He was glancing round the Badlands scape, his arms curved at his sides and—

Something white flitted across the visz screen and, as the lenses tracked the movement, they lost sight of Gabriel.

When they returned to where he'd been standing, there was nothing.

Taraline darted to the ladder faster than I'd ever seen her move. So fast that her veils caught on the edge of one of the hooks that had held my old weapons, and it tore the coverings clean off her head, revealing her face and more in the lantern light.

Webbed skin that stretched over a few reconstructed cheekbones, an emerging nose . . . She *was* partially healed. And for the first time, I saw her hair, tufts of blond struggling out of her skull in patches.

I crawled to the viszes, next to Taraline, the closest thing I'd ever have to progeny, just as the lenses finally rediscovered Gabriel in the visz closest to the homestead.

He was on the ground, wrapped in silver chains, some of which were against his neck, sizzling against his skin. His fangs were bared at two Witches—a boy and a girl—poised above him.

"Subject 562, where?" the boy said to him, and all I could concentrate on was that peace sign burned into their foreheads, marking them as products of General Benefactors.

Before Gabriel could answer, another human strolled into view of the visz.

Johnson Stamp, using a crutch to balance.

And he had his chest puncher out, targeting Gabriel.

"Looks like I'm just in time for the fireworks," he said.

He meant the moon's peak. Taraline had said that Stamp was using it against the Witches. He was hoping we'd engage with them, keeping them busy while he got a straight shot at Gabriel.

He was using *everyone*, and he was going to come out of this alive, as he always did.

But not if I could help it.

I dug dirt to the ladder. The moon's peak was coming.

Any second, I was going to burst open, becoming that other beast.

But . . . Gabriel. I had to get to him *now* . . .

"Taraline," I groaned, starting to strip myself of clothing for the change. "You need to hide."

"No—I need to—"

"Just do it!"

The moon finally gave a mighty push in me, freezing me, and all I could do was watch those visz screens as two more humans—a nearly bald woman dressed in old leather and a one-eyed man—backed up the Witches, their chest punchers out and pointed at Gabriel.

Had Hana and the oldster resurrected their visz screens wherever they were hiding? Were they watching this, too, as they went through their were-changes?

Then I remembered that they would never come to Gabriel's aid again.

What about Chaplin, though?

I reached up to the first rung on the ladder, but that was when the full moon really got me, punching from the inside out like a rounded baby that wanted to emerge no matter what.

I broke the rung as I pulled back with the shock of feeling. I roared just as the long hair shot out of my skin, as my eyes went vertical, my sight rushing from blue to violet to red, my mouth expanding along with my teeth, limbs, torso, tongue, and multiple arms.

Gabriel!

I thought it more than said it, because I couldn't create words anymore.

My link to Gabriel burned as I saw him on the viszes, looking into the lens, smiling as if I shouldn't worry, his fangs showing. That smile was for me.

Only me.

I loomed to my feet while Taraline shrank back from me, not even bothering to put her veils back on. She had that same look of devotion and terror that the guardian vamps had worn last night, when Gabriel and I had left them with 562.

On the viszes, the two Witches disappeared from view, almost as if they were ghosts.

Stamp looked after them with a wry grin and muttered, "You sure you want to go down that door to meet the rest of the weres?"

Witches were coming, and Stamp was leading them right to me.

This was one time I wouldn't mind helping him out, but Gabriel came first.

Then the door opened in my ceiling, giving way to two white streaks that darted down the ladder. Two shots—swish, swish—and I was bolted against the dirt-packed wall.

It'd happened fast: silver spears in two of my arms, bloody pain.

Within the next second, the same agony split my other set of arms, and there I was, pinned like a bug fit for study.

I didn't know where Taraline had gone, but she sure wasn't here anymore. On the visz, I heard Stamp's voice cursing a holy diatribe, then shots being fired.

Then silence.

I still felt my link to Gabriel, so he was as alive as he could be. Somewhere. And I needed to trust in him to stay that way.

The Witches were lowering their weapons, assessing me, and I didn't assess them in return, because I was already thinking of something else. Blood. Bad-guy blood.

And more kinds of blood than even that.

The hunger was even worse tonight, escalated. Was it because the moon was at its worst?

In my red view the Witches came into better focus: two preteen kids with big pale eyes. Little dolls, mementos from a stealth nightmare.

My split tongue flicked out of my mouth, but I couldn't get to them. They were calm, though, probably wondering why I wasn't wriggling round from the pain in my arms or screaming for mercy.

"Subject 562, you?" the boy asked me, and his gaze was preoccupied, as if he were accessing something in his brain.

When he glanced at his partner, it seemed as if they were sharing information.

Then, without any warning, the girl unleashed a taser-whip from behind her, flung it out, and lashed my tongue with it.

The electric charge buzzed through me, and I gurgled low in my throat.

It tickled.

The boy repeated, "Subject 562, you?"

I laughed, and it sounded like a thousand snakes hissing in a pit.

"No Subject 562, this," the girl said, doing that glaze-eyed thing that made her seem as if she were looking up inner data.

Maybe they had mental pictures of the real 562 in the asylum during its own full-moon changes, and I didn't match up.

The boy looked real hard at me, and I realized that I couldn't move. Not anywhere.

A psychic hold?

"Civil, you?" the boy asked me.

"No Civil, this," the girl said. *"Red."*

"Not vampire," the boy said. "Not tik-tik, not gremlin. Were-creature?"

I was getting tired of this verbal biopsy, but with my tongue lashed and my body pinned, I'd have to gather some strength, maybe even get them a little closer to me, to do much about it.

Then something weird happened—the silver-poisoned blood in my body seemed to gather itself up and rush up my throat.

I spit a bunch of gunk at the Witches, the blood burning at their feet.

No vampire or were-creature or *any* Red could do that, to my knowledge.

Now the girl looked hard at me, too, and I felt my mouth being jarred open.

She was launching a psychic attack . . .

My jaws kept being pushed apart until my mouth covered my whole face. The hinges cracked as they kept pushing, pushing . . .

Enough.

I roared, yanking my arms from the wall while bringing up my legs, pressing my feet against the dirt, then pushing off so that I tore my speared arms out of their traps at the same time. Then I wrenched my tongue out of the taserwhip's hold.

Everything stung—from the gapes in my biceps to the electric buzz on my tongue—but that didn't matter as I jumped at the Witches.

They were fast enough to fight a regular vampire or were-creature, but not me, and with the split of my tongue and my two sets of arms, I had them in my grip within a blink.

I held both Witches across my body, like a human X, and ripped them apart.

They hit the walls with a wet smack, more red than white now as their blood covered my floor. The dirt absorbed it, as if it were just as thirsty as I was.

Blood.

More.

Any blood.

I dove into it, glutting, reveling in the hot mess of it. Human blood tinged with vampire. They weren't related to me—they'd stolen that blood, so it wasn't like I was feasting on progeny.

When I was done, I licked it from all my fingers, shuddering. Last night, the Civil blood had extinguished the need for one type of taste, but it hadn't been sufficient. I heard noise from the viszes, and I turned, my arms and tongue waving. I stood tall, and I could almost believe I was the blood goddess the vampires thought I was.

The screens weren't blank anymore, and what I saw made me roar louder than ever.

A bouncing, stalking were–mule deer.

Hana.

She'd gotten out of wherever she'd been hiding, and she was hunting down Gabriel.

I knew he wouldn't have gone far—not with me still feeling him nearby: a pounding connection, a live wire that might make me go dead inside if it ever flamed out.

I went to the ladder, my body already healing, the holes in my arms sucking into themselves. Avoiding the first broken rung, I slipped upward until I went out of the exit.

It took only a second for my eyes to adjust to the moony night and my skin to acknowledge the pressing warmth, and in that moment, I spied Gabriel on top of a small hill, laid out flat.

I tilted my head when I saw that Taraline had made her way out here, too, and she'd thrown herself on top of Gabriel, covering him and holding up a spear.

And she was doing it because Stamp, the bald woman, and the one-eyed man were circling the hill, their chest punchers still out.

But Taraline was smart—she knew that Shredders had taken an oath not to destroy humans, only monsters, and she was using her body to shield Gabriel.

Her cleverness wouldn't last for long, though.

Hana was fast approaching the hill, too, and I had no doubt that my neighbor was moon-crazed enough to attack, whether or not she was with child.

I barely heard the rustle of some shades' wings as they circled nearby, attracted by the promise of violence and carrion. I looked round for the oldster and Chaplin, but they weren't here.

Weren't anywhere.

Anger bit at me. Cowards.

And I thought of blood . . . their blood.

Shaking the notion out of my head—not Chaplin, I couldn't think of him that way—I bounded out of my doorway and went at that hill at full speed, my hair streaking in the night.

When I reached the top of the hill, beating Hana with my speed, I plucked Taraline off Gabriel, threw down her spear, then pushed her down the other side, where she rolled out of danger.

Then I hunkered in front of Gabriel, my blood, his blood as my pulse echoed into him. I swayed, growling, looking straight into the faces of every single enemy so they'd see what they were up against in these diamond-sharp glowing green eyes of mine.

Hana arrived, screeching at me, her were-deer teeth like little needles compared to mine.

I roared at her, so forcefully that she slipped backward, down the slope, her legs flailing. She'd better run, I thought, because I wouldn't have minded tasting her blood.

Or her baby's.

The tik-tik sentiment shook me, but why was I surprised? With 562's influence, I was a were-creature, a vamp . . . and maybe even a little bit tik-tik and nasty gremlin.

Gabriel must've felt this in me, and he touched the back of my leg, balancing me, as if knowing I'd never be able to live with myself outside the full moon if I let myself go like I wanted to.

Peace, I thought. Was he able to give me the peace again during the full moon?

He'd done it when we'd first met, back when everything had been simple between us—a man and a woman who didn't know how complicated it'd get when vampires and were-creatures mixed it up.

One Shredder, plus Stamp, had their punchers trained on me now. The other was targeting a frothing-at-the-mouth Hana.

Stamp, leaning on his crutch, lowered his puncher, as if he'd formed a different plan in his devious mind.

"Stand down," he said to his partners. "These weapons aren't going to do any good on her, and I'm going to make a wild guess that the Witches are dead, anyway."

The one-eyed man swallowed hard. "Just what *is* that?"

"A whole big splat of shit if you don't play nice with it," Stamp said. "I mean it, Dicing. I've seen Mariah in action at the asylum. We haven't been trained to deal with its like, so it's retreat time. For now."

The two Shredders didn't lower their punchers from me or Hana. Stamp tightened his jaw.

I laughed, if you could call it that.

Then Stamp cast me a look so loaded with hate that I almost counted that as his mightiest weapon. I was the only thing standing between him and Gabriel, and he knew he'd be dead in a croaking second if he crossed me.

But I had no doubt he'd be back if we didn't do something about him. With the Witches dead, he'd just wait for the full-moon phase to go by, and now that he'd found Gabriel again, there'd be no stopping him.

Near him, Hana panted, her vaguely human face just as rancor-filled, her lips twitching. Near some scrub brush, I saw a shadow.

Taraline had changed position, and her spear gleamed.

Hana, still under the spell of the animal moon, bounded back up the hill on all fours toward Gabriel at the same time the one-eyed Shredder fired his chest puncher at me.

It smacked into me, mooring into my chest, prying it open, and then the attached stake lit up in readiness to puncture and torch my heart.

At the hiss of fire, I tore at the moorings, yanking them out of me. Blood splattered as I threw the fiery projectile back at the male Shredder.

He ducked just as the lady Shredder turned her sights on me and fired.

I dodged the projectile just as Hana reached Gabriel.

Now that everything had fallen apart, Stamp was on his way to Gabriel, too, using that crutch, making faster headway than anyone might've expected from him while aiming his chest puncher.

Already, I was healing, my chest sucking together so rapidly that it was almost as if my body couldn't stand not to be melded together. It hurt, all right, and from the way Gabriel was bent over, I think he felt it just as much as I did.

The Shredders were already drawing out more weapons—guns that probably had shredding bullets in them. I had just enough presence of mind to spy a flash of movement beyond the brush, near where the oldster's domain door was located.

Was he loose?

I had just enough time to pull Hana by the neck away from Gabriel, and I held her in the air.

Then, with a whoosh, she was taken from me.

I looked to the right, where a blur of preter speed marked a were-creature's progress into the night.

The oldster. He'd saved Hana from me.

I don't know if I would've hurt her—I still had some kind of conscience, even in this body—but thank-all he'd finally come out.

Taraline was running for my door, so I turned my attention to the Shredders, opening my arms, daring them to shoot.

They sure enough did, and I twirled out of range of their ripping bullets before springing down to my enemies. It was easy impaling the woman with my tongue and twisting the one-eyed man like a pretzel with all my arms before they even had a chance to fire again.

I tossed the bodies a decent distance away, and some shades swooped right down. Gargoylesque, they plunged their beaks into the bodies, their pleased cries like nails on metal.

The taste of the Shredders' blood made me roar to the moon, then turn to Gabriel, who was engaged with Stamp as the Shredder screamed holy curses at him. I closed my eyes, using our link to block his hearing.

His body, my body.

It worked, because Gabriel snapped out of his temporary freeze, swiping at Stamp, then grabbing him by his one leg and holding him upside down. Blood was seeping through the Shredder's beige clothing, red gouge marks on his chest.

Gabriel had struck skin, and it looked deep.

"Should I get this over with?" Gabriel said. "Or should I prolong it like you would've?"

"Do it like a man," Stamp said, snarling.

Gabriel hesitated, and I felt the confusion in him. Without

our link, he wouldn't have cared about being a man. But now, with the return of what I gave to him during the full moon, it mattered.

I considered running from him, far enough away so he might lose his connection to me. He needed to be a vampire right now.

But Gabriel had already dropped Stamp to the ground, running a reddened gaze over the Shredder's single leg.

"It'd be like killing a wounded puppy," he spat out, turning his back on Stamp.

Don't do that! I thought, readying myself to interfere.

But I didn't have to when a voice rang out over the night.

"Mercy!" it cried. "Please, mercy!"

We looked over to the east, but there was nothing. To the left, though, more shades were flying lower, preparing to challenge those already on the ground for the Shredder carrion.

I screeched at all the shades, and they took off, scared to death of me.

When the voice came again—"Mercy!"—the speaker finally revealed herself over the rise of another small hill.

I recognized her. Mags, Stamp's partner.

At first, Stamp looked as if he'd been given a gift he'd always longed for. His fathomless gaze brightened.

Both my and Gabriel's pulses picked up. We knew that look.

But then Stamp got panicky. "Get out of here, Mags!"

Yet she just kept walking toward us, her hands up. "Please. Don't hurt him."

Gabriel's vitals reacted to her plea, and it pulled on me, too. But when I tensed up, it caused him to do the same.

Is this one of Stamp's traps? I thought to Gabriel.

Must be.

But then he looked at Mags again. They were near enough for eye contact, and when they locked gazes, Gabriel took on a whole new posture: acceptance.

I read what was going on between them in Gabriel's shared thoughts, and I couldn't believe it.

Mags had a secret, and it was only because of this that we let her go to Stamp, kneel next to him, touch his face.

She moved with the easiness of someone like Gabriel, graceful in the night, and Stamp was acting as if he didn't know why.

Or didn't want to know why.

Blind, I thought to Gabriel. *Love can be so blind.*

When we looked at each other, we knew it was just as true for us, too, because when the full moon deserted us, we wouldn't connect anymore. We'd be further apart than ever.

Faintly, I thought I heard a barking sound from my quarters below the earth, and I sucked in a heaving breath.

Chaplin.

I thought of blood.

Any blood.

With one more glance at Gabriel, I took to my feet, speeding over the Badlands dirt.

I traveled miles to get away from my dog, and when I finally stopped, I turned to the blood on my hands from the Shredders I'd terminated. I ate it up, trying not to think of any other blood.

Shivering, I stayed away from our hideout until dawn, when I would return to myself.

And my much less disturbing appetites.

26

Stamp

This time, when Mags touched Stamp, he didn't shy away. It hurt when she laid her fingers on the gouges that Gabriel had mired into his chest. Funny, but he'd barely known that they were there before Mags had come along.

She glanced up at the shades in the sky, the carrion eaters returning to circle and circle above, but they hadn't attacked again. Stamp was also faintly aware that Gabriel had already sped around outside to bury the dead so deep that the shades couldn't get at them anymore. He'd gone through Mariah's door, leaving them alone.

"We should go inside, too," Mags said.

"Not with him around."

She didn't listen, as usual, dragging him quickly to a door that he supposed Gabriel had left open for them before he'd retreated to Mariah's place.

After Mags turned on a solar lantern—she'd found it in the dark—he saw that they were in a room with branches and structures sticking out of the walls. One of the old quarters that the Bloodlanders had lived in and deserted once upon a time.

"The shades can't get at us now," Mags said.

She bent to him again, looking at the blood on his chest. He'd lost more than he'd thought, because when he attempted to sit up, he couldn't.

Mags held him, enveloped one of his hands in hers, pressing it to her.

Cool skin, Stamp thought. He'd never noticed that about Mags before.

He tried not to notice now, just as he'd told himself not to notice a lot of things that'd happened recently.

"You took long enough in getting here," he said.

"I had to track you."

"The zoom bike . . ." He took a breath. It wasn't coming so easy ever since Gabriel had cut into him with his lengthened vamp nails. "The bike you took from the shack should've made up for lost time."

"I didn't take any zoom bike."

There'd been four bikes at that shack; he and his party had made off with only three of them after they'd heard one roar away.

Stamp turned his face away from Mags. Taraline had gotten to this homestead even before he and the others had. *She'd* taken that bike, not Mags.

As she looked down on him, he saw that her gaze had that red reflection that he'd seen the other night, and it wasn't any projection from his bloodlust.

Mags was scenting the blood on him.

It felt as if something were scooping a hole straight through Stamp, and he grimaced, pushing away from her.

"John—"

"God-all, please tell me you didn't do it."

She opened her mouth to talk, and he saw the fangs— small, almost ladylike as she put a hand to her mouth, just as if she were surprised they were there.

He'd denied it before, but there it was—evidence of what'd happened when the asylum vampires had taken Mags away to be "questioned."

I'm tired, she'd told him one time afterward. *Really . . . tired.*

She must've been weary enough to already have given up to them at that point, given in to the monsters without telling her partner, the guy she was supposed to have trusted through thick and thin.

Bile crept up his throat. He was sick all over.

"When?" he asked.

"Not long ago. They were questioning me, wearing me down, and . . . Well, after they turned me, they kept me in the holding area, nursing me until I was fine to go back up and interact with everyone else."

Stamp worked some saliva up in his mouth, and he spit on the ground.

Mags seemed to pity him. "They wore me down to the point where what they had to offer seemed like the only choice if I wanted to go on. But it was the right choice, John. You'll know it's the same for you, too."

All those humans who'd been led out of the cells—they were vampires, just like Mags.

The whole world was going to go monster.

Stamp pulled himself as far from her as he could. He was going to get away because he couldn't even look at her now, but he couldn't help glancing back all the same.

Under the faint light, her hair was loose, darker and shinier than he ever remembered. Her eyes, already shaped at an exotic angle, would go red every time she got excited from now on.

Stamp's throat burned, just as it had whenever he remembered his parents, but this was worse. This had turned into a different kind of affection, and he'd never even asked for it.

"You'd better get out of here," he said.

"Because you're going to kill me now?" Mags smiled sadly. "You wouldn't do that, even if you could in this state."

"What . . . makes you so sure?" Even harder to breathe now.

Mags looked ready to punch him. "Stubborn ass. Even with you bleeding out, you won't say it."

Nothing to say.

She reached down and yanked him back to her by the shirt. He sucked in air, agonized.

"Here," she said, trying to touch his chest again.

"Don't."

"I can heal it."

"Don't."

At the venom in his voice, she cowered. For a vampire, she seemed decimated.

Feeling. She was still in the early stages, where she would be clinging to humanity. She'd be like that for a while, but Stamp wouldn't be fooled.

"Do you know what I did for you, John?" she asked. "How I even came to be here?"

"Don't tell me you turned vamp for me," he spat. It felt as if more blood were leaking out of him, his life going with it.

She was trembling now, and it was because she scented her next meal on him.

"I did what the vampires asked," she said, "just to save your life. They wanted to kill you, straight out. They weren't going to give you any chance to convert whatsoever because they thought you'd never willfully do it. But I suggested a way."

As she lavished a look on him, Stamp thought how breathtaking she was, even with those fangs and reddened eyes.

Mags whispered, "I told them I would recruit you."

"You—"

"You're not the only one who's ever come up with a plan." She reached out, touched his hair, shrank back before he could protest again. "The vampires need everyone they can get, and they knew that if you could be turned, you'd be a formidable ally, with your Shredder knowledge. They told me not to let you know that I'd been converted—not until I persuaded you to be with me, and I couldn't do it with sway, either. Deep down, you had to *want* to be with me. Otherwise, you'd be a vampire no one would want around GBVille."

"And that's what you were counting on—that I'd want to be with you so much that I'd give up everything else."

"Wouldn't you?"

A small, hidden part of him said, *Yes.* But then there was the rest—the boy who'd watched his parents die, the one who'd grown into a slayer who clung to his job—his salvation and sanity—more than anything else.

Mags said, "They let me free you from that cell, knowing that I was going to come back with either a vampire or a dead man. And I wasn't going to allow it to be the latter."

"You shouldn't have bothered."

"I suppose I shouldn't have put out the effort to play hide-and-seek with the Witches back at Goodie Jern's shack, either, just so you'd have some time to talk with your Shredders. I knew you'd come up with a scheme. You cared enough about life to do *that*."

Stamp pressed his lips together. Mags hadn't attacked the Witches because she knew they could easily take on a regular vamp. She'd cared enough to live, too.

His chest was numb, and he pushed his hand to it. Blood soaked his shirt, and Mags groaned, turning her head away.

"Let me give you life," she said between her teeth.

He heard how much she loved him in her mere voice. But with a vampire, love wouldn't last.

That was what his brain told him, but his heart . . .

It was begging to give itself over.

"John . . . ?" she asked, as if sensing him coming around.

She got to all fours, bending over him, her loose hair brushing his chest.

Now he started to shake, caught between what he knew was right and what he knew was wrong.

She opened her mouth, her fangs glinting . . . her eyes red and full of blood promises, just as brutal as the splash of gore that'd covered him in the marketplace that day his parents had blasted apart from a sympathizer's bomb, right along with the only normal world he'd known . . .

With the last of his strength, Stamp took hold of a

grenade on his belt, one filled with silver shards and designed to disable any vampire or were-creature.

He hugged it as he pulled out the pin.

"Run," he whispered, barely able to say it with his throat closing up as it was, bringing wet heat to his eyes while he closed them and pictured the Mags he'd known before they'd gotten to GBVille.

She hissed, but it sounded more like a tiny cry, and then she was gone, the door in the roof banging behind her, the wind whooshing around him, leaving the air empty.

Stamp thought of how many humans he'd saved in his short lifetime. Now he was only saving one more, and it was the one that counted most of all.

He was still embracing the grenade, and his convictions, when it exploded.

27

Gabriel

Third Night of the Full Moon

At dusk, Gabriel woke up to the sound of screams.

He bolted from the couch in Mariah's domain, springing fang, on reddest alert, already crouched and ready for trouble.

Under the trapdoor, on Chaplin's blankets, Mags was letting loose, and Mariah was standing away from the new vampire as Mags flailed and made an earsplitting racquet.

Gabriel sped over to her, taking the young vampire's wrists in his grip and pulling her off the blankets. He peered into her eyes, consoling her.

Calm . . . calm down . . .

Going limp in his arms, she slumped back to the floor. He checked her eyes. Misty.

He allowed his fangs to recede and backed off.

Just what they needed—a fledgling vampire in distress.

"Mags was with Stamp just before he died," he said to Mariah as she stayed near the wall. "After he did himself in last night, she zoomed back in here and raged about it until she went dark at dawn."

He glanced at Mariah, who must've changed into human-like form and waited until after the same sunrise to sneak back into the hideaway. He hadn't seen her do it.

Now, she'd already dressed for the day, but she hardly looked put together. There were dark smudges under her eyes, as if she were plumb worn out. And in those eyes, he could see that his aloof explanations about Mags disturbed her. That she wished the moon were still full because that was the only time she knew him.

But just being this near to him, her vitals were also pumping, spelling out her desire for him.

As if to remedy that, she glanced at the visz monitors, breathing deeply. The views were peaceful, revealing an expanse of Badlands dirt that had settled back into place after the showdown last night.

"How did Stamp die exactly?" she asked.

"He loosed a grenade on himself while they were down in Zel Hopkins's room. When I read Mags's mind after she fled the scene, I could see all of what happened. But even before that, I felt the explosion."

"Suicide?" Mariah asked.

Gabriel recollected that the same madness had engulfed her father after he'd grown weary of taking care of his wayward werewolf daughter.

"Yes," Gabriel said. "Stamp chose to remain what he's always been instead of switching sides. He couldn't stand a world where he'd have to be one of us. He was dying, anyway, from the wounds I gave him, and he didn't want Mags to heal him or exchange with him."

Gabriel was still holding Mags's hand, and he let go of it. There was no reason to be touching her now since he'd swayed her.

As Mariah stayed quiet, Gabriel relaxed, noticing with one test of the air that Taraline was somewhere within the domain. The direction of her scent indicated that she was probably in the bedroom, no doubt still sleeping off the trying events of last night. Humans—or even creatures with a lot of humanity still in them—weren't as stalwart as vamps.

Gabriel jerked his chin toward the door that led to the common tunnels. "I've been meaning to see what kind of destruction the grenade left, and what's there of Stamp, too."

"You're going to bury him?"

"There's probably nothing left to put underground."

She wrapped her arms around her middle. It clearly hurt her to be near him, with her blood simmering and the threat of a full-moon change creeping up on her for the third night in a row. Most of all, it had to hurt that he didn't want to touch her anymore, that he had no need to.

Mariah shirked off his gaze, concentrating on Mags, whose dark hair spread over the floor, her gaze still sedated.

"How long will she be swayed?"

"I gave her enough for about an hour." He shook his head. "When she first came to us last night and told us her secret, I knew it'd bring no good with it."

"I think Taraline knew what Mags is," Mariah said. "Or at least other shadows did. They know everything."

Gabriel had never given Taraline a chance to explain when she'd brought up Mags last night. There'd been the Witches to plan for, as well as Stamp. Plus, he just hadn't given a shit.

Mariah started walking away, then halted. "She's going to need help, you know. Just like you did when you became a vampire and your maker wasn't round to teach you."

Gabriel knitted his brow. He'd never wanted children, and even if this one consisted of a vampire in her late twenties, he couldn't see himself raising anyone.

Mariah didn't pursue the subject, though it remained in his mind. Maybe Mags could just go back to GBVille and be taught the ways of vampires there.

"God-all," Mariah said, hugging herself harder as Gabriel flinched from the curse.

Her inner pain was just about radiating off her.

"Are *you* okay?" he asked. Then it occurred to him that she might've somehow run into trouble when she'd deserted him to roam free under the moon last night. "Did the shades harass you while you were out there?"

"No." She sent him a glare, as if he should know better. "You don't understand anything anymore, do you?"

Yeah, he did, but he just didn't feel it. He was even starting to wonder why feeling for someone else even mattered when it threatened your survival, just as it obviously had done with Stamp when he'd chosen to die instead of accept Mags's offer of long life.

"Why're you still even here with me now if you couldn't care less?" Mariah asked.

"Because the last of the full moon's tonight."

Her voice shook. "And that full moon gives you a rush, but only because of me, doesn't it? Is that why you're staying?"

He'd be able to explain it to her later, when they were both in a better place.

"It's not worth this," she said, her voice gritty. "Staying with each other just for the sake of a three-night rush."

"Why not?"

"Because either we'll be at polar ends for the rest of our existences or we'll be bad for one another in so many other ways." She wiped a hand down her face. "You're at your best during our full-moon link—you're basically back in your gloaming phase—and I'm at my worst with my four arms and that sharp tongue. And when the moon *isn't* full, you don't want much to do with me while I sit here aching for you. Our imprint still works on me, but not you, unless there's that full moon."

She sighed roughly. "I shouldn't want to be anywhere near you, but here I am, wishing for it, wanting to die rather than knowing I don't mean a thing to you at any time other than when I go into 562 mode."

"We'll find a way to work with that."

Was he saying it just because she wanted to hear it? Because the words reminded him of platitudes that you gave someone who had something you wanted, and you were only holding them off until you could get it again? For him, it was the promise of those three addictive full-moon nights in the future.

"I don't think there's a way this time." She sank back

against the wall again. "You don't love me anymore, Gabriel. Liam told me that you wouldn't be able to. You can devote yourself, but it's a gesture, not an emotion. You've evolved into something I can't understand."

"We all evolve. You're even doing it with every full moon."

"Is that how you see it? An evolution instead of a devolution?"

He cocked his head, which seemed to make her angry again. He could hear it in her raging pulse.

But maybe it wasn't just about him.

"However you want to put it, Gabriel, I have . . . cravings. And not just for Civil blood. Last night, I . . ." Shame seemed to color her face. "I started thinking about Chaplin."

Instead of shock, a comparison hit Gabriel: 562 had never gotten along with Chaplin—it had even attacked him on the first night they'd met—but the origin had never eaten the Intel Dog.

Was Chaplin a lot like a Civil monster in 562's mind but, because it had wanted to win over Mariah, it hadn't devoured the canine?

"I'm becoming more like 562 every time," Mariah whispered.

"No. You don't have its full blood. You weren't born a 562, only made into something like it."

She turned those watery green eyes on him. "There's more to it than that. I've never really fit in anywhere—not since I was bitten. And I wanted to so badly. But finally, *finally*, I found a place where people looked at me without having that *Why don't you just go away?* cast to their gaze. And I found it with you."

"In GBVille." Where she was the power-blaster heroine, the goddess of the Reds. And he had worshipped her there, too, in his own way.

"I can't go back there because I'd only end up stirring up the Reds again, and that'd lead to me putting another wedge between them and the Civils," she said. "And I can't go back to what we had there, either."

"We can go other places," he said.

Mariah paused. "Are you saying we should just keep running together like nothing's wrong?"

He assessed that, and her expression fell. It was his coolness again.

What they had now really wasn't enough for her. But he couldn't give her more than those three full-moon nights, and she'd told him that all she'd ever wanted was to belong. Now, with his gloaming over, she didn't even belong in *his* world, not as she wanted to.

He made her so sad, he thought as he watched her hold back the tears. And she was too human to want to live with that kind of isolation when she still loved him so much.

"We're always going to lose to the monsters in us, aren't we?" she asked.

Without waiting for an answer, she went to her room and closed the door behind her.

Gabriel stayed by the viszes, knowing that whatever he might say to her wouldn't change a thing. She was right—the monsters in them would always win. It would either ruin everyone around them or ruin *them*.

But those three nights . . .

He stood in front of the viszes, as still as the dusk on the screens. An hour passed without him moving a muscle and without her coming out of the room. Then another. Mags rested through it all because he kept going back to her and swaying her, dreading the noise she would make when she woke up again.

Eventually, a knock sounded on the door that connected the domain to the common tunnels. He went to unlock it, opening it to the oldster, who was still wandering around without clothing.

Nodding in greeting, the man didn't seem to mind that he was buck naked and skinny as a whipcord to boot. The were-creatures he knew had been pretty free with their appearance after coming out in GBVille, unlike most vampires, who didn't destroy clothing upon going monster.

When the door to Mariah's room opened, too, Gabriel

switched his gaze there, expecting her to wander out. But it was only Taraline. She'd put her veils back on, even though everyone knew what was beneath the cloth now. With her, it was a matter of propriety.

She came close to Gabriel, and he saw that she was jittery. He knew why. Last night, when he'd come back inside, she'd seen the blood on him from where Stamp had sunk teeth into a spot by his ear. He'd hadn't even noticed it was there until she'd skimmed her finger over it before it'd healed, then put her finger into her mouth.

She wanted more now, did she? Not for survival, just for that rush.

Made sense that she'd have a yen for it, after going so long without it following Mariah's 562 infusion the night of the asylum rampage.

The oldster spoke. "Just wanted to see if everyone is recovered."

"For the most part," Gabriel said.

"Mariah's sleeping," Taraline said. "How's Hana?"

The oldster shuffled his bare feet. "She's good. Chaplin's with her. Like Mariah, she's sleeping it off. Being pregnant might be starting to take a toll on her, but I've already got her restrained, just in case she wakes up and takes it into her mind that she needs to work her way out of the chains like she did last night and continue this vendetta against Gabriel."

"A vendetta you seem to condone," Taraline said.

"Listen, I realize it looks bad for me and Chaplin to have sat out that fight with the Witches and Shredders, but we knew Mariah would take care of them."

Taraline said, "You're only the peacekeeper."

"How could I possibly have picked sides last night? If I'd taken up Hana's back, I would've been choosing Stamp, too. And if I'd gone the other way—"

Gabriel interrupted. "You would've chosen me."

"That's right, and against Hana, that struck me as wrong."

Taraline folded her hands behind her back. "A world of gray, not black and white anymore. Even Mariah has had moments of being just as bad as any bad guy out there, although her intentions are good for the most part."

"Good power can still corrupt," the oldster said, "and I've been working round to teaching her that."

"So has Chaplin," Gabriel said.

"Well, he comes from a different place, as far as I can tell. Chaplin seems to believe that suffering redeems, and Mariah hasn't gotten to a place where she's done enough of it."

Gabriel talked before he thought. "That's hard-core, Michael."

"Chaplin's a hard-core dog."

Chaplin. He'd decided not to defend Mariah last night when that was all he'd been doing his entire life.

"Does he think Mariah still doesn't need him?" Gabriel asked.

"She's gone beyond him, Gabriel."

He knew that telling everyone what Mariah had relayed to him a couple of hours ago would be for the best, so he did it without compunction. "When the full moon hits, that dog needs to steer clear of her, oldster. Her appetites . . . I think her brain is starting to see Chaplin as something like a Civil monster, just like 562 might have. I figure this because Intel Dogs and Civils are both more powerful than humans, something different from humans or Reds . . ."

The oldster gasped. "She gets hungry for him?"

"I can't say." Gabriel looked to her room. "But even if Chaplin were to change his mind about Mariah, it might be best to keep him away from her altogether, especially during the full moon."

"Wonderful," the oldster said.

A few moments passed, and he went to stand in front of the viszes.

Taraline took a spot next to him. "At least those Witches and Shredders are destroyed. Do you think that was the last of the Witches?"

"It depends," Gabriel said. "We don't know how many died in GBVille or how many there were to begin with. If these were the last two, I'd count ourselves lucky."

The oldster said, "I can't believe Stamp's done."

"You were still out with Hana when it happened," Gabriel said.

"We saw evidence enough of it since Zel's door was blown open to the common room. I cleaned up after our return and the full moon released me." The oldster kept watching the screens. "Too bad the same doesn't hold true for those 'bots I mentioned yesterday. If only they'd be dead, too. That way, we'd take out a couple of the government's precious little tech pets. From what we know via those GBVille reports, the gov don't have very many operational 'bots—just these new Monitors that were put into place after the Indian sanctions were lifted. They cost an arm and a leg—"

"—and it'd take a chunk out of the government's improving resources if they *were* dead," Gabriel said, his mind gearing up. "It'd be quite a statement."

The oldster was still just complaining. "I'm thinking that we shouldn't even be hanging round the Badlands if there's any chance that they're patrolling. What if they registered those shades circling above our bloodletting last night?"

"It's completely possible they'll be here soon, then."

"Fuck. Fuck a duck."

Taraline sighed. "Fuck is right."

As the oldster gave her a curious look, Gabriel remained calm. After all, he and the oldster were monsters. They could take down humanity, so why couldn't they do the same to a couple of 'bots?

And it was the final night of the full moon, when most of them were at their sharpest.

The oldster's eyes got kind of bright as he watched Gabriel. "What's running through that vamp mind of yours?"

Gabriel smiled. "I don't know about you, but I've got an itch to scratch, and I'm sure Mariah will need something to occupy her, too. Are you up for some running around tonight?" He paused, then added, "In the open?"

Then Gabriel told him everything, and the oldster liked the idea well enough.

So they waited for the night to deepen and create its magic with the moon, waited for Mariah to awaken. Then, knowing that they'd probably never be on the same side again, the three monsters set out into the Badlands to take care of the last of their business together.

28

Mariah

One last hurrah.

We were patrolling the perimeter of our homestead, with Gabriel using his senses to see if there were any 'bots about. The oldster and I let him do the work for now, seeing as the moon still hadn't peaked.

That was when we'd take over.

Hana was back at the homestead with Chaplin, and Taraline was keeping Mags company in my domain just in case the were-deer caused any trouble with my dog. We didn't really expect that, though, since the oldster had lied to Hana about Gabriel being staked by a Witch last night. She'd wanted to see a body or at least some evidence of this on a visz recording, but we'd reminded her that, unlike a werecreature, vampires imploded to nothing upon termination, and besides, Gabriel had been ended out of the visz's range of view.

This meant, of course, that Gabriel wouldn't be going back to the homestead. Wherever he headed, though, I knew I shouldn't go with him. Not after that talk we'd had.

Following the full moon's demise tonight, there'd be nothing left for us except the hope of next month and, meanwhile, I couldn't live with his distance while I yearned for more from him.

I'd probably be happier on my own, without all the heartbreak we caused each other. Sure, I kept asking myself why I just couldn't suck it up and deal with the troubles we caused one another during the rest of the month when there wasn't a full moon, but the way Gabriel looked at me now . . . the way he *didn't* look at me . . . Well, if you've ever been in love, you'd understand. You need to have it returned or else you feel like you don't even exist, or worse, that you do exist and you're worthless. It tears you apart just to think that you're nothing in someone's heart and mind.

The oldster and I, both out of our clothing in anticipation of the change, watched from behind the rise of a hill as Gabriel darted here and there, trying to lock his heightened sights on any signs of 'bots.

"We've been out here for a while," the oldster said. "How long do you think this is going to take?"

"I don't know, but when the moon pulls, you, at least, won't be able to think about what you're doing."

"I guess I won't be so interested in 'bots then since they don't have blood."

Gabriel disappeared behind another gathering of hills, and I could feel the oldster latch his full attention onto me. Great.

"I been thinking," he said.

I sighed.

"Someone has to do it." He scratched at his whiskers. "Where're you gonna end up, Mariah?"

It went unsaid that none of us would stay together.

"I'm not sure yet." I didn't tell him that I wasn't certain just where I belonged anymore. All I knew was that Liam had told me I should stay separated from 562. Everywhere else but GBVille was open to me.

Yup, there were lots of locales to go from here. Maybe I'd even head to a random hub farther east to see if more places had fallen yet, just like GBVille. Or maybe I should go to old D.C., where the major action was probably happening even at this moment, with monsters trying to take down the bigwigs.

For the first time ever, I sure wished my dad hadn't extracted the personal computer from my arm and patched it up by allowing my were-healing to mend me. And I wished that computer would get reception in the nowheres. I would've liked to see if any rumors were flying round the Nets about mosquitoes and the like, and if the government was acknowledging that the diseased killers had gotten to old D.C.—which would mean that the monsters had taken over communications.

The oldster flopped from his belly to his back. "After this, I'm gonna take care of Hana."

I smiled at him, mostly because of the determination in his tone. "She's lucky to have you."

"We'll see about that. I'll have to find someplace decent for her to give birth. I'm thinking of that outpost near the Badlands borders, the tent city. Hana and I can manage there, just until she has the baby."

"And then?"

"Then I'm considering going back to GBVille. Hopefully, she'll want to come with me."

GBVille? Where Pucci had died?

But there was something about the oldster's moonlit expression . . .

"What's back in GBVille?" I asked.

"Possibilities. Even after everything that went on, I still think we monsters can make a go of it. By now, I'm sure the Civils and the Reds have gone to council. I bet they've got their priorities halfway straight."

"The vampires are in charge. It'll be their way or no way."

"I've come to accept that it'll be the same case in every hub we take over. Vamps have powers I can barely even imagine—powers I don't think I'd want. And, frankly, they can have the reins as long as they don't ever mind-wipe me."

He slid a glance to me, almost as if he were lending

assurance that he wouldn't ever ask for a taste of my blood, as I'd once dreaded. The oldster was fine as he was.

He added, "I've got someone on the inside of GBVille who might go a long way in letting the vampires know that I can be on their side."

"Someone?" My voice caught on the word.

"Falisha," he said.

The name seemed to linger in wistfulness on the oldster's face for some reason, but he sat up before I could really be sure. He was frowning, as if he didn't want to be thinking about her, and I could see why. I didn't know her well, but she was a tik-tik.

"It's good you're going to get Hana out of here," I said, changing the subject, much to his obvious relief. "The only thing holding Gabriel back from killing her has been our full-moon link, and I'm not sure he'll last much longer if she attacks him again. *I* might even hurt her."

"You came close last night."

I didn't apologize. Hana had run on the wrong side of me, and nature had almost taken its course.

"You'll look after Chaplin?" I asked.

He rested a hand on my bare arm. "Just as if he were my very own."

I breathed out, then in, telling myself I wasn't going to cry. The oldster held tight to me, as if knowing that it was the only thing I had left—a touch from the person who felt like my last friend on earth.

"You'll find others," he said. "Don't you worry about that."

"But I won't have Gabriel."

I tried to smile, yet it broke somewhere along the way, and I lowered my head so my chin-length hair covered my face. Maybe this way *I* wouldn't break altogether.

"And what about Taraline?" he asked.

"I'm hoping that if Gabriel decides to take the new vampire, Mags, under his wing, both of them might escort Taraline to 562. She'd make a good day guardian."

Before this, I'd told the oldster about hiding 562 with the

guardian vampires. I didn't tell him where they were, though, or how much I wanted to see the origin again.

"She might be happy there," he said. "She and 562 always got along. She was almost like another daughter."

"She would've been if me and Gabriel hadn't put a stop to the rampage." 562 hadn't attacked Taraline for blood back at the asylum—she/he had wanted an exchange. Was it because 562 felt for wounded women, like the tik-tiks she/he had created from the corpse of a female who'd lost everything?

I didn't add that I suspected Taraline might be desiring Red blood soon. If she agreed to day-guard 562, she might be perfectly happy with Liam and the twins lending her a blood treat every so often. But that'd be up to Taraline. After 562 had tried to exchange with her, I'd realized that she wasn't out to give up her soul just so she could become a vampire and heal that dymorrdia of hers; she'd never wanted to live eternally, just fully.

As the oldster started to say something, he stopped himself, looking right above my head.

He didn't have to say who it was because my pulse spiked.

Gabriel, standing on a rise of hill above us.

He'd sneaked up, just like a breeze that suddenly comes and whips to nothing. Had he been close enough to listen to us?

I folded my arms over my chest, trying to control my battering reactions to him. "We were just talking about Taraline and Mags."

His essence tangled into me, wrestling with the tug of the moon, which was gathering strength by the minute.

But his gaze was still a million miles away.

"I heard you," Gabriel said, but he didn't add any more. Stranded, alienated. There I was once again.

He looked out over the hill, his profile etched in rough lines, honed from each blow that life had delivered to him. "If you two are still interested, I located two 'bots about twenty miles yonder. From where I was, the acoustics helped me hear them moving around, even from way off."

"What're they doing?" asked the oldster.

"Traveling this way, and they're going at a good clip. If there are still operational satellites, I wouldn't be surprised if they're using images from last night. But they were far enough away to need some time to get here."

The night and moon were starting to do their work on me, pushing, making me feel as if I were ready to expand.

"It's almost time," I said.

"I can feel it," Gabriel said.

And our link blipped, gaining power. My Gabriel was on his way just as surely as lunar time. Here for a short while, only to be gone all too soon.

The change didn't happen right away, but, within a quarter hour, it burst upon me—eyes, arms, hair, tongue.

Gabriel was the first thing I saw after the change, the first thing I identified thundering through my veins as he smiled down on me.

Then he reared back his head, opening his fanged mouth, basking under the moonlight and the returned gloaming within him.

My blood, his blood—crashing toward each other, making us as near to one entity as we could be.

After the oldster was moon-pulled into his were-scorpion form, we all sped off into the night, not quite as fast as yesterday, when the moon had been its fullest, but rapid enough to leave flares of sand in our wake. We brushed over hills and gullies, and I had to keep tabs on the oldster because he kept mindlessly veering off to hunt.

We made it to where Gabriel slowed us down near an old highway that crawled over a rise.

There was nothing round us except for that.

They know something's on its trail, Gabriel said. *They're fleeing.*

And we took off again, on their tails.

Blood—I wanted it now . . .

All kinds.

But the 'bots were foremost on my mind, and they led us a merry chase. We spent most of the night after them. It got to the point where our efforts even became a game instead of a life-and-death mission.

I grabbed wildlife along the way, munching on it, offering some to the oldster and Gabriel, too, before we put on our speed again. Once, after I'd given Gabriel a sand-rabbit dripping with blood, he looked into my eyes, love shining from his own.

It wasn't just devotion right now, either, thank-all.

The moon was already getting weaker, though—I could feel it in me—and Gabriel ran a hand over my face, as if mourning what was going to occur all too soon. I shied away from him, too beastly to imagine that he could enjoy touching me in this form.

Mariah, he thought, almost like a beaten sigh.

The oldster had been ripping apart a blackmole with his mouth, which was no more than a slash through the exoskeleton covering his face, and he grinned a bloody grin at us. His limbs waved just as my arms did, ready to pluck and smash.

He ran off again, and we had to follow.

It didn't take long for our preter senses to detect a whining from the 'bots. We were getting close.

Very close.

Soon, we found them cooling their engines near a bundle of high rocks, where the elevated pitch of the machines was louder than ever. The sound gouged my ears, going lower, through my chest and limbs.

I had to kill that sound.

The oldster and Gabriel seemed to have the same idea, and we zoomed ahead, charging them.

Their bodies, which resembled little versions of those old stealth airplanes you'd see on the Nets, weren't facing us, and I got to a 'bot first and grabbed it by the wings, raising it over my head.

Gabriel and the oldster took the other Monitor, but I got too busy to mind their fight.

My 'bot changed color, from sand to dark blue, as I raised it toward the sky. A pair of mechanical beaks snapped out of its casing, slicing toward my arms.

I heaved the thing toward the ground, but before I jumped at it, the 'bot blasted laser shots at me.

I took offense at that, mainly because this 'bot was a representative of the government. The enemy. The big bad guy.

I flipped away from every laser shot as the 'bot recovered well enough to jet off the ground, aiming its beaks and its sharp nozzle at me in a burst of speed. At the same time, it captured my image in its lens with a revolving click.

No matter—we'd be gone soon, anyway. If the government was still functioning, they could chase us all they wanted to.

I sprang into the air, thrusting my tongue out at the machine, taking it by the nozzle, holding it high once again and banging it into a nearby rock.

Its plates flew off, revealing the naked form beneath—a buglike mass of gears and parts spiked by those beaks that sought me out again.

Everything on it started whipping round then, just like fast-motion blades, as it came at me.

I spread my arms—*come on, come on*—while it zoomed toward me, my sight isolating each blade until its movements were reduced to slow whirs in my reddened sight.

I shot out my tongue, grasping the head of the 'bot, and it was as if time sped up when I threw it toward the rocks again, pulling back my tongue before it got sliced off. Just as rapidly, I hopped after the machine, grabbing a rock in each of my four hands.

Right before I smashed the bitch to smithereens, I saw the recording unit glowing in the 'bot's middle, red, like blood.

Hunger needled me as I thought of what I could be feasting on: blood, bad guys, animals, Civils.

Chaplin . . . ?

Full of rage at that, I opened my mouth wide at the exact same time I brought the rocks down on the 'bot, one-two-three-four times with all my hands, over and over again, freak strength. Just as its blades stopped whirring, I clamped down on its nozzle with my teeth, chewed on it, then spit it out.

Its innards were strewn all over the place, and I ran my tongue over my teeth. None broken.

But I did have a cut or two that were already healing on my body.

Inside me, I could feel the moon beginning its retreat and, taking advantage of what I had left, I turned my attention to the oldster and Gabriel, who were playing a match of dodge with their 'bot. With a hissing laugh, I jumped at it, hopped on its back, grabbed onto its wings, and rode it for a few seconds, just before its beaks and blades came out.

The thing must've been wounded by something Gabriel or the oldster had done to it, but it still had enough feistiness to rear back and forth so much that it jarred me, making one of my huge teeth dig into my lip.

Blood wet my mouth. It was just enough to tick me off again, and ignoring the blades, I jumped off the 'bot, turned it over like a turtle, then jammed a clawed hand under its casing, disemboweling it.

The 'bot dropped to the ground, and it made a terribly humanlike sound.

"Meh-meh-meh," it said in its death throes, just before it went dark.

I smiled big for the dying 'bot's lens as it clicked to termination.

That entertained the oldster and Gabriel, and their laughter—wheezy animal cackles from Michael and a warm zing of feeling from my vampire—cleansed me. At least for a time.

But then the oldster ran off again, taking advantage of the full moon's last moments, after more blood.

That left me and Gabriel there, and neither of us was laughing anymore.

We looked at the damage round us, and I imagined how, inside of him, he was about to get just as cold as these gutted gears and parts.

He walked toward me, and I backed away again.

Don't, Mariah, he thought.

I let him take one of my hands, and he didn't mind the claws, didn't mind my other appendages waving round.

But the night was already backing off the moon, leaving it weaker.

Still, Gabriel kept holding me, looking into my eyes for as long as he could, my body, his body . . .

When I finally dropped to the ground, I pulled my claw through the dirt, as if I could grab onto what remained of our disappearing connection that way.

Looking up at Gabriel, I saw that he was experiencing the loss, too.

Mariah . . . he thought to me, but this time, there was desperation. He sounded like a man who was being pulled back into hell after being granted a few days out of it.

The moon lost more power. My extra set of arms drew back into me, just like my long hair. My eyes rotated back to their normal shape, my mouth and teeth shrank, along with my tongue . . .

All the while, Gabriel seemed to be slipping further away, although he was right here.

I was halfway human now, and with the last of my strength, I wrapped my two remaining arms round Gabriel's legs, and he got to the ground and clung to me, too.

The last thought I heard from him was, *Remember how much I love you right now. Never forget* . . .

Then he was gone—not in body, but in here: my chest, my hollowed-out center.

He pulled back from me, frosty, distant, with a look in his eyes that told me he felt nothing, even with my bare skin against him. He glanced at the blood on my lip, where I'd bit it earlier to create a wound that had already healed.

Only the blood remained, and I knew he wanted it.

Knew it would make him sick if he took it.

Even as my body beat for him, post-change pain flowing through me and making my aches that much worse, I saw in Gabriel's gaze that he was a stranger now.

When he stood, I knew he only had to leave to complete the journey.

"There's always the next full moon," he said.

I shook my head, unable to stand the thought of this torture month in and month out. I poisoned him, but he poisoned me just as much.

He tilted his head, as if digesting my reaction, and then without even a good-bye, he sped off for parts unknown, seeking shelter before daylight broke.

I never even had time to call out for him to come back.

After about an hour of rest, I found the oldster nearby, and he was in no shape to were-change again, so before the sun could get too hot to endure, I took it upon myself to change into my nonlunar form, in spite of my keening joints and muscles.

I took him in my arms and sped back to the homestead, entering my domain and setting him down on my bed, then slipping back into my human state, my body one big pile of hurt.

He was already asleep, and I kissed his forehead. My own last hurrah with a good friend.

Holding back the tears yet again, I went to my living area. My place was deserted: No Mags. No Taraline.

No Gabriel.

He must've come here straightaway, extracting Taraline and Mags before dawn fully broke. They could've even gone to our second homestead, where there'd be water and shelter and no Hana to contend with, but I didn't pursue him.

I couldn't bear to.

Taraline had left a scrawl in the ground, though, and I kneeled down to read it.

> *Gabriel is taking me to the place*
> *where I'll be safe and happy. Mags, too.*
> *Thank you, my friend. I'll always remember*
> *how you saved me.*

I didn't move from that spot for a while. I guess happy endings did that to you, made you choke up just as surely as sad ones. And, if I could judge by this note, Gabriel had taken Taraline to 562, and she was pleased about it.

She'd always liked taking care of others, following them, and her path had taken her to a being who needed another guardian badly. A being who had cared for her during their calmer moments together.

I lay down right there, my head near Taraline's words. Sleep claimed me right away, and I didn't get back up again until the next nightfall had introduced itself.

The oldster was still tuckered out as I cleaned myself up, fortified myself with water, filled up a few canteens of it, dressed, then gathered some supplies.

I left the oldster slumbering, left without a word to Hana or Chaplin, neither of whom would care where I went, anyway.

As I climbed my ladder for the last time, then shut the door behind me, I looked west toward the setting sun, with its colors inking the sky. I set out the opposite way, east, drifting just as aimlessly as Gabriel had when I'd first seen him on the visz screen.

But I didn't let that get me down, because I was going someplace. Old D.C., most likely. Along the way, I'd try to catch news of what might be happening there. I'd look for fellow monsters, but I wouldn't fall in with any.

I was going it alone, and I didn't mind so much.

Well, not too much.

I walked that night. My body was too worn out from the full moon, too hammered from so much else, for me to change into nonlunar form. I walked the next night, also, and the next.

On the fourth night, I was strolling through a gully rife with weblike loom trees. Night birds whirred and made sharp chirps, warning me off. Little did they know that it wasn't wise to smart-mouth me.

When I caught the sound of rock sliding against ground from above, I glanced up, my body tensing, ready to were-change if need be.

But I didn't see a thing.

I walked some more, and after a few moments, I heard it again.

This time when I looked, I saw a silhouette against the waning moon.

A dog.

And he was just as tense as I was.

Emotion itched in my throat, my chest wrenching together.

"Chaplin?" I whispered.

He barked, a lonely sound that echoed through the gully. *Mariah?*

God-all, what was he doing here?

Had he come because Gabriel wasn't round to corrupt me anymore?

I stood my ground, tried to seem mean, tried to seem that I was glad we'd been separated.

"Get on," I said. "Go back where you should be."

Bark, whine, mumble mumble. *I couldn't let you go for good.*

Now tears were at the corners of my eyes. Great, like I could waste any water, out here in the nowheres.

"I mean it, Chaplin—git."

The oldster told me about your cravings for me during the full moon, he said. *But we have a long time until you need to worry about that again.*

"But," I said, words nearly impossible through the scraped alley of my throat, "I might eat you."

The words, ridiculous as they sounded, just hovered—hauntings that were never going to go away.

I'll just leave before each full moon, Chaplin said matter-of-factly.

The dog thought he knew everything.

I swallowed and swallowed, fighting the hardest fight I'd ever taken part in.

Funny—Chaplin wanted to be with me during the times Gabriel emotionally couldn't be. And when Chaplin couldn't be round me during the full moon . . .

Well, Gabriel could've been there.

But he wouldn't be.

My mutt must've known that it wasn't in me to turn him away, because he scuttled down to me in a tumble of dirt and rock, hardly breaking speed as he jumped at me.

I opened my arms to him, taking him against me and thudding to the ground with him, crying, never letting go. As I hugged him, my eyes fixed to another spot high up, where it was dark and murky.

I thought I witnessed another silhouette.

A man . . . ?

But as I sat up to see better, I realized that my eyes were only playing tricks on me.

Embracing Chaplin again, I buried my face in his fur.

"It's just you and me," I said.

He barked softly, but he wasn't really saying anything. It was just Chaplin's way of sounding content.

After that, me and my dog walked the gully together while the moon spied on us. But I kept looking up, expecting to see that other silhouette again.

Even though I didn't, I took solace in imagining that I'd seen a vampire.

A man in a long coat and battered clothing, even now watching over me, showing me that even though we were far apart, there was still a part of him where I belonged.

29

Gabriel

Whether or not they were meant to be separated, he would always be somewhere near, watching over her, and maybe, during the next full moon, he would get even closer.

Three nights out of a month when they could connect.

The thought was a drug that sang through a vampire's veins just as surely as blood while he used the rock as cover. Though Mariah wasn't a part of him right now, he craved the next moment when she would be. It had been enough to make him decide to leave Mags with Taraline as she settled in with 562 and the guardians. It had been enough to bring him here.

A breeze blew past him, ruffling his long coat, his short hair, bringing her scent downwind to him. He could hear her body, too: a frenzied orchestra of heartbeats and blood.

As she and the dog disappeared into the loom trees at the far end of the gully, Gabriel stayed on higher ground, following at a distance.

Following because, more than she knew, she would always be what he needed, even if it was only for a moment in time.

*In the Bloodlands, sometimes the monsters
don't even know themselves. . . .*

CHRISTINE CODY

BLOOD RULES

A Novel of the Bloodlands

After the vampire named Gabriel came into her world,
Mariah Lyander was forced to face her true nature and
admit to the terrible things she had done—things that
Gabriel could not forgive.

To redeem herself and recover her own humanity—
and Gabriel's love—Mariah sets out on a perilous journey across the haunted land, in search of a rumored
cure. And Gabriel, blood-bonded to her, is compelled
to follow.

Together—yet not together—they will face danger and
death. And what they will find is not a place where monsters can be cured—but one where they are born. . . .

M892T0511